THE DREAM AND THE DESTINY

For six days now it had not rained.

It rained once, I recall, and Bricko shrieked, "Look, it is raining!"

But it wasn't raining on us; it was raining on the scattered remnants of the Sixth fifty yards behind us. We ran. The man from Kwangtung was leading. And, as he chased the rain, begging for it to stop, it receded before him. Little Ball was there, leaping from tuft to tuft over the bogs, shouting with his bowl thrust out to catch the sparkling water. But the rain eluded him, sweeping with increasing speed over the shouting column, to vanish over the horizon. The sun burned down. We fell on our faces, sucking at the putrid mud.

The Dream and the Destiny

Alexander Cordell

CORONET BOOKS
Hodder and Stoughton

For Donnie, who made it possible

Copyright © 1975 by Alexander Cordell

First published in Great Britain 1975 by
Hodder and Stoughton Limited

Coronet Edition 1977

Printed and bound in Great Britain for
Hodder and Stoughton Paperbacks,
a division of Hodder and Stoughton Ltd.,
Mill Road, Dunton Green, Sevenoaks, Kent
(Editorial Office: 47 Bedford Square, London, WC1 3DP)
By C. Nicholls & Company Ltd.,
The Philips Park Press, Manchester

ISBN 0 340 21833 9

I am grateful to Mrs. Lois Wheeler Snow and Victor Gollancz Ltd. for permission to include an excerpt from Edgar Snow's *Red Star Over China*, and to the Oxford University Press for the poems *K'unlun*, *The Immortals* and *Loushan Pass* by Mao Tsetung as translated by Mr. Jerome Ch'en and Mr. Michael Bullock and adapted from *Mao and the Chinese revolution*, by Jerome Ch'en, © Oxford University Press 1965.

My thanks are also due to the librarians Mr. Michael Elliott F.L.A. and Mr. W. J. Jones A.L.A. (Llandudno) for making available to me important books of research, and to Mr. O. Vaughan-Jones F.R.C.S. and Mr. D. G. Edwards M.P.S.

To James Hale of Hodder and Stoughton I am grateful for valuable editorial work and suggestions.

'Adventure, exploration, discovery, human courage and cowardice, ecstasy and triumph, suffering, sacrifice and loyalty, and then, through it all
like a flame, an undimmed ardour, undying
hope, and the amazing revolutionary optimism
of those thousands of youths who would not
admit defeat, either by man or nature or God or
death – all this, and more, is embodied in this
Odyssey unequalled in modern times."

Edgar Snow

The year is 1934. For two thousand years China has been governed by a feudal system punctuated by scores of unsuccessful peasant rebellions which resulted in further repressions and the advancement of the wealthy and powerful.

Chinese communism, founded in 1921, became an active political force six years later when Chiang Kai-shek, then China's nationalist ruler, carried out a bloody coup against the radicals which threw up three main leaders – Mao Tse-tung, Chou En-lai and Chu Teh: by 1931 these men controlled a peasant army of 300,000. In this year Japan attacked China's northern territories, but Chiang Kai-shek ignored them and turned his great Kuomintang armies against the communists.

For three years he pounded away at the rebel forces in what he called 'Bandit Extermination Campaigns', leaving the Japanese menace to grow apace. By the end of 1934 he had bottled up what was left of the Red Army into a single province. Here, in Kiangsi, a million peasants died in a year of siege. In order to survive, the last hundred thousand of Mao Tse-tung's forces broke through the encircling Kuomintang armies.

Thus began *The Long March*.

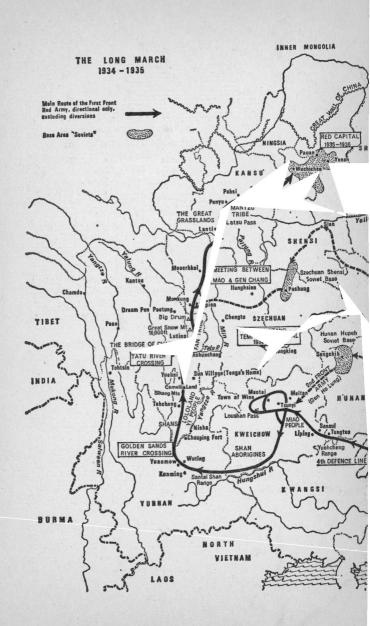

THE LONG MARCH
1934-1935

Main Route of the First Front
Red Army, directional only,
excluding diversions

Base Area "Soviets"

ONE

Outside my window the snow is falling. Beyond the love-pavilions the fields are white; a mantle of snow covers my mother's grave.

In Laoshan the snow falls in great wavering flakes as big as orchid petals, the bamboo bows to the frozen river. A bird is calling from the woods of Shengsu where Pipa lived; a dog is barking; somebody is knocking at a door. The village is deserted, the world holding its breath.

Sounds appear muted in this room where my mother used to sit to escape the vulgar peasantry of my father. She was fond of the place, and her tastes were delicate. Nor was it tampered with during the Revolution – the occupants being gracious enough to leave the decoration as my mother designed it. The walls are of silk, wonderfully preserved, the ceiling high and plain. The small peony fairy standing on the ledge of the window reflects my mother's love of poetry.

There is little left of the original furniture, of course; the local bandits saw to that. All that remains of the Kuomintang looting is the cracked Peking vase which Lu, our servant, hid for me. The Tientsin carpet, for instance, is a recent acquisition; as is the rose-wood desk, where I am writing this.

My father, who was executed by the Red Army before I returned to Laoshan, is not buried here in the ancestral home of the Chans, but I do have my mother; her grave, as I said, is in the garden. In summer it is covered with lotus blossom, her favourite flower. And, at every Ching Ming festival I sweep her grave as she would have wished, for she was a reverent Taoist.

Certainly, she is worth more than a passing mention.

A bondmaid of a wealthy shopkeeper of Homan, my mother was so poor that in her sixteenth year she worked in the fields with but a rag to cover her nakedness. Escaping from her master, she begged her way south during famine and entered this house as a second kitchen-maid; the men servants had their way with her, as was then the custom. And, in a moment of drunken rage, my father sought from her a son, since all he could begæt from his wife and concubines was daughters.

Now, my mother, though not beautiful, had a brain of some intellect. She was a tall, angular woman, with big shoulders and large, veined hands calloused with labour. At the nape of her neck she wore a bun which shone like black silk. Once I saw her combing out this hair: certainly it was splendid hair – better than Su-tai's, my father's favourite concubine. Also, my mother's feet had been expertly bound; tiny for such a big woman.

It was from my mother that I heard of the poets. Having taught herself to read and write within a year of taking to my father's bed, she attended me many hours each day, reading to me such books as *The Romance of the Three Kingdoms* and quoting the poems of Li Po, such as *Drinking Alone under the Summer Moon*. It was from her that I learned the subtle dynastic changes; the differences, say, between the Sung poet, Yeh Li, and his contemporaries. My mother was a valuable woman.

Although my father rejected poetry, he respected it: finally, so impressed was he with my ability to quote yards of it while I was attending Shengsu Middle School (and it was here that I met my lovely Pipa) that he divorced his wife for gossiping and married my mother, naturally taking care, of course, to retain his concubines.

When I was eighteen, I left Laoshan and took my place in Shanghai University with a grant to study medicine for the next five years at Chiang Kai-shek's expense. I scarcely repaid this generosity because three years later I returned to Laoshan and joined Mao Tse-tung's Red Army.

Two months before my arrival home, my mother died.

Many relatives attended the funeral, said Lu, our servant; whenever there's a will there are abundant relatives.

My ancient Aunt Tezan came – she who despised my mother for her childhood poverty. She wore upon her cheek a cluster of rubies to conceal a disease contracted from my Uncle Soon, a rare old roué, even for Hunan. Some cousins on my father's side came too – one of them a landlord who used whips on his peasants. But most of the mourners were my father's courtesans;

12

these arrived in best white funeral clothes with their many children, every one a female.

My father, apparently, did not come in immediately from the burial in the garden, but stood astride my mother's grave with his hands clasped, staring up at the sky. The rain poured down, said Lu, and the relatives hammered at the window, telling him not to be a fool, or he would be next in the grave. But he did not obey: for hours he stood there, said Lu, staring up at the rain, and his face, with his lips curled back, was the face of a wolf.

This servant, now long dead, told me that the lavatories had over-flowed and that a smell of boiled chicken and rice polluted the incense of the mansion: also the children were howling and being smacked by their painted mothers.

When my father came into the house he was dishevelled: even the hem of his gown was stained with mud from the burying, yet about his appearance he was at all times particular.

Coming into the hall, said Lu, he turned and flung wide the great, double doors and pointed at the garden, crying:

"Out!"

At this the mourners were outraged and they gathered their children about them, nudging and tossing their heads indignantly. And, when my Aunt Tezan stamped her ivory stick on the floor, cackling, my father approached her threateningly.

"*Out!*"

They flew before him, followed by items of furniture.

Then, Lu told me, my father went full length on to the couch in the room where I am writing this, and wept, crying:

"Sula, forgive me, Sula, forgive me," which was not my mother's name but the one by which he called her.

Within a week, said the servant, he was back with his concubines.

So now I am writing this in the place my mother loved, remembering her.

Before me are the musty, rain-stained sheets of my *Long March* diaries (and the special entries, of course, for the Paoan-Yenan route, for which I am responsible to the Party).

Sitting here in the dusk with Kwelin asleep in the chair, I recall the lost years: amazingly, by some trick of the ear, I can hear my mother's voice – reading passages from *The Water Margin* and *All Men are Brothers*.

Earlier, the house was a bedlam of noise, with people clattering about and children shrieking: it was impossible to write under such conditions. But now the guests have gone, if not the ghosts, and the room is quiet again.

There is no sound now but the hissing of the fire, and Kwelin's breathing; in this firelight her face is young again.

The dusk grows kinder. I can hear the wild geese calling from the village. The house is talking to itself in creaks and whispers, as houses do at night; the wind is sighing down the road to Laoshan where the ravens fly. And strangely, even as I pick up the brush to write, I can see an ocean of camellias: they stretch across the Sikang Mountains where Pipa lies, to Laoshan, the hills of home.

TWO

In the Autumn of 1934, aged twenty-one, I returned home from Shanghai University in my third years as a medical student. China was at war with herself, this time with communism, and rumours persisted that Chiang Kai-shek was beginning a new purge of the radicals. It was also the Mid-Autumn Festival, when the wife of the Celestial Archer swallowed the potion of everlasting life and became the Queen of the Moon.

Such was the charming rubbish believed by people like my father.

No such immortality was conferred on Old Teh, my friend the Laoshan water-carrier: he had just been sentenced to death for protesting about his rent.

It was because of such injustices that the Chiang Kai-shek clique was faced with the extremism of progressive thinkers: violence alone, they claimed, was the only outlet for complaint. But men like my father, bound by the old ideals, had neither the compassion nor sense to realise the outcome. He said, soon after my arrival at Laoshan:

"Old Teh, you ask? He will have to die. The mandarin has sentenced him, it is the law."

"It's cruel and unjust!" I said.

"It will be cruel and unjust if others follow his example: soon we'll have peasants refusing to pay rent at all." He eased his great shining backside into a cane chair on the verandah. "It's all the fault of these damned communists, of course. How are the medical studies going?"

Later, the moon rose over the paddy fields, and the stars shimmered over the rim of Big Wall Mountain. My Pipa would be finished teaching in Shengsu village by now; even if I couldn't borrow a horse, I could walk and run the distance between us in well under an hour.

Su-tai, my father's eldest concubine, younger than I, was lying in a wicker chair beside me, her eyes like the stars above. She

15

was bewitchingly beautiful; her skin was of the same languid whiteness as the orchid from which she took her name.

"Lin-wai," said she, "aren't you going to Shengsu tonight?"

"At the moment I'm more concerned with Old Teh's murder," I replied.

"The old fool parades his communism – what do you expect?"

"Anyone with the smallest protest is always a communist. You may be advanced in certain subjects, little tart, but not in the Manifesto."

Rising with easy grace, she joined me at the verandah rail and stared up at the moon, saying, "Old age is boring, Lin-wai. An hour with me would be more entertaining than a dozen political speeches." She winked with pert charm. "Your father is visiting the mandarin tonight to confirm some sentences. Is Shengsu village still attractive?"

I did not reply.

"It is amazing to me how your perfect Pipa gets away with it," said she, adding, "the way she's been behaving while you've been away, you certainly need to make the best of her."

"What do you mean by that?"

"For all her breeding, she's not above the law. Tang Fu may be the secret communist agent in these parts, but Yang Pipa's an open agitator; your father, you know, would scarcely approve." She smiled at me, her head on one side. "I will even change this dress for a red one, if that suits you better?"

I did not look her way.

Pipa was small and her skin was golden. Her god, said my mother once, had cooked her beautifully in the oven of the sun, enhancing her quaint beauty. Her hair was black and plaited either side of her face; she possessed the high-boned cheeks of the blood Cantonese. Also she was finely educated, though her blind Aunt Lei was notoriously poor: the whole of Shengsu wondered how she had ever afforded it.

"In fact," said Su-tai, "I will change into nothing at all if you find that preferable."

Her skittishness was hard to ignore; all over the land it was happening – young concubines, tiring of fruitless service to aged masters, were seeking out sons.

"Mine's a very unsatisfactory existence, Lin-wai," she said now. "Do you realise how unrewarding it can be?'

"Somebody's bound to come in in the middle of it," I replied. "Best I go to Shengsu."

"Then watch your Pipa's Aunt Lei," said she. "Blind she may be, but she has ears to hear brown grass growing, take it from me. Meanwhile, Chan Lin-wai, you are a pig's arse."

It was a reasonable statement, all things considered.

I bowed to her.

"I love you," said Yang Pipa.

The little red-roofed cottage in Shengsu was a haven after the discord of Laoshan.

I said, "And I love you, but when will your Aunt Lei be back? Ever since I got home I've been dodging somebody."

Pipa replied, "When she comes she will tap with her stick; we will hear this – be peaceful."

"People say she isn't as blind as she makes out."

Pipa replied: "When Yang, my namesake, the queen of all concubines, was born in the year seven hundred and eighteen, her parents in Shensi saw a star fall out of the sky: later, when she died for encouraging her emperor's folly, a dynasty collapsed about her." She looked at the window moon. "Important as you are, Lin-wai, I can't think this would happen if Aunt Lei found me in bed with you. But I'm fortunate indeed to own such a lover." She opened wide, beautiful eyes in the dim light, adding, " 'Yang Pipa,' I sometimes say to myself, 'you are a fool. You are in love with this Chan Lin-wai, a common medical student of Laoshan, and he comes to your arms but twice a year. What will you do for a lover for the next six months?' "

I answered, "You'll teach at Shengsu Middle School and continue your studies in nursing until he returns from Shanghai with his doctorate in two years time. Then you can be his receptionist."

"Another two years? *Aiya!*" She showed her straight, white teeth. "Meanwhile, what would he do if I presented him with a baby?"

"He'd discuss it with you at the first opportunity. Aren't you his wife in everything but name?"

I paid her the respects of my body, and there was warmth in her and a trembling; she caressed my face in sighs, saying, "You don't much flatter the woman who is your slave, do you?

17

Couldn't you tell me that my lips are carmine, my skin like jade, and that my eyebrows curve like a willow tree?"

"Your mirror tells you you are beautiful, Pipa. Need I waste words while others are dying?"

"Let's not forget Old Teh, Lin-wai – just for a minute?"

So I made her one with me. A night-bird sang from the thickets of autumn.

"My Aunt Lei would be appalled," said Pipa.

Soon, I thought. I will carry this one in a red sedan chair and a scarlet marriage gown to my father, presenting her to him for naming as wife, and she would kneel before him in Laoshan. In days this would happen – long before obtaining my doctorate as planned – while the big carp slept in the pools of the garden under the big autumn moon.

"Not before time," said Pipa.

THREE

The Confucian doctrine of Social Status governed our house in Laoshan, therefore Su-tai and the other concubines sat at my father's table, but in junior status to my Aunt Tezan, who was staying a few days. *The Book of Rites*, the directive on the subject, was explicit about this; it was an abominable enemy to China's social progress that instructed everybody on how to behave.

It may not have been in accordance with the *Origins of Culture*, but I desposed my father; he epitomised for me all that was wrong with the old system of parental advantage. Life for him was legitimate loot. Under the junta of the Chiang Kai-shek clique, the regular verb, 'I steal, you steal, he steals, they steal, we all steal', was the dominant precept of his existence: it applied to humans as well as to syntax. The peasants chained to their carts like animals, the exploitation of children, barbaric foot-binding and ferocious punishments for minor crime were a result of Confucian interpretation of religious principles – all in conflict with the gentler Taoism practised by the masses.

The Confucian injustice that forbade family argument, for instance, had degenerated into parental domination. The ancient Chinese saying that the country was like a box of sand, each grain representing a family unit, no longer applied. Under the law of filial piety, my father, I considered, had died in a morass of corruption, China's oldest disease.

The intelligent young of 1934 were at war with the old: it was a widening generation gap that only violence could bridge. The masses were dying in millions of famine, pestilence, war. Men like Marshal Chang Tso-lin, the warlord, lived like Indian maharajas and the poor lived with pigs. The governor of one province alone was worth thirty concubines and thirty million dollars, but the peasant who spat at the feet of a landlord died for it. Martyrs, as always in times of revolution, proliferated.

Life in Laoshan, like other southern villages, was one of un-easy quiet; Kwangtung province, with its ever-rebellious capital, Canton, was afire with a new spirit, and the Old Order war-lords put down violence with growing malice. Flogging to death, once a punishment reserved for banditry, was now the sentence for even minor crimes; burying alive was reserved for non-payment of rent. But Mao Tse-tung's Red Army of over a hundred thousand peasants, surrounded in their Juichin Soviet in south-east China, was threatening to break out, and peasants were flocking to their Red banner.

Old China, with the last fling of the ruling class, was like a hog being fattened for slaughter. The mocking smiles of Taoism, the peasant religion of millions, tolled the death-knell of old Confucius, who was dead, said the workers, but wouldn't lie down. The mass murders of seven years ago in Shanghai, when twenty thousand progressives died, became the spark now spreading a flame over the southern provinces. Little rebellions, breaking out like bonfires, were instantly put out by the Kuomintang, Chiang Kai-shek's nationalist army. Hundreds of thousands of peasants died in a last attempt to extinguish communism. With the fall of the City of Wuhan, when a Red Army was routed, Chiang Kai-shek began systematically to soak the land in blood.

Old Teh, my friend the water-carrier, about to die, was the way in which Laoshan paid for what the communists called the New Ideal.

FOUR

Next day, at sunset, my father led the family down to the village square, there officially to witness Old Teh's execution. The villagers of Laoshan were already assembled, many of them Tanga and Hoklo people of the sea; others were land Hakka, the Guest-People, who had fled south from other butcheries.

As I took my seat in front of the crowd facing the execution stake, I was surprised to see Old Teh sitting with his back to a tree near the mandarin's justice seat. With his legs crossed and his knees cocked up, he scarcely looked the victim; he was reading *Six Chapters of a Floating Life*, a classic he had borrowed from me and failed to return. We all sat in silence, awaiting the mandarin. Flies buzzed, frogs croaked, cicadas sang. My father sat in sweating obesity, wiping his florid face. Old Teh, after a glance in our direction, went on reading.

When the mandarin's procession came into sight, we rose. Preceded by his bodyguard of fifty Kuomintang soldiers, he came in his crimson sedan chair and the twelve bearers carrying him were naked to the waist. The personification of wealth and power, he descended from the sedan in tottering age, and was helped to the Chair of Justice; there his white and purple robes were arranged before an open grave. When the soldiers were ranked behind the mandarin's chair with the usual bawled commands, Old Teh momentarily looked up, made a wry face at the disturbance, and went on reading.

Indeed, he made no protest when the executioner touched his shoulder, but followed the soldiers to the open grave before the mandarin's chair and sat on the edge of it, swinging his legs in it, still reading. Captain Pai wheeled his big brown horse before the crowd and shouted:

"The man sitting before you has protested about an increase in his rent, the amount of which has long been recorded as less than is the landlord's due. This is mandarin land; it is fairly distributed – it's only through your lord's good offices that you are paying rent at all." He trotted the bay back to the mandarin's chair. "It's clear that the prisoner has been reading communist

21

posters about land reform: let his execution for an attempt at propaganda be a lesson to you all."

The soldiers heaved Old Teh to his feet. Rising, I walked slowly to the mandarin's chair, calling, "My lord, I would speak with you."

The mandarin's eyes drifted over me and he waved away the two guards barring my approach, saying, "You also protest about your rent?"

I replied, "My Lord, I am the son of your Laoshan agent. I pay no rent."

"Then why present yourself unbidden?"

"To make a request for the prisoner.'

He was intrigued. "A request of a common labourer?"

I said, "The book he has there belongs to me."

Old Teh, still reading, glanced over his shoulder, crying, "Don't worry, lackey, you'll get it back."

The mandarin asked, "A rare book, young man?"

"The thing's a classic. I lent it in good faith and I'm entitled to have it returned."

He made a wry face. "It's astonishing to me that people steal books, yet wouldn't dream of touching an umbrella."

This was the Pig of Kwangtung, the representative of Chiang's Central Government in Nanking. His breeding was stained with royal blood, for he was related to the old Dowager Empress, a sow of the first order. The opium which had destroyed his body had earned him princely wealth, for he had soaked Kwangtung in the blood of the poppy. He ate from beaten gold, slept on silk. Ten concubines and a eunuch had he, none of whom he could serve, and his wife, as ugly as a Tibetan monkey, had contracted Mandarin's Disease: the poor enjoy their private revenges. Now he said:

"A peasant actually reading?" He added, drolly, "Doubtless one of the eight-legged essays of the old Imperial Examinations?"

"*Six Chapters of a Floating Life*," shouted Old Teh, pushing away the soldiers.

The mandarin answered, "*Six Chapters*, eh? By all the gods!" And he quoted cynically, " '. . . touched by autumn, one's figure grows slender. Soaked in frost, the chrysanthemum blooms . . .' He wrote it, they say, between bouts of needlework, and I can

22

well believe it. It doesn't compare with the *Dream of the Red Chamber*."

"That," cried Old Teh, "is your bloody ignorance." Followed by the disconcerted soldiers, he came closer to the mandarin's chair, saying, "*Red Chamber* isn't literature, man, it's an ode to the barbarism of Confucius. Do what you want with my body, but don't insult my intellect."

Reaching out the mandarin took my book from his hands, saying, "Ah yes, I know it well enough, but it's a very poor edition." He flapped its pages. "The construction's poor, the crises few; it has a beginning, a middle and an end, but nobody could call it literature."

Old Teh snatched back the book, crying, "Good writing is life, it has no rules." He spat. "Had you read this instead of rubbish you might have ended up a water-carrier instead of a mandarin. So piss off, and take your *Red Chamber* with you. Confine yourself to rent-collecting."

The mandarin said, obviously trying to keep his temper, "Frankly, I'm getting tired of this conversation."

"Me too," I said, "for I still haven't got my book," and Old Teh angrily shouted, "By my grandma's arse, you're nearly as bad as him." He took a stance. "I shan't let it go until I've finished it. It's outrageous to be denied the ending of a book."

Allowing freedom to literary discussion, the mandarin sighed deep. "All right, all right, how much more have you got?"

"Five pages."

"Then don't take all day about it, and when you've finished it, give it to its owner – there's thieves all round us when it comes to books."

So Old Teh shoved the soldiers aside with unprintable curses and sat down with his back to the tree again, and the mandarin, the garrison commander, fifty soldiers and 600 villagers waited in silence until he had read the last five pages of the classic. The sun burned into dusk, the birds sought their nests, the cicadas began in triumphant chorus. And, when he had finished reading, Old Teh rose, handed the book to me, bowed to the mandarin and said:

"In the Tang dynasty 1,000 books a month were published – not that you'd know this. In my grave, unhampered by gentry louts and mandarins, I will read the lot." He turned to me. "My condolences to your father over there – may he continue to exploit his labourers until the communists come and take his head, and my curses on the soul of this generous old fool." Having said this, he went to the soldiers, calling over his shoulder as they bound him hand and foot, "Goodbye Chan Lin-wai I prefer the friendship of your childhood . . ."

I interrupted this by shouting to the mandarin. "My lord, this execution is against the Law!"

"Don't you plead for me," said Old Teh as they carried him away.

Before the mandarin's chair, I shouted, "The government lays down certain punishments for certain crimes. Non-payment of rent attracts only a few months imprisonment . . ." Hearing this, Captain Pai shouted:

"Kwangtung is under martial law; the mandarin's jurisdiction applies."

I yelled back, "But only after reference to the Nanking judiciary!"

My father, behind me now, wailed, "Lin-wai, *please* . . . !"

Recovering himself, the mandarin said, "I will deal with this outrage later. Meanwhile, I am master here – even the son of my agent would do well to remember it."

I shouted, while the soldiers restrained me, "He is dying because he read a poster. For communism he can be beheaded without trial and by mandarin's command, but first he must appear before the Provincial Court and guilt reasonably proven."

In the following momentary silence that followed, Old Teh, shouted, "I am dying because I'm a communist. With luck, the young will follow my example."

I said, "I'll tell them that you died for China."

The soldiers lifted Old Teh, carried him, laid him face down in the grave and buried him alive.

I knelt above him until the struggling earth had tired.

FIVE

I was awakened next dawn by sounds of firing, and Su-tai shaking me by the shoulder.

"Lin-wai, get up?" cried she.

"What is happening?"

"A messenger is here, waiting on the verandah." This was a different Su-tai; gone was the artless languor.

"You know him?" Out of bed now, I was dressing swiftly.

"Everybody knows the communist messenger." She stood aside as I went through the door. "Good luck."

"You're a strange one," I said.

"We live in strange times." She drew her robe closer about her.

I had seen the messenger before, one thinned by heroin; his rags fluttered in the cold dawn wind. Gasping, he said:

"I am come from Tang, the agent, to warn you. Last night many villagers signed government repentance slips, promising to deny communism; they betrayed themselves. Now the Kuomintang are rounding them up and shooting them in batches. Many in Shengsu have been buried alive."

In Anyang County whole families were murdered on suspicion alone; slaughter was wholesale over the southern provinces, ordered by Chiang's Nationalist Government in Nanking.

I said to the messenger, "How do I know this isn't a trap?"

With surprising verve, he replied, "You do not, Chan Lin-wai, but if you wait here for Captain Pai you'll very soon find out."

"Is this man Tang in Shengsu?"

Su-tai said, behind me, "Comrade Tang is everywhere. Go, Lin-wai." She handed me an envelope. "Don't waste time reading it now. Collect your woman – she, too, is in danger."

"There are communists here in this house?" I ran past her and she followed me into my room, watching while I finished dressing.

"Of course," said she.

"They're a strange brand."

"That's the art of being a communist." She winked at me.

The messenger was still awaiting me. I looked back once, I remember. Su-tai was standing motionless on the verandah under a lightening sky. I waved: she did not wave back.

Fires burned on the outskirts of Laoshan, ragged firing grew in the middle of the village; faintly on the wind came the shrieks of women and the bass shouts of men. The messenger and I began a jog-trot into the hills, taking the road to Shengsu.

I was not surprised to find Pipa awaiting me in the yard of her cottage. I asked her if she knew what had happened, and she replied:

"All last night they've been rounding up the villagers who signed repentence slips. Look, I have food and a water-bottle. Tang, the agent, said you would have a letter of introduction – who to?"

The messenger gasped, "Don't waste time reading it here – make north to Juichin, and watch the nationalist patrols."

"Why Juichin?"

"Because Mao Tse-tung is in Juichin Soviet – if you are good communists he's your only hope." A sudden burst of firing came from Shengsu village outskirts. He jerked his head towards the sound. "If you are half communists, stay and die."

Pipa whispered, her face pale in the dawn light. "But Juichin is encircled – the place is under siege – a million people have already died in Juichin Soviet!"

The young man spread his hands. "Then what is two more?"

"Come," I said, and seized Pipa's hand.

"But Aunt Lei, Lin – I must say goodbye to my aunt!"

"To hell with your aunt," I said, and towed her away, ignoring her protest.

"Good luck!" called the messenger.

Later, I heard they caught him a mile outside Shengsu, warning other communists, and beheaded him. And for harbouring a communist they sought – Yang Pipa – the Kuomintang also beheaded blind Aunt Lei.

Although bathed in an Indian summer of late September, radiant and golden, this was vicious country.

Ever since the birth of Mao Tse-tung's Red Army – the first Red uprising was at Nanchang but 100 miles north, in 1927 – this was an embattled area constantly patrolled by the Kuomintang, Chiang Kai-shek's nationalist army of millions. Kwang-tung, like her sister province of Kiangsi, was a land of bayonets; occupied territory where every village was an armed outpost and every town a bastion against communism. True, there were large areas of verdant country between us and Juichin that had seen neither communist nor nationalist, but most nights the Kuomintang army patrols 'yelled the road': even in deserted areas, their terrifying howls reverberating in the hills; a prelude to plunder and burning. And so communists, suspected or real, ran to safety; one place was the sea, and escape by junk to Hong Kong and Macao. Others, like us, ran to the protection of Mao Tse-tung's Red Army besieged in Juichin, a fortified soviet area which Mao had announced as the Red capital of China, about thirty miles north of Shengsu, Pipa's home.

"And when we reach there, what then?" asked Pipa now.

"When we reach it the task will be to enter," I replied. "There are four Kuomintang encirclements around Juichin, and we are now walking in the second. The defence will get thicker the farther north we travel – and even when we're through these, we take the risk of being fired on by Mao's Red patrols."

"It might have been wiser to try to reach the sea?"

This I pondered, for it was sense, but it was nearly 300 miles to the coast and we hadn't the food.

"Read that stupid letter again," said Pipa, and sat upon a rock.

Beside her, I took the letter from my pocket, squinting at the white sheet in the incinerating blaze of the sun. It was an excellent day for dying, I reflected, and read:

To General Peng Teh-huai,
Commander Third Corps,
First Front Red Army.

Receive into your force one Chan Lin-wai, son of Laoshan agent to Mandarin of Kwangtung. A medical student, he is not lacking in courage, if gentry born, for which I apologise. Long live the Red Army.

Tang (Code, Laoshan-Shengsu Area Comrade)

30th September, 1934
The sun was above us in a molten sky as we took the road to the north.

This was autumn patchwork country, a coloured quilt in a grandmother's fingers; the dying gold of an ungathered harvest was stained with the blood-red roofs of the empty labourers' cottages; the deserted farmsteads clustered around the shining river bends as if cringing in fear. High about us steepling hills flanked the valley, their dull vigour guardians to the lowlands where sweeping grasslands sparkled with encrustations of mother-of-pearl; oyster beds claimed from the sea, before the world was young. Few birds sang here; it was a phenomenon I noticed later, the closer we go to Juichin, where only buzzards and hawks used the sky. One might travel through this second encirclement with comparative safety, providing one kept a watchful eye for Kuomintang patrols. For this was fortification by isolated pockets, not the crystallised trench system of barbed wire and land mines: it was the country where Kuomintang outposts were linked by telephone and heliograph, leaving vast tracks of province clear of marauding soldiery, and I knew it like my hand.

I put my arm around Pipa's shoulder and we plodded onwards in the heat of the freak September.

By dusk we came to a place of water; shadowy country in a defile between rocks. Here we rested for the night, making a little arbour in the bushes beside a singing river. We dared not light a fire lest it attract the attention of enemy patrols, but we ate a little of the bread Pipa had brought and refilled the water-bottle. Wild berries grew in profusion here and we ate until we bulged, then lay together on the lush grass, listening to the chatter of the river.

Luckily, Pipa – ever the same, demanding Pipa – did not sleep.

"Lin-wai, are you awake?"

The night was hot; even the cicadas were too boiled to sing. I heard, in a sleep of starts and fumbles, the distant croaking of frogs and the tumbling splashes of nocturnal fish. I opened my eyes; Pipa was bending above me.

"Go to sleep, girl."

"Sleep? I can do that in bed back in Shengsu!"

"*Tin Hau!*" I exclaimed, "don't you ever tire?"

It was as if the sky had dropped quicksilver rain over the

rolling country, and the river flashed and sparkled near us, throwing up white arms to us. An orb of a moon of frightening immensity sailed over the star-swept land. And, as the sleep left my eyes, I saw that Pipa was naked. Reaching out, I drew her against me and her body was icy to the touch. She whispered, her wet hair against my face, "Come on in, lad, you can sleep any time! Come on in!" She put her arms around me, heaving me from the bushes, and we rolled, locked together, one over the other, to the edge of the river.

Standing now, I flung off my clothes and dived into the river, losing all my dreads in the icy plunge. With her ungainly dog-paddle, for she was no swimmer, Pipa plunged towards me, catching me around the neck, and her delighted shrieks echoed in the defile: I heard this, I knew the danger, yet did nothing. Her wet kisses, as we rolled in water, seemed to wash away the killing. It was a cleansing after the horror of Old Teh's execution, the heaving earth. Now we floated on our backs, hand in hand, staring at the stars.

I heard the clatter of falling stones almost as an echo – it was a sense rather than a sound that brought me upright, and I pushed Pipa away, instantly alert. She whispered:

"What was that?"

"Back to the bank," I said, and swam, and Pipa floundered after me.

And the moment I scrambled out, the bullet the soldier aimed from the rocks flung up earth and water.

"Come on!" Stooping, I hauled Pipa after me to the cover of the arbour.

Rigid, we listened. Another shot; this ricocheted and whined eerily into the night.

But I had seen the flash of the pistol: it was at least fifty yards away. Whoever was firing at us was a fool; in this light one couldn't hope to score a hit at such a distance. Pipa whispered, "But why shoot at us?"

"Quick, put your clothes on." This we both did in gasping haste.

"Kuomintang?" she chattered with fear, not cold.

I said, "He aimed at me, not you; you realise that?"

She began to tremble; the trembling began on her lips and slowly enveloped her. Trying to speak, her mouth opened and shut like the mechanical contrivance of a puppet.

Pipa was remembering a trick of the Kuomintang: after the rape they fired a bullet up into the body through the vagina.

"Wait here," I whispered. "You hear me – *wait*!"

Her eyes were wide in the watery mask of her face.

A wandering soldier? A deserter, perhaps; or a patrol?

I did not know, but had to take the chance; running to the edge of the river, I flung myself down behind a boulder. And, even as I gripped it for cover, I heard the stinging impact of the bullet on the rock and the song of the ricochet. Pipa moved in the bushes. I called softly, "Don't move, stay there!"

Pipa was on her knees, staring at me. I heard the man reload. Another burst of fire came; sparks and debris shot up. I waved at Pipa and she sank low, seeking cover, now understanding the ruse.

I lay still, listening to the rustle of the attacker's feet on stones. Nearer he came, nearer, his confidence growing; clearly he believed he had hit me. Instinctively moving around the boulder, I saw him.

No Kuomintang soldier, this one – a bandit. I recognised the ragged tunic, the home-made bandolier that crossed his chest.

He was a big man, and bearded – unusual in the Chinese. Hatless, his unkempt hair fell to his shoulders. Wading ankle-deep in the shallows, he was staring up and down the river. Momentarily, I saw his face; incredulity at our disappearance was growing on his flat features, and I knew his tragedy. This was a Moslem horse-man, one turned out by the Kansu cavalry: Kwangtung was littered with them; men turned bandit to live.

Now he was hunting money and a woman, in that order.

With the pistol stuck out before him, he came warily towards the bushes where Pipa lay, the shore gravel crunching beneath his feet. Incredibly, he called, in Mandarin:

"*Hei! Ni zai nar?*"

His voice echoed above the surging river, and he cried again, wandering about, "*Hei hei?*" He was floundering in sand now, on the other side of my boulder. "*Ni jiao shenme mingzi?*"

He knew Pipa was near; he was asking her name.

To my astonishment Pipa sat up, replying:

"*Wo jiao Yang Pi'pa . . .*"

Instantly he lowered the pistol.

I saw his face in the moment before I leaped upon him from cover. The gun clattered away. In a cross-stretch I gathered his arm, turned it in the Judo and heard his forearm crack in the lock. He screamed with pain as I butted him, catching him with a sweeping hand-chop as he fell. And the instant he hit the ground Pipa was above him, and the stone came down. All in a flurry of action. Her stone again descended; the bandit sighed, and slipped easily into death.

Kneeling, Pipa stared at the stone in her hand, and then at me.

"*Tin Hau!*" she whispered.

I rose, taking the stone away from her, but still she stared at the dead man's face.

"I've killed him," she said.

"Either him, or us," I answered, and took her arm. "Come." I took the bandit's Luger and counted the bullets in his bandolier.

It was no place for midnight bathing.

We travelled all that night, seeking the old Hakka salt trails that led north to the imprisoned Red Army up in Juichin.

Here the country was ragged, heavily spiked with craggy outcrops, every one of which might hide a sniper like the Kansu bandit – men who took off the finger for a ring.

Remembering the dangers now, we travelled with care, coming at dawn to a rocky outcrop in an isolated place by a stream.

Thinking to rest there during daylight hours, we entered a cave and sat down on the edge of its yawning blackness. We had actually settled to sleep when I abruptly sat up.

A fat man stood within a yard of my head: behind him was another who seemed a giant in comparison, bearded and stripped to the waist. From between them peered down an imp of a person with a stricken face, and he was clad in rags with a knife at his belt.

Bandits, without a doubt.

I sheepishly rose, getting Pipa behind me.

Within touching distance, there was no escape. The fat man said, jovially, taking the pistol from my belt:

"*Hei wei*, Bricko, what have we here? A 1,000 dollars ransom for a poof and his sleeper?"

"Let me have her and you keep the poof, Jo-kei." The face of the small one was scarred by fire; welts of his burning ran like vipers from throat to forehead. "*Aiya*," he ejaculated, limping slowly around us, "Dressed good, I could get 500 dollars for her in the city of Changsa; now old Mao's around the women raise the price!"

The giant moved ponderously before us; a dim glow behind him reflected his massive size: his red beard was proof of Mongolian extraction.

Jo-kei, obviously their leader, smoothed his stomach with large, fat hands, saying:

"Where did you spring from? – and no lies!"

My throat was dry, and I could feel Pipa's trembling. I did not reply immediately.

"You are running with the Kanchou gentry?" His voice was cultured, belying the grossness of his features. The giant behind him made a strangled bass sound, staring at Pipa. I replied, "No, we are from Laoshan, and as poor as you."

He fingered my tunic, "Names?"

"Chan Lin-wai – this is my woman."

"In silk, and as poor as we?"

The glow brightened beyond them; I saw a face riven with excess and bearded with rough sleeping: his appearance conflicted with his obvious education. The little man, Bricko, cried in a strange falsetto, "Gentry bastards, Jo-kei – on the run!"

The fat man said, "Is it true?"

"I am a student, my girl is a teacher," and he instantly groaned:

"The gods plague me – more wind-head intellectuals, and I could do with soldiers." Turning, he bellowed into the cave, "Muchai, Muchai, some of your kind have arrived – students and teachers – soon we'll be opening another bloody academy." He waddled away; the big man's eyes drifted over us with a strange serenity for one so fierce.

There came from the glow a fourth man and he was old; one tall, aristocratic in bearing, and his voice was deep and pure, "You are a vulgar devil, Jo-kei." He bowed imperceptibly to us. "Do not heed him, you are safe here."

"But there's a need to ask good questions, remember!" came Jo-kei's warning from the darkness.

"Ah, yes." The elder addressed me, smiling. "The name of the military commander in Laoshan, please – this I happen to know, so be careful."

"Captain Pai," I replied.

He nodded faintly, stroking his straggling beard; he was of good age for asking questions, this one, and of quiet, educated charm. "And the name of the mandarin's agent who lives in your village?"

"Chan."

He smiled. "By coincidence the same as yours?"

"You know, don't you? – Yes, I am his son."

He regarded me. "That was brave – there's a ransom about if Bricko finds it attractive – it is good that you told the truth instead of a lie. Jo-kei dislikes lies."

"You know my father?"

"I have – shall I say – contacts with your family in Laoshan. Also I have served with him on the Mandarin Register, having been on the Nanking Committee of Rotation Planting." He peered at me, adding, "His family suffered as well as his labourers; scarcely a man to be recommended, you think?"

We weighed each other in the faint light. He added, "Probably the most unpopular agent in the province of Kwangtung?"

"We do not boast of him."

"That is wise, with your name."

He did not move; the shapes of the others behind him were motionless. It was a delicate situation, and I was leaning on the integrity of the elder: doubtless they were bandits, but banditry could be an honourable profession, a school in which criminal and intellectual enrolled side by side to save their necks. Men such as Chu Teh, Commander-in-Chief of Mao's Red Army, were bandits in youth. The old man asked:

"And you are running from Laoshan?"

"From the Kuomintang there: Captain Pai is burying communists alive."

He made an impish face, calling over his shoulder, "They are telling the truth, Jo-kei; I know these facts – be lenient."

Jo-kei, preceded by his stomach, returned to the foreground. "Then perhaps we can use them – you, your trade or study?" He prodded me.

"I'm a medical student."

"That's convenient!" Jo-kei asked, "When do you qualify?"

"I am in my third year – Shanghai University."

"And your woman?"

"She could go for a nurse – she has first-aid experience."

"Heaven's blood – a doctor and a nurse – will you throw in with us?"

I said "But we are going to Juichin."

"They'll find the Red Army quicker with me, eh, old Bony?" He tugged the old man's beard, then made a swift sign language with his fingers before the big man's face: grabbing Bricko by the collar, he thrust him towards the mouth of the cave. "Quick, Eunuch, the mules; find them, saddle them – Big One will lift the loads. You two now . . ." and he gripped us, pointing within the cave. "In there is food and water. Go and gather it; fill the bottles, carry all outside and wait there for me." He waved us away.

Deep in the cave, gathering up the food, the water-bottles and cooking pans, Pipa whispered:

"Lin-wai, do you trust them?" Her face was shadowed in the red glow of the fire.

"Only the elder."

"He knows of your father, it could be dangerous."

"He knows too much about me to be healthy."

"And Jo-kei, the fat one, he is the leader?"

"Of course."

Jo-kei, appearing from nowhere, was standing above us; the dying fire played on his wide expanse of chest and the sagging muscles of his tremendous stomach.

"Later you will discover how well informed we are," said he, and gave me back the Luger.

SIX

Within the Kuomintang encirclements the mountains of Kang rear upwards from the plains of the lovely Meilin River, impassable to an army but not to partisans. We took the narrow tracks from the valley, over rock-strewn ground, thumping the flanks of the four mules that staggered under the weight of submachineguns and automatics, making enough noise to awaken dead ancestors, said Jo-kei, and as we climbed ever upwards we watched the crags and boulders for ambush.

Many decomposing bodies littered the trail, lying in clutches, proof of ambush: some were skeletons, partisan dead from battles of earlier years, a few finding their graves in trees, rags fluttering on their bony limbs. These seemed to watch us as we passed, their crow-clawed sockets staring at something living in this dead place, the graveyard entrance to Kuangchang where Mao Tse-tung, but weeks back, lost 4,000 peasant dead, and Chiang Kai-shek's Kuomintang blew open the gates of his Juichin Soviet base.

We went in single file; Jo-kei in the front, Muchai following, a swaying figure strangely elegant in his long, black gown; behind Pipa and I came the four mules in a rope-train, obedient to the shrill commands of the little eunuch, while Big One, his great body swathed with ammunition bandoliers, brought up the rear.

On a tiny plateau in the mountains, we rested; the mules grazed in meek contentment; Jo-kei, able to sleep at any time apparently, fell asleep in raucous snoring. Bricko the eunuch talked in high whispers at the sky; the giant beside him sat hunched, staring into the valley in moody contemplation. Murchai, stretched out near by, said to me:

"Consider him, the big man; his must be a strange world. He climbs, but does not know why he is climbing. Soon he will die, and will not know why he is dying."

I replied, "He cannot communicate at all?"

"He possesses a tongue, for I have examined it, but little brain:

35

there are many such as he, mentally deficient deaf-mutes, in the country of Hingsi – major inter-breeding."

Pipa asked, "Why did Jo-kei enlist him– just to die?" and Muchai said softly:

"The scars you see upon his back are healed, but not his mind. When Jo-kei freed him from bond-service they had him in the shafts of a cart and were beating him like an animal. For me Big One is China, the sprawling, suffering edifice. Two years ago Jo-kei found him, and taught him the Hingsi sign-language – a limited communication, but it suffices. He adores Jo-kei and another called Tenga, from whom, apparently, he is borrowed. Raise a hand to either, I hear, and he will kill you."

Pipa asked, "And you, old man?"

Muchai's sallow face creased into a smile. "There are times when leaders seek intelligence."

"The eunuch?"

"Pity him, he is scarcely twenty. Jo-kei's partisans routed a bandit lair on the road to Yutu a year ago; they were having sport of the boy with knife and fire."

Jo-kei stirred from bonds of sleep and rose in heaves and grunts, sinking down beside us, saying, "The old one gabbles, eh? It is the privilege of age, but do not heed too much – he's as raw a recruit as you – but a month or so he has been running arms. Think of it!" He bowed in mock servility. "A professor of literature and communist beliefs? It is unsavoury, children – and a 1,000 dollars reward for his head, put there by the Whampoa Military Academy."

"And what of you, Jo-kei?" I asked.

"The eulogy must be limited, with a little bitch around."

"Do not spare me," said Pipa, and Jo-kei belched deep, patted his stomach and turned his face to the dying sun, a face despoiled by heroin. He said:

"I am a fool, if you want the truth: the biggest fool, surely in all Honan, where my large head killed my mother. Once I was a bandit, later a little war-lord. I fattened on looting, lived in a mansion, ate fine foods and owned seven concubines, one of whom I filled each day of the week before breakfast – an idyllic existence."

"Honourable indeed," said Muchai, drily.

"Now I am tired of soft living, easy money, women. Older, I

36

seek idealism to account for sins, and find it in communism. You believe this?"

"It is possible," I said.

"Communism is dogma, and dogma I distrust. For instance, I do not entirely trust Mao Tse-tung – certainly not since the Futien Mutiny, when he sent Chen Yi to shoot his own soldiers. But I give him the benefit of the doubt – somebody must do something to build a better China."

"To whose degeneracy he has amply subscribed," observed Muchai.

Jo-kei made a wry face. "Ah, true, but now I repent. A man must have a goal in life as a reason for staying alive."

Muchai said, "In latter years he has deeply considered Confucius. Forgive him if you find it sickening."

"And we? What do you plan for us?" I asked.

"Service to the partisans first, then service to Mao, and a dignified death if you prove loyal. If you are disloyal between here and Juichin, an undignified passing, for I will personally cut your throats. Does that suffice idealists?"

Later, with the coming of darkness, we camped in a little fertile place and chanced a fire, sitting around it like Tartar bandits while Muchai, first watch, stood like a sentinel on a crag, etched black against the big, October moon.

On the third day of travel, now dodging Kuomintang patrols as we entered the First Encirclement (an area of thin defences), we came to a place called the Country of the Blind, a land east of the Kan River where, through constant malnutrition, eye disease affects the people. We halted the mules on a crag and looked over a scene of utter desolation.

Jo-kei said, "This is near the coffin they call Kuangchang."

"It's an old place for a stink, mister," cried Bricko, suddenly beside me. "Worse than before, eh, Jo-kei?"

The wind was sickly with the smell of corpses as we made our way through the shattered hamlets where Chiang's last great battle against communism was fought. Howitzer muzzles raked the sky, twisted in the hands of giants: from green pond-craters protruded the skeletons of men caught in cross-fire.

Here, Muchai told us, the Red Army had been systematically decimated by a German-backed scientific war at odds of ten to one, and a legion of communist soldiers had committed suicide rather than submit to torture. Here, too, deserters in their thousands had been executed by Chiang Kai-shek's Kuomintang because they were Reds, or recaptured by the Reds and executed because they were deserters. Domestic pigs and wild dogs roamed here at will, fat and slothful in their savaging of the dead, scarcely turning to the clattering hooves on the metalled road.

It came, of course, our first Kuomintang attack: even considering the great distances involved and the impossibility of defending every square mile within a defence encirclement, we knew a challenge to our wanderings had to come. But according to Jo-kei it came sooner than he expected.

Darkness was falling over the land. We had entered a trenched area six miles into the slaughter-ground of Kuangchang when it happened.

Here we had to cut through barbed wire in depth to pass the mules. It was fighting country and the trenches were littered with fresh dead, mainly communist. Jo-kei said, within shelter of stricken trees:

"This is the middle of the First Encirclement; be on your guard – anything can happen. I know this place like my garden back in Honan, but where have all the soldiers gone?"

Even as he spoke, a low whining came from the north.

"Here's your answer," I cried, and gathered Pipa and pushed her flat, throwing myself down beside her. In shrieks of torn metal the earth around us plumed upwards, combed by big-calibre mortars. Instantly, a mule was hit. Its belly ripped open, it crazily wandered about us, shedding blood. The barrage increased, lighting the dusk with stunning, vivid flashes; the ground beneath us heaved and bucked. Bricko, lying beside me, leaped up and raced after the panicking mules in a hail of mortar splinters. And to this, the moment he showed himself, was added the rat-a-tat of distant heavy automatics: how he survived this I do not know, but despite Jo-kei's commands to 'forget the bloody mules' he managed to collect them, run them downhill and tether them in a nearby hollow: on his way back he shot the wandering mule, and returned, gasping, to my side. It was truly conspicuous bravery.

Later, on Jo-kei's command, he lay in a shell-hole and kept up a rapid fire at everything that moved in the moonlight, drawing upon himself intermittent barrages of mortar and automatic fire from the distant Kuomintang post; taking risks of being surrounded by a patrol as he retreated from one position to another. And in the hour of respite he earned, we crept away, led by Jo-kei, into the shattered country of Kuangchang.

At dawn, undaunted, he joined us.

"What the hell you been doing all this time?" demanded Jo-kei.

All that day we travelled, seeking the cover of trees and low places: Bricko cut down branches and with these we camouflaged the three mules so they appeared like walking bushes: gay ferns of autumn, green and gold, we stuck in our clothes, and we travelled even more warily while in the Encirclement area for fear of ambush. But darkness protected us, and soon we entered the actual village of the Kuangchang area, the accepted centre of the No-Man's-Land between the opposing armies; here we chose a derelict cottage and crept within. Bricko lit a fire. Muchai gutted and cooked a captured cockerel. Pipa lay in my arms while the others pressed on the *k'ang* bed about us.

Strangely, though weary, I could not sleep. Lying there amid the fitful breathing of Muchai and Bricko, I watched the pale profile of Pipa's face; beyond it the window was filled with stars and the incandescent flashing of the guns of Juichin. Faint rumbling filled the room as the siege bombardment began a dawn crescendo.

The room spoke of the grief of war, the disordered flight of the villagers. Broken chopsticks were scattered about, a headless doll, a baby's rattle; in one corner stood the little red altar of the Kitchen God, whose lips were annually smeared with honey that he may feed the mouths within – a sour priestcraft of Confucian law that did nothing to protect the inhabitants from the sad absurdities of fratricide.

Suddenly, Jo-kei began to snore in guttural groans that increased to gasps and shouts, an impossible noise. After an hour I could stand it no longer, and rose carefully so as not to awaken Pipa.

It was cool in the little street outside and I wandered aimlessly until a sound sent me into the shadows of a building; there, with pent breathing I watched three men in the darkness. Moving silently, they were lifting off the doors of the abandoned cottages for beds – an old trick of the Red Army. When they disappeared into another cottage, I turned back to warn the others.

"Keep still," said a voice. I felt the prod of a gun in my back. I kept still.

Reaching around me, a hand took my pistol.

The face of the child was little higher than my belt, but he held the rifle with soldierly intent as he backed away, eyeing me. I judged him as one of the thousands of Little Red Devils of Mao Tse-tung's army, but was not prepared to take a chance – in peasant dress he, and the others, could reasonably be bandits. His large, child-like eyes moved over me.

"Deserter?" he asked, treble.

"No. I am on my way to Juichin."

"O aye?" And he looked at me very old fashioned. "Anyone else?"

"No." I was not prepared to commit Jo-kei and the others.

He jerked his head and gestured with the rifle. "Get going."

SEVEN

Clearly, I had arrived at this outpost on the main Juichin fringe at an opportune time, for the main attack forces for the impending break-out were already on the move in bulk, and I wondered if Jo-kei realised the imminence of the action: these were early days in October.

Along the dusty road where the little Red Devil took me, assault troops were already bivouacked, awaiting the command to advance.

In view of the coming interrogation, I wondered if it would be wise to mention the presence in Kuangchang of Jo-kei's party, or not. Why had not Jo-kei brought us these few remaining miles, if this was truly a Red Army outpost? Would mention of partisans bring military reaction – possibly even an attack, on Jo-kei's men, and danger to Pipa? I did not trust Jo-kei. It could even be that he was working for the enemy of communism – Chiang Kai-shek.

I decided to keep my mouth shut on the subject of Jo-kei and Pipa.

"In here," said the child, and propelled me into a hut.

Everything about me smelled of danger: I knew a sad finality, a sense of losing my girl in everything I did.

Later, perhaps, when I knew the situation better, I would begin talking of Jo-kei and his partisans.

The young captain at the bare table looked up with an expressionless face; his grey uniform was stained by rough sleeping, his hair starched with dirt. Yet the weariness of his eyes was countered by a faint humour, and he said, impatiently, "My grandma's minge, Trip – must you root out these running dogs at a time like this?"

"Got him in Kuangchang, Captain," the boy announced brightly, placing my pistol on the table before him.

"You were sent for doors, not bloody deserters." The officer picked up a brush. "Name?"

"Chan Lin-wai."

"What were you doing in Kuangchang?"

41

"I was on my way here. And I am not a deserter."

"They never are – occupation?"

"Medical student – Shanghai University."

"Are you indeed – when do you qualify?"

"Two years from now."

"You'll qualify here. What brought you?"

"The garrison commander was murdering communists." Stuttering machine-gun fire echoed in the hut; a bombardment began along the defences, growing in severity; high above us a shell began its dreary whistling; he did not look up from his notes. Bringing out the letter, I tossed it before him. "Here's a testimonial from one of your Area Comrades, perhaps this will impress you."

His expression was unchanged. "Half the gentry in Kwang-tung have comrade recommendations, it isn't important." He read the letter and put it in a file. "Leave it with me. It may guarantee your life but not a single privilege – |personally, I'm sick of you pseudo-intellectuals."

"Are you not one?"

"But of a long line – ten years of solid communism, father, son, brothers – not a bunk at the first bloody shot fired.'

"You were born fortunate."

"Next you'll tell me you had a Chiang Kai-shek bursary."

"I did."

"And you square that with conscience?" He stared up coldly, then rose, pulling open the hut door, shouting, "Vanguard!"

Another little Red Devil entered, one of portly fat, as broad as he was long. The captain said, "Another gentry volunteer, Little Ball. Take him down to the mules and give him to Tenga." He slid my pistol towards me.

As we left the hut, the boy asked, "Mules, mister? You volunteer for mules?"

"Apparently." We threaded a path through thickening wedges of soldiers going up to the front. It was an inauspicious begin-ning; every yard I walked took me further into obscurity, and I was now seriously worried about what would happen to Pipa.

Bugles were sounding as I followed Little Ball to the quarters of the Fifth Muleteers under a waking sky. Gun-carriers of the parent Sixth Regiment crawled like snakes from caves honey-combed in the hills; motor-cycles wending paths through marching men: the morning made shape in washes of sunlight, the day threatened rain. Little Ball, now walking beside me, fidgeted and grumbled like a veteran in the crush of men and animals and the full light of morning slowly etched in shape and size the smashed fortifications of Yutu, the most westerly outpost of Juichin.

Here, resting after repulsing the Kuomintang's attacks, the soldiers moved with the lethargy of men half dead: weakened by malnutrition and lack of salt, they stared at us as if perplexed by the futility of war, a contrast to the fresh attack troops nearer to the front.

"Sixth Regiment," announced Little Ball, "the best in the army."

They didn't look it. Many, I later discovered, were either Kuomintang deserters, or had run before the White Terror, one of Chiang's communist purges when a million peasants died. Earlier, as a marauding free-foot army under their legendary Chu Teh, they had known constant victory. Taking as their motto the old *Red Eyebrows* revolt cry, 'Share the Land' they were once the nucleus of communism. Now, in Yutu, the advance defenders of Juichin Soviet, they had tasted gall, and before them stretched an ignominious retreat.

"This way, gentry," said Little Ball, "but first we see the wounded."

Clearly, he had brought me this way to impress me.

There came on the wind a tuneless sighing.

Before us stretched a minor sea of litters, the wastage of the Encirclements. The child said, more seriously, "This is Casualty Hospital – we got 6,000. There's another 13,000 back in Juichin City, and more in between."

They lay in the cold without blankets, these wounded, all without drugs, and they were calling for water; pure water was scarce.

There came from the stretchers a moaning chord of sound, with white bandages heaving accompaniment; there was a tang of urine in the wind and the odour of bowels turned to water.

"All these will be left behind," said Little Ball. "Mao can't take wounded on the march."

Propped against rock walls, lying on their backs, they howled at the morning, these men, or lay with ashen faces, indifferent to the Young Vanguards and orderlies racing among them with trailing bandages. Pipa, I thought, would be sickened by the sight of such carnage.

Their uniforms loaded with blood, the men stared listlessly when the wounds were fatal, though many called to me, faintly raising their hands. A boy soldier, squatting on his haunches, rocked to and fro, speechless; his bottom jaw was shot away. Near him, contained, perhaps in the same detonation, five others lay dying; sacks of humanity in blasted clothes, the live, pink bones thrusting up through their rags. Another was mad, shrieking from an astonished face as if for my benefit; under a girdle of trees doctors were operating without anaesthetics, kneeling over victims on doors.

One of the wounded – a child of the mines of Wuhun, he said – called to me and I knelt to him.

"We got to go, mister," said Little Ball. "These doctors see you messin', and you'll have it."

Slackening the brutal tourniquet around the amputated stump of the boy's leg, I removed the filthy bandages loaded with suppuration: slackening the tension, I watched the blood congeal.

A Young Vanguard raced past me and I gripped him, snatched a roll from his pack and bent to the boy again, re-dressing the wound.

"Doctor comin', soldier," said Little Ball, ominously.

He had come. I saw his feet. The wounded boy smiled at me.

"What the hell are you doing?" asked the man.

I rose.

He was thick of body and speech; his eyes moved sullenly from the child to me.

I said, "Whoever put that thing on was a bloody butcher," and returned his stare.

"You a doctor?"

"No – a medical student."

"He just come in," said Little Ball, screwing his hands.

"Has he been through Political Protection?"

"O aye! The captain's put 'im with Tenga."

The doctor bent, examined the dressing, then rose. To Little Ball he said, "Take him over to the Fifth."

Automatically, I followed the child; every move now, every action I made seemed to be taking me farther and farther away from Pipa.

"Tenga, Tenga!" cried Little Ball minutes later, and the corporal turned, bending a thick mule-whip in his large, hairy hands.

"What you got there, Vanguard?" His voice was bass and coarse.

"Gentry muleteer from Political Protection." The boy stood to attention.

"Guts of grandma, he don't look a muleteer to me."

He was a stocky gunk of a man, evil-smelling, a sack of strength. He had a wife in the Kuchi-Yi, and she was Tibetan. His legs, heavily bowed, were clad in torn leather breeches gaitered at the calves; his arms were long and thick. Upon his powerful body he wore a calf-skin jacket furred at the neck (and roped at the middle) which he had stripped from a dandy Tartar officer whose throat he had cut. The stink of him crept out and owned me.

"Where you from, gentry?"

"Laoshan, in Kwangtung."

He put his fists on his hips, and spat. "Another educated puss – when do I get muleteers?"

Little Ball said, "A doctor, remember – he ain't the same as Pansy Yung I brought last."

Tenga said, "You piss off, lest I hand you worse than mules."

I returned his hostile stare.

The drovers gathered about us, streaming from the cave stables where ostlers were polishing and blacksmiths shoeing in a clanging of iron. It would do my lovely Pipa no service to bring her into this.

These were drovers, the dregs of the southern provinces, and usually most brutal of bandits. Now they ringed me, bawling in a high-pitched chorus around another prize. The corporal struck a path through them, gripped a wandering mule by the ear and dragged it before me. "You see this mule, gentry?" The thing struggled away and he caught it again. "*Hei wei*, you old bugger, come here." He twisted up its face to mine. "You see that eye, mister? She's Tojo, and she's evil. You like her?"

I nodded, and he shouted, "Then she's yours. Food she don't need – just plenty of whip – but cut her an' she'll have your balls off, eh, me fancy?" He thumped the mule on the nose, sending it scampering. "You'm a medic, eh?" He peered up at me, fighting for intelligence.

"A student doctor."

"Then you doctor here on Tenga's mules." He bellowed laughter, scratching vigorously under an arm. "She's coot lousy, and you'll be too, but she's a good old buggering mule, ain't you, woman?" The mule regarded me with glinting eyes.

It was a long cry from Shanghai University.

EIGHT

I saw Mao Tse-tung for the first time about a week before the break-out from Yutu, a move delayed owing to repeated feints by the Red Army, and the transportation into the Kiangsi mountains of the 20,000 wounded. Mao, I remember, was pale and huge-eyed after three weeks of malaria – in poor condition for a man about to begin a forced march.

It was on this short tour of the defending outpost that he visited the Third Army Corps, and by this time I was seriously keeping a diary; recording, for instance, that the early opponents of the Bolsheviks were to be left behind at the break-out to defend the host of wounded and sick – one method, apparently, of ridding the Party of undesirable elements under the flag of eternal glory.

One to be abandoned – presumably to make the sacrifice credible – was Mao Tse-tan, Mao's younger brother; nobody could accuse Mao of preferential treatment of relatives and friends.

An early entry in my diary was made while sitting outside the cave where Tojo, my mule, was stabled; well beyond reach of her heels I wrote:

October 10th, 1934

I have been in Yutu, this advance post of the main Juichin Soviet for three days now, and all about me there is talk of partisans who are expected to arrive with more arms, to organise the peasants in outlying areas. Hearing this, I immediately reported to Political Protection. (Happily, the hostile young officer I saw had been replaced.) It was a relief to be told that Jo-kei is known to the military here; that he is working for communism. There was much talk that he might have taken his arms direct to the partisans waiting to support us at the crossing of the Hsiang River. All this should be comforting, but I am sick with worry about Pipa.

Now orders have been received to stand by for the break-out. The waiting column, men say, is twenty miles long, stretching right back east of Juichin City. Today, on the advice of the doctor I met, Tenga, the corporal, has appointed me doctor-student to the Fifth Muleteers – a savage lot. I'd have preferred a higher authority . . .

Three days before the break-out the morning was grey. Thunder threatened throughout the day of unceasing toil and dusk came prematurely with sheeting rain. Where was Pipa, I wondered that wet evening.

There was in the lines of the waiting that convulsive quiet that comes before action; the peasant soldiers seemed to seek relief from tension by raising their voices; the spasmodic bombardment of the nationalists had unaccountably completely ceased.

Our Third Corps, under General Peng, was to be the vanguard, and of this vanguard the Fifth Muleteers, supply carriers, were to follow the Assault Cadres in service to the famous Sixth Regiment, all Mao's veterans. None appeared to know where we were going, the main purpose being to escape from the advancing Kuomintang and the graveyard of the old Juichin Soviet.

This news brought to the peasant soldiers a surly aggression; Mao's invincibility had at last been disproved. Numbed by body ulcerations through lack of salt, dysentery, typhoid and mountain sickness – protected by only a 1,000 dollars purchase of medical equipment – they infected their ranks with a cancer of mutiny.

Until then Mao Tse-tung had been their chosen leader: now, with the evacuation of the base organised by one, Otto Braun (a German expert sent in by Stalin) the rank and file of the Red Army found themselves controlled by a higher oligarchy in a distant land. It annoyed them, drained them of confidence; they were peasants and of proud Chinese origin: it induced in them fear and bred in them aggression. Foreign interference meant loss of face. To them it appeared that they were about to die – not for Mao Tse-tung, but for something Russian.

On the eve of the evacuation, with still no news of Pipa, I was sitting with Yung, a new-found friend posted in to the Fifth Muleteers a few days before me. Watching the soldiers at the collection points, he asked:

"Why are you fighting, Chan Lin-wai?"

I was strapping Tojo's harness with an eye out for a rampaging Tenga, for everything in the Fifth Muleteers was going wrong, said he. I was already tiring of his questions; I ached for Pipa.

"For my son," I replied, "and against Confucius."

"Confucius is dead." Could it be that my Pipa was no longer alive? I wondered, replying:

"That's the trouble, he's not."

"You have a son, Lin-wai?" His young face was eager.

"I am speaking figuratively." Would we, I thought, pick up the partisans after the break-out?

"You appear a lonely man, Lin-wai."

I watched him in the faint moonlight; rain clouds had blown clear of the mountains and the air held a hint of frost.

Yung possessed the classic features of the aesthetic, almost feminine in refinement. Like me, his education had put him among Tenga's muleteers; we would educate the muleteers, they would humble the intellectuals; it was an ethic later to become a parable.

A swarm of fierce-looking peasants thronged past the stables, coming from the issue ordnance after collecting uniforms and provisions. Each man shouldered a carrying-pole, from which hung large tin cans containing the standard issue of six pounds of rice, hand grenades, rifle ammunition; in the pack of each was a blanket, a winter uniform, three pairs of cloth shoes, a drinking cup, chopsticks and dried peppers. Each soldier had a rifle, a wide-brimmed sun-hat and a paper umbrella.

Yung said, "This isn't an army, it's a gathering of rustics."

He was mainly right. It was a force of fighting peasants whose loyalty, until now, had stood staggering reverses – not least Mao's incompetent handling of his Hunan guerrilla campaign of two years earlier.

"They look like bandits to me," Yung added.

Many were. To enroll such cut-throats, Mao Tse-tung had defied the conservatism of the Central Committee's beliefs, the Party machine tail which so often wagged him. Seven years earlier, in 1927, he had arrived in the Chingkangshan mountains a defeated man after the overthrow of his Canton commune idea. Here, in an area of volcanic peaks, a debased society had flocked to his banner – thieves, beggars, murderers, prostitutes: these swelled his depleted army to some 1,500 men and women. The Committee (in which Chou En-lai was then serving) was finally outraged by his acceptance of the followers of notorious secret societies like the *Kê Lao Hui*. Fearing a tainted communist army, the Committee sent against him a newly approved army led by the redoubtable Chu Teh, a leader making a name for himself by routing war-lords who were devastating China. Chu Teh, tracking Mao's force to Chingkangshan, was about to engage him when both armies were attacked by the Kuomintang at the very moment of battle. It was an error from which Chiang Kai-shek never recovered. Uniting against the common enemy, the Reds defeated the nationalist Kuomintang by a combined effort.

At Chingkangshan Mao Tse-tung and Chu Teh formed a union of communism that was never to falter or break.

All this I explained to Yung, and he replied, "They are largely bandits nevertheless. It needs an intellect to know how to die."

"Also a belly."

"Many of my Buddhist relatives died under the Manchus eighty years ago. You agree that history might repeat itself, Lin-wai?"

I strained at Tojo's girths and she snapped viciously over her shoulder. "If it does, then all is lost. Because 100,000 were slaughtered on the Tatu River, need we die? The ideal is to stay alive. You are morbid, Yung, we are useless to China dead."

Later, while we watched the Sixth Regiment streaming past, he said, "It was from my uncle that I learned of communism. He served with Chou En-lai in the same military academy; Chou escaped the Shanghai purges of the intellectuals, but my uncle was captured: he and 600 others were shot on the Bund after torture. I was fifteen years old at the time. My uncle's courage impressed me. At the first opportunity I left Canton University and came to Juichin."

Tenga waddled past us, swearing obscenely, cracking his whip over his head. Ignoring him, Yung continued, "Back in Chekiang I lived in a mansion. My father was a court official, so we ate while others starved. In my village the labourers are so poor that they will strangle a baby for the coral necklace it wears. Once, while dining with my parents I watched the villagers stripping our trees of bark; this they mixed with mud to feed their children. Next day my father's agent impounded their bowls for rent reparations, and our servants actually used them in our kitchen. You don't have to be poor to die in Chekiang."

"Your province is no different from others."

He smiled at his thoughts. "My whole family is tubercular, you know. And my two remaining brothers will die in silk, no doubt, with great attendance and much official wailing – on our verandah, facing the moon; three have already died this way. The villagers will be ordered to attend each death, kowtowing their respect, but one can die better with comrades around – my brothers would not deny me this October moonlight."

I was tiring of him; he was too morose. He added, "The well-bred man should not waste away."

"And your uncle's ideals? Aren't you making a convenience of the things he fought for?"

"Perhaps. It's good heroics." He smiled bitterly.

"But bad communism."

Anticipating the lack of anaesthetics, I had enrolled Yung into the task of poppy-gathering; this, the remnants of the old harvest lay scattered for the winter rot. The method of dispensing the drug was scarcely new; both Yung and I had known it since childhood.

Gathering the poppy heads we filtered out the seeds into one container and pressed out the pod juice into another. And in this, before it solidified, we rolled each of the larger seeds with care, leaving them to dry in the wind. It was the old quack method of gauging the opiate – the smaller the seed the smaller the dose; China had been using the method for centuries. Also by hollowing out a seed it was possible actually to enclose a larger quantity for the deep coma necessary for important operations, and these we carefully labelled.

"You realise," said Yung, "that we're breaking the law?"

"Of course."

"You're prepared to take such a risk, Lin-wai?"

"I am."

"And the chance of creating serious addiction?"

"I'm having no man screaming in my hands. What do you suggest – butchery?"

He gave me his slow amiable smile. "I had hoped you would not mind me giving the warning."

I looked at him in the glow of the stable lamp; his hypersensitivity was apparent in his every move, particularly in the transient, nervous twitching of his fingers. Earlier, Tenga had told me to select a medical assistant; Yung, on first sight, might serve me; a happy contrast to the average muleteer.

A brisk activity now began to grow about us, as if the tensed spring of the break-out was at last unleashed. Long cobras of mule-teams, Assault Cadres with their bristling guns thickened about us, cramming the roads and tracks, heading for the perimeter wire of the forward trenches. And, as if anticipating the imminence of the attack, the Kuomintang siege guns began their baying and thundering beyond the distant wire. From the depth of the First Encirclement shells began the familiar intermittent whistling; in the vast discord these grew into screams, exploding behind us: then, as the Kuomintang gunners got the range, the bombardment plummetted the earth about us in vivid, orange flashes that split the dusk, and through the fury of it I heard Tenga's voice:

"Mount the Fifth! Up off your arses, you lucky muleteers!"

Darkness seemed to strike us instantly, and I saw Yung's white face in staccato flashes of the shells.

This, the forward base of Juichin, was not alone in such treatment. Suddenly the bombardment abruptly ceased, switching north.

We moved out of the forward base on reed-soled shoes, with canvas wrapped around hooves and wheels plaited with bandolier pouches; alongside every cart the infantry danced beneath their shoulder-poles with their strange, mincing gait, and their rifles, back-slung, stabbed the faint stars. On either side, as the hordes silently advanced from Yutu the secret societies came the late arrivals of the Five Villages – supporting Mao as they had earlier done after the failure of his Autumn Rising. Now they sent their wives to help the walking wounded, running through the ranks of the grim Sixth Regiment like coloured fingers: Young Vanguards like Trip and Little Ball, the messengers of the Red Army, suddenly appeared among us, distributing leaflets. Seizing one, I read in the faint light:

> If the enemy advances, we retreat.
> If the enemy halts and encamps, we harass.
> If the enemy seeks to avoid battle, we attack.
> If the enemy retreats, we pursue.

Faintly a bugle sounded the retreat, reminding us that this was not a victory, and past us in the dark marched the 7,000 soldiers detailed to defend the wounded and keep open the gates west of Juichin City until the lumbering Headquarters was clear. Later, we learned that half of these died in the final Kuomintang assault months after; hundreds more, together with officers of the calibre of the famous Kung, their Chief of Staff, deserted, and over 1,000 were ceremoniously beheaded by the victorious Kuomintang after watching their wounded shot on the stretchers. Only a handful escaped.

It was still night when the vanguard under Peng of the Third Army Corps reached the river beyond Yutu and was not attacked.

That night we in the Fifth Muleteers pulled off the road to Tenga's command and watched more of the vanguard march past in the pouring rain – the assault engineers in their hundreds with their explosive packs and pole-charges; the wire cutters; the fierce veteran infantry of the Sixth with their pack-loaded, sure-footed little donkeys, hides steaming. All about us was the dull thundering of the cloth-wrapped wheels, the slithering of reed-soled sandals on the muddy road. Next came the mass of the Sixth infantry, and these were whispering hoarsely from beneath their little sea of oiled-paper umbrellas. The rain ran in streams from their straw sun-hats, their field grey uniforms were soaked, and I heard the outraged exclamations of soldiers going to war. The incessant creaking of their shoulder-poles was like the song in cicadas in the blackness; the rain beat about us all in pelting blusters.

A man called, "Where the bloody hell we off to, Corporal?" and Tenga bawled back:

"I tell you that an' you'll be wiser 'an me, soldier."

All that night we followed them: the bombardment of northern Yutu continued with unabated ferocity as the army pulled out, driving west, but still we did not come to battle: it was as if the Kuomintang had faded away before us. And, with dawn, we reached the river beyond Yutu and stared about us at the vast concourse of men and material; at the deserted Kuomintang trench network; and listened to the assault troops mopping up isolated enemy patrols. It was astonishing, but it was true: apart from minor, thin patrol defences, the Kuomintang had vanished as certainly as if it had retreated pell-mell before us.

But it had not retreated. It had been outwitted by the military genius of Otto Braun, who organised the break-out. Diversionary

53

feints had pulled the bulk of the army to the north, south and east, leaving behind only minor patrols to cover the roads to the west.

All that day was spent building log rafts: the engineers bridged the river in furious haste, the day faded into dusk and still the Kuomintang did not attack. Their bombers, under the pall of mist and rain, apparently could not find us.

The river was bridged before darkness. Mao Tsetung, men, said, walked with long strides along its bank, a man possessed by his own thoughts. Then, before light faded completely, he raised his hand and slowly turned, swinging it to the west. The waiting army stirred in the rain, the whips came out.

Local commanders peered through the rain at sodden maps, noting the main, heavily defended area at Hsinfeng, the crystallised defence line of Chiang's First Encirclement.

Vainly, in the faint light of a misted moon, I looked to the south and Kuangchang, where I was leaving Pipa behind.

The thought had a curious effect on me; I felt no longer whole.

It was the sixteenth day of October, 1934.

The Long March had begun.

NINE

After the first three days we also began to march in daylight, but with more frequent breaks for food; squatting on the road verges and shovelling in the weak congee of rice and cold water, our feet stuck up to revive the circulation. A thin trickle of blood was running down one of Yung's legs, I noticed, yet he did not complain. My own feet, after the first seventy miles, were no longer recognisable as feet: the instep was scarred deep with the abrasing leather thong and mud; the soles a single, shallow blister that extended to the heel.

I was in agony.

When it rained we always marched. Even at a given period of rest, if it rained we were immediately off again, for rain brought poor visibility for marauding nationalist 'planes. It was imperative, the pamphlets said, that the lumbering Head-quarters should be brought as clear of Juichin as possible, for there a fierce battle was now raging between our rearguard and the outwitted Kuomintang. And it was vitally necessary, we were urged, that we should breach the First Encirclement before the enemy could reform: this was the Hunan-Kwangtung line of concrete and wire, with interspersed pill-boxes. Before the town of Hsingfeng we attacked this line by night while the Kuomintang defenders were playing *mahjongg* and drinking in the surrounding hamlets.

The Sixth Regiment, rejuvenated by movement and the promise of fighting, cut through the defences with pole-charges and flame-throwers and led us through the gaps into the open plains beyond. And now, our escape discovered, our light artillery was brought up to carve a path through stiffening opposition.

Heavily camouflaged, we moved ponderously under the heavy bombing of the nationalist 'planes. And, once the First Encircle-ment was breached, we split into two columns to confuse our pursuers, for the pressure of the two armies was coming from the east and north, snapping at our tail. South-west we drove, crossing the Hsingfeng River by the unprotected ferries, and the unreliable Kwangtungese war-lord troops swelled our ranks with desertions.

After taking a batch of these prisoners down to Political Protection, Yung said with prissy charm, "I took the opportunity of enquiring the whereabouts of your woman and her friends, Lin-wai."

"That must have delighted them – every day I'm down there pestering."

"The only hope you've got, apparently, is that they've joined with the Yu partisans behind the Hsiang River."

"I knew that days ago."

Perceiving my abruptness, he said, hurt on his face, "You have no objection to my asking?"

I didn't reply. His pedantry, his impeccable manner savoured of affectation; more, it bordered on effeminacy. These days the tough muleteers greeted Yung with the soprano cries reserved for male daintiness, and the fact that he had stitched himself to me involved me in the ill-bred game. Their attitude angered me and I told them so, to no avail; they could not comprehend that behind Yung's refinement, there existed the masculinity of his breeding. Doubtless, I reflected, they would learn of this when the guns really took over, for China's gentry had long known how to die. Meanwhile Yung appeared not to heed the jibes, and this evoked in me an intolerable sense of shame.

And now I was beginning to fear that I'd never see Pipa again. To enlist with the fervently patriotic partisans, who hated the intellectual classes, was practically a death sentence: nor did I trust Jo-kei, who obviously had a roving eye. And if the scholar, Muchai, interceded on her behalf, his protest would be frail. Bricko I distrusted, Big One I feared.

I replied to Yung now, "I am sorry. It was good of you to ask."

By the first of November we were fighting off minor attacks on our flanks, still dragging behind us the elephantine Headquarters like a wounded beast drags a leg, so much of the heavy equipment was shed in the mountains; printing presses being distributed among the villagers, where instructors were left for local propaganda; tailor's dummies and sewing machines went next, and the villagers took these over, together with tons of uniform cloth to be claimed later. Surplus arms were unloaded from carts and mule-panniers, and buried in mountain caves.

Every village we passed through greeted us as heroes, for we gave, taking nothing. The army, with each succeeding mile of these early days, became lighter, more mobile. By the time we crossed the Hsingfeng River unopposed, our numbers had risen to 120,000, replenishing losses on the march.

New, modern equipment – Chiang Kai-shek's military aid from both Germany and America – was daily being captured and put to better use.

I was marching at Tojo's head over rough country, the cart behind us crammed with wounded, when Tenga appeared beside me. He said, hoarsely:

"Commander Ma's sayin' you come from Jo-kei – you know Jo-kei, that old bastard bandit?"

"I do."

"His Yu fighters should 'ave come to us this side of Yutu, people say."

"I didn't know that," I answered.

"Your woman with them – and you don't know?"

"I know nothing of the partisans."

"Is Jo-kei having a big fool fella wi' him at the Kan River blow-ups?"

"Yes, he did – a man he called Big One."

"An' he speaks to him a language of fingers?"

"Yes. The man is deaf and dumb."

Tenga broadened his chest; his big, yellow teeth appearing in his hairy face. "Then he be still twittering, eh, the big fella?" He thumped his fist into his hand, "Now, ye watch, soldier – when we push over the Hsiang River, Jo-kei's rebels will be there waitin' us – bootin' old Chiang Kai-shek up the backside while we do 'im up front!"

"An attack in the rear."

"That's what partisans are for. Then Big One will leave that old bastard Jo-kei and take care o' Tenga again."

"He's your servant?"

"Since the peace days o' Juichin, but I lent him to Jo-kei, and the fat sod hangs on to him, don't he?"

"And what about my woman?"

"She be safe, too, unless old Jo-kei thinks to 'ave 'er, of course."

"I'll kill him if he touches her," I said.

"Oh, aye?" He grinned evilly from the corners of his mouth.

We marched together in a new friendship, our feet squelching in the mud. Tenga said, "Only two people I trust – the big chap and me son, Hu. I got a pretty little woman – but I don't trust her. In Sun Village, these two – a six year old and me woman. She made him straight an' tall in her belly, didn't she? A flower of a girl – a little dark Tibetan. I'd bleed for her, but a man can't beat his friends. Like Big One – I lends him to Jo-kei, but I wants him back whole."

With this, he left me, glowering, on his thick, bowed legs like an overgrown Tibetan monkey.

Yung said, joining me, "You've been having an intimate conversation with our mule-skinner, I notice."

Of the two I preferred Tenga.

The rain sheeted down; the earth-bound tracks became quagmires. From the east came the rumbling of nationalist cannon, the deep roars of subterranean explosions. With the rain running down my body I listened to the rat-a-tat of rifle-fire – the forward patrols loosening snipers; the sky bulged, fat-bellied in pulsating redness. Clear of Yung, I sat under Tojo's cart, dried the blotted paper of my diary with medical wool, and wrote with a stub of brush:

3rd November, 1934.

We have crossed the Hsingfeng River, the First Encirclement defence, without serious opposition. Surely the Kuomintang must now accept our escape from Juichin. The Sixth Battalion captured Kupo and Wangmu ferries intact; today Tenga spoke of Big One as his servant. Where is Pipa tonight? I wonder.

Yung said, creeping under the footboard, "You are writing to Pipa, Lin?" He opened a book beside me.

"I am writing in my diary. What are you reading?"

"*The Romance of the Three Kingdoms.*" He showed me the cover; his teeth were chattering and I could feel his thin body shivering against me. "Tell me of Pipa," said he.

"She's as incurably romantic as you."

The Third infantry were streaming past us in the rain, hauling their guns, and the mules were taking it hard; it was a bedlam of whip-cracks, shrieks and commands. Discretion had vanished now, the enemy listening posts ignored; the artillery hauled and cursed and flogged the guns down, scarecrows of mud in the hammering rain; this incessant rain drowned my soul, beating in the watery cavities of the brain. Yesterday a man had gone mad with rain, throwing off his clothes and floundering about naked in the mud, flinging up his arms and whining at the sky. Yung said:

"This Pipa of yours – is she beautiful?"

"Men look up from eating when she passes."

Isolating myself from the agony of the mules, I dozed in the damp steamy haze of soaking clothes, chin on chest.

"Are you sleeping, Lin-wai?"

I wished him to the devil; why the hell couldn't he shelter under his own bloody cart? A corporal on the road was shouting shrilly, cursing and lashing at everything in sight, and he cried, "Come on, come on, get those fuggin' mules out of it and head up the guns, come on, you Cantonese bastards!"

Pipa's mouth, I remembered, was beautiful when she smiled.

Yung said, "You prefer not to speak of your woman, Chan Lin-wai?"

Now we swirled like a giant cobra over the winter roads of Kwangtung, with General Peng's vanguard leading us in a north-west march, striking over the Chang River for distant Chengkuo, while a second prong thrust for the Chingkanshan mountains, Mao's old bandit lair; cutting through the Second Encirclement defences of the Canton railway with ease.

During the third week out of Juichin's Yutu I stood on a rock and watched the Red Army on the march. Before we went the Red Cadre assault companies with their red flags streaming in the wind: we, the Fifth Muleteers carrying ammunition and forward supplies, came next in the column (each regiment – and we supplied the Sixth – possessed a muleteer company of some 300 men) and then came the bulk of our Sixth infantry – about 2,000 men in all. But they did not march in a formation of trained soldiers: the peasant army travelled in the manner of China's centuries – each man with the same lilting trot, his slung rifle and shoulder-pole hung with his personal provisions, grenades and fifty rounds of ammunition. His own rice he carried and cooked on the way in the communal section cooking pot, to which he subscribed a daily handful; he carried his own water; his titbits, which every soldier managed to scrounge on the march, became his own property as personal as his letters home. His lavatory paper he carried in his oiled-grass sun-hat, his needle and thread could be seen pinned to its brim. The Red Army soldier was a self-contained unit in every respect; his rifle was as much his personal property as the pack-blanket he used for sleeping and in which, if his stars proved unlucky, he was buried.

Behind our Sixth Regiment the main column, now unidentifiable as individual units, streamed away over the countryside with the other regiments comprising our Third Corps. Lin Piao's First Army Corps stretched ten miles over the horizon, followed by the Central Column commanded by Chou En-lai. Last came the rambling General Headquarters sandwiched for protection between Tung Cheng-tang's Fifth Corps and General Lo Ping-hui's Ninth, the fighting rearguard. And this army of over 100,000 men was commanded by the Central Revolutionary Council, the political arm of which General Chu Teh was Commander-in-Chief.

To see this aggression snaking over the plains, spitting fire from its flanks on the march was a sight to be remembered. And it was a cock-a-hoop army. Success was in the air as fears of Chiang Kai-shek's Encirclements were dispelled; united at Linwu and sandwiching between our prongs a host of prisoners, we split yet again and attacked towards the next Encirclement defences, the broad Hsiang River.

It was at Linwu that we shot our first landlords; eight of them, ashen-faced and old, indicted by the townsfolk for crimes against the people. Dragged to the execution posts, surrounded by wailing relatives and friends, they kowtowed and begged for their lives. But we shot them just the same, and, as far as I know, without giving them a hearing. It was a popular decision with the crowd. Ragged volleys split the dusk; eight old landlords jerked their fleshless limbs to the impact of bullets and floundered about.

This had the desired effect, the pamphlets said next day: landlords in the path of the victorious Red Army were now fawning over their tenants. Instructions as to how to treat the peasant population were, however, a little different.

"Order of the Day Number 17!" yelled Little Ball, racing along the muddy streets. I took one of his pamphlets and read the order aloud:

The following rules will be learned; all ranks will be expected to repeat them by heart:

1. Obey orders.
2. Do not take anything from workers or peasants.
3. Hand in everything taken from landlords and gentry.
4. Put back all doors used as bed-boards.
5. Replace all straw borrowed for bedding.
6. Speak politely.
7. Pay fairly for what you buy.
8. Return everything you borrow.
9. Pay for everything you damage.
10. Do not bathe in the sight of women.
11. Do not search the pockets of captives.

Yung said, sarcastically, "Those landlords would be the first to agree, you know – it is a most idealistic war."

On the march to the Hsiang, with Tenga's help, I managed to exchange Toja's large ammunition carrier for a long-cart – a broad, deep-bellied affair covered with a removable hooped canopy. Into this we fitted rought litters: full, it could carry twenty men in comfort and thirty at a push. Indenting for surgical instruments to Third Headquarters, I was astonished to see these arrive – later, I learned that a rampaging Red Cadre had captured a coach of an ambulance train near Linwu, for bandages and surgical equipment were comparatively plentiful.

With Yung an unofficially appointed nurse, and Tenga on call to hold the patients down, I was able to carry out minor surgery while actually on the march – pulling out of the column and operating at frantic speed, then whipping up old Tojo for a gallop back into position. And the patients (I was responsible only for the Fifth – about 300 men) gripped by Tenga for minor cutting, would howl at the winter sky.

My first important operation in the new ambulance cart was a back wound: the bullet had taken the soldier high, neatly razored away his tunic and shirt and inflicted a shallow gash from bicep to bicep. Now the man lay on his stomach at the end of the cart and watched the column pass with calm eyes As Yung mentioned later – quite out of context – he really was extraordinarily handsome. I cut away the blood-stained shirt and bared the wound while Yung opened his notebook on the footboard.

"Name?" said he.

He got no reply.

Yung shrugged. "Number?"

"And I have no number," replied the soldier, "am I cattle?"

Yung was nonplussed; I was interested. This one was educated for a soldier of the line. I said, "Opium . . .?" and offered him a seed.

"No opium."

I said to Yung, "Then call Tenga to hold him down."

"And no Tenga – that mule's not putting his hands on me."

I cleaned the wound and poured on iodine: it ran in a little surge along the red channel of the wound. The soldier bowed his head, but made no sound.

I said, grimly, "This needs stitching. Will you change your mind on the opium?"

"Just stitch it."

The muscles of his back were like iron under my hands. I sewed him from shoulder to shoulder, and he pushed Yung away as he tried to help him out of the cart. The wounded watched him with astonished eyes.

"Thanks," said the soldier, and pulled on what remaind of his coat.

I called from the litter, "Be reasonable – I must have a record, soldier."

Turning, he bowed slightly, saying bassly, "I am the man from Kwangtung."

"He's a bit of a mouthful," said Yung, glumly, writing.

"He's a bit of a man," I said, watching him disappear.

Next morning I saw him back in the column, actually carrying his rifle slung.

I did not know then that my destiny was linked with his.

In the little town of Amor I washed myself with hot water for the first time since leaving Juichin Soviet. Tenga was drunk that night, dancing in the light of the fire, surrounded by 100 clapping muleteers, who roared his bawdy song in chorus. All down the line, now that the rain had stopped, men were cleaning equipment, feeding the animals, and as the column crammed into the little market town, I saw away to the east a line of fiery torches of regiments which had not yet arrived.

The Mist and Flower bawdy houses were crammed; music filled the narrow streets of mud-walled houses. Within them the little painted flowers of prostitution tiptoed on dainty feet to the playing of the *pi'pa*: the cymbal clashing of a Cantonese opera echoed from the square where more landlords had died.

Yellow lamplight shafted the rutted streets. Bright were the stalls of the tiny market-place where the traders, astonished at being alive, cried their wares under the hissing naphtha flares, bargaining for the sulphur-drugged cobras being skinned alive, the flat, roasted duck and dried fish strung in rows, their phosphorescence glimmering in the dark.

Here were the ragged orphans of war, the widows, the aged grandmothers and grandfathers pinned on sticks in a travail of hunger – the bony specimens of Chiang Kai-shek's Old China. Beggars called to me for alms, holding before me scientifically crippled children, their tools of trade: dogs that had so far escaped the club roamed here in starving desolation, cats darted from kicks, rats watched from shadows. And there was in the night wind that sweet-sour, onion smell that will be for ever China – boiling herbs, manure and incense of the joss – it was the smell of Laoshan, and its perfume took me home.

And I thought of Pipa, needing her in longing.

A young communist of the Sixth, already tipsy, lurched past me with a girl: she was young, and there was in her an urgency of youth that I had seen in Pipa; though hunger had savaged her body, there was in her face a cool, exquisite beauty, and about her a coyness that reached out and touched me. Obviously, she was one of the hundreds of prostitutes serving the Kuomintang: I wondered if she would fare much better with the idealistic communists. Disease, I reflected, would begin to take its toll of the Red Army as the occupation of towns and cities increased.

Malaria, meningitis and trachoma were the scourges at the moment: mountain sickness, always with us, was usually mild. Feet ulcerations grew with the forced marching, of course, yet, curiously, certain sicknesses were prevalent in certain provinces, according to the pamphlets I weekly received. Thyroid troubles occurred later in the province of Yunnan, for instance, probably through lack of iodine; cholera and syphilis outbreaks appeared in Shensi. But of all diseases, venereal cases were the most rare:

less than a score of Red Army soldiers were so infected. This was probably because most of the soldiers were very young, therefore sexually inexperienced. Also, with a marching average of twenty-six miles a day since the Juichin break-out, the troops were too tired to indulge in anything but sleep, the ironic battle cry of the Sixth being, 'Don't go to sleep beside her, go to sleep on her.''

The young soldier I met with his girl was obviously an exception: he was leading her to a bed with the brooding intent of the hunting male: vaguely I wondered if he would appear before me within a week: in the event, he did not come. Next time I saw him he was face down in the mud of the Hsiang River.

In retrospect, I hope he enjoyed her.

Every woman I saw that night, every female voice I heard, brought to me an overwhelming longing for Pipa.

TEN

Recoiling like a spring from Amor, the Third Assault Engineers led us over the plains of Hu towards the wide Hsiang at a gallop. Yung shouted to me above the beating hooves:

"Soon there'll be big fighting, Lin – Tenga says the Kuomintang will make a stand at the Hsiang," and a soldier lying exhausted in the rain cried:

"Not at the Hsiang, friend. Word's come down from Peng's Headquarters – Mao says he'll fly over us like 100,000 birds."

"Like 100,000 camels," yelled Tenga, jumping from his cart. "Get off those bloody footboards and leg it with the mules!"

The word went down the line; rumour was at it again: an army marches well on scandal: Otto Braun's wife, Peng's wife, Mao's wife.

"She's with child again."

"Who?"

"Mao's wife."

Work the dates back, shout them in the line. "They say she's marching with the rest."

"Then she's no more'n three months away – I remember my missus."

"One thing's sure, lads, Mao ain't marching."

Yung said, "The man's ill."

In truth, Mao's wife was carrying heavily; and that morning after racing out of Amor, a nationalist 'plane had strafed the column, blasting the Central Headquarters caravan where she was lying – twenty-four pieces of shrapnel in her body. The woman, said Mao in an Order, were displaying amazing courage; the wife of Chu Teh was another example. Her name was Kang and she was built like a wrestler: a fighting brigade commander, she marched every inch from Juichin to Paoan, often carrying a wounded soldier.

Still striking north-west through daily bombing, we were yet pushing everything before us, the pace increasing to get the fighting rearguard clear of ancient Amor. And the rain, as ever, sheeted down, a constant water-torture drumming on our wide-brimmed sun-hats so that we marched and jog-trotted in its constant dripping thunder. In Kwangtung it had been a deluge; Kwangsi province, looming up from the west, promised little better. It teemed from glowering clouds, it bucketed in tub-washes of water, soaking men, animals, filling the carts, loading the bedding: before us stretched an ocean of water inches deep: it was eternal, unrelenting: we sloshed along in it, blinked it out of our eyes, spat it from our mouths. Our flesh was bleached white by water – faces as white as fish bellies loomed from under the sun-hats; foot blisters rumpled and opened, abrased with the unending mud; the leather throngs of our sandals twisted and cut into our insteps; our reed shoes dissolved and floated away; unprotected, we slithered in the quagmire, the hidden flints of the broken roads slitting our feet. And, when men faltered, the cry went out:

"Mao's wife, Mao's wife, Mao's wife!"

"To hell with Mao's wife!"

"Sod Mao's wife – you too, Tenga!"

The pace increased; the exhausted mules, horses, donkeys were flogged into a canter, and we raced after them, whips cracking behind the bucking carts, splitting the cries of the tumbling wounded. A corporal of Peng's Headquarters, galloping down from Headquarters, bawled through the rain, "Get on, get on, the column's bunching!" and he shouted into Tenga's face:

"The rearguard's trapped on the bunch in Amor. General Lo's holding off two Kuomintang armies east of the village – get on, you mad bugger, do you want them slaughtered?" and he wheeled his mare and galloped along to the vanguard: out with his own whip, then, flaying the leading mules, and Tojo collected more than her share, until Tenga got after him.

Exhausted scarecrows no longer recognisable as men were falling out of the column. The lead animals of the Assault Cadres were being beaten to the point of collapse, the stinging water spraying from their flanks to every slash of the whips.

"The Kuomintang are coming!"

"They've encircled the rearguard!"

"Do you want disembowelling? Get on, the Fifth, get on!"

Tactically, speed was a necessity: it would get the vanguard over the flooded Hsiang River and allow the column to stretch: bunching, jammed roads in the rear echelons were the constant fear.

So we raced out of Amor and down to the basin of the Mother Hsiang. And on the night of the second day, the Fifth, following the Cadres, reached the river: I saw it in the glare of the watery moon, one strangely brilliant for the season. In now thunderous rain, I saw the gleam of the great Hsiang. It was claiming by flood acres of the soaked countryside, a lake of mirrored brilliance. To cross this meant temporary safety for the whole Red Army, for the Kuomintang armies had been preparing, men said, to pincer off Lo's Ninth Army Corps. Its Red Cadres were selling their lives in vicious fighting nobody else had known, to keep us clear of encirclement.

I sank down beside Tojo's cart into the mud of the river, letting the rain beat over me, listening to the shouts of the Sixth pushing up. All about me animals sank down in the shafts, refusing to rise despite pitiless beatings: the Fifth Muleteers rocked on their buttocks, holding their bleeding feet. That night and all next morning the First Front Army poured in its fighting men to the bank of the river – the Cadre corps specialists under General Chen, the First Army under Lin Piao and the Fifth Army under General Tung who got bunched outside Amor – all flocked down to the Hsiang in a broad front, calling for raft-pontoons, hauling the artillery into position for a covering barrage. Only at dusk on the second day did the feverish activity cease.

Afterwards I checked the distance and time against a map.

In a fourteen-hour march we had covered eighty miles.

"I have never force-marched before," a young corporal of the Cadre Corps said to me, "and I shan't do it again – not even for Mao Tse-tung."

Away from eyes, I sat beneath the cart after feeding Tojo – she didn't require watering – and gently removed the remaining shreds of my reed sandals. The bitter November wind, though shivering my bones, brought instant relief to my feet. I moaned as I washed them in a pool of water, for they were humped with swellings, the skin split, exposing the red flesh of the soles.

Bandaging them, I fetched medical supplies from Tojo's cart where she was standing in splayed dejection. Limping around, I went to the crippled soldiers. The first I tended was a man of the Fourth battalion. He was no longer young: sweating with pain, he yet greeted me as I knelt before him.

"I was once a farmer of Peiha," said he, "and walked my share, but this is madness."

I washed his lacerated feet with care; even when I poured iodine into the wounds he did not complain. I said, "Your little toe is hanging on your right foot, do you know it?"

He did not reply, but Tenga, visiting his muleteers, shouted, "More than one toe off and you ride, lads – feed them to the mules. Dropping big toes all the way through Kwangsi, eh?"

I said to the peasant farmer:

"Look the other way. Concentrate on that fool, Tenga," and I cut off the toe, cauterised the stump and plastered it.

Tenga bawled lustily, aping the soldier's pain – indeed, I could have done without him.

"Another forty miles tomorrow, muleteers, remember!"

They bantered with him, but it was fitful humour.

On the bank of the Mother Hsiang, I took them off: young toes, old toes – toes of every size and shape could be found on the road to Amor, said the Young Vanguards coming up from Third Headquarters. But there was also a sweet rumour floating down the line: Ho, the wife of Mao Tse-tung, had given birth on the march.

Men snatched at it, nurturing it, repeating it with praise. With her body peppered with shrapnel, she had given Mao a daughter.

It was true, and excellent propaganda.

"If she can birth a girl on this march, you can walk on a few toes less," bawled Tenga.

How long, I thought, would Pipa's feet stand this sort of treatment?

Mistakes were made, and paid for. The stupid Third Battalion, thinking they were miles from the Hsiang River, came down to the river with torches blazing, a snake of fire across the hills, and the Kuomintang gunners on the far bank opened up on us from point-blank range.

Technical mistakes cost us deadly. The Bridging Section got their sampans and rafts bogged down in the mud six miles east, and did not report it. So we sat in shivering misery on the river bank awaiting assault craft that did not come while the earth erupted around us in showering sand and stones. Tenga, the first to show his head, was wading knee deep among the mule-carts shouting his head off, and I saw him shake a fist into the face of a staff officer, crying, "We done our bit – we got here like you ordered. Where's those fuggin' boats, then – where's your fuggin' guns?"

The barrage laid about us from oriented guns: yard after yard of us being slowly decimated as we scrambled with bare hands into what cover we could find. Mules were somersaulting, carts overturning. Men were shrieking about me; animals, out of the shafts, were floundering girth deep in mud, fighting to be free; mules, horses and donkeys were crying. And Tenga stood on a cart with shrapnel whistling about him, yelling, "Hold the mules! *Hold* them! Is this what I taught you?" Now the gunners came with their own mule-trains, flogging them down to the river's edge, and this added to the confusion, for the mud took them, sucking them down: false tides, caused by short-falls, wallowed over them. The cry went up from hundreds of men, "Where's the boats? Where's the boats?"

Confident now, the enemy barrage increased; small arms fire added to the holocaust. Whistling iron cut men in half, and disembowelled animals. The whole of the Sixth Regiment were stuck as effectively as flies on fly-paper, cowering under the barrage from the enemy bank. In the flashing light, oblivious to the explosions (for the closer they are the more silent they become) I saw a mule-train charging down the road towards us with assault log-rafts bucking behind them. Men shouted, "The boats are coming!" And I saw the raft, the four mules and their muleteer disappear in the red blaze of a direct hit. Men were falling from exhaustion now; others, abandoning their mules, fled, their stuttering faces shouting unanswered questions. Up on the top of the bank mules were stampeding; free of the shafts they raced along the dry flats of unchurned earth, trailing their traces and the bodies of their drivers. Automatic weapons raked us as bank fires confirmed our position, their tracer blazing across the glittering Hsiang, for now the moon had risen, as if to watch the decimation of the Third Corps. Yung staggered through the swamp towards me as I fought to get Tojo clear. I saw him through curling, red smoke, and he was coughing: blood was on his face as he yelled something unintelligible; we were confined, alone, doomed to isolation in the clamouring, unheard cannon. All about me were uniformed wraiths of grey lit occasionally by

69

pulsating orange light: men staggering, men falling, running in howls in the pealing of the guns. Yung was gesticulating before my face now, his mouth opening and shutting mechanically against a jumbled mass of mules, limbers and men dancing in space. Tenga was hit in the head, yet amazingly survived, leaping about grotesquely, cursing vividly, his hand clapped to a shredded ear. And the bombardment grew slowly to a crescendo, a deafening concussion: then abruptly ceased.

There grew about men an eerie silence, as if great hands had put sand-bags on the world. In this melancholy respite there was no sound but the crying of men and animals.

Tojo had actually come down on top of me, and I was lying with my legs under her belly when man hauled me out. The Kuomintang were silent; a man said they were cooling their guns. Another beyond Yung leaned over and whispered hoarsely:

"I was on the top, you see – *wei*, *wei*, I had it bloody terrible; as fast as he took me up he hit me down."

Another said in the silence, "My mate in the Sixth has gone, you know. Both legs were off him, you hear me?"

"Yes," I replied.

Yung said, "You all right, Lin?"

I nodded against him.

The first man said, "I'm having an awful fuggin' war, you know. Nobody in the Third is having a worse bloody war than me, doctor." His face, broad and plastered with mud, was split by his toothy Cantonese jaw. "You got an opium seed for me, mate?"

On the wind I heard them, *Aiya, aiya, aiya* ... and said to Yung, "What happened?"

"You got stuck under the mule."

A voice said, "Yen was his name and he come from Canton – my friend. He had a sister five years old. His father's dead with the Cadre, he said – there's a muleteer down there with a blown-up belly – sod, he looked awful. As I tied him together he called me Mao." The voice fell to chuckling softly, holding its face. I said to Yung, "Are you all right?"

"Got it through the arm."

Tenga was wading around us, shouting, "Get off the bank – up on the dry, ye fools – come on, come on." He swayed towards me, stooping, holding his ear. I said to him, "What's wrong?"

70

"What's wrong? Somebody shot me fuggin' ear off, that's what's wrong."

"Let me see."

Yung said to Tenga, "He can't do it yet, Corporal – the blast got him."

"Then haul him out, before it starts again."

In the silence that followed, they bent above me, pulling me out of the mud, and the first thing I heard when I opened my eyes was a voice saying, "Oh, *aiya*! Nobody's 'aving a worser war than me."

With my senses returning, I propped myself against Tojo's cart: its load of wounded were miraculously unhurt. Tenga said into my face, "What about this bloody ear, then?"

"What about it?"

"I want it off."

Sickness was welling up in my throat and I swallowed it down. I said, turning his head to the moon, "It will stitch, you know."

"I don't want it stitched, I want the bugger off."

A man said, "I was here before him, you know."

"Maybe," shouted Tenga, "but I'm a bloody corporal."

They stood in a swaying line before me, muttering, grumbling their tales of war. A man called from the back, "Cut his bloody throat while you're at it, Bone-man, never mind his ear."

"Are you all right, Lin-wai?" whispered Yung.

I cut off what was left of Tenga's ear with bandage scissors, all I could find, and he roared and danced before me: men were laughing, despite their wounds, floundering about me in the moon-shot smoke like dogs circling a kill; one, I remember, had a single eye gleaming in his head, the other was a socket of blood. A man was calling, "Who'd be with the bloody Fifth? Who brought us down here?"

"That bastard, Tenga!"

"It was terrible, you know. I suffered a lot."

"I got a little woman in Miao Country, Doctor."

"Mine will never believe it – missed me cock by inches."

"Call her lucky."

"She's left Canton, you know."

"Got his ear shot off."

"Serve him right, the sod."

They danced before me, yelling while I dug out shrapnel from one and another, and I was making a ghastly mess of it. Yung said, "Careful, Lin, you'll have his fingers off."

I said to the man, "It won't hurt much now, I think I've cut the nerve."

Somebody said, to a background of high whistling, "Here they come again!"

"Scatter!" bellowed Tenga, up on the cart beside me.

The bombardment had started again. This time the shells were landing behind us, bringing the same roaring confusion to the Seventh Regiment coming up; vaguely, I was glad it wasn't us. Yung shouted into my face:

"We'd best find some cover. Can you walk, Lin-wai?"

The concussion had iced my brain: I reeled, and Yung, with amazing strength, held me with one arm; the other hung uselessly beside him. His body was soft, like a girl's. It was a delicious sensation amid such carnage, rather like being against the body of Pipa. I said, "That arm . . ."

"I'm all right," said Yung.

In wet grass, I knelt beside him while the shells of the Kuomintang planed and whistled in the moon-lightening sky: I saw his face, smooth and unlined, and the white sweep of his throat; he said, "*Tin Hau*, when morning comes they're going to plaster us."

It was strangely pleasant in the warmth of him; automatically, I pulled myself away, sank down on the stones; with regaining senses, I stared about me in the moonlight.

The river bank was strewn with men and animals, limbs entwined. Upon the faces of the dead was a careworn age; they lay in disordered postures, leap-frog statues with their clothes ripped off.

"Come," said Yung, and pulled me to my feet again; he led me down to water. And we stepped through the dead and badly wounded with careful tread, lest we should awaken them into a yowling protest from sleep.

All about us was the wastage of the bunch, the spillage of men and machines halted in an onward rush. And now, with the assault boats being rushed down to the bridgehead, faint cries came from under the raking hooves and wheels. The raft-pontoons heaved like bulky ghosts on the face of the river.

And as we knelt, Yung and me, washing clean Yung's wound,

a soldier of the engineers deliberately dropped a bridging plank, reached out with his foot and toppled me over. "The sampans are coming through," he said, "you can't stay here."

"You running dog!" yelled Tenga, coming up, holding his ear. With his free hand he raised his mule-whip. "Take your dirty hands off my muleteers!"

The night was alive with incandescent flashes, the river glowed with light and blood; the earth below us heaved.

ELEVEN

We lived through the numbing November night with the wind coming from the east across the flooded river, waiting for dawn and our massive attack. We muttered about the inefficient bungling that ordered us into a river swamp when we could have stayed 200 yards back, in the dry – under cover, instead of exposed to enemy fire. We debated, in the mud and rain, the incorrect timing, the lack of covering fire, the lateness of the assault craft, the absence of artillery.

Yung said, "It's the administrative mind. A retreat like this can't pull a caravan behind it – Otto Braun is mad."

"Don't blame him – ain't this Mao's soddin' army?"

Another said, "It's the non-combatants that does it. It takes three of them to keep one of us in the field – the Red Army University, the Red Revolutionary Council – no wonder everything's red around here."

A third muttered (and he was a peasant farmer of Kiangsi), "Then there's the Central Bloody Committee, the Young Communist League and the anti-Imperialist something or other – every one of them think they're the biggest thing on the march."

"We lost a couple of printing presses and a tailor's dummy," replied Yung, sarcastically, "but the Headquarters is still as big as an elephant – sandwiched between the Seventh and the Ninth to keep the bullets out."

"Oh, what a bloody army," said a man. "I fought with Mao before, but it isn't the same this time."

At dawn light the Young Vanguards came up to the river, giving the time of the attack.

The Third Corps died in the river, their frail rafts shot from under them in the continuous waves of assault; many swam, and were shot like turtles within the first 100 yards. They died in each other's arms, swept away by the Hsiang flood: on the pontoon decks they died, sitting on logs or in the few assault sampans the bridging sections hauled up – the farmers of Hunan and Kwangtung, the fishermen of Foochow and Swatow who could handle boats: some even reached the far bank, shouting their *Internationale* into the muzzles of the nationalist guns.

Some died under bombs, for the Kuomintang 'planes had found us now; others by execution, being hauled out by the enemy on the west bank and shot in batches. But still the infantry poured in, sent by a military contraption numbed by mounting losses. And, while panic and recrimination continued in the tented Headquarters, the rain sheeted down, turning the mud of the home bank into a swamp and more of the Red Army died, by suffocation.

By midday, with the massacre continuing, the Third and Fifth Corps began to falter, so reinforcements were sent up. But we were still short of assault sampans, so regimental messengers went galloping down the line.

The last reinforcements now came from Lin Piao's First Corps.

In their thousands they waded into the mud, walking scarecrows, strangely tufted: re-forming, they shivered in the swamp, their hopes dashed by the complete failure of our first assaults: as dead men they lay, numbed by the Kuomintang bombardment, with the rain hammering on their backs and the shrapnel whistling above them.

I lay beside them under the barrage with what remained of the Fifth, for the Muleteer Supply Unit could not move until the infantry had got a bridgehead.

They were men of the farms, mostly, these of Piao's First, the pride of the army; coarse, rangey men and tall, being from the north. Many were new to communism; few were afire with wild ideals.

But they were patient men, worthy of the land.

Beyond the marching, the blood of the long campaigns, there was locked in them the lust for peace and a longing for home: they dreamed, generally, of a hut and six *mou* of land, a woman, rice, the cicada's song: these banished the fears of the stumpy amputations, the beggary of the city walls. Fiercely critical, they were yet Mao's veterans: despite his military errors, they followed him: they even sought excuses for his execution of thousands of their comrades in a blood-bath of three years before, their Futien mutiny of 1931. Mao Tse-tung was right, they claimed – in the end; Lin Piao was their commander,

Chu Teh their Commander-in-Chief; these they trusted and loved, but they didn't compare with Mao.

Now they hadn't seen him for a week: it unsettled them, it made them uneasy.

"Where the fuggin' hell 'as he got to?" someone asked.

"The sod's always up wi' the forward Cadres – one of these days he'll bloody catch it," said another.

"I reckon he's dead," said a third.

This silenced them; his continued absence at the Hsiang pestered them, for things were going wrong. They were becoming as jumpy as alcoholics.

Nobody dared tell them that Otto Braun, the German, was directing the Hsiang assault; that Mao had malaria.

By nightfall of the third day before the Hsiang River the flashes of the Kuomintang guns, the blood, were wine-tinting the flood. The sodden remnants of the Sixth Regiment, backed by units of the First Corps, moved in a mud-plastered phalanx down to the river. And Trip, the Young Vanguard who had captured me in Kuangchang, was shouting shrilly:

"Tenga! *Tenga!*"

I pulled him clear of the men. "Get back, lad. In two minutes the barrage starts again."

An orthodox German thoroughness, free of variation, was now to be found in the tactics of the Kuomintang: you could put your watch right by their bombardments. Trip cried, shaking himself free, "I got to find Tenga. Headquarters wants your carts back there, the baggage train's been hit!"

"Bollocks to the baggage train," said a voice from the ranks.

"Otto Braun himself, remember!" cried Trip.

"And Bollocks to Otto Braun," said the voice. The men laughed with surly aggression, shouldering past in the endless mud. I said to the boy:

"Leave it with me, I'll find Tenga – go on, out of it!"

Red flares glittered from the enemy bank; a shell exploded near by, the air stung with cordite. Then a Very light shot up, suspended against the stars, exposing us: I saw the wan faces of the new waves of attackers, the hollows of their eyes and sunken cheeks. They looked as men do when facing the firing squad, already dead but moving with the relentless vigour born of self-discipline, their wading feet leaving deep swathes in the mud. The light spluttered out, bringing darkness. Tenga, as if bidden, called from the darkness, "Where's the Fifth? Where's my muleteers?"

"Here!" I replied, and found him. "Message from H.Q., they want the mules and carts back there."

"*Aiyo!*" He gripped me. "Get medical packs – we'll need first aid."

Cupping his hands, he shouted, "Gather up the Fifth – give your carts to the Vanguards. Muleteers, muleteers!"

"*Wo*, Tenga!" They cried back from the darkness, "Tenga, Tenga!" His name was becoming a password of authority.

"Over here, over here! Come on, lads, we're away with the infantry." Tenga fired a pistol into the air and they sought the flash of it, pressing about him for safety. I heard my wounded shouting for me as Tojo and the cart went to the rear. Yung came up, one arm in a rough sling.

"What's that?" demanded Tenga, peering through the gloom.

"A flesh wound," Yung answered.

"Good lad. It's through the head that counts." He gripped us both. "Over the pontoons, eh? The pair of you follow the run – first aid on the bank, remember – it'll be days before the Third medics get over."

His last words were almost obliterated in a roar of our own artillery; darkness was shattered by brilliant flashes: ten pounders whined above us, landing on the enemy bank in vivid balls of light; dull reverberations echoed in hollow clatters over the river. And, as our bombardment increased I saw, with astonishment, a make-shift raft pontoon bridge stretching like a rod from our own bank; on it, their naked bodies reflecting red, the bridge engineers, the army élite, were working with precision: around them swarmed a small navy of sampans with stores. The sight of it galvanised the Sixth into action; rising from the mud, they swept towards the bridge in clamouring excitement.

Seeking cover behind a fallen tree, Yung and I watched the main assault on the Hsiang.

Our artillery grew into a full, bass song; along the bank behind us new groups of black muzzles were appearing every minute, joining the snouting fire, and the heat of their discharge scorched us. Ten minutes later, with fresh infantry rushing past us towards the sampan bridge-head, the line of dim earth that sheltered the bulk of the Red Army danced and glittered in the discordant crashing of guns. I saw nothing as vicious in the Long March campaign. Within minutes the whole of our own front was alight, a constant horizontal bonfire along the river interjected with stabs of concussive explosions. And in this inferno the shapes of the gunners writhed and twisted like men being consumed: the smoking muzzles of the big ten-pounders spoke deeply; the heavier fire of the two-point-fives snapped like angry terriers, a brighter hue, and the steady rat-a-tat of the heavy machine-guns compounded all into a sustained roar. The earth bounced and quaked beneath us in the fire-power of the new Red Army. Men about me were shouting deliriously, slapping each other's backs, moving in a thick wedge of bodies towards the engineers' bridge-head. And suddenly, knifing the staccato broadsides, I heard Tenga's voice:

"Come on, lads. It's Tenga, *Tenga!* Over the bridge wi' the Fifth, eh? – come on, come on!"

Yung whispered urgently, "Is it us, is it us?"

"No, we wait till the bridge-head is secured."

A suspended rocket-light brightened the face of the Hsiang. I saw the clustered sampans, the flashing paddles, the high plumes of the erupting water, then the light died. The entire Red Army, as far as I could see, was rising from its initial shock and loading into the river.

"Who's that madman?" yelled Yung into my ear, for an officer was riding a big brown charger in front of our guns, risking decimation: now the horse slithered down the bank into the mud, and floundered towards us. I saw his waving sword; he was shouting as he threaded through the milling infantry, "Where's my Third Corps? What are you doing lying here?"

"It's Peng Teh-huai," I shouted.

And they rose to him, reaching for him, scrambling out of the craters like startled rabbits: bare areas of the mud became alive with hiding men. Grabbing his stirrups, many ran beside his horse, courage replacing fear now that their General Peng had arrived. And there began on the river bank a harsh, discordant cry that challenged the guns:

"Peng, Peng, *Peng!*"

"Now that's a bloody general!"

Another wailed to me:

78

"*Ayia*, it's an awful war. Why do I get it so hard?"

I momentarily saw his face in the flash of the bombardment; smoke-blacked; his features were twisted with fear in the glare. Head down, squealing, he ran, flopping about.

Now billows of smoke rolled over the enemy positions and our chattering rifles began a sustained roar as the infantry sought targets. Behind us the forest cracked and snarled, trees toppling to the scything iron as the enemy 'planes joined battle; a row of poplars laying themselves flat like a line of shot soldiers, displacing high flames. And in the fierce blaze I saw a band of scarecrow men, black imps dancing in hair-raising yells as the bonfires flushed them out.

Now the counter-bombardment grew apace; explosions, air-blasts so linked that the night became a deep-throated cauldron of sound and heat; a blaring orchestra of flame, smoke and whistling steel.

We ran together in a primitive lust to survive. It was neither courage nor patriotism which drove us, making us as one with the lurching infantry fighting along the bridge: it was a rush for cover after nerve has gone, an escape from turmoil.

All about me were mud-encrusted faces, a foliage of open, red mouths chattering with the strains of fear. Now, jammed together impossibly at the bridge entrance, men were reacting to their own convulsive heaving, fighting for the middle of the bucking footwalk. Some just shrieked; others, furious at the constraint, were actually fighting with their fists. And about me danced their eyes, huge, dark circles lit with terror in the pulsating shoots of the guns.

"Forward, forward! Get on, you bastards, get on!"

They were crying a song of attack, others howling laughter, some weeping: they pushed, slipped down and went through the rails into the river with washed, gulping faces: many fell and we trod over their backs. Tenga was standing on a rail, his squat body swinging in the wires, and he shouted, "Over the bridge, come on, over!" and he flailed his mule-whip high in the red glow, cracking it down above us. "Where's my Fifth?" and he leaned down to me, "Come on, you bloody infantry!"

Seemingly indestructible, he was bawling his obscene humour as he drove us on. Being taller than most, I saw above the heads of the men before me grey surges leaping before the sparkling enemy guns, and the flashing of bayonets in a vicious hand-to-hand. Now air and space was rushing about me as Yung ran clear, and I leaped after him down into the shallows of the enemy bank. Something scalding gushed to my right; men screamed as the flame-thrower enveloped them: men alight now, staggering about me; others had their hands clapped to their faces. The flame-thrower sent its lazy spouts across the emptying bridge-head: in its lull I dashed forward, swerving to the left, following Yung; above me a stick grenade somersaulted, landing with a deafening concussion; liquid fire sprayed attacker and defender. Men on the ground now, rolling with their clothes ablaze; torches of men were blindly running like devils in the dark.

A man was crouching to my left in the shallows of the river: instantly, I recognised him – the man from Kwangtung: his mud-spattered face opened and shut on the pin of a grenade; rising, he flung the bomb high, and the flame-thrower exploded in a sheet of fire.

Tenga was shouting hoarsely, "Into them, the Third. Now then, you Kuomintang bastards!"

Another, "Opium Peng, Opium Peng!"

"Give it them, lads! Let them have it, lads!"

Before me, at the junction between bridge and enemy shore, a mass of bodies was mounding upwards. Water gushed over me. I knew a sensation of light and firmness as my feet struck mud. Inflamed faces were all about me, hands clawing for the climb over dead and dying; above my head was an exploding crimson of nothingness, a shell detonation that blew me side-ways. Drilled by bullets, men fell about me with astonished expressions: stoic and coward, they always fell with the same profound amazement. And as I counted the pall of bodies, firing at the enemy trenches, the whole world grew in a singular, glorious brightness. Set against a flashing sky, men were locked together in small, squawking groups, a mêlée of bayonets and rifle-butts, and I glimpsed beyond them a rush of civilian men darting into the Kuomintang infantry with knife-like ease, their war-cries shrill, splitting the bass thunder of the guns. It was the unmistakable voice of the partisans, a wild, victorious acclamation.

I knew the bridge was won.

Men around me were sinking down, exhausted by the charge, gasping on their faces in the dull, red soil like men being flogged:

one knelt with his arms wide, hilariously laughing at the sky as his comrades staggered past him.

A pitiful lamentation came from the wounded as the bombardment slowly died. Lying on my side I saw the bridge crammed full of advancing soldiers; unhindered, they were spewing from the open footboards and leaping into the river shallows, wading ashore, their hip-held automatics chattering fire into the packed Kuomintang ranks. All about me were the bodies of men; motionless, or gently heaving, they littered the foreshore. I vomited, kneeling in the wet earth. When I raised my head a wounded Kuomintang soldier was crawling weakly towards me. His outstretched hand was more a threat than a supplication; taking deliberate aim with my Luger, I shot him. Falling flat, he began to cry faintly, his accent Cantonese. After a few moments he began to sigh. I was kneeling, now grieving for him, when Yung ran up.

"Are you hit, Lin?"

I stared at his blank face. "No, I don't think so."

"The partisans have come, you hear me?" He shook me to make the sense of it. "Look, look!"

"The partisans?"

He called above the desultory firing, "The partisans, you fool – the Yu people!"

He helped me up. The sickness of the bomb blast still contained me. "Look," said Yung, excitedly pointing, "to the left of the bridge-head!"

I followed his pointing finger.

It had happened as Tenga had told. The Yu Partisans, gathered by Jo-kei, had attacked the Kuomintang in the rear as we were forcing the bridge. Thronging along the river bank, they were now gathering at the bridge-head where our transport victoriously rolled across towards them, their coloured clothes and gay-neck-scarves identifying them from the grey-clad infantry of the Sixth, who were greeting them joyfully. For the first time I knew the importance of Jo-kei, the leader. More than 1,000 insurgents from the Yu mountains were now cheering lustily as the Red Army landed.

The facts grew into me, hammering through the heady swims of the concussion. I remembered Pipa. Her face made shape in the mist of my mind.

I started forward: seizing my arm, Yung ran beside me.

"Pipa, *Pipa*," I cried, and we raced together, through the littered dead and wounded of the bridge-head.

On the edge of the crowd now the partisans turned, making a path for us, slapping our backs in welcome. We gained the middle of them, a medley of dancing insurgents and Red soldiers yelling with incoherent joy.

"*Pipa!*" On tiptoe, I looked over the massed heads of the crowd. First I saw Big One. He was there in the thick of it, head and shoulders above everybody, grinning at the people swaying about him. Then I saw Jo-kei, turning in a circle of laughter, a woman partisan held high in his arms. Muchai I saw next, standing apart in silent contemplation. Near him, Bricko, the eunuch, was yelling in his strange falsetto.

And then I saw Pipa.

She was standing with other women of the Yu detachment, and she was obviously looking for me; but it was a very different Pipa from the one I had lost. Her face was blackened with powder-flashes, her quilted tunic was torn; her hair, once her pride, was cut short to her skull; there was about her, even from this distance, a new reason for living – that of a fighting partisan. Bursting through the crowd, I stood before her, and there grew upon her face inexpressible joy.

"*Lin-wai!*" She ran into my arms.

TWELVE

"Big fella'!"

Tenga came from the crush of soldiers but a moment after I had discovered Pipa. Shoving aside partisans he came, shouting bassly from the crush. And Big One saw him and ran to greet him, swinging people aside: they gripped each other; astonishingly, Tenga was bright-eyed.

"What about me, then, Yichi Tribesman?" asked Jo-kei, his arms outflung.

"You piss off," growled Tenga, pulling the big man away from him.

"You've not missed your old friend, Jo-kei, my Yichi mule?" Jo-kei begged in mock appeal, sweeting his lips, head thrust forward.

Tenga scowled and put a fist under Jo-kei's chin. "You not bring 'im back, I kill you. Two weeks, by seed-fall, I said, didn't I? Ye keep him six bloody *months*! – you sodding Kiangsi farmer. Perhaps one day I kill you anyway."

Pipa turned to me; "What happens now?"

Yung replied, "We go back across the river for Tojo and the wounded."

"Tojo? . . . Wounded?"

Yung said, pompously, "Don't you realise that Chan Lin-wai is a power in the Red Army? Doctor-student to the Fifth Muleteers?"

"I did not know," said Pipa, her eyes swept over me.

"He talks too much," I said to her. "Come."

After the initial attack troops had crossed the bridge, Pipa, Yung and I forced a passage back to the home bank and returned with Tojo and her cart-load of wounded, all miraculously free from further wounds. When we returned to the Fifth Muleteers, we found our battle losses replaced by Jo-kei, Muchai, Big One, Bricko, and no less than 100 partisans – men of the sure-footed little mountain donkeys they had brought from their villages.

"And I stay too?" Pipa asked Tenga, with a frivolous smile.

"You, too," growled he. "All the devils in one net." His mood alternated between pent anger and pride. "What that gun-runner Jo-kei brings, Tenga keeps – the fat-belly Cantonese pig, eh, *eh*?" And he staggered around holding up his stomach, grunting and snorting to the laughter of his muleteers.

"Pig, pig, *pig* Jo-kei," cried he.

"Make the most of it, my bandy Yichi Mule," said Jo-kei, eyeing him.

The following two days we rested in bivouac, seeking shelter from the bitter east wind – moving only sufficiently away from the river bridge-head to accommodate Second Echelon troops – and, of course, the giant Headquarter Commission, which made no reference to the sorrowful losses we had sustained. Yung said bitterly, "They should have been with our Third and Lin Piao's First, then they would have seen some dead," and Jo-kei replied:

"But be fair, gentry boy. Is it good strategy to announce such losses?"

"The army knows," I replied.

There was little more to be said, though Muchai, I noticed, was actually weeping; even Bricko, the usually excited eunuch, was quiet as we buried our dead.

In single graves we laid them, mainly alongside the river, in the harvested fields too, to enrich the soil of ancient Hunan, deeper than the reach of the plough and stamping oxen.

We hauled them away in the ammunition carts, laying them side by side as comrades, in the bleak hills of Tupang Ling Sin-tien, which, to many, was home. Later, as the days wore on, we buried them less decently, layer upon layer, in great pits, and we estimated the total as some 15,000. But this did not account for the hundreds who had been swept down-river to gasp out their lives on the flat-lands of swamp, or those who had dragged themselves away to die in some forgotten place.

And, as I went among the wounded of the Fifth with Pipa and Yung, operating here, comforting there, more died under my hands; others lived, becoming addicts of the opium seeds I fed them in place of anaesthetics.

Later, when the dying became too great to handle, we dragged them like strings of beads roped to mules, across the frosted land for the inevitable cremation – night-signals, in themselves, for the Kuomintang bombers.

"How many, would you say?" I asked Muchai.

He shrugged. "Ten thousand – a rough estimate."

"A bad guess," said Jo-kei, "double it."

Both were wrong. On the afternoon of the fourth day of the crossing official estimates (but not in writing) put the figure at 22,000. Nor did this include the losses of the second column that had crossed farther up-stream, we learned, where the Hsiang was even wider.

"Call it 40,000," said Jo-kei, putting down his brush.

"Call it minor losses," said Yung. "One must pay lip-service to the Party's propaganda."

The final death-roll was over 50,000.

It was a loss from which the Red Army never recovered.

Although we buried them for three days with indecent haste, I stood with Pipa and looked upon a minor sea of corpses.

It was difficult to forgive ourselves for being alive.

My greatest opportunity for extensive surgical experience came during those five tragic days spent on the bank of the Hsiang River. Pipa, at my request, was transferred from the small women's section of the Partisan Detachment to the Fifth Muleteers as a nursing orderly, replacing a reluctant Yung in his role of male nurse.

It was necessary that I should have Pipa with me now I had found her: my need of her was the need of a man for his wife, and the very sight of her during the endless batches of incoming wounded brought me to a new and joyful expectation. Having her by my side seemed to banish some of the weariness, and even when the batches of walking wounded increased to a flood (as casualties from a second, up-river assault were brought down by raft) I found renewed strength in the constant operating. Pipa, however, wilted early, and I had to bring back Yung.

On the third night in Casualty Clearing, with Yung in the next canopy attending to some lightly wounded, we crouched under Tojo's tent affair (an enclosed awning designed for re-attachment). Despite our tiredness we were on the edge of love-making when sounds outside told of the arrival of more of the heavily wounded. The return to normality was a most frustrating business.

Usually, I attended light wounds: at my level, the intention was to get a man quickly back into the column. Anything more important than flesh wounds I sent down the line to the Casualty Clearing of the Sixth Regiment.

Paradoxically, however, impossibly wounded men I was also expected to attend, 'there being little point', said the Surgeon-General, 'in sending to higher echelon an armless man who couldn't fire a rifle'.

At the Hsiang there was no discrimination in the severity of the wounds. I was one of the forward doctors; initially, I saw them all.

Pipa said, with a groan, "Bless my womb!" and turned away her face as they carried in the litter.

The soldier upon it was young – scarcely more than a boy. The high velocity anti-tank bullet had taken him low, through one hip and out of the other, castrating him on the way. He lay with the ashen face of a man already dead, his hands deep in his abdomen where his entrails bulged. Pipa sank to her knees, staring with eyes of horror. I said to the soldier:

"You have no pain?" I knew, of course, that he had not; the wound was too severe.

He actually smiled, shaking his head.

Turning away for the opium seeds, I said softly to Pipa, "Tie him as best you can."

Sweat grew on her face; she began to shake.

I was a little surprised at this reaction: all that morning she had been working with quiet effect, handing me instruments for the neat, blue bullet holes, bandaging flesh wounds with apparent unconcern. I reflected that little more than this had been required of her during her nursing studies back in Shengsu. A major casualty such as this took her into realms of horror, the heady sickness that precedes the faint.

There was no sound but the metallic clashing of the army, the drumming of hooves, harsh commands, and the faint, hoarse breathing of the dying soldier. When I looked again, Pipa was on her knees, the bandages faltering in her shaking hands. The soldier was watching her with eyes of calm resignation. He said, and his voice was strong:

"I am going to die?"

I whispered to Pipa, "Quickly – outside and bring Yung." To the soldier I said, lifting his head, "Of course you will not die

– here, take these. Within days we will have you back with your people." He swallowed the opium seeds, unaware that they would kill him, and he was still watching Pipa.

Somehow she got to the door. I heard strangled ejaculations as they carried her away. Moments later Yung came in.

"*Wei, wei,* old soldier," cried he, grinning down.

"Strap him, Yung," I said. "He needs the support."

Within minutes the soldier died.

Yung said, wiping blood from his hands, "Pipa is ill."

"She will come to it."

"I doubt it." He raised his eyes to mine. "She is not this kind of nurse."

I went outside to Pipa. She was just coming round. I held her on the stubble grass. "It's all right, my love, it is all right," I said.

She turned away her face.

On the sixth morning of the bridge-head Mao published an Order of the Day, commanding a push towards Sangchih, the headquarters of the communist Second Army under the General Tiger Ho Lung. That evening, with the Red Army still skirmishing on the flanks and our rearguard fighting desperately to disengage from two Kuomintang armies, we whipped up the Fifth to Tenga's commands and struck north-west towards the Kwangsi border. It was the nearest we got to Sangchih.

When the march was not forced, the journeying was wonderful indeed, especially if there was a moon and a gentle wind blowing, and now, with the Hsiang slaughter behind us, whole companies of men began to sing – even the wounded – and others in the rear would answer at times, a pleasing echo. It was as if China had suddenly forgotten winter, it being quite warm, with only a threat of December.

These were the days of hope and even gaiety. The long trudging of the march was lightened with the happiness of having Pipa always beside me. And nor did her presence appear to annoy the soldiers; they had long since learned that Pipa was no prude. The obscenity of their expressions she didn't appear to hear; her short white coat which she wore for dressings earned her the nickname of 'Little Fifth Nurse'. Automatically (and, I hope, because they respected me) they accepted her in the ranks of marching men even more readily than they accepted,

Yung, the effeminate. Our positions on the march were accepted, too: Yung walked behind Tojo's long-cart of wounded, Pipa and I marched with Tojo's bridle between us.

With my arm over her shoulders we marched, or even hand in hand.

"I love you, Lin," said Pipa.

And, had this been overheard, there would have been no sniggers. The average Chinese peasant is as earthy as the soil he serves. The Doctor-student was a good young chap, and this little beauty was his woman. And Tenga, as usual, was the earthiest of all.

"This Partisan girl belong your piece, Bone-man?"

It was at a night halt; aided by fit men, the wounded had been laid on the ground in a line, in a place of shelter clear of the wind; Tojo's long-cart was temporarily empty, and Yung was industriously sweeping it out. I replied:

"She was my piece, as you call it, long before I came into your Fifth Muleteers, Corporal."

He glanced about him. "What you waitin' for, then?"

I smiled at him in the moonlight. Pipa passed us with an armful of dressings, humming happily a child's melody of home. Tenga said:

"I ain't short o' a woman, ye know – I got the likes of her east of the Shans near the Lolo Yi . . ." He looked at the moon. "Don't you think 'cause you got your piece that Tenga don't 'ave his, an' she comes pretty smooth in the belly . . ."

"Are we thinking the same thing, Corporal?"

"You're being plain daft if you ain't thinkin' the same thing as me. Who's to know? Get her up in Tojo's boards and gi' the girl a treat."

I shook my head, smiling.

Later, with Pipa's hand in mine, we kept step with the column, and Pipa's face was shadowed in the light of the torches, for the moon had faded and the bamboo frays were alight, sending up sparks at the stars.

There was an expression in Pipa's eyes I had not seen before. The wind took her hair, blowing it over her shoulders. I saw the men watching her with unusual intent.

That night she was incredibly beautiful.

I always loved these night marches when we could take our

time; it gave a marvellous impression of strength to see behind us a dragon of fire snaking over the hills and plains. Behind us, General Lo's rearguard was still heavily engaged, with rockets and shells decorating the night. Before us the vanguard stretched over the white, untouched fields of Hunan.

"It is like walking into the future," said Pipa.

When hard-pressed by the pursuing Kuomintang, we often marched in day-time too, and, at such times, the Chiang Kai-shek bombing formations would pound us: each time we would scatter, afterwards reforming to resume the march. Our dead and wounded, even in the skirmishing, were many – there was scarcely a man in the Fifth unbandaged after the Hsiang, and Tenga looked a fool with his Tartar fur cap perched on top of his head bandages, cursing eternally with the pain of his lost ear.

The peasants in the villages through which we passed always helped us as best they could, and nor was this through fear, for we took from them nothing we did not pay for. Of money we had plenty, for Mao never lost the chance of capturing an important hostage, and corrupt high officials of the Nationalist Government were worth more alive than dead.

"The brother to a Kuomintang general brought a quarter of a million in ransom," announced Jo-kei, now very much at home with the Fifth Muleteers, "and Mao needs every cent. This was precisely the amount paid to the governor of Kwangtung to get us through Kuomintang lines without a fight. It is merely taking from one to give to the other – an ear will always hasten payment."

"Bribery and blackmail – is that good communism?" asked Yung, and his face was shadowed in the light of the flares.

"And the two missionaries, Bosshardt the Swiss and Hayman, brought us four coolie loads of silver in Kweichow, they say," said Muchai, ignoring him.

I was worried about Muchai; on the short twenty-mile march from the Hsiang bridge-head, he already appeared to be failing.

"Do not talk, old man," I said. "Save your breath for marching."

"So where," asked Yung, "are the fine ideals?"

"Ethics aren't involved," replied Jo-kei. "Your head wouldn't be on your shoulders if the Central Committee didn't bend the rules."

Bricko cried, falsetto, "They say Mao's brother runs the mint – I'd give my cock to be Mao Tse-ming."

"Cheap at the price," said Jo-kei, and began to sing then, his voice bass and pure, his face upturned to the moon.

Yung said quietly, "Lin-wai, your Pipa is coming up the line."

It was obvious. Every muleteer in front was turning to look.

I did not question where she had been – probably she had visited friends in the Women's Detachment of the partisans, commanded by the giant female Shao Shan. She said softly:

"Oh, Lin, I am ashamed." She caught my hand, pressing it against her.

"Of what happened this morning? You have no need to be – it could happen to anyone." Away from watching eyes, I kissed her.

"He was such a terrible sight." Pale-faced, she drew away from me.

"Forget it, he is at peace." I took her arm. With Yung on the other side of her we walked together with Tojo's head nudging my shoulder, and the night was fine with a canopy of stars, filled with the sound of marching men and the creaking canvas over the wounded behind us.

Yung said, "You do not mind me walking with you and Pipa, Lin-wai?"

Come dawn, I reflected, I would be alone with Pipa. It was an idle promise because, come dawn, Yung was still there, and still watching. Desperately I wanted to make love to Pipa.

I began to wish Yung to the devil.

It was ironic, I reflected, that the only one truly to understand the situation, was Tenga, the ignorant muleteer.

In these marches we also captured many prisoners, Kuomintang soldiers separated from their units. Food was always scarce but to abandon them was also dangerous since they could betray our logistics.

Sometimes Tenga would send a message back to Headquarters Commission, asking for a prisoner's release in the next village we passed through, but always the same reply came back, "No, he must be killed." Then the guards would become excited and jostle around Tenga, crying, "Let me do it, let me do it," or, "It is my turn now, he killed one yesterday." Hearing this the captive would beg for his life, but he would be shot just the same.

Jo-kei once said, "Isn't it more humane, you fools? Would you leave him to be eaten by wolves? Or to be tortured as a deserter by the Kuomintang?"

It was much the same with animals on the march, but we did not kill them because they were useful. So, while stragglers caught on the march were usually killed, a wounded animal was given a big feed and tethered within reach of water – fresh meat for Lo's rearguard.

Just east of Thunder God Rock we captured seven Kuomintang deserters living brutally off the peasants; six were immediately shot because they were not worth enlisting – a deserter will desert from anybody. The seventh, a boy of fifteen named Po Ku, we spared because of his youth, but after ten miles of marching he began to falter.

Muchai said, "He has been interrogated, remember – Political Protection is enough to weaken anybody."

Po Ku lay by the roadside, weeping large tears.

It happened that Sho Shan, the mountainous woman commander of the Partisan Women's Detachment, was passing down the line.

"Put him in the cart," said she.

Nobody moved, so, stooping, Shao Shan gathered him in her arms and tumbled him into the back of my cart. Po Ku was happy at this and stopped weeping. Meanwhile, I had treated Po Ku's feet; they were nearly stripped of skin. Po Ku said, "In five days before I was captured, the Kuomintang marched us eighty miles, and on this journey I had one bowl of rice. When you halted at the Hsiang, we came to Maoan Village, and there deserted because we wanted to join the Reds."

"You knew about us?" I asked, as I bandaged.

Po Ku said, "The Kuomintang told us terrible stories. Our officers said you were blue-nosed creatures who gouged out the eyes of their prisoners. I am happy to be with the Reds now."

I thought: perhaps you will be less happy when Tenga returns from his inspection up the line with our Company Commander. Within an hour he came, saw Po Ku sitting in Tojo's cart, and demanded, "What the hell's he doing up in there?"

I replied, "Shao Shan commanded it."

"I do not," said Tenga, "fetch him out of it."

Po Ku ran beside us limping, crying aloud. The bandages around his feet were stained with blood.

Pipa, coming from the long-cart, marched with me, saying, "Oh Lin, help him, please help him – he is only really a boy!"

Tenga's attitude was brutal, but it was the law; without a depth of ability to think for himself, the corporal worked by the only rules he knew – those of military expediency. What was of use to the Red Army was allowed to live; that which was useless was better dead. Meanwhile, Pipa was running alongside Po Ku, helping to support him, and she was calling me from the verge:

"Lin-wai! Lin-wai!"

When I did not answer her she came to me and took my hands, shouting into my face in English, "If you love me, do something! If you do not care about the boy, then care about me – look, I am weeping for him!"

Still I did not reply, but I think I loved her in that moment more than at any other time: her outraged sense of justice, the compassion of her womanhood reached into me more deeply than any worship of her body.

"Oh, darling," whispered Pipa, "look at his poor little feet!"

Drawing Pipa aside I called:

"Corporal Tenga, you are shameless to behave like this."

Tenga did not reply to this.

"To which I would add that he's a bloody bastard," observed Jo-kei, arriving in a sweat. "Put that lad back into the cart."

Obviously the corporal was affected by this statement, for he rubbed his bad ear and swore ineffectively, waving his thick arms about in a sort of futile desperation.

I called to him, "You told me once that you had a son. This child's feet are terrible."

For Tenga all this opposition was a great dilemma. Eventually, he said, "Send it down the line."

Reluctantly, Yung wrote on a slip of paper and Little Ball, who was passing on a horse, took it back to Third Headquarters. Meanwhile, the pace increased, and still Po Ku marched, with a hand on Tojo's harness, and no one prevented this.

Tenga lurched beside him, scowling and holding his head, for the wound was septic: I knew the pain was bad because when I dressed the wound he did not complain, and he was usually protesting over something.

That evening Little Ball galloped up and handed him a message. This read:

> Po Ku, captured at Maoan; Sixteenth Regiment, Kuomintang. Unsuccessfully interrogated. Shoot him.

Bricko, knowing this, waited, watching Tenga's face. And Tenga crumpled the paper in his fist and bowed his head.

"What did you expect?" I asked.

Bricko cried, "Let me do it, Corporal, let me do it."

Others heard this and soon Tenga was surrounded: jubilant, they jostled him, begging with their hands. Pipa said, softly:

"I am ashamed of being Chinese."

Tenga nodded to Bricko.

Po Ku begged, but to beg of the eunuch was useless. Bricko shot him in the head, turned to Tenga and said, "Are these .303?" And he took from Tenga's bandolier a bullet, ammunition being scarce.

It was but three days after this event that our leader of the Fifth, Commander Ma, appointed Tenga to the rank of sergeant.

Muchai remarked, drolly, "This could have been because of your gallantry at the Hsiang crossing, Sergeant Tenga. On the other hand, could it be a reward for the murder of Po Ku?"

Tenga did not answer this. For many hours we did not see him in our section of the line.

"What is wrong with him?" I asked.

"It would appear that he has a soul," said Jo-kei. "Until today I had seen no sign of it."

On the night of the fifty day of the march from the Hsiang River, Tenga sent Yung back to Third Headquarters with a message, and Pipa and I were alone, free of the resting army.

There was a lane of poplars where the moon raced in gaps among high branches; distantly, we heard the bawdy shouts of the soldiers; saw their little cooking-fires blooming through leaves.

Here the brown refuse of old autumns whirled in crisp eddies about us; the low sighing of the poplars above us brought to us a deeper remoteness: all life seemed to flood past us in the moment I took her into my arms. The pain of marching, the sweat, the blood, all was lost in the finality of our long waiting.

"I love you, Lin-wai," said she.

The kisses are quiet in the beginning when clothes uncover lovers. Trembling hands seek warm places in enveloping blackness: the breathing is pent, the pain grows where the loins are forged, in heat and shape, together: explosions bloom in growing redness here, the mouth is hot, the ears contained in an unknown silence amid a muted chanting of the guns. The soldier knows no pity: his body wounds. After this comes emptiness, a requiting piece. I put my arms around the softness of her, kissing her mouth until the world about us made shape in etched shadows of waving poplars in the yellow decoration of the moon. The air was cold on our bodies. Pipa, hugging herself, giggled softly against me.

"Dear me," said she, making eyes, "that was a step in the right direction – we're enjoying more of it now than back in Shengsu dodging my old Aunt Lei. Do it again, Lin-wai? And do it harder?"

Strangely, the face below me in that moonlight was suddenly not the face of Pipa.

I did not reply to her; to have done so would have broken the gossamer thread of my existence, and made her into another, a woman of the Street of Tits.

Later, when we rose together, we saw the shadow of a man standing at the end of the poplar lane: so still he stood, as one frozen by the moon. It looked to me very much like Muchai the Elder.

Yung, returned to us, was asleep with the others around the dying embers of the fire: Tojo drooped near by, contained in her mule's nothingness: the wounded were sighing, dull snores came from sleeping soldiers.

Only Muchai, the respected scholar, was absent. Soon he came back to the fire, bowing to us as he took his place.

"It is a most lovely night, Muchai," Pipa said blithely.

"I am delighted you both enjoyed it," replied he.

THIRTEEN

Now, with forward battle action daily diminishing, and Kuomintang air attacks lessening, we breezed across the northern neck of Kwangsi towards Kweichow Province and distant Tsunyi, leaving the Ninth rearguard to fight off our pursuers. And, as the foothills of the Yuehcheng mountainous regions approached, we spoke of Old China and her legends; told romantic stories of the past to kindle our spirits: we even talked the old solar measurement of time, the Joints and Breaths of the year, and of 'Li Tung weeks' as the beginning of winter.

The omen for Old China was good, explained Muchai, the old scholar.

Listen, said he: amid *Cold Dews* the Red Army had escaped from Yutu, the outpost of the old Juichin Soviet: in *Hoar Frost Falling* it had marched to its first great battle, the Hsiang. Now, in *Early Snows*, there stretched before it Thunder God Rock of Old Mountain; crystal white, she speared the blue-enamelled sky in a white vastness.

"Look!" cried he, pointing.

Once across Thunder God Rock of the Yeuhcheng Range we will shake off the pursuing Kuomintang, said Muchai – in the ancient books this is written: beyond the goal of Yenan we will get to grips with the hated Japanese.

For all his scholarly benevolence, Muchai was a riddle. Nor were his qualifications restricted to teaching English at the Whampoa Academy; Muchai was a herbalist of knowledge; as such he had become indispensable to me in the short time I had known him. Scarcely a day passed but he brought me ancient remedies gathered by the way. Rhubarb he brought me, for tonics and treatment of diarrhoea: cassia he gathered as a tonic, ephedra for asthma and hay fever, prevalent in the south; the gum-resin for Gamboge, a purgative; other cathartics, he found, also Ginseng root for stomach infections. These he undertook to dry and store, presenting them to me in neat leaf packets tied with raffia.

Nevertheless, I was certain Muchai had been watching Pipa

and I making love: nature-lover or not, I decided, henceforth, to keep an eye on him.

Days later, at a brief stop to water the animals at a stream, I noticed the old scholar sitting alone on the bank; I said, to open the subject, "How are the plates, old gentleman?"

"If ever I weep, I do not weep for feet," said he.

Earlier, I recall, he had wept for Po Ku, whom Bricko had executed.

"You're doing passably well."

It straightened him. "Don't underrate the old, young Doctor; when it comes to stamina we'll always see you off."

I said, "Jo-kei tells me you lectured in English literature at the Whampoa Academy."

"It is true."

I sat beside him while Tojo drank near by; as far as one could see the animals were drinking, and the snake of the Third wended to the east across the frosted hills: with their feet stuck up, men dozed in the weak, winter sunlight. I said, "But surely, at Whampoa, they teach only the literature of the guns?"

Pipa, sitting near by with the women partisans, waved gaily to us: we waved back.

The old language delighted him, and he replied, "Not so, Chan Lin-wai, the great academy is also culturally endowed. A good officer must have recourse to the classics if only as a diversion from the art of killing." He added drolly, "It always astonishes me how one appears to go with the other."

"You must have taught great men."

"Greatness isn't easily defined." His voice was deep and he gathered about him his mud-stained gown against the wind. "I prefer to say I have had some meritorious students – men like Chou En-lai; also notorious ones, such as General Wang, the governor of Hupeh. The first was an intellectual whose favourite reading was *The Magic of Common Sense*; the other, as a pastime, filled the sing-song girls at 100 dollars a time – the annual wage of a peasant farmer." He made a wry face. "There are compensations for tutorage, of course; for every 1,000 dunces and lechers one occasionally surprises an academic genius."

"You became a radical?"

He nodded. "After I abandoned Confucius I found myself

delivering personal views during my lectures, when I should have been compounding irregular verbs."

I asked, "You lectured in English?"

"Passably well – I got my degree at Oxford."

"But at Whampoa they arraigned you?"

Muchai sighed deeply; his old, lined face was beautiful in the sun. "The decorum was perfect – you can't drag a venerable old scholar from his platform and flog him in the street, you know. I was warned of the perils of diverting from the accepted Chiang Kai-shek line – this was reasonable since it was his Academy."

"And they threw you out?"

"Eventually. I protested, naturally, talking of freedom of scholarship, but the committee was a military one: it was like decorating swine with pearls. Pigs, as you know, don't appreciate jewellery."

"And then?"

"Once beyond the precincts, I ran. About this time Chiang was feeding communists into locomotive boilers and blowing whistles to each new head of steam as a warning to others. Somehow I escaped, though many did not. Jo-kei, running guns to Red partisans, found me on the road."

There was a silence between us. He said. "And you, Chan Lin-wai–"

"You know most about me, it would appear." I eyed him.

"Enough for comradeship. Had I not known less, I would have congratulated you on possessing a beautiful wife."

"But Pipa isn't my wife– you know this."

He said, blandly: "Then the ceremony's a little overdue."

"How dare you spy on us, Muchai!"

He emptied bony hands at me. "I do it for your sake."

His eyes, strangely opaque in that brilliant light, were steady on mine. He nodded towards Pipa, who was calling to me from the little clutch of women partisans, and said, "Bring your woman to us, Chan Lin-wai."

"Bring Pipa? Why?"

"Call her – it's important to you, but more important to her."

All around us was the slow activity of a resting army: muleteers attending the shoes of the drooping animals, a bell-ringing of hammers: girths being tightened, rifle breech-bolts oiled in a hammering rat-a-tat. And there floated down the line from the tough Red Cadres the music of comradeship; the laughter of

97

men at rest from war. I said, "You mind your business, old man, and we'll mind ours." I made to leave, but he stilled me, saying:

"I demand your respect of my age, young man. Do you really think I'm concerned with morality at a time like this? This time tomorrow we could all be dead. Call her."

I did so.

Muchai said, in a place away from the resting column, "What is your full name, young Doctor?"

"You already know it." I replied testily; there was growing in me an indefinable fear.

"Please," said he, "if I am to help you."

"Chan Lin-wai."

Pipa cried, joining us, "You want me, Lin?"

Muchai patted the grass beside him. "Sit, child, be patient." Of me, he asked, "And you are the only son of Chan of Laoshan, he who is agent to the Mandarin of Kwangtung these past thirty years?"

I nodded; Pipa whispered, "Lin, why these questions . . .?"

Muchai said to me, "Let me be accurate about this – you are the child of one your father called Sula, his second wife?"

"I am," I replied.

"She who died some three months back in Laoshan?"

I said, "My mother died just before I returned home from Shanghai University."

"Forgive me . . ." he began. "She was at first a concubine to your father?" He spread his hands delicately, "Please . . . this is legally acceptable under the law of Ching."

I said, tersely, "My father divorced his wife and married my mother. But I can't see where all this is leading us."

"And what has it to do with me?" asked Pipa.

There was within me a mounting fear; my bowels shrank as he turned to her, saying:

"Your full name is Yang Pipa?"

She smiled wonderingly. "It is – you know my clan name?"

"And you lived with your aunt in a cottage in Shengsu, a mile or two from Laoshan, Lin-wai's home?"

"Why, yes, but . . .?"

"The cottage has a red roof and stands by a stream? Jasmine and smartweed grows in the garden."

"You know Aunt Lei?" Pipa was delighted.

I was ill with fear. Realisation was growing with his every word. He said, "And neither your aunt, Pipa, nor your father, Lin-wai, knew of the love you hold for each other?"

"I tell my father nothing of my business," I replied.

"This is a pity," said he. "Certainly it would have been better had you done so." He sighed deeply, lowering his face. "Let me out with this and quick – the pain will be easier. .." Reaching out, he took our hands. "From the moment I met you I became suspicious that you were lovers. But it was not until a few nights ago, when I followed you among the poplars, did I have this confirmed ..." His expression softened, his voice grew faint. "This cannot be, Chan Lin-wai – neither can it be for you, Yang Pipa. Listen to me." He smiled into her pale face. "The woman, Lei, who raised you, is not your aunt – she is a gentry woman of lost fortune employed by Lin-wai's father at your birth. Your mother, his first wife, played beautifully on the *pi'pa* – so after this you were named. Nor is she dead."

"You know my mother?" Clearly, Pipa had not realised the import of what he was saying. Muchai answered:

"Her company was a joy to me. One day, if I am spared, I will return to her in Canton where she keeps my house."

I heard myself say, "Then Pipa and I are related."

He nodded. "She is your half-sister – you are sprung from the same loins in Laoshan. This you must know – friends you can be, but never lovers. Obviously, you are unaware that you share the same father."

There was building within me both shock and horror: I had lain with my sister. The sense of indignity slowly replaced the enormity of my loss; the degradation struck me like a fist in the face. And yet, withal, I knew an overwhelming pity – not for myself, but for Pipa: I had transgressed her body; it was greater than a theft of virtue. Head bowed before Muchai, I knew self-loathing. The children of her womb would be tainted by her father's blood. And if she had conceived ...? The thought brought me to near panic. I said, softly, "By my mother's honour, the gods pity us ..." but nobody heard me.

I stared at Pipa's white face and my body said, "I love you, I love you ..."

I rose uncertainly. Distantly, I could hear the harsh commands that preceded the order to march. Muchai watched us both. Pipa was standing with her hands over her face, sobbing quietly. I touched her, but she did not turn to me. Muchai said, from the grass, "I realised you did not know ..." He added, "For the sake of your children, I would be doing less than a common duty ..."

I closed my eyes. "You are certain it's true?"

"I know it."

"You will speak of this to nobody?"

He rose. "I swear it."

"*Ngoh sahphan gamgik*," I whispered, which, being translated, means, 'I am very grateful.'

But Pipa turned in pent fury, shrieking, "Why didn't you leave us alone, old man. I curse you, you hear me? I curse you!"

She wept aloud.

It was a rewarding halt – for others; people took advantage of it beneath the varnished blue of the sky, though a bite in the wind foretold snow. The Confucian religious, also Taoists not yet baptised into true communism, were burning paper money to little red tablets of their ancestral gods and preparing for them little dishes of rice, which they themselves, by the generosity of such gods, would afterwards consume. Heads were being shaved against the onslaught of lice by two cocky barbers with flashing razors, their victims sitting in stare-eyed apprehension. The Cadres were instructing new intakes in the technique of the Kupassa automatic, hundreds of which had been captured at the Hsiang battle. One could have mistaken this halt as a moment of peace: an oasis of communism within the heart of nationalist China. The wounded watched dully as Red Army regulars, in the high shrieks of children, played leap-frog in the sun.

For my part, I wandered, desolate.

Later, when the march recommenced, I marched at Tojo's head with Yung, and Pipa did not come. After a little while Yung said:

"This is so sad, Lin-wai – where is your beautiful Pipa?"

I did not answer.

Within hours there had grown an unclimbable wall between us.

All that night we marched, and Pipa did not come.

On the 23rd November I wrote in my diary:

We are now striking towards the Yuehcheng Range that guards
the Kweichow border; already the advance is slowing in a land
of littered boulders, and the nationalist 'planes are pounding
us relentlessly, plucking great, bloody gaps out of the column.
As fast as I get one batch of wounded down the line to Sixth
Casualty Clearing, the long-cart is filled again. Yung spends
much time up with the forward Assault Cadres; it's my guess
that Pipa is also there. Today Tenga asked where she was, and
I lied to cover her. One thing is sure, I can't go on much
longer without assistance.

Two days later, Tenga said, "Your woman's playing the tart
up with the Assault Cadres, you know this?"

"She was here this morning," I said.

"She bloody weren't, and don't you lie!" He wagged a big
finger before my face. "I got bombing and I got wounded, and I
ain't pissin' about wi' half-chat nurses – yesterday I see her up
with the Cadres, didn't I – an' I reckon they're nursing her."

Muchai said, "Forgive him, Lin-wai, he is not himself today."

Tenga raved at this, and I cried, "All right, all right – leave
my woman to me."

Jo-kei, lounging against the long-cart, said, "She'd account to
me if she were mine, young doctor. I had her before we joined
you on the Hsiang, remember? Within hours she was in trouble
with the partisan women."

"But not with the men, so leave it," I said, and climbed
through the canopy door of the cart to the wounded. They lay in
lethargic postures, grey-faced, their eyes opening as I crawled
among them, steadying myself to the lurching of the cart. Jo-kei
appeared at the back of the canopy, briefly riding on the foot-
board as the march began again.

"*Because* of men," said he.

I laced the back of the canopy, shutting him out. The wounded
muttered amongst themselves as I began the morning dressings,
raising their spirits for the usual morning banter that somehow
reduced the pain. I had one with a smashed knee and he was
moaning unintelligibly as I changed the bandages; calling for his
mother at times in the picture stages of his opium dream. I had
seriously addicted him and the responsibility was frightening.

Sometimes I wondered if it was kinder to let them moan. Washing my hands, I went back to the driving-board and Jo-kei was there with Tojo's reins.

He said, "You've caught a tartar in your pretty Pipa – why not realise it?"

I didn't reply, and he added, "She was well away with my partisans and now she's starting it here. What's wrong with her –doesn't she get enough?"

"You've got a filthy mouth, Jo-kei."

"Perhaps, but I recognise my kind. You're living in a dream, man. Don't you know she's up with the Cadres?"

The man with the smashed knee began to cry aloud above the pounding of Tojo's hooves. I began to wonder if his wound was gangrenous; until now the swelling had been minimal. If it got any worse I would have to take the leg. He was a farmer of Kwangsi; this was his province. If I sent him down to the Sixth the surgeons would put him on the road for the villagers to find, then he would surely die of gangrene. I began to wonder, with the state of his leg, if he was really my responsibility.

Jo-kei said, as he screamed again, "*Seeds of piss* – he makes enough noise for a sow on hooks – for my sake, put him out, the poof."

We sat together while the Kwangsi farmer howled. Hunched, moody, we stared at the sky for bombers. Suddenly Jo-kei said:

"There's a new nurse coming up from the Ninth tomorrow, have you heard?"

I shook my head.

"Tenga's fixed it – he looks like a mule but he's a sergeant when it comes to his wounded. For your sake he's let your bloody Pipa have her way, because if you can't handle her, Tenga soon will."

He talked more, but I wasn't really listening for I was desperately worried about Pipa. And the thought that when she returned to the Fifth she might hope to continue our love-making brought to me an inner coldness. Also, what astonished me more was that her continued absence pestered me as one is pestered by the absence of a beloved relative. It was an enigma; I couldn't rationalise it. My relationship with her, once essential to my existence, had switched to a protective aura. Indeed, I was now actually comforted by the knowledge that wherever she was, Yung was probably with her: a week ago the possibility would have infuriated me. Jo-kei said, breaking into my thoughts:

"She worries you, lad?"

"I am not her keeper."

"Aye, then, that's better. Give her time up and down the line and someone will loose her out of her drawers."

I turned upon him. "Will you shut your mouth!"

"Ay ay – I was only mentioning it – she'll be off your hands, you see."

"Wish she were in mine, though," exclaimed Bricko, appearing from nowhere with Muchai. "You talking of that Yung? Don't you fret, boy – that little pansy Yung can't do up your woman any better'n me, eh, Muchai?"

Muchai, marching near, lowered his eyes from mine.

Tojo plodded on. The wounded man behind me shouted his way into his lidded, opium sleep of gardens and cool waters.

Distantly, as if sounding an end to the drama, the column air-raid hand-bells began to jangle, increasing to a blaring, discordant medley. The cry went down the line, "Bombers, bombers, *bombers*!" and I drove Tojo pell-mell to the cover of nearby trees. Crawling into the long-cart, I sat among the wounded: there was never time to off-load them into cover before the bombs came down.

They plastered us that afternoon; they straddled and raked us: somewhere up with the Assault Cadres, where Pipa was, an ammunition cart blew up in a sheet of flame, showering the column with the debris of shrapnel, shattered mules and bits of men. The wounded around me began to whimper apprehensively as the bombs came nearer. It always amazed me that, under stress, the wounded invariably returned to their frightened childhood of bruises and grazed knees. Now their blanched, fearful faces stared blankly at me; features grotesquely twisted in the concussive flashing of the bombs.

"It will be all right," I said. "They are going now." And, as I said this, a hole appeared magically in the canvas awning beside my head: I saw the crying soldier momentarily stiffen, then relax. Blood began a slow trickle down his ashen face. A man beside him raised himself, saying in the moment the bombing ceased:

"He's dead, Doctor. Would you believe it? The poor sod's kicked it."

I nodded, covering the dead man's face. Not all my worries, I thought, would disappear quite so easily.

When I took the long-cart back to the column, Yung was awaiting me, and his face, usually pale, was white with anger. He said, "You're back safely, then. Are you sure you're unhurt?"

Putting Tojo back into the line, I faced him. He said, "You seem to be taking care of yourself well enough – did you spare a thought for Pipa?"

"These days I leave that to you," I replied. "Where the hell have you been, the pair of you?"

"That's our business!" he straightened, prettily defiant.

"And Tenga's – he's been asking for her – luckily he doesn't appear to have missed you much, and neither have I."

"One thing's sure," said he, and came nearer. "From now on, Chan Lin-wai, neither of us are answerable to you. I don't know what happened between you and Pipa, but I tell you this – you have hurt her bitterly."

FOURTEEN

At a brief halt in the foothills of the Yuehcheng Range, on the
road to Tungtao, our officer, Commander Ma of the Muleteer
Companies, came on a tour of inspection with a scowling Tenga,
who, said Jo-kei, considered the unit his personal property and
disliked interference from higher authority. Indeed, Tenga made
it clear that he held no brief for officers of any rank, but it was
obvious that he respected Commander Ma.

"Line up!" he bawled.

All down the line I could see the anti-aircraft quick-firers
taking their stand in their little fighting groups, the muzzles of
their big calibre machine-guns circling at the sky: and as far as
I could see beyond the Sixth Regiment, the battalions were being
roughly lined up before their commanders.

We rarely saw our Commander Ma; he left most things to
Tenga, being mainly engaged in ordnance liaison. This was the
business of getting our mule-carts replenished with ammunition
for the forward artillery and the Sixth Regiment's provisions. I
guessed him to be of Anwhei blood; certainly he was too large a
man for the famine-cut Cantonese, and his complexion was fair,
proof of his northern extraction. There was about him the inborn
charm of the well educated, and he treated Tenga with the
smiling courtesy of his good breeding; tolerant of his peasant
vulgarity. I had met such men before: they came from military
wombs, professional soldiers of China's more enlightened gentry.
Amid the corruptions of war they knew how to die with aristocratic understatement.

Behind me Pipa and Yung were sweeping out Tojo's long-
cart. With its hooded canopy over the wounded on the grass to
protect them against the fierce wind, they worked with their
usual silent efficiency. Brought closer by my alleged defections,
they had for the past week reduced conversation with me to
essentials.

The hurt was deep in me. To protect her own emotions, Pipa
was making me a scape-goat, prospering Yung's obvious need of

her in the process. I didn't understand it, nor did I try. Yung, for his part, induced in me a sense of safety, a convenient foil for the pair of us. Both Pipa and I knew that a single moment alone together would open the flood-gates of the old, resistless desires.

Yung assisted me at the more important operations; Pipa did the cleaning and washing and changed the dressings. Gradually the impossible situation became acceptable. One thing was sure – Jo-kei's allegation that Pipa had earlier been disporting herself with the forward Cadres was unfounded – Yung, I discovered, had been with her all the time. And the passing days further assured me – he was instantly, deeply in love with her.

And Pipa. What of her?

What of me? I did not truly know.

I knew only that should she come to me, begging to ignore all barriers of relationship, I could not accept her now – far too much had risen between us. And yet, if a morning passed without my seeing her, I was in a fever for her safety. Were she to lie hurt, I would have shouted them all away, taking her into my arms, kissing her mouth. Desperately, I tried to analyse the conflicting emotion that attracted and revulsed me; it was a contradictory anguish much deeper than the fear of making an idiot child; it was purer than physical wanting. It was not based on brotherly affection. It was indefinable, and it tore me. It made me one with her in a deep, abiding love; it induced in me a physical sickness at the thought of her touch.

But one thing was certain.

Pipa was mine and I belonged to Pipa.

Yung knew it, she knew it, so did I.

Now Commander Ma called us in a great half-circle about him, and said: "I will not keep you long. Headquarters has ordered local commanders to instruct their units on what is happening. Can you hear me at the back?"

Men raised their hands in mute assent, and he continued:

"On the face of it, this march is a madness, and it needs to be explained. Every man has the right to know his future, and as we stand now, it is nothing to boast about." He bent his riding-crop into a bow before him, his eyes sweeping the eager faces about him. "The most optimistic among us claim it is a victory – well, perhaps it was a major victory in getting safely out of

Juichin – but ever since leaving the Yutu advance post we've been engaged in a headlong retreat; this is not victory."

He paused, staring distantly, a man suddenly isolated in contemplation, then continued, "So, why are we marching? Let's come to it ? because if the Kuomintang encircle us, they will kill us – this is Chiang Kai-shek's stated intention – to wipe out communism wherever it is found. But a retreat can be turned into attack if it has another purpose, and this one has – it is the right for men like us to live decent lives with a promise of the future – and this is not the future of a class-ridden China of starvation, death, disease. But will we always be retreating, you ask? – I tell you, we will not! This constant running will end when we have beaten off our pursuers and gained time to es- tablish another protective soviet. It may be within a week from now, a month, a year – I do not know. And nor will it be like the old Juichin where a million peasants died in order to keep alive the things for which this army stands. It will be a model soviet, an impregnable fortress from which the ideals of communism can expand. And, however long the traitors to our country chase us, whatever weapons they bring against us, we will withstand them because right and truth are on our side. And, one day, when our new home is established – be it in this province – if the Kuomintang sicken of the chase – or 1,000 miles north, we will regroup and strike northward again to do the job Chiang Kai- shek should be doing – fight the invading Japanese." He pointed to the north-west. "Look – those are the mountains of the great Yuehcheng Range – cross them and you will be in Kweichow province. Perhaps there, around the city of Liping, we will build a new soviet – perhaps we will be driven from Liping, I do not know. What I do know is that one day we will turn and fight – like the famous Ninth Army Corps is fighting daily to prevent our encirclement by these white brother bastards. You hear me?"

Silent until now, they rose to him in a body, shouting assent, as every unit down the line was also shouting. He had got them going now, and knew it, and he yelled, his fist swinging before their faces:

"We are not alone – did you think it? The tiger General Ho Lung with his Second Front Army of another 100,000 is driving towards us from his Sangchih Soviet in the north: General Chang Kuo-tao is fighting out of his Hunan Soviet south of the

Yangtse-kiang and will link up with us – then we will see some bloody encirclement – the encirclement of the Kuomintang who chase us from pillar to post! Think of it, eh? Who will be the tigers then? Will it be Chiang and his Kuomintang rubbish, or will it be Mao Tse-tung, your leader who has never lost a battle!" He glared at them. "Now then – fight and run, run and fight, and soon commanders like your own Chu Teh will lead you north in an army of a million to sweep back the Japs! You are already the victors. We are not retreating, do you understand? We are advancing to fight the Japanese!"

They enveloped him, slapping his back.

Ma yelled, "A year from now we will invade Japan!"

Discipline was forgotten. And, all down the line it was the same: the speech, timed to a second, repeated 100 times, brought instantaneous applause; every unit from the vanguard Red Cadres to the rearguard Ninth seemed to be cheering. Thousands of voices were shouting, "*Jih pen, Jih pen!*" (Japan, Japan!).

"Right!" roared Tenga, "back into line. Get those wounded back into the carts – come on, me lucky muleteers – back on the march to Tokyo!"

They joked with him, yelling their obscene banter; they cracked their mulewhips high, shouting good-byes to Commander Ma who was now striding back to his Sixth Headquarters, leaving us to Tenga. Muchai I found standing quietly; in his face was an unquiet resignation.

"What do you think of it?" I asked.

He said, shaking his head, "It is terrifying – but more so since they actually believe it. No army can exist for long on lying propaganda – we aren't even retreating before Chiang – we're being decimated."

Pipa was standing as if awaiting me; for some reason Yung was temporarily absent. "Lin . . ." she said, her hand moving to mine. She looked like a Young Vanguard standing there in her crumpled grey tunic. Her hair was black in the weak sunlight; her collar was open at the neck, showing the white, upward sweep of her throat, and her eyes were bright.

She was at once the same, beloved Pipa.

But the wounded were calling to me from the stretchers, so it was convenient not to reply to her. Knowing a mixture of love and shame, I did not trust myself to touch her.

Had Kwelin not come I could not much longer have borne the knowledge of Pipa's presence; it was as if the fates brought her to me.

Kwelin's joyful personality unravelled the conflicting emotions of conscience, duty, love. Her initial impact on the Fifth Muleteers, a mass effect, diluted my personal complications; her infectious humour bred abandonment; it spread new hope.

The coming of Kwelin, a nurse of the fighting Ninth Corps under General Lo, the army's present hero, was made singular by the way the men received her. Carried behind a mounted Young Vanguard (who galloped his mare to the rear of the Fifth Muleteers) she came on foot along our column to Tenga. Of the legendary Ninth, the corps that was saving our lives with its courage, she was wearing, by Mao's command, the scarlet necktie of the respected rearguard, and in her cap was the white flash stained in their blood. Seeing her coming, the muleteers yelled their admiration – the average life of anybody in the Ninth was now down to a fortnight, and this applied to nurses too.

She was a girl dressed in the uniform of a boy – it never suits. But no Young Vanguard I had met enjoyed her gay, child-like beauty; nor was this sullied by a bad hare-lip, though her smile, like her speech, was unaffected by the curse. Seeing my shoulder-flashes and the wounded in the long-cart, she stopped before me.

"Doctor-student, Fifth Muleteers?"

"Yes," I replied.

She bowed, almost imperceptibly. "I am Kwelin, Ninth Headquarters."

"If you are, you've seen some action."

She made a wry face. "Too much, they say. Male nurses are replacing females with the Ninth."

"There's not much going on here – our troubles are mainly bombers and feet."

She was disappointed; I could see it in her face. "But the Medical Commission told me you were performing serious operations."

"When there's little hope of survival: it's not a romantic existence."

We automatically walked together to the wounded.

Here she paused to admire the removable hooped canvas

canopy, Bricko's conversion of the medical long-cart into an American Mid-western wagon.

Bricko's fame as an inventor was spreading; his latest genius being the construction of what he called his 'Brown Contraption' – a sort of six-hole lavatory, easily carried and unfolded, to span a handy brook or gulley: "A balm to what is left of my dignity," Muchai had said. "Does the Red Army really expect a venerable old gentleman to squat upon his heels?"

Kwelin said now, prodding the hooped canopy, "This has been taken up by the Ninth, did you know?" she wandered around the long-cart.

"Anaesthetics?" she asked.

"Opium, the usual."

"Isn't that against orders?"

"Of course." I pulled back the rear awning; the wounded raised their heads to her. I said, "What we don't kill we manage to addict. Meanwhile we only have a few patients; things are pretty quiet."

"It won't be so quiet in Kweichow," she said.

We looked at each other, the conversation dying; her smile faded. As if aware of the blemish, she lifted a hand and covered her mouth.

"Come," I said, "I will take you to report to Tenga."

Pipa and Yung came to the long-cart; holding aside the canvas, Pipa mounted the rear foot-board and disappeared among the wounded.

Kwelin said, "Who's she? I thought the only women up with the Sixth Regiment were with the few partisans."

"Pipa and Yung have been helping me with the nursing. Both are unqualified."

"Pipa . . .?"

I thought; best let her have the truth of it. And to hear it from my own lips would be for me the first confirmation of the true relationship.

"Pipa is my half-sister, but this isn't common knowledge. Yung's in love with her. Any time now he will make this apparent."

She laughed with a sudden abandon. "Romance in the Mule-teers? It's more than I knew in the Hammering Ninth," Smiling whimsically into my face, she added, "But by your manner you don't approve of the match."

"Later you will meet them, but now I must take you to Tenga."

Pipa was standing on the cart foot-board; Yung spoke to her, but she did not answer him; quite still she stood, her eyes upon us.

"One thing's sure," said Kwelin, "you've got a very beautiful sister."

I shrugged, suitably non-committal. Intuition warned me of the possibility of externalising my growing sense of guilt, and I was glad, also for Pipa's sake, that I had told the truth of us; it would diminish the strain of us all working together: the ones to suffer most from discord would be the wounded.

Now, having found Tenga, I was wondering if he might consider transferring Pipa back to the Women's Detachment under the command of the dominant Shao Shan. The fact that this would remove her from Yung's company – for he would stay with the Fifth – was not absent from my mind.

Expectancy, jealousy, joy were quarrelling within me in quick-silver, changing moods.

"No," Tenga muttered now, eyeing Kwelin, "you'll want all the nurses you can get once we're over the big Yuehcheng – hang on to the little tart and keep her under your eye. If I give anyone a boot it'll be that pansy, Yung." He put a huge arm around Kwelin's shoulders, almost enveloping her. "You'm a good one – you come from the Ninth – now you nurse the mules, eh, my sister?"

Kwelin raised an eye at me.

On the way back to the long-cart, with the muleteers shouting their rough greetings to her, she said, "You seem to be having trouble with this beautiful Pipa!"

"It looks like rain," I said at the sky.

Now, with the Yu partisans flanking the mule-train; in the company of Jo-kei, Muchai, Big One and Bricko, we marched together with a new intent towards the bastion of the Yuehcheng Range, and there came upon the men of the Fifth an unusual gaiety. For, while the rearguard was still locked in combat with the pursuing Kuomintang, the vanguard, spearheaded by the Assault Cadres, melted all before us. And new tactics were ordered by Headquarters; henceforth guerrilla methods were not to be absolute; diversions would be cut to a minimum.

The united fire-power of the Cadres and the partisans was to blast a path through the weak provincial troops to speed the advance.

"Averaging twenty-seven miles a day, who can go faster?" asked Muchai.

"You'd average forty with the Kuomintang behind you," growled Tenga.

"We have got to disengage Lo's rearguard," said Jo-kei. "Word comes that they're losing 100 men a day."

"I'd double that," said Kwelin. "The last three miles of this army is white with bandages."

Within an hour of joining the Fifth she knew every wounded man in the unit. Into everybody's business, she would run up and down the column, swinging herself up into the carts, talking with everybody, but always returning to join me in the morning and night inspections. There was about her a gaiety that translated itself to the men. Nurse one moment, entertainer the next, as she marched backwards along the mule-train teaching us the 'bus song of the famous Ninth. And soon every muleteer was roaring it:

> There's a 'bus coming up, a Number Eleven.
> And Mao Tse-tung says the seats are free.
> So spin me along with a girl on my knee,
> Me shins cocked up and me feet in heaven.
> Cool me shifters, boys, count me toes,
> There's a 'bus to Peking, a Number Eleven,
> Which no bugger's seen and no bugger knows.

And the ditty (not entirely Kwelin's version) known to the mule-train as Kwelin's song, was adopted by the Third Corps instantly. The Assault Cadres in the van bawled it, the flanking partisans and Lin Piao's First Corps repeated the chorus of the last two lines, echoing them over the foothills of Old Mountain and Thunder God Rock looming out of the winter mist. The Central Column marching under Chou En-lai heard it and sent it down the line to the Fifth Corps under General Tung, and these repeated it so that the Ninth Corps, still desperately fighting, heard their song and shouted it in the confusion of the battle. The Kuomintang heard it and adopted it, making their own versions but always it was the song of the Number Eleven bus. Friend and enemy, mechanically fighting for ideals forgotten, made this marching song the music of the *Long March*. Rumour had it that Otto Braun was singing it. Even Mao Tse-tung sang it, men said. It walked, this song, from Kwangsi to Yenan, in unprintable versions; it was the song that won China to communism.

But we did not sing while climbing Old Mountain of the Yuehcheng Range, the highest on the Kwangsi border. On the night of December 10th, squatting on a ledge 2,000 feet up, I sheltered from the wind and sleet and wrote in my diary:

Yesterday we climbed Old Mountain. It was a bitter experience; we lost, in slips, scores of men and animals. Several days ago, Kwelin and I, with medical packs, climbed with the Cadres – lent to them by Commander Ma, for the Fifth Muleteers were taking the longer route through the lower passes. Tojo kicked at everything in sight when she saw me leaving, and Pipa was slightly hurt. I trust Yung cares for her. All day the Cadres, fanatical young fighters, have been flushing out snipers. The only casualties we treat are from frost-bite, as expected. The heights are terrifying – I have no head for them. Kwelin doesn't seem to mind – she leaps over gaps with sickening drops – an incredible young woman . . .

Later, we returned with the Cadre soldiers to an ice-road 2,000 feet lower. This was supposed to be at a more reasonable level, but the challenging mountain roads, snow-covered in dizzy whiteness, were still almost too much for my uneasy head. Here we met the carts of the Fifth again, curling around a precipice on the mountainside. Instantly, I recognised Tenga's commands, and soon the muleteers' torches came into sight.

"Is that you, Lin-wai?"

I called a reply in the dark, and Jo-kei shouted, "Watch the bridge, the planks are rotten," and he waved in the moonlight to Big One, who was carrying a man.

It was dark.

The rain was beating down, bringing misery and confusion. Donkeys were crying under the whips as the Fifth hauled up stores for the Regiment. The fourth night on Old Mountain we spent in the open, crouching under our oil-cloth umbrellas, Kwelin shivering against me.

With the first light of dawn staining the clouds, Jo-kei stood on a little plateau and beat himself for warmth.

"No farther, Lin-wai – to hell with daily orders."

"Sleep," said Kwelin, and sank down in the lee of a rock.

Muchai came, followed by Big One and Bricko with three walking wounded, all of whom were exhausted. The rain had ceased, the wind dropped. Word came up to bivouac until daylight. Yung and Pipa were last to arrive.

I unrolled my blanket and spread it on the rock floor; our breath steamed like smoke in the frost; all about us, now the rain had stopped, the crags began to paint themselves a delicate whiteness.

"Will you sit here with me?", I asked Pipa.

"That is the nurse's place," said she. "I am perfectly all right with Yung."

Later, Kwelin, who seemed to notice everything, said, "She may be very beautiful, Chan Lin-wai, but she's not a very affectionate sister."

"Relatives are entitled to tiffs," said Muchai, as if he had said nothing in particular.

Although the wind was bitter with the advent of dawn, there was a fine security away from the fighting, and the respite from the march was welcome. And, as we sat there watching the dawn come up, the sky cleared and the moon appeared so round and big that you felt you could reach up and touch it. The stars were like festival lanterns set against black jade; all about us the peaks of higher Leikungyai were towering black giants spearing a jewelled sky.

Kwelin, wrapped in her blanket, was asleep beside me: Pipa was sleeping in Yung's arms, and Muchai muttered from a frozen face:

"It is like sitting at the bottom of a well, eh, Lin-wai?"

I did not answer for I was watching Kwelin's face: her feet were actually jutting into space over the ledge: moving closer, I linked her arm in mine. Muchai, chuckling, said softly:

"It is good policy to take care of the nurse – to say nothing of the excellent diplomacy."

Jo-kei said, "He is a wicked old bugger, Lin-wai, do not heed him."

114

Hearing us, Bricko crept along the ledge holding another by the hand.

"Fool, my friend," he said. "Here's Lin-wai, the doctor, also Jo-kei and an old one: everything is here, I tell you – if you're sick on the march, even a nurse for a bit of bloody comfort." He bent low in a mock bow. "Gentlemen of the Fifth, meet me friend, Fool?"

The man by his side was tiny; his rags hung on his skinny body and he hugged a tiny mongrel dog in the crook of his arm: from his mouth hung spittle and he looked more dead than alive. I sat up, and Muchai said, "Bricko, what the devil's happening?"

"This peasant man and his dog called Kau Kau I have found; they're following the Red Army for food."

Jo-kei said bassly, "Let him loose, Eunuch, the man's an idiot."

Bricko's voice rose shrilly. "I found him, I tell you; he'll fall at this height!"

The man by his side made a wild, incoherent sound, his face haggard against the moon.

Jo-kei rose, his fist against Bricko's nose. "Then sleep now, the pair of you. One more squawk and I'll put you two and your wonk over the edge. In the name of Buddha, where do you find such rubbish?"

At this Bricko sat, rocking the little man in his arms, and, to my astonishment, the man drew from his rags a flute; putting it to his lips he played strange, tuneless music, and the mongrel, on its hind legs, danced.

"That is excellent," cried Bricko. "See Jo-kei, my little man plays the flute of a beggar? And Kau Kau, his mongrel, dances!"

"By the blood of Confucius!" roared Jo-kei, getting up again.

Up and down the narrow ledges I saw fires being lit by men who could not sleep because of the cold. Down in the unseen valley there moved a serpent of light; the last of the Third streaming up to Thunder God, curling its tail in flares to a black horizon.

All about me men were snoring: Tenga was actually sleeping in Big One's arms; I wondered about this strange relationship: Fool, the new man, was mumbling nameless sounds; Pipa's face was pinched with cold.

All down the track men were asleep in the crevices; others were still talking in whispers, yet the silence was so great that I heard their words clearly. Suddenly, Pipa said, over the space between us:

"Lin-wai, have you forgotten me?"

"Sleep," answered Muchai, his hand raised between us. He turned to me, "You also," said he. "Sleep. It is better that way."

But I did not sleep and soon the dawn came up red and raging, bringing to life the mountain in all its crystal enormity: scarlet and gold, the Kwangsi dawn shot blood across the world.

The voices about me died to whispers: the heavy breathing of the sleepers, motionless beside their dead fires, beat about me in echoes; the sound of a complaining spring now; later the murmur of a distant ocean. Now loudly, at other times so faint to my ears before I slept, that they were like silkworms munching banyan leaves.

FIFTEEN

The morning was bright with winter sun; the ledges of Thunder God Rock were coated with ice: distant Sansui was like a beleagured ghost town on the horizon, the roofs glittering like diamonds.

I was stiff and cramped, my arm around Kwelin; when I rose, I looked out on to a world of ice and fire.

The young cadre soldiers, impossibly brave, moved first; using a heliograph to flash our position, and the Fifth Muleteers' carts slid down to the western plains.

With Tenga leading us again and the Assault Cadres wheeling north-west for the city of Liping, we marched under a fine sun, our sandals beating a roar on the frozen ground: making for the Great Snow Mountain where the peaks were so tall that you had to take a donkey's saddle off to get him under the sky.

On a ledge of Thunder God Rock lay a dead woman.

"What she is," said Bricko, kneeling beside her, "is one of them camp followers."

As such, she was also of no consequence.

"Tip her over," commanded Tenga, coming up.

"She is a peasant," said Kwelin, furious, "you will treat her with respect."

The woman had been dead for many hours: plainly, she had frozen to death, probably in the business of climbing the Yueh-cheng to sell herself for food, a bargain common to the Kuomintang. Her face, embalmed in frost, was stark and beautiful in its marble whiteness under the moon.

Tenga swore and said, "All right, then – rope her, you two, and slide her down."

This Bricko and Big One prepared to do, and we stood in a little group looking down at her, now with pity, for she was impossibly young to die. And Kwelin said softly, "You will be careful of her face, Bricko?"

And as the men looked up Kwelin added, "Do take care, please?"

Tenga spoke first. Shifting his feet in the snow, he said, "Go gentle, then – you watch it. Treat that corpse proper or ye'll never hear the bloody end of it, understand?" and he blustered about.

They treated the starved woman of Leikungyai as if she were Kwelin.

"Did you notice, Lin-wai," said Kwelin later, "she had the most beautiful mouth . . . ?"

The pace increased. The rearguard, again, was heavily engaged: political workers ran up and down the line, encouraging us to greater speed. In the first three days after leaving Thunder God Rock the vanguard marched and ran no less than ninety miles, and it was feet, feet, feet once again, said Kwelin. Every night, pushed to the limit of human endurance, we lay where we fell, exhausted; in the open, under the carts, digging ourselves into the loess hills when the ground was unfrozen, seeking the shelter of a hedge, a rock, a boulder – anything would do. Very often, when we could get Tojo on to her side, Kwelin and I, Pipa and Yung would lie with our backs to her warmth, away from the prevailing wind. Yung, I noticed, had begun to cough at last – any time now I had expected this. His fine looks belied his stamina; he and Pipa always walked behind the cart these days, seeking shelter from the wind howling with the threat to freeze us alive.

Thus we force-marched on to the town of Sansui, splitting the army, for a second column went full-pelt for Chien-ho; a ruse that confused the pursuers, and the pressure on Lo's rearguard slackened once again.

Sansui, which we entered at midnight, storming the main gates, was a scene of desolation. All down the crazy little alleys the doors were ajar, the cottages plundered. Bodies were lying in heaps, the refuse of landlord slaughter, not even children had been spared. And the retreating Kuomintang had taken the women at will, some not even bothering to pull off both trouser legs for the rape. The deserted streets were littered with fragments of discarded uniforms, smashed weapons. One by one the townspeople came out to greet us, but there was no enthusiam; it was as if the soul had been battered out of Sansui, not a drink given, not an offer of hospitality. The people lined the streets and gazed apathetically; a town of living dead.

It was a night brilliant with frosty stars. Kwelin had been temporarily sent down to the Headquarter Commission, and had not yet returned: sick of the constant bickering among the wounded, for the more the wounds hurt the more indecent the quarrelling became, I left them to Yung and Pipa after doing my evening round of dressings and inspection.

Now, under a curved roof by the western wall, I found a warm place by an oven in a deserted baker's shop; here was a smell of humans, wheat and corn. Mice watched me from the corners as I settled myself to read; I opened *Six Chapters of a Floating Life*, the book Old Teh had returned to me before his execution. In a shaft of moonlight, huddled against the draughty cold, I read:

The bride's companion asked us to go to bed, and Yin, my young wife, asked her to shut the door and retire first. I sat down by my wife's side on the bed and we joked together like old friends after a long separation. Touching her breasts was like magic; I felt the beating of her heart and there was sweetness in it. I asked, "Yin, why is my sister's heart beating so fast, is it because she has a need for me?" She smiled, not replying, and we were carried away in the arms of love. Later, we went into the bed; all too soon came dawn.

A shadow crossed the smashed floor of the bakery. Pipa, closing the door behind her, said, "Kwelin is at the Headquarters, yet I was available, but you sit alone. Have you not a moment for me these days?"

"It is best we stay apart, Pipa. Surely you know that?"

Her eyes were shadowed in that dim light; her face that of a starved ghost, the skin stretched tightly across her pinched cheeks. This march, I reflected, was slowly killing the women.

"It is best because you say so? Have I no word in this?"

I replied testily, "It's old ground, Pipa, there's no point in stitching its wounds. We're finished – you know it as well as I."

A silence of broken friendship came between us; she joined me in the unspoken sadness; then said, her voice brittle:

"I'm with child."

As if unheard, this seemed to beat within my head. Rising, I took her hands. She said, smiling up, "You're surprised? And we were once such lovers!"

I did not reply; turning away, she added, swiftly, "Amazingly, the child is Yung's."

Beyond the window, in the moonlit streets, the flower of the army, the Assault Cadre storm-troops, were thronging shoulder to shoulder in search of food and rice-wine, an impoverished consolation. What women were left alive in Sansui that night were in no fit state to entertain soldiers

I said flatly, "It can't be. You've scarcely known him a month."

"He's known me longer than you think."

I said bitterly, "Then you didn't waste much time!"

It turned her, instantly furious, her hands clenched. "So I'm a whore now, eh? I can bed myself for your enjoyment, can't I, but I'm tarty when I give myself to Yung?"

"I didn't say that."

She wept. I held her and she sobbed against my coat. The very touch of her brought to me the old unfathomable excitement. I said: "Tell me the truth, it's important to me. Is it really Yung's?"

Pushing me away she went to a corner; ceasing to cry she replied, "I should know, shouldn't I? If you prefer your medical facts, it's the second month."

"*Tin Hau*," I said. "The Party won't thank you for a baby on the march."

"To the devil with the Party – what of Shao Shan, the women's commander? She's six months gone, isn't she? And what of Ho Tze-nien, Mao's wife?"

"Mao's wife didn't march, she was carried. As Yung's woman you'll birth in a ditch like an animal."

"And as Yung's wife?"

"As Yung's wife they'll billet you in the nearest town to wait your time."

She said, reflectively, "We Chans carry small, they won't know until it's too damned late."

I said, wearily, "You've told Yung?"

"Of course." She was smiling through her tears, wiping her face with her hands like a child. "And he is delighted."

"It's scarcely a convenient time, Pipa."

I was instantly aware of the platitude.

"Yung gave as much thought to that as you."

It had been a mistake, I reflected, to bring her to the army.

In all, there were some thirty-five women officially on the march; this included Mao's wife, Chu Teh's, a few other wives and the woman of Otto Braun, a union that had not been blessed; she deserted the March long before Paoan. There were the few women partisans, of course, commanded by the big Shao Shan, whose husband, the hero of her conception, was five-feet-four, and therefore much respected. Shao, these days, was a barrel on legs, being three months from her time: her approaching confinement was of torrid interest; but it was doubtful if the same kindness would be paid to Pipa.

There was hope, I remembered, in the coming union with the Fourth Army marching towards us from Hupeh. General Chang, later Mao's political opponent, had in this army a women's detachment some 2,000 strong: Pipa's predicament would be lost among such numbers.

But now I wondered how Welfare would handle this confinement if she was delivered while serving with the Fifth. At worst a death in labour; at best a litter on Tojo's cart with a baby squalling in the ranks: the Party, as prim as ever, had small patience with unmarried mothers.

Pipa said now, "You have no love for me now, Lin-wai?"

I gripped my hands. The old emotions began to sweep over me: strangely, in that musty place, I smelled the sweetness of her hair, a faint but pleasing perfume that not even the trudging march, the sweat of rough sleeping had managed to dilute. It took me back to the moon-ridden nights of Shengsu, when we made love. Getting up, I stared at her in the dim light, silently begging her not to approach nearer. I said:

"I'll always love you, you know that."

We stood motionless; people afraid to move. It took all my strength to stay rooted there, yet I knew I could never take her into my arms. She said, "It's ridiculous, you know. I am now Yung's woman, but even while Yung was in my body I begged in my heart for you. Oh, Lin-wai! Will you not love me now, darling . . . ? Once more?"

I ached for her, yet was sickened by the emotion.

She said from the smudged shadows of her face. "We're two different bodies, aren't we? The world wouldn't know. Just once more – please?" she came closer; I turned away.

When I looked again the tears were on her face. She said:

"I'm in pain for you, Lin-wai . . ." She opened the door. "I'll always be in pain for you though you do not want me – don't forget my face . . .?"

The thought repeated itself in my head – *an idiot child*. And if Yung really believed the baby was his he must be simple in the head.

SIXTEEN

It was north-westward now, headlong, driving before us the greater army of General Chih-tan: darting a feint at the capital of Kweichow to throw our pursuers off the scent. Confused, they roared west to protect the city, so Mao Tse-tung took us directly north for Tungtao and Liping.

There was now a new strength and purpose in the ranks; we were retreating, true, but we were retreating north for the purpose of an army – to shake off Chiang Kai-shek and fight the Japanese.

Despite casualties, for we were averaging a bombing, skirmish or minor battle every two days, we were now numerically stronger since leaving the Juichin Soviet; the peasants of the towns and villages through which we passed were flocking to the Red Flag, for this was an army which gave and did not take. Unlike the pursuing nationalists, we did not rape and burn.

What we needed we bargained and paid for: in the village communities we organised defence against the oncoming Kuomintang, gave political advice, formed military cadres and centres of welfare. While we publicised the benefits of enrolment into the army of New China, we did not impress soldiers; indeed, if a man was the sole breadwinner of a family, we did not trouble him. The only item we insisted upon having was doors; in Chinese villages these are easily removable. Under their cover a man could lie protected in the winter's rain and frost, and we returned these to their owners before leaving in the morning. We gave medical advice to villagers; if hungry, we shared with them our rations of rice, each man subscribing it in grains. This countered Chiang Kai-shek's Nationalist Government propaganda that we were bandits. The only member of a community having cause to fear the Red Army was a landlord, and even he, were his record reasonable, was spared. Unreasonable landlords we imprisoned in their own jails, freeing the peasants: the landlords who had viciously exploited the peasants we shot in batches.

Our Fourth Army under General Chang Kuo-tao was sweeping all before it as it drove south towards Tsunyi, the next big city in our path: with Ho Lung of the Second Army decimating Kuomintang opposition, Tsunyi City loomed up as a meeting point of armies.

Tsunyi, Tsunyi, *Tsunyi*! The name was on all lips. Jo-kei said once, and he was proved right, "The Long March, my friends, began in earnest from the city of Tsunyi."

At Liping, on the road to Tsunyi, I knew the comfort of a woman.

All that morning, after entering the outskirts of the city, I had been performing minor operations under the long-cart canopy, assisted by Yung. Kwelin, still down with the Military Commission, was now temporarily attached, and I protested vigorously to Tenga about it without effect. This gave licence to Pipa.

Said she, "A qualified nurse who isn't available, Lin-wai? You might be down to the hacks again, but at least we're here. One wonders if you've got your Ninth Corps heroine or not."

"She'll be back," I said.

Pipa swabbed the injured man for stitching; it was a minor wound, the shrapnel had opened the flesh at his groin. Yung could have stitched it. Pipa, as she gently swabbed his leg glanced sensuously up at me, then slyly lowered her face. I turned away.

Jealousy flowed in Yung; he made no attempt to conceal his dislike of me. This did nothing to improve his efficiency; these days he made elementary mistakes. Also, the wounded were now openly hostile to his attentions; his latent femininity, increased by the nature of his care, induced in them the rejection of the healthy male. Conversely, he was in no way timorous: his doe-like exterior was the fur that hid the tiger. Not a man there, including me, sought an outright confrontation with Yung, the hybrid of the species.

And he was undoubtedly playing the man with Pipa. Knowing about the child, apparently believing it to be his own, my presence was infuriating him, and I longed for Kwelin's return that I might somehow be rid of him.

"Qualified nurse, did you say?" he enquired of Pipa now. "What this unit wants is qualified doctors," and he winked at the wounded man.

The atmosphere, by the time we reached Liping, was not conducive to healing.

Liping, our final major halt before Tsunyi, was a town in the grip of soldiery. Down in the bazaars the naphtha lamplight swung yellow rays on to the faces of thronging men; the arm-linked razzle that every soldier knows: Red Army songs battered down the clay-walled alleys. The town, shut-black and still at our first approach, now flung wide its doors to the jingling pockets of the invaders. Traders arrived with squawking hens tied upside down in bundles of six; the scarred refuse of the ancient city spewed out on to the winter pavements crying its wares, indicting with derisive shouts the grocer who over-charged, the shaved-bald women who had consorted with the fleeing Kuomintang. Down in the village square the execution squads drove stakes into the frozen ground, each bell-clang of the hammers tolling the death-knell of more shivering landlords. Drinking hot rice-wine in a teashop, I decided to forget them all – landlords, Yung, Pipa, the war, and go down to the Headquarter Commission to try to find Kwelin. But the warmth of the wine crept into my bones and with this came images of Pipa. So later, when a woman called to me from the darkness, her voice confident and clear on the frosted air, I turned.

"Kai-yan! *Kai-yan!*"

I went to her, seeing behind her peasant's tunic and trousers a room with a fire; the blankets of the bed *k'ang* were of excellent quality. "I am not Kai-yan," I said.

She was probably twice my age, yet the brightness of her eyes belied their grieving lines; ten years ago she might have been beautiful. Now she said, her plain face upturned to me:

"Forgive me, you are the image of my husband in uniform: now you are close I see you are young." She drew away from the street lamp brightness.

There was a warmth about her; the room beckoned with the smells of Laoshan. I said, "There cannot be two such as I in the Red Army."

"It was a trick of the light," said she.

I thought of a soft place to rest; of Tenga's muleteers and their feast of drunkenness, of Pipa.

"Will I not do?" I asked, and it brought her to a womanly aloofness.

"I am not a sing-song girl," said she. "A year ago my husband volunteered with the Red Twenty-Fifth, yet he is not a real soldier. Indeed, he is a craftsman, making peony figurines in ivory and sandalwood."

"It appears a waste," and I bowed to her. "Such a man deserves a better life than uniform grey. And, in your arms he could still enjoy his soldier's dream."

In the doorway, she replied, "Then why does he not return to me to dream again?"

"Perhaps I am he, then?" I whispered confidently. "It's inconceivable that such beauty should be denied a man about the house."

I waited.

Not a woman of the brothels, this one, or a window-knock lady designed for a brief, ecstatic contemplation; this one would have to be handled like an injured cricket.

Opening the door for me to enter, she gently said, "My name is Mrs. Soong, but my friends call me Lu. Come in from the cold."

"And I am Chan Lin-wai – Surgeon-General to the First Front Army – doubtless you've heard of me?"

She said she had not, so I added, "I come as your protector, Soong Lu; any complaints about my soldiers' behaviour you will of course refer to me."

"Welcome to my house, Chan Lin-wai."

In quick, before she changed her mind.

Even Pipa would have approved, I told myself, beset as I was with an empty belly, maltreated feet and a vow of celibacy diluted by wine. And, though Soong Lu was scarcely beautiful, women on the march become prettier every minute.

At her bidding I seated myself on her warm *k'ang*. Leaving the room, Lu returned in a scarlet gown, and her glance of sweet expectancy moved me to say, "You are beautiful, Soong Lu."

"Thank you."

"Do I smell noodle soup on that stove?"

"You have an excellent nose, Chan Lin-wai; in truth, I was preparing it for my husband."

"Does he appreciate your good cooking?"

She replied, her eyes slanted away, "He is a man of tremendous appetite."

"Not necessarily reserved for noodle soup?"

She smiled most prettily.

Later, the shadows deepening in the room, I lay on the warm *k'ang* with Soong Lu's hand in mine and listened to her voice above the clamour of the billeting army; the hunting soldiers, the shrieks of willing females. Lu said, "My husband, you know, was previously married by vendor's contract; his wife, he said, was beautiful. Of silk embroidery she could stitch an inch a day, spending much time with paints and powders. Indeed, my husband never quite knew where she was, for men desired her." She sighed against my face. "Soon she died."

"And then he married you?"

"He did, after just two days. Then my husband said, 'No more silk-stitching, no more paints and powders, no more beauty. I will marry Lu, the miller's daughter: of plain darning she can do a yard a day; being prominent in the breast, she will doubtless milk well: being plain, men will not desire her'."

I commented, "He is a good enough philosopher."

"But with little knowledge of women, you suppose?" Her arms went about me hard and strong.

"Kai-yan," she whispered, and her body was trembling against me, "you realise, don't you, that were I not able to mistake you for my husband, I wouldn't be doing this?"

"I appreciate the honour, Soong Lu."

"Indeed, I would die of shame if ever I was tempted again."

I did not answer, for at that moment entered her, and she moved her face away from me, saying in tears, "Oh, Kai-yan, *Kai-yan* . . . !"

The night streets of bawdy soldiers battered its wine-breath on the window. Soong Lu wept.

Knowing that tears are often joy to a woman, I reflected that she was lucky that I happened to be passing; loneliness is the toll of war; women pay the most. Her husband, also, was fortunate; at least he was decently represented.

In the dim light of the fire her eyes moved over my face, and

127

I saw in their depths an unusual light that could have been madness; this I had not seen before. She said, kissing my lips, "Oh, Kai-yan, my sweet, my precious . . ."

"My little Pipa," I said, but this she did not hear.

There was little conscience in it for me. After all, I told myself, obedience to marriage vows and chastity are only commended under the laws of Taoism, not exacted. To assist her conscience, I mentioned this during loving her, even while seeing Pipa's face.

"But I am a Buddhist," Soong Lu protested, "I am no pagan Taoist. My vows are important to me. So have no fear, my darling, that I would ever betray you as your first wife betrayed you – I am no loose wife for men and sweet foods."

Gently I drew from her loins, kissing her brow, a husband's respect to a dutiful wife.

"Do not leave me, Kai-yan." She wept. "I beg you, do not leave me again, I cannot bear it."

Clearly at times of mental incoherence, she truly believed me to be her husband.

While dressing, I saw on a mantel the official Red Army notification of his death – apparently, he had been killed but a week before, fighting with the Twenty-Fifth Army in the counter-attack at Lushih.

Kneeling beside the k'ang, I kissed her small hands.

"Goodbye."

It was raining in the street.

The naphtha flares struck me in the face as I went back to the bazaar: beneath the slanting, rain-shot beams the dried fish gaped at me in regimental deaths of mute surprise as I got into the Hankow brandy, the brew Tenga loved: cold tea in the bottle, it was fire in the belly. At a table beneath a ragged awning I drank steadily amid the bedlam of thronging, bawling soldiers.

In time of stress, in the vomit and groans, in times like this a face always returned to me; it was not the face of Pipa and certainly not Kwelin's. A young soldier, apparently recognising me, held his bandaged arm closer against his torn tunic and gazed at me in recognition. Lifting my bottle, I waved him away.

There was, a week or so ago, another boy aged thirteen, a Young Vanguard of Perhai, who had limped into Casualty with a minor wound in the foot. The shrapnel had taken him cleanly, neatly slitting the skin at the back of the heel: his ragged shoe, I remember, was filled with blood.

"Wait," Pipa had said, "I will swab it clean."

To the boy I had said. "It's nothing, lad. Look, turn your back to me and take your weight on the injured foot," and this he had done.

"Now raise your weight and stand on your toes – one foot only."

He had done this, too, and the Achilles tendon, half cut through, snapped at the heel and flew up the back of his leg like an elastic cord, gathering in a great, purple bunch behind his knee at the moment of his scream.

We hadn't done a lot on Achilles tendons in Third Year Shanghai University. I sent him down the line to Dr. Nelson Fu, to whom I sent all my other mistakes. Later a note came back to me; it read, 'In future keep away from Achilles tendons'. It was my one and only reprimand.

They got the tendon down, of course, but he never walked again.

Last time I saw him he was sand-bagged on the road verge, his rifle cocked up, a sacrificial sheep for the oncoming Kuomintang.

Now, under the naphtha light the wounded boy-soldier returned, held out his bandaged arm and said, "Thought it was you, Doctor-student – this is coming on good . . ."

"Piss off," I said.

For, deeper down the bottle of brandy I was seeing the Vanguard's face: yet it was Pipa's face that made shape through the soaked, grey shapes of barging soldiers: I heard her voice above the raucous cries of the stalls.

"Lin-wai," said Pipa.

This one was Pipa in the flesh.

Unsteadily, I rose, putting down the bottle.

"I followed you," she said.

The rain teemed down from a splintered, opal moon, deluging in spouts from the edge of the awning, running in sheets to the gutters where beggars waved wet, drum-stick limbs, spiking the flooded road.

I smiled and reached for Pipa and she snatched herself away as if insulted.

"Don't you touch me," she whispered. Making a fist of her

129

hand she pressed it against her belly, "I carry your child in here. You know it, I know it, yet you go to the house of a whore."

"She was not a whore."

Swinging back her hand she struck me in the face. "A whore! Yet I am here?"

A silence grew about us: intent faces of compassionate soldiers stared at us through the rain. I lowered my head, needing her warmth more then than at any time I had known her. Pipa said, softly, "You devil, Lin-wai ..." She thumped herself. "You only had to ask!"

Turning from the table, I left her, wandering aimlessly in the fug of the brandy. And I saw before me not Pipa's face, but the Young Vanguard lying on the road verge; hatred was in his eyes.

Pipa was now before me again, whispering as I walked unsteadily, "Right, then, from now on I'm Yung's tart, not yours. Two hours I waited outside that whore-house – *two hours!* Was she better in bed than me?" Her face was wet with rain; her eyes were diamonds in the garish light of the lamps.

I stiffened before her, gripping my arms lest I put them about her. Pipa said, softly. "All right, then – now I know. I'll go to Yung tonight – *now*, d'you hear me?"

"Goodbye," said the Young Vanguard, holding his bandaged arm.

Neither Pipa, Soong Lu or he deserved my kind of bastard.

SEVENTEEN

Onward, ever onward to the Wu River: walking, trotting, even running in the snow; an hour walking, an hour trotting, an hour running: on, *on*.

The Assault Cadres, tough and strong, often used to discipline the line, fists up, threatening the soldiers.

"Get on, get on, you bloody two yards of cloth! The Japs are coming down from Manchuria – what are ye waitin' for?"

Another cried, "If you bunch here the Ninth and Fifth have to stand and fight – get on, get on, you lazy bastards," and he swiped at Tojo's rear and Tenga yelled:

"You keep that whip off my fuggin' mule or I'll land you one."

"How dare you, Sergeant! Do you know who I am?"

"I do, and I piss in your mother's milk!" and Tenga came out of the cart-line with his whip flying and we didn't see Red Cadres for dust. "And I'd do the same for Mao Tse-tung – you leave my unit be!"

Leading the Kuomintang a dance like a monkey baiting a cow, Mao led us now to the Wu River of the Wumeng mountain range, the gorges of Yunnan Province that leap at Kweichow. Here was thickly wooded land, the home of the Miao aborigines, a minority who hated Chinese. Up came the sappers to bridge the river with their centipedes of rafts and canoes, also a detachment of strong swimmers hand-picked from the Sixth Regiment.

The heliographs flashed the message from the surrounding hills where the propaganda scouts were breaking ground; the Young Vanguards shouted it, and it was always the same: faster, faster, *faster*.

We forced our way over the bitter Wu River, prepared to blast from our advance every Miao pigmy in sight; we laid barrages across the surrounding hills to silence the sniping Kuomintang. Mobile heavy machine-guns from Russia had joined the First Corps, and these raked the sky during the bombing raids; in multi-purpose now, firing over open sights at the Kuomintang tanks, for these were after us now. And always we expected attack from the Miao.

But the Miao did not come as enemies; on the banks of the Wu they came as friends, with their swift little skin-canoes to aid us. And on the third day of January, the Second Division of Lin Piao's First Corps rumbled past our muleteers at a gallop, whips flying, a glorious confusion of activity and sound: up came the forward artillery, the mobile machine-guns, the bridging sections with their centipede rafts of bamboo and kerosene tins. More strong swimmers of the Fourth followed in their bright yellow skull-caps, passing us swiftly, though we were at the trot. The pain of rubbed abrasions and raws was forgotten. It was onward, ever onward, racing the Kuomintang for the fertile plains of the Wu basin: once over the plains we would be safe, they said, for the Ninth rearguard was locked in bloody battle with armies.

Free of the restricting mountain passes and fears of ambush, the pace slowed at last. Over the snow-covered wastes there came again the methodical tramp, tramp, tramp of feet. With breath recovered the Third began again a new marching song, lately learned for the benefit of Otto Braun:

We don't know where we've come from,
Or where we've been today.
We don't know where we're going,
Or why we've come this way.
But when we get to Tokyo,
Herr Otto Braun will say:
"*Mein Gott, Mein Gott*, what a bloody fine lot,
for *Gott's* sake go away."

Undoubtedly composed by an intellectual of the Headquarter Base, the muleteers bawled it over the arctic-like wastes of the Wu Basin: without an idea what '*Mein Gott*' meant translated, they shouted it above the tramping sandals back to the main Third Corps who flung it to the First Corps under Lin Piao, the Ninth, the Seventh, the Fifth: there it was bellowed around Braun's lumbering Headquarters.

Later a recitative was composed, which was especially performed for the benefit of Otto Braun himself, on the rare occasions he was seen in the line.

Otto gets chicken and bean-curd soup.
But what do we get? *Congee!*
What does he get?
Fried pork and eggs, fat beef and chilli,
And what do we get? *Skilly!*
He gets tobacco and sweet pearl barley,
White bread and rice. And what do we get?
Lice!
Oh, what a fuggin' awful war, mates!
Oh, what a fuggin' awful war!

It is a lucky thing for us, said Muchai, that the German doesn't speak Chinese, though they call him Li Teh.

This, of course, was the trouble.

He didn't speak Chinese.

The sin was unforgivable.

A word about Otto Braun.

At this stage of the march we had covered nearly 1,500 miles from the Juichin break-out – a military miracle which this German organised. We had averaged twenty-six miles a day, which included rest periods and almost daily bombing or fighting: Otto Braun, the adviser to Mao sent by the Russians, had not marched one, according to reports coming down the line. And his meals were fast becoming a legend among the hungry soldiers, it being said that he consumed a pound of pork at a sitting, wouldn't eat rice, had a baker appointed to him and drank wines especially brought in from Hong Kong by messenger.

Yung said, "They say he's over eighteen stones, can't march because he can't see his feet, and is either on horseback or carried on a litter by four coolie bearers."

"Why the hell does Mao allow it?" asked Jo-kei.

I shrugged. "Probably because he's got no alternative. If he wants the active support of the Russians he's got to take what Stalin sends him."

"We've got to have someone to blame when things go wrong," said the man from Kwangtung. "I suppose it was Braun who messed it up at the Hsiang river."

Jo-kei said, "Rumour, rumour, but I think I believe the latest. Chou En-lai has officially complained about Braun to the Central

Committee. In future the German will be denied the small Cantonese ladies he so much prefers."

"Aren't you all being very unkind?" asked Kwelin, walking up. "I've actually met Otto Braun in General Headquarters, and the man's a gentleman." She added, "You slander him because he cannot speak Chinese? The only woman I have seen him with was his wife."

"Then where do all the rumours come from?" demanded Jo-kei.

"You started them," answered Kwelin, "it wasn't me."

She had at last returned from Headquarter duty. Her face was bright with expectation that sunny January morning outside Tsunyi: despite the scar of her lips, I thought her beautiful. Big One, I noticed, watched her with his heavy smile, alone in his silent world.

"It's untrue, Kwelin?" I asked.

She made a wry face. "Of course it isn't true – you know how these things start – somebody makes it up and it immediately becomes a fact. Have you missed me?"

I was glad she had returned. She brought with her the assurance of her ability and her strength of character, and I was sick of the wearing atmosphere of having Yung and Pipa in such close proximity.

Even in Kwelin's absence I sensed the growing bond between us, and, now she was back, it was strengthened. I knew it, so did Kwelin; it was an emotion beyond friendship, having no need of words.

"It's a very pretty situation," said Pipa.

I did not reply.

Later that day I sat in a deserted cottage outside the enormous gate-towers of Tsunyi, and recorded in my diary:

7th January, 1935.
Tsunyi, they are saying, is the turning point of this march. It was captured by the genius of Lin Piao, the commander of the First Army Corps. When he routed its outskirt battalion he ordered Comrade Tseng to take a small force of scouts and buglers to the city's gate disguised as Kuomintang. While the regimental buglers created a commotion, one of the scouts begged entry, shouting that the Red Bandits were upon them.

134

The sentries of the gate then asked the name of his company commander: this was given by a Kuomintang prisoner with a knife against his throat in the dark. The sentry cried, "Don't tell us they're already over the Wu River mate – nobody moves that fast." "these buggers do " shouted Comrade Tseng. "Here they come now the Peasant Army of China."

"The defenders were caught with their trousers down and before they could pull them up we were through the gate-towers and into them " said Lin Piao.

Kwelin said entering the room "Lin-wai nothing seems to weary you. What are you writing?" She squatted cross-legged at my feet smiling up at me.

"A diary of events."

"On the march? Isn't this being done by official historians?"

"No doubt perfectly " I replied. "This one I am doing for my ripe old age if I live to see it."

"For your children?" Her eyes, I noticed again, were ever-moving, swift in changing expressions, the jewels of her face that hid the scar.

"For the Party," I said.

"Dear me," said Kwelin, bored.

Later, while at the market in the city, I heard talk that the army was soon to come through, so I returned to the cottage by the gate-towers because it was a vantage point.

Here, to my surprise, I found Kwelin, and she was kneeling before her god, Kuan Yin, a deity created by the God of the Western Paradise. Yung, I reflected with a sigh, was also a Buddhist; this made two of them.

"Lin-wai . . . ?" said she, to the creak of a board, and turned.

I had not suspected her of Buddhism; any who worshipped the Party and served it as did Kwelin was naturally assumed to be an atheist. I said, "I am sorry to have disturbed you," and turned to leave

"But stay," said Kwelin, "or do you disapprove?"

"Of course not. If this is your belief, I respect it."

"But you are surprised?"

"I thought you a good communist."

"But I am. Must I reject all teachings before I can serve the Party?" She rose from the altar. "You have no beliefs at all?"

"In the nation."

She approached me. "For a woman, China isn't enough. So I return to the consolations of childhood – the gods I learned of at my mother's knee. It is harmless enough?"

"It is not in accord with the teachings of the Party," I said.

"Well, well," said Kwelin, "you are very stuffy. I'd never have believed it. Do you even know of Kuan Yin, the Goddess of Mercy?"

I replied, "Better than you would believe. Originally a male divinity, she was introduced here by Mahayana Buddhist missionaries, and epitomises womanly virtues – gentleness, filial piety, beauty."

"You're well informed, I am surprised."

"And I'm surprised you should believe such bourgeois rubbish."

Kwelin replied with a smile, "I prefer Lin-wai the doctor to Chan the communist." Standing at the window overlooking the gate-towers, she was silent. I recall the stillness of the room, the beauty of Kwelin's profile: beyond her were the crammed outer city streets; the merchants bargaining in Kweichow shrieks; the playing of the one-stringed fiddles in a market-place mantled by snow. The whole of existence seemed to throng outside the glittering gates of Tsunyi, leaving us bereft in the hurt of a lost friendship.

Kwelin said:

"Don't underrate my intelligence, Lin-wai – Kuan Yin exists in my fancy, but she keeps me sane. There is little in communism that consoles the individual." She touched her mouth. "Look at this face, the social outcast."

I had no words for her.

"Kuan Yin is the sunshine of my mind – she who can see at once both ends of a stick. You will not take her from me unless you replace her."

"You're not short of friendship here. And you are needed even more than Pipa."

"She has the edge on it. Pipa is loved."

The bedlam of the street below beat about us. Kwelin said:

"Yesterday I saw Yung kissing her. It may be frowned upon by the Party as a disgusting habit; strangely people still do it." She added, "But what man would want kisses from the mouth of a rabbit?"

136

It savoured of self-pity; I didn't like it, and said, "When I was young my mother told me of the Architect P'an Ku who sprang in evolution from the Great Monad of Yang and Yin, the female principles; the shell, the egg. From the interaction of these, the Greater and the Lesser, the architect was hatched in chaos. You know of this?"

She laughed from the shadows and I heard it above the city clamour.

I continued, "But one planet, Earth, he built only for China. His breath became the wind, his head the mountains, his voice he transmuted into thunder. His limbs were the four quarters of the globe, his beard was the tangle of the stars: his left eye he flung into space as our sun, his right eye became the moon. His blood was the rivers, his flesh the great rice territories, the forests his hair: his skin became the weave of silk-worms, the rain was his sweat in all these labours. Man himself was the parasites of his body." I took Kwelin's hands. "In all this I once believed: now I tolerate its romance."

Kwelin did not reply, so I said, "But one thing more. Within his Creation ran a hare, ancient before China was born. Indeed, because she was so inoffensive, *P'an* selected her as the expounder of his scriptures. One night, walking in paradise, he became lost and cried to the animals in his thirst and hunger. The otter brought him fish, the deer her milk, the jackal his kill, but the hare presented herself empty-handed, saying, 'Grant me, Great Buddha Allah Jesus, whom men worship, the honour of being in your service, I who have nothing to give you but myself'."

Bending, I kissed her. Her eyes opened wide with astonishment and she covered her mouth with her hand.

"One god at a time," I said, "communism. Come, we will return to the wounded."

But Kwelin did not immediately move.

As one deeply in thought, she said at the window, "You realise, of course, that Pipa's being married to Yung soon?"

"Of course."

Kwelin turned, her eyes moving swiftly over my face in mute enquiry. "I ... I heard that she is marrying into Buddhism – this, like mine, is Yung's belief. You have no objections?"

"Life can be short these days. It is Pipa's life, not mine."

She pondered this; these were difficult questions for her, and I knew what she was wondering. Kwelin said:

"Muchai says that it will be a simple ceremony – at the western temple – by the other gate; this city has two gates, you know. You will not be there?"

I shook my head.

"Won't this hurt Pipa? True, she is only your half-sister, but would it not be kind . . .?"

I put out my hand to her; together we went back to the wounded.

I do not remember Tsunyi for the manner in which we entered it so much as for the conversation that preceded this. Looking again at my diary, I see that it records:

10th January, 1935.
This morning, an hour after the dawn, the Red Army entered the city. There are plans, I hear, for General Chu Teh to address a mass meeting in memory of Rosa Luxemburg; also there will be a convention of the Politburo of the Party Central Committee. Rumours tell of a political split in the Party, that Mao Tse-tung's leadership is now threatened. It is the usual political haggling, of course, and the common soldier is little concerned. Mistakes like the Hsiang crossing are being labelled as Leftist failures; the critics are being called Rightist opportunists. Mao's position as Chairman might have been strengthened by the Tsunyi Resolutions, but it is significant that, since the Tsunyi Conference, we now have attached to the Fifth one who henceforth will watch our movements: the muleteers have named him Political Chang. The feet are bad enough without having to put up with these political bastards.

The conversation in the cottage overlooking the gate-towers of Tsunyi on that cold January morning was anything but political.

Bricko, the eunuch, said, "Ay, ay, and when I gets to the Golden Sand River I'll get cut o' this bloody army, buy five *mou* of land and set up house wi' a dumpy little woman," and he stroked Fool's mongrel lying in his lap.

"It is an admirable ambition," said Yung. His eyes were shining from his pinched face: Pipa slept beside him, her face upturned in the dim light.

138

"Ay, indeed," continued Bricko, his arm around Fool. "I'll turn up a marriage vendor and buy myself a good clean man with a big ball set on him, and he can lie in me bed and knock out sons."

"An unusual wedding that," observed Jo-kei, and he folded his hands on his stomach and smiled at the ceiling, and I heard the distant clattering of the preparing army: red light was flashing in the room from the drum-fire of the Kuomintang guns. Kwelin breathed softly beside me. Muchai said:

"Without a penis, does he have any option?" He sighed. "Life after all, is a question of priorities."

The man of Kwangtung, lately with us, said quietly, "Does it matter from whose loins a child springs? My father was sterile. For her harvesting sons my virtuous mother paid a dollar a time to passing soldiers."

"Mind you all," said Bricko in his shrill falsetto, "I used to get a lot of pleasure out of mine. What about you, Doctor-student?"

Kwelin was apparently sleeping, but I didn't entirely trust her. I said, "It is there for procreation, of course.'

"A medical opinion," said Yung. "On this march it is the tool of rape."

Muchai stretched his long body on the boards, and said:

"It's astonishing to me that such a ridiculous organ should qualify for ennoblement. The poets are mad. Li Po, for instance, sings of love as if it never descended to the business of erections. He's got the Fragrant Concubine's corpse flinging up rare perfumes in the Valley of the Eastern Tombs – something quite out of accord with her Emperor's middle leg, of which she was extremely fond."

"It can have no place in literature," said Yung.

Muchai turned over. "Frankly, I've never had any time for mine. The bandits were perfectly justified in cutting yours off, Bricko – you can manage all right without it."

The door opened softly and a Kuomintang deserter stole in, whispering, "Is the Doctor-student here, lads?"

"Bugger off, Hop-cock," muttered Jo-kei, "this isn't the field hospital."

I sat up, beckoning. "I am here, soldier," and he knelt on the boards beside Kwelin, his hands out to me, whispering, "You remember me up on Old Mountain, Doctor?"

"I do."

"And that I nearly fell on Thunder God Rock?"

"No."

He covered his face. "Oh, servant of man, I'm 'aving a dreadful bloody war. Look at me shiverings."

"We're all cold," I said.

"And the lice . . ." he scratched under his rags.

"And we all have lice."

"You seen me feet?"

"Not at this time of the morning."

Kwelin opened her eyes and said, "You trifle with him, yet you know his trouble?"

The soldier said, "Horses' arses, I'm 'aving it bloody terrible, Bone-man. Nobody's 'aving a worser war than me. Just a little seed . . .?"

The guns hungered and reverberated. I saw the deserter's face more clearly, the humped, bruised cheeks caused by the face-slapping, a trick of the Kuomintang caught from the Japanese up in Jehol. I saw his bitten lips and the drooping eyelids of the opium addicted.

"No," I said. "I need it for the wounded."

This sat him up, his arms out-flung. "But I been wounded up in Jehol, and twice 'afore that in Chingkangshan with Chu's Fourth – I been fighting wi' China before you was born!"

"No," I said.

"He's your responsibility, you addicted him," said Kwelin, severely.

The man began to cry and Jo-kei sat up, bellowing, "Piss off, Opium – go and yell in the road outside!"

Leaping up, I dragged the soldier to the door and propelled him through it. As I lay down again, Muchai said, "As a three-year student you are a wonderful doctor, Lin-wai; as a human being, you lack humanity."

I did not reply but lay there, hugging myself against the cold.

"He will die out there," said Kwelin.

Later, the man from Kwangtung said, "You, Bricko, at least will be faithful to the mother of your sons. In my life I have known many women, and have been faithful to none."

"Go to sleep," said Jo-kei, and Big One, lying beside the sleeping Tenga, snored bassly from the darkness.

The man said, "I was first married at eleven – the same age as Mao Tse-tung when they contracted him a wife, so we have something in common. Mao, they say, never consummated his early marriage, but I did; a fine achievement at such a tender age. My wife was sixteen – five years older than the groom according to the custom then prevalent. After a year she came large with child, but the midwife had dirty fingers, and at the time of the grain rain my little wife died."

Nobody spoke. But Political Chang, a little fat one in the corner now attached to us, stirred in sleep. The man from Kwangtung continued, "I grieved for her. She was as delicate as a lotus petal and had tiny breasts that did not fill my hands. Her feet were most successfully bound, and were a joy to me."

Observed Muchai, "Lucky for you, Political Chang is asleep."

"But I am not a communist," came the reply. "I don't fight for Mao but for the freedom he promises. And I don't give a damn for Political Chang – back in Canton I am rich."

"His masters – Political Protection – will be interested in you," murmured Jo-kei.

"Is it politics now to state that I used to kiss my little wife's feet every morning?"

"It's very much safer to kiss the political arse."

Kwelin said, "Can you imagine the pain of bound feet, Kwangtung soldier?"

"I know the pain of communism," came his reply. "Once we win we'll be worse than the nationalists."

"Really?" said Political Chang, apparently awakening.

"Back to sleep, you political pimp," said Muchai.

"What is your name?" asked Chang, sitting up.

Said Jo-kei, "He has no name. He is the man from Kwangtung."

"When did you join this unit?" asked Chang, his brush and notebook out.

"In time for the battle of the Hsiang River," said the man, "when the likes of you were bloody head down while I was wounded twice."

"And before that?" asked the agent, unmoved.

"Before that I was serving with your enemies, the Kuomintang ... up in Chahar during its rape by Japan. But when Chiang Kai-shek withdrew us to fight against you Reds, I deserted. Now I wonder if it was so wise." He took a breath. "Tell me the difference between Chiang and Mao in term of tyranny. In Chahar I shot communists – now I shoot landlords."

Jo-kei said, "By my grandfather's balls, soldier, I admire your stomach."

"Please continue," said Political Chang.

"Not six months ago, when a Kuomintang corporal, I put a communist general in a bamboo cage and took him around the towns of Kiangsi in chains. Later, we beheaded him before a crowd. Before he died he cried, 'China, China!' So he was not dying for Mao."

"His name was Fang Chih-min?" asked Political Chang, now taking notes.

"Yes. And when I deserted and joined the Red Army I was officially congratulated upon his death – apparently he had made a mess of things and was out of favour with the Party, so continue to take as many notes as you like."

"You're a ripe one," said Muchai.

"I have had to be. I've been in the stench of it, the flies, the bleeding. I've watched the Japs rape and fire – inflict every kind of filthy treatment on women, for this terrifies men. Mao, by comparison, only shoots landlords."

"You criticise the actions of the Chairman, also?"

"I reserve that right."

Chang shouted, waving his book, "You are all renegades here! You are grooming base reactionaries and following the bourgeois line. How can the Party exist on such muddle-headed revolutionaries and truthless contradictions?"

Jo-kei said, getting up in grunts, "Now it's blowing wind from its political anus. You, Bricko, begin your original theme again – how a man can live in the absence of a penis – personally, I worship mine."

"Such immorality!" cried Chang, strutting about and waking Big One and Tenga. "You are all the enemies of communism. I shall have to report it, of course."

"You, my friend," said Jo-kei, drawing his belt-knife, "will report nothing, or you will end up like three brass monkeys looking for a welder." Rising he caught the agent by the tunic and twisted him close. "Hold your water, man – we're all here for a variety of reasons, but with you nothing is free. A word of what you've heard in here – opium and all – and your privates will decorate the door."

"Let me go! Let me go!" cried Political Chang. "By the gods, I curse you all! May your fathers speak through the holes of dogs and spit on the bellies of your mothers!" And he shook in Jo-kei's grip.

"At last we understand each other," said Muchai.

The First Front Army was moving towards the gates of the great city.

From the mist emerged a great concourse of men and animals, and the red flares above them tinged the frosted land with rosy hue. Fifteen abreast the infantry came, the flower of Lin Piao's First, their great bulk growing in shape. And in the street below the urchins of Tsunyi began to dance in shouting expectation. The mist slowly disgorged an army of standard bearers, rank on rank of fighting coolies with their shoulder-poles and raking rifles. In their strange, skipping gait they came, with red flags streaming above them, their flares painting up the snow. And the mist about them slowly dispersed to the heat of them, exposing the packed ranks of the peasant army.

Political Chang was forgotten. Cramming at the windows we stared; the Red Army was entering Tsunyi; it was unforgettable.

Now the mist lifted in a rush of dawn sunlight, and the army magically came to life; the infantry with their outriders trotting, the gun-limbers with their mortars rumbling: now the snouting two-point-fives who had won the Hsiang.

They came with military precision, the provision carts, ammunition carts, water-carts – the Cadre Assault Battalions came, the cream of the infantry; the engineers carrying their explosive pole-charges at the ready, their pontoons and make-shift rafts following. Behind these were the ragged civilians, the artisans of the road with their tools of trade, and they numbered thousands. And, as the sun burst through we saw the caravans of the Staff Headquarters, the military factories, Administration Corps, the Red Army University. The Young Communist League was in the van, men of fine military bearing, the Central Communist Committee marched in civilian clothes.

The sun blazed, forgetting winter, and in its golden light we saw the lumbering caravans which Otto Braun prized, their canvas hoops ripped by battle: the mint came, guarded by armed horsemen; members of the Soviet Government marched erect, the technicians and military advisers Mao scorned: the printers came, walking with their mule-hauled presses. As if alone in their own importance there marched the Anti-Imperialist League and the Young Communists with wonderful precision. Behind them was the Sanitary Department with its white-coated doctors: their 500 stretcher-bearers were an army in themselves.

Now a detachment of Young Vanguards marched along the flank to the gate of Tsunyi, and there stood at ease. Beyond them I saw tents appearing along the ramparts: smoke from field-boilers began to brush the sky. No official entry into a prize city was going to stop the midday rice. Then a bugle sounded and the gate-towers were suddenly alive with Red soldiers manning the turrets and embrasures. Chains rattled, locks shot back. The city gates swung wide, exposing the great market-place within.

We followed Tenga down into the street.

Standing at the very gates of the city was Pipa. It surprised me to find her alone, for these days Yung was rarely far away from her.

Kwelin, with her usual diplomacy, drifted away with Tenga and the others when Pipa called to me.

She was lovely indeed that morning; there was about her face the usual beauty and serenity which Nature employs on women who are carrying: her hair, as if brushed especially for this meeting, was tied with red ribbons and lying in plaits either side of her face.

"Well, then, what do you think of it?" she asked, happily.

Despite the regal entry into Tsunyi, the waving banners, the blaring bugles, I knew what she meant. I answered:

"It could never be, Pipa, and in your heart you must know it – it is a wonderful day for a marriage, and I'm glad you've accepted Yung's religious beliefs."

"I'm in love with him, you know."

"I'm glad – that's how it should be – certainly he's in love with you."

She said, abstractedly, "It . . . it wouldn't have worked with us, you know. I mean, even if it had been possible . . ."

I did not reply.

We stood uncertainly, as wordless as strangers; the splendour of the victorious entry beat about us. When I looked at Pipa again, tears were in her eyes. Softly, she said, "It . . . it will be at the western temple, near the other gate. Do not come, Lin-wai. Please do not come . . ."

Yung arrived like a man seeking his bride, and put his arm about her.

Empty, I left her.

EIGHTEEN

That wide entrance to Tsunyi, where history was made, will stay for ever in my mind.

The market-place was crammed with townsfolk attended by elders in their ceremonial robes; Taoist priests nervously made their signs of Temple Guardianship, fearful of Red atrocities; Buddhist monks, their treasures hidden from the incoming barbarians, stood in a bald, mystical calm, passive in the face of the expected tortures.

Side by side with European missionaries were foreign women, their arms protectively around their children. Surely all the nationalities of the Orient were in Tsunyi that morning; the coloured turbans of the Tartars, the saris of the barter Indians contrasting with the dull grey of the surrendered Kuomintang. These, in their hundreds, lined the processional route, each soldier on one knee facing the Red Army, face low, right hand over breast, left arm hanging loosely: the kowtow of complete submission. Yet, in victory, such as these 'yelled the road' – the bandit-soldiers' cry that terrified defenceless civilians. Few of these, I reflected, would live to see another dawn – all would be indicted by the city elders.

"Here comes Mao," said Muchai.

In a clattering of hooves a party of horsemen arrived and took its place at the head of the procession. Mao Tse-tung I recognised immediately. His shaggy Tibetan pony moved with the same listless manner of its rider. The conqueror of Tsunyi and the Five Encirclements drooped in the saddle, his face yellow and grimed with sweat and dust: malaria, his usual curse. Behind Mao, also mounted, was Chou En-lai, commander of the Central Column, and Cheng Kung of the Cadre Corps: Lin Piao and our Peng Teh-huai on their sprightly brown chargers looked positively cheerful, men refreshed by war. General Tung of the Fifth and Lo of the Ninth were absent.

Behind these five rode Ho, the wife of Mao. Astride a donkey she came, and in her arms she carried her child, the symbol of her courage.

Otto Braun, the German adviser, came in state, lolling in his great wooden litter, carried by four bearers.

Dressed in his plain communist grey, he looked like a Roman emperor entering a city for spoils. Cheerfully grinning from his flabby face, waving delightedly to the watching crowd, Braun aped and acted, calling to children, winking at the Europeans who regarded him with astonishment. Had his bald head been garlanded, said Muchai, he could have been a modern Nero.

Pickpockets were on the streets of Tsunyi, ragged urchins scampered among the legs of the crowd or cart-wheeled in the gutters in the hope of flung coppers. Mangy cats and flea-scratching dogs slunk and grinned in the alleys, shying from kicks. And in the middle of the bustling, pushing crowds of peasants free of their confining cottages, the street hawkers bellowed their wares.

Steam-rollered ducks were here, their brown-baked, biscuit bodies flashing in the sunlight: here were the noodle-laden tables and fat wives, the old crones with their bars of dried salt fish; the merchants of the sea-board towns who followed the path of the Red Army with their bales of silk and cotton and prettily coloured streamers. Hens clucked and scratched for food, others hung upside down, eyes glazed in the strangling approach of death: pigs, long-hidden from the thieving Kuomintang, were being slaughtered in shrieks and screams.

Here went the Confucian scholar, the rolling drunk, the opium vendor after his pipe-relief from pain. Here the vociferous peasant mother, a baby on her back, one by the hand and one in her stomach, reviled and bargained and bartered as her kind had done for 4,000 years.

Once suffocated by the Kuomintang, Tsunyi now flung off her cloak of suffering. The prisons opened, her convicts barged out into the clear winter sunlight: European priests who feared the communists, political prisoners with their scars of torture, spies awaiting execution, beggars, pimps and thieves flooded down to the market-place, always the beating heart of a Chinese city. One-stringed fiddles were playing, melodions singing from the bazaars; in the gutters beggars cried for alms, holding out for pity their stumpy, near-dead children.

147

To bawled commands of the older Vanguards the Kuomintang prisoners went two abreast, followed by shrieking hags who didn't know a communist from a nationalist. Down at the southern gates two bandits were being flogged to death – the accepted punishment for molesting travellers.

The sing-song bawdy houses were crammed with eager soldiers, impatient before the inevitable closures. Down in the Street of Prostitutes the tinsel bars were full, freed prisoners gulping at the hot rice-wine or cool Maotai before the inevitable restriction by the military street-squads.

The same old communism, I thought – prim in public, amorous in private.

It was snowing again when Kwelin and I came to the low, broad one-storey house where the landlord trials were proceeding. Manacled in the snow outside, some fifty landlords, awaiting their turn, shivered with cold and apprehension; around them clung their weeping relatives. In a greater circle, penning them in despite the efforts of the Red Army trial guards, were infuriated peasants of Tsunyi. These, and they were hundreds, yelled their threats and recounted the crimes with waving fists.

"If the guards weren't here," observed Kwelin, "they would be torn to pieces."

A man shouted, waving a paper of indictment, "Peng Teh-huai's in there, you landlord bastard. He'll give you crimes against the people!"

"Our own General Peng?" I said to Kwelin. "Can the justice be so rough?"

"We can go inside and see," said she.

Crowding into the court-room with others, we passed another dozen manacled, white-faced landlords.

We sat on open forms before a little table on a dais: at the table sat General Peng, the idol of the Third; on either side of him were his legal advisers. It was a military court in the usual tradtion; the farcical trials of 1,000 landlords who had died under the guns between here and Juichin. Not a man there, I reflected, had doubts about the outcome of this particular case; such trials, we had learned on the march, merely filled the military requirement lest the charge be made that we condemned on the spot and shot men out of hand.

One landowner, the mandarin of Tsunyi, was of fine bearing.

Looking neither right nor left he stood before the tribunal of three with dignity. He was no longer young. Stripped of his robes of office, his coolie rags did not demean him. Nor did he show the slightest fear. Rather, it was with disdain that he stared around at the jeering peasants, held back from attacking him by the crossed rifles of the Political Protection guards. The hall was a confusion of bawled insults; the public denouncements allowed at such a military trial.

The charge being read by General Peng, he required the prisoner to remain standing. Then an elder of the city, one Sun Yi-Fu, rose to give evidence on behalf of the people of Tsunyi; these, now silent, sat in happy contemplation. Of great age, this elder unfolded a paper, raised his face like a Christian baptised. This is what he said:

"My name is Sun Yi-fu. I live in this town and I was born in it. I am of the clan of Sun, being much respected. I now report on behalf of the people.

"When I was five years old my father sold me for five dollars, one for each year of my age, to the mandarin of Tsunyi, the father of the accused. Upon the death of his father, the prisoner became mandarin by title; upon him devolved the responsibility for his peasants: it was he who made the law." Turning, he momentarily addressed the crowd in the hall, saying, "When I was twenty years old I became the property of this man – he was then aged twenty-six. Now he is aged seventy-two and I am sixty-six. Who here could not imagine this man to be my eldest son?"

There was a murmur of assent.

General Peng raised his face, and the elder went on:

"Look well upon us both, Tsunyi people. His has been a life of ease and luxury, mine one of unending labour. Once I possessed two sons. My elder son ran away from Tsunyi; I have not seen him since. My younger son he executed at the age of seven for stealing wild apricots . . ."

"By his personal command?" interjected General Peng.

"By the sword of his executioner."

Peng sighed. "It is allowed, pray continue."

The elder said, "In times of plenty, when his granaries were full, my wife grew ill through starvation. Once, in harvset, his agents dispensed with mules and put his bondmen in the shafts; they whipped us like animals."

"He knew of this?" asked General Peng.

149

"This I doubt." The elder stripped off his tunic and vest; the scars of a whip were white on his back.

"You doubt that he knew?" asked Peng.

"Possibly not, he was away in the town of Liping." The elder continued, "I have a cousin who was neutered at the age of fifteen in his service as a eunuch."

Apparently unmoved, Peng asked, "You are now discharged from the prisoner's service?"

"I am."

"Do you pay taxes to him on land you rent, Elder?"

"I do."

"In fact he granted you licence to use this land?"

"He did."

"Are you in debt to him through taxes?"

"The taxes are impossibly high."

"Yes, but are you in debt to him – come, you are an educated man."

"My education has not served me, gentleman."

General Peng shifted impatiently. "Perhaps, but I did not ask you that. Do you owe the prisoner money in taxes?"

"I do."

"For how many years in advance has he claimed this tax?"

"Twenty-six."

"You are telling me that you have paid taxes to this landowner for twenty-six years in advance – to the year 1961?"

"Not exactly, gentleman, I have paid to the year 1960 – I owe him for one."

Peng rubbed his mouth, saying drily, "Count yourself lucky, old man. I know of taxes demanded sixty years in advance, the grain being distrained for non-payment. The gentry, it appears, are reasonable in Tsunyi." He examined the elder with kind eyes. "Your judgment first, then?"

"Death," said the Elder.

This was the signal to the hall. The crowd reacted like a cut spring: leaping to their feet the peasants rushed the dais in jeers and waving fists. Peng shouted, with commendable calmness, "Now . . . wait and be calm before you pass judgment – I am not listening to a rabble." He stared at them and they retreated to their forms again, muttering low. Waiting for silence, Peng said:

"Your elder is beautifully educated. You are fortunate to have such a man speak for you. But he speaks of his own tribulations, remember, not of yours. Also, before you watch your mandarin die, remember that he stands for a system that has prospered in this province for 3,000 years. Is he guilty of being your mandarin – is this why you shout for blood?"

A peasant in rags behind Kwelin bawled, "He fuggin' starved me an' mine – what else do you want, soldier?"

Peng answered quietly. "It is not enough. I need his guilt of murder. So far you have given evidence of one death only – the execution of a child for stealing wild apricots. Isn't there another here who can confirm the truth of your Elder's statements?"

His imperious manner was beginning to anger me, let alone the peasants. In retrospect, of course, I realised that he was after the most solid evidence, that it may later stand him in a court of appeal. But now the crowd was jostling with growing indignation, and one, bolder than the rest, sprang down to the dais; raising the stump of an arm, he shouted, "Then look, gentleman – see this? He 'as it off me because I run – I run from Chan-tai, the walled village, because his agent flogs me – an' he fetches me back in harvest month, an' has this bugger off me, and nigh a hundred watch. So me and the childer starve, same as Sun's wife – him, the Elder. And I may not be much, but I were raised by Chi, the cousin of Sun who stands there talking: and this one, he were cut in the groin o' his bollocks on Insect Feast Day – no, the day before, because he was pretty and the prisoner was queer. So he prays on the block, like me, before me arm comes off, and that bastard standing there, he watches ... yes, he watches an' waves a scarf an' we wiggler and scream, but no bloody mercy does the sod show us." He was panting with emotion, the stump raised. "*Aiya, aiya*, I remembers that real well, Soldier General."

Another came forward, saying haughtily, "It is right that he should die because he is a landlord."

Peng retorted, not looking up, "You may be peasants, but you are not fools – listen to me. The prisoner stands accused of unjust laws, of allowing his agents to beat his labourers, of unjust collection of taxes. He is accused of maiming a servant for leaving his place of employment, of neutering to provide a eunuch for his pleasure. None of this is enough – such crimes are standard in the provinces. I will pass sentence if need be, but I prefer evidence of murder. On one charge only am I truly impressed – the execution of the child ..." He regarded them, his expression wry. "Is there one man here who was witness to this murder? One who will swear on the body of his father . . . ?"

They leaped to him. Chairs and forms overturned in the rush: they swayed in a bunch before the dais, shouting into his face.

"I thought as much," said Peng. "Death by shooting, take him out."

"I spit on your justice," said the mandarin of Tsinyi.

The peasants seized him, brushing away the guards, and dragged him from the court-room.

Later, we saw this man, the fifty-eighth to die; he did not speak when the soldiers tied him to the execution post, one of four standing in line.

Their faces were already the faces of corpses, I remember; their sunken eyes held a dull, monastic look as the crowd danced behind the clasped hands of the soldiers holding them away. Amazingly, as if in accompaniment to the macabre scene, three vultures sat screaming on a bare, winter tree like rusty hinges on a gate. All about the square, totally ignoring the executions, soldiers sat around cooking-pots, hands warming to the fires.

The exploding guns splitting the dusk, the wailing relatives, the heaped bodies, the black posts against the virgin snow, all made a scene of carnage within a vast, white eating-house.

In a narrow street I took Kwelin's hand, saying, "Look, I know Tsunyi. Once, when I was young, my father brought me here on business. There is a place of quiet, if it is still there, where brown ducks swim on a pond."

"And a tea-house?"

"*Tea of the Mountain Clouds above Hunan*, if they still serve it."

"That," replied Kwelin reflectively, "is truly excellent tea."

"Kwelin No Other Name, it is nice having you around."

"And that is even better than tea," said she.

"And you like me?" The sunlight was white in snow-glare. There was no blemish on her face that I could see.

She did not reply.

So I took her to the Blue Flower pond and the *Teahouse of Abiding Joy*, named after a garden in lovely Wuhsi. Here were the curved pagoda gables of a summer house. Gilt and golden it was, garlanded by snow and the curved beauty of cypress trees. It will be understood that this was not a place for common soldiery. I said, as we sat at a table in the sun:

"Today is historic for my clan."

Kwelin sipped her tea. "You approve of Pipa's marriage, Lin-wai?"

"She should marry within her station. The name of the Yungs is known beyond Chekiang; my father will not be displeased."

"Your father, doubtless, is great and famous."

"He's agent to the mandarin, it is enough to command respect. He possesses a mansion, much money, many concubines. Yung's family will never match such eminence."

"You are cynical about your father?"

"Of course."

"And what of filial piety and respect for parents?" Her voice was pert.

"There's a difference between us, Kwelin – you are a Buddhist."

"Unless you show respect for your father when you're with me, the difference will be wider than that."

She was annoyed: it brought to her a new beauty. Her eyes, I thought, were the loveliest I had seen: her hair, well-washed for this occasion, possessed a blue-sheen blackness. Her high-boned cheeks made her a woman.

"Tell of your childhood." She was still aloof.

I said, "In childhood I was lonely; many children sprang from my father's bed, but only I was a legitimate child. In this loneliness I found a friend and his name was Old Teh. He was the village water-carrier and died at the age of eighty, being buried alive – the first communist martyr of Laoshan."

"More about you, please, Lin-wai?"

I shook my head, watching her over the brim of my bowl. "You know enough about me – something about you for a change?"

She shrugged prettily, and smiled. Her teeth, I thought, were more even than Pipa's.

"My name is Kwelin, isn't that enough?"

I caught her hand and kissed it, an astonishing thing to do in public, and she snatched it away, staring about her.

I gasped at the steam of the bowl, watching her as she told me.

"I joined the Red Army from the town of Hengyang," said Kwelin, "after much sorrow. For the Kuomintang came and trapped us in the town – me, my parents, my baby brother. They breached the town walls with bombing, ran in the streets slaughtering everyone they caught. Because I was nursing wounded in the central-headquarters, I was not at home when the soldiers broke into our house. All my family, including my brother, were herded into the square with many other civilians. After the usual brutality, each was publicly beheaded – my father with his son in his arms. The young women, such as I, were forced to stand against a wall and watch . . ."

Her voice was flat, without emotion, her eyes were dull.

"And you?" I asked.

"When the Kuomintang came to the central hospital to kill the wounded, I hid in the basement with six other nurses, but all of us were captured trying to leave the town. The soldiers tied us and took us to the square where 100 others were waiting: older women were taken from the group and shot. Only thirty were alive after these executions, and they were spared because of their good looks . . ." She faltered, adding, "It was dusk, you understand, and they did not immediately see my face . . ."

"Tell me, Kwelin."

She closed her eyes, saying, "Of the thirty remaining, twenty were immediately sent to the town brothels, were priced, and ringed by the necks in windows; this I saw next day, when the merchants took us out of Hengyang; one, my friend, raised her hand to me. To her husband, killed the day before, she was priceless, yet around her neck was one dollar twenty."

I turned away.

"Don't blame the nationalists," said she, "blame Chiang Kai-shek; this was his method of area depopulation – it was he who gave the orders."

During the Fifth Anti-Red Campaign of the Nanking Government, of which Chiang was then head, open directives were issued (some are still framed in private homes) that in areas once occupied by communists the civil population was to be systematically reduced by mass executions.

Kwelin raised her face to mine. "What kind of a world is this, Lin-wai?"

I answered, "Chiang Kai-shek has a policy of scorched earth, and the wheat is human. Under him this has been a disgusting country – something had to be done."

Thousands of children had been transported to sea-board cities – a Yellow Slave Trade – and there sold for free labour in factories owned by foreign capital. Tens of thousands of women and girls, even now, were being driven around the countryside in open trucks, to be sold into *mui tsai* for the sport of gentry sons; many were taken into schools, there to be educated in the sexual perversions of the war-lords.

Kwelin said, "There is a reason why I talk of these things, Lin-wai. It is necessary that you know of me."

"I want to know," I answered.

She took a deep breath. "It was a stupid decision to take refuge in the hospital basement, of course: they prised us out with ease, and we all knew what would happen. It wasn't just a question of being raped – every girl over the age of eight in Hengyang expected this – mothers in the town had even instructed their daughters what to expect, begging them to lie quiet under the pain of it, in the hope of staying alive. Listen to me. . ." She stared up, her face white. "I have seen mothers waving to their daughters from a forest of legs, calling them to have courage and to please the rapist ... and save the bayoneting. Every woman in my town expected the bayonet after Japanese rape, but few expected it of Chinese soldiers . . ."

I thought she was going to cry. Trembling now, she continued, "Outside the town the Kuomintang officers began dividing us up – we were then in three groups – the young, the middle-aged, the pretty ones. I was with the pretty ones, because now it was dark and they peered at us in the light of lanterns. Then women with short hair and without bound feet were shot since this, the soldiers said, was proof of communism. My feet were unbound, but I was with the pretty ones – the rule did not apply to us, apparently . . ."

The chatter of the tea-house beat about us. Officers of the First Front Army had entered and their talk was mainly of women and politics.

Kwelin said, "Then the Kuomintang general came and picked out two girls for himself – one was eight years old, then the officers had their pick. My hair was over my face, and when one pulled me out he first kissed me, learning the shape of my mouth; pushing me away, he stared and spat. So much was happening then that nobody heard his shouting, so when the officers went I was left with eight others among 200 men. I was raped six times that night: one girl died from loss of blood.

"When morning came some merchants roped us together and we were marched to the railway station. We thought we were going into the locomotive boilers for their sport, but, after locking us in a guard's truck, the merchants left us. One or two, their clothes ripped away, were nearly naked, and it was autumn: also one of the girls still had her baby – a little boy of four months. We all gave our clothes to dress this girl, whose name was Wei, I remember, because she was on the feed. The baby cried all night. In the morning the merchants came again."

"It is already enough for Tsunyi – there will be happier times . . ."

Her eyes moved over mine, "You asked for it all, you will get it all, then you will know of me, Lin-wai."

The brown ducks were on the pond, in a little place unfrozen; their chattering came to us on the frosty air. Kwelin stared down at her fingers.

"The merchants ordered us to strip, and we stood on the railway-line holding our rags about us. I thought I would die of cold. A railway worker walked past us as we stood there naked, I remember, and he went along the rails tapping them for fractures as if we were part of the equipment. One of the women said we were, and we laughed at that, although it was freezing." She smiled faintly. "I never thought one could be so cold and live. Despite my mouth the merchants put a price of ten dollars on us all – I never realised I was worth that much. Then servants from the gentry houses came for us with clothes, and a merchant told me to pull my hair over my face. This I did, and I and another girl aged about eleven spent the night together on a warm *k'ang* in the servants' quarters. For two days nobody came into the room, which was beside the kitchens, except the house servants, and they ignored us. But on the third night a man-servant led me up to the rooms above and into the bed of the eldest son of the family, a youth under instruction for marriage. But he could not know me, being young and shy. In the morning the father entered the room to learn of his son's successes, and he saw my face. Shouting, he beat me out of the house and the servants threw my clothes out into the garden."

"And then?"

She made a faint gesture of helplessness. "Then I walked night and day on the beg, looking for the Red Army. On the third day I met out-riders of the Ninth Rearguard. It was a near thing. I was then two miles behind the Kuomintang lines. The rest you know."

In the following silence I heard the rumbling of the Kuomintang guns. She said:

"That is my story. Never say you do not know of Kwelin."

"You must despise men."

She made a wry face, "A few I've met have minor compensations."

I rose, but she did not move.

"Before any man touches me again he must remember that I am second-hand," said she.

I drew her to her feet.

When Kwelin and I returned to the cottage by the gates of Tsunyi, it was clear that Yung and Pipa had married.

Muchai and Jo-kei were asleep side by side; Bricko and Fool were snoring in quiet harmony. The man from Kwangtung, ever watchful, opened an eye as we quietly entered: Kau Kau looked up from the arms of Fool.

In the middle of the room, surrounded by rough screens, was the litter-bed where Yung and Pipa lay: lucky red paper was pinned to the floor round it; silver talismans, crushed gold paper and artificial blossoms, symbols of longevity, were scattered about. And, at the head of the litter where Yung and Pipa lay, was placed the Pa Kua of the Eight Diagrams, the ancient tokens of creation, also a pomegranate to betoken many sons. Muchai said from the wall:

"Now they sleep – leave them," said he. "Today they were married by the Buddhist priest; this is Yung's religion."

"It is not Pipa's," I said.

"It is now. Leave them."

Kwelin touched my arm. "Come," she said softly. "This is the end of it, Lin-wai. She belongs to Yung."

Soon she was asleep against me, but I could not sleep.

Through every booming chime of the Tsunyi clock, into the hours of the young red dawn, I stayed awake, staring at the silent bed before me.

There was within me an overwhelming sense of loss.

NINETEEN

Kwelin said, "I shall remember Tsunyi, not for its Fourteen Resolutions, which I have yet to see published, not so much for the twelve days' rest – not even because of Pipa's marriage to Yung ... I shall remember the place for the smell of cordite, the military courts, the mounds of landlords' bodies."

In this mood of sombre realism, we turned our faces to the wind, and with the Fifth near the van again, took the road north for Tungze.

In my opinion the Tsunyi halt had proved a waste of time. True, Mao had confirmed himself as the army's political commissar: but it had achieved little save the opportunity for Chiang to rush in fresh divisions from Nanking. Finally, the intention to form a great new soviet in Yunnan, the adjoining province, was proving just another exercise in propaganda.

Like the other dreams of Tsunyi, it never materialised.

What materialised was felt more painfully by the common soldier. We were still being daily bombed. Lo's Ninth and Tung's Fifth Corps were still fighting to keep new attackers at bay: the General Headquarters, beloved of Otto Braun, still required a full army corps to protect its lumbering flanks. Casualties were rising from constant ambush, for now the Kuomintang were around us: scabies and lice were eating us raw. And feet, the most important of all, had been softened by the twelve days of rest. It was feet, not the political in-fighting of Tsunyi, that would rid China of Chiang Kai-shek, said Muchai, and he was right.

Feet never ceased to astonish me.

Later I calculated that, in marching 25,000 *li* – the European measurement being about 8,000 miles – the average soldier put each foot to the ground some 20,000,000 times: it wasn't surprising, said Kwelin, that some feet so changed in shape that they ceased to be feet at all.

The feet of many had now become calloused, stub-toed,

natural boots – akin to those of the webbed ducks of the marshes of Amoy – no other description fitted them: the soles were armoured from slipping on the rough-plaited sandals (these always soaked away at the first hint of rain) – the upper insteps so grooved by the sandal-thong that the upper bones were deformed. Foot wounds I had found very difficult to heal. To sew together corns and callouses harboured infection; to cut away the hardened skin lengthened healing.

My own feet, since I often rode while tending the wounded, were not so badly punished; neither, usually, were the women's, because of their lesser weight. But Jo-kei's feet (he could have marched bare-footed on tin tacks) were in the last stages of deformity – no longer feet. Bricko's were but stumpy amputa-tions that thumped the road: most women with bound feet on the march had long since dropped out as sport for the oncoming Kuomintang.

On the fifth day out of Tsunyi, Shao Shan visited my medical tent.

"Shao Shan, Women's Partisans," announced Kwelin.

Shao Shan, preceded by her stomach and the threat of confinement, stood before me in gasps and wheezes; never had I met a woman short of quadruplets carrying as large as Sergeant Shao Shan! And from under her brawny arm, fixing me with a stare, was a Kweichow duck.

"A present for the doctor-student," said she.

Lately, the majority of my stomach cases had been caused by Kweichow duck.

Every abandoned farm we came across produced a mint of them; every scheming merchant with an eye on Red Army con-tracts arrived with carts of them squawking. Glut was a major irony of the Long March. One day we would be starving, next day feasting on the produce of a particular province: later, in Yunnan, it was hams. Over-running the factories of the rich Yunnanese packers, we ate ham until we looked like ham. In Kiangsi the produce was war, and of this we also had a surfeit. In Juichin, and later in Hunan, thousands died for lack of salt – now we were walking on sacks of salt in the store-houses, used to salt the hams. At the break-out three months ago we had 1,000 dollars' worth of medical supplies for 100,000 men: now we had captured enough in Tsunyi to care for three armies, though still no anaesthetics. This was the way of it – shortage or glut.

Bowing to Sergeant Shao Shan, I took the duck from her and gave it to a reluctant Kwelin.

"What can I do for you?" I asked Shao Shan.

"It is the boys," said she.

Trip and Little Ball, vibrant with health despite their hardships (for they marched like the men) came first, beckoning. Around the tent door crowded fifteen others.

These were the youngest conscripts of Tsunyi, the street urchins of the City of Gold. Rarely have I seen children in such a sad condition.

It was Mao's stated policy to try to save the children; this he achieved by taking them into the Red Army. Naming them 'Young Vanguards', he elevated them from the refuse bins to a new self-respect. "My only sadness," he once said, "is that I can do little to save the girls." Now these Little Red Devils, as the Red Army soldiers knew them, crowded together around Shao Shan, seeking comfort from fear by each getting hold of some bit of her clothes – candidates for soldiering, children still.

They were the by-products of misrule and opium, the dereliction of the towns and cities, who crowded around the tea-houses begging for scraps. Mostly orphans of the constant warring, even Chiang Kai-shek's wife considered their condition so bad that she included them in her *New Life Movement* for State adoption, but their numbers were too great for mass rehabilitation.

In every population centre the recruitment officials used to take a handful; they were found where there was hope of food. Most as naked as birth, they hadn't seen a bath since the midwife. Victims of mange, trachoma, scurvy, they would perform their happy acrobatics in return for a copper, eating from the road like starving dogs.

Trained, they became Young Vanguards, a necessity to the army's existence: their incorrigible humour and roguish antics matching their courage under fire.

Now they stared up at me with frightened eyes, shivering in my hands.

Most were in advanced stages of scurvy; for these I prescribed tinned tomatoes – vitamin C. The capture of a canning factory on the outskirts of Liping had given us this in plenty. Trachoma affected a few; two had mange; this I had no hope of treating.

"Uniforms," said Shao Shan; she rarely wasted words.

"You won't find them here – take them to the tailors."

"No cloth," said she.

"What do you mean – no cloth? There was miles of it in Tsunyi."

Their fears abating, the boys gathered around me. Kwelin added, coming in. "You can take it to the top: Vanguards are priority."

Shao Shan said with hostility, "Why do you think I'm here? I tell you, there's not a yard of cloth in the regiment – I've already been to the tailor."

I shouted, "But Political Protection recruited them, didn't they – what did they do about uniforms?"

"You're responsible for Young Vanguards, you tell me."

"I'm getting to the bottom of this one," I said, and wrote a memo to the Third Corps Political Commissar, saying, "Take this and don't come back without a reply."

As Little Ball and Trip raced off with the note, Shao Shan said, "It's a scandal – they can always find uniforms for the men," and she gathered the brood about her, glaring at me with hostility. She was no longer the commander of the Women's Partisans, but the centre of the world.

Two days later the reply came back: the memo, it appeared, had in error been sent right back to General Headquarters: the reply read:

To Doctor-student Chan Lin-wai. Fifth Muleteers, Sixth Regiment, Third Corps.
  Indent for uniforms in normal manner; in future do not apply direct to Political Commissar, Headquarters.
              (Signed) Ho We-tei, Captain, Third Ordnance.

Then arrived another:

To Doctor-student Chan Lin-wai. Fifth Muleteers, Sixth Regiment, Third Corps.
  Indent normally for Vanguard uniforms, giving sizes. Direct application to Political Commissar unnecessary.
              (Signed) Peng Teh-huai, General, Third Corps.

Then came a final field memo:

To Doctor-student Chan Lin-wai. Fifth Muleteers, Sixth Regiment, Third Corps.

Uniforms for fifteen Vanguards, various sizes, being despatched immediately. If you don't get them, let me know personally.

(Signed) Mao Tse-tung, Political Commissar,
General Headquarters, First Front Army.

Copy to Peng Teh-huai, Third Corps:

And tinned tomatoes, Peng – a crate a boy. *Vitamin C.* What the bloody hell is happening?

On a halt on the road to Maotai, I treated the Young Vanguard sick parade.

"My name," said one, "is Shang Chi-pang, Doctor-student; it is not Shang Chi-pa."

I replied, "I will enter it carefully on the sick list."

Kwelin, on the other side of the medical tent, had turned away, shaking with silent laughter.

"Now, Shang Chi-pang, what is the trouble?" I asked him.

Aged ten, smartly to attention, he stood before me with his greatcoat down to his ankles. Like the rest of them, I was pouring orange and tomato juice into him; now, on the twentieth day out of Tsunyi he was still suffering from recurrent head-boils, the result of malnutrition.

"Just these?" I asked, examining him.

"Only the head-boils, Doctor-student."

Kwelin had previously shaved his head: now he looked like a little Taoist mystic.

The cure for head-boils was to raise the scabs, press out the pus and inject; the wounds would then be dressed with antiseptic fermentations, a painful business.

The child's comrades were peering expectantly around the door of the canopy, their ears tuned to sounds of cowardice; this Kwelin allowed, but was careful to turn away the victim's face so tears could be shed in secret.

"This," said Kwelin, "is a very bad one," and she lifted the scab and squeezed out the pus. "Are you all right, Chi-pang?"

He wept large tears: Kwelin, his face held against her coat, soaked them up, whispering to him in his Cantonese dialect. He, for his part, had each hand gripping her, his mouth against her breast.

"*Hei, hei*," I said, prising him away.

"It is all right," said she, in English, "he is really only a baby."

"Only one more," I whispered. "Hold it, lad."

Later, medicated, mopped dry of tears, he said at the door, "You'll be sure to get my name right, Doctor-student? – Shang Chi-*pang*."

"See now," said Kwelin, "I will check it," and she read with emphasis from her register, "Shang Chi-pang, aged ten, of Huisa, Canton?"

His face was bright with sudden smiles.

There being a world of difference between Chi-pang and Chi-pa, the latter meaning penis, as he explained.

"All right, Prick, I'm next," said one of his mates, coming in.

In the next twelve weeks, we marched and counter-marched, striking north for 100 miles to feint at Sungkan, meeting opposition; melting away to threaten distant Weisin, leading our Kuomintang pursuers a February dance in the foothills of Taloushan. Marching south-east, we crossed the River Wu again; swinging in a wide arc of encirclement, we drove the Kuomintang before us. Storming in panic over an old pontoon bridge, they left 1,000 of their number on our bank; these we got into with our Cadre broadswords, and the enemy bulk, rushing about in aimless droves, trampled their wounded to death. Recrossing the river we were now chasing our pursuers, dividing them, decimating them in short, vicious fights, before retreating once more into the frosted Kweichow box. Splitting into three columns we raced; one for a feint at the great Yangtse-kiang, our next big obstacle: the two remaining columns, of which we were one, spread fiery fingers through the white-blue, icy land.

An entry in my diary, dated February 15th, 1935, states:

Surely we are lost. Each day eternally the same. It is now a soldier's hobby to calculate where Mao will land us next. Dreadful country. Weather appalling. Bricko brought Fool in this morning – minor frost-bite; his chilblains have opened and he moans with pain. I gave him some ... It considerably relieved him, poor little man. Even Kau Kau, his dancing dog, had a frozen tail – Kwelin thawed it out. There must be an error in Shao Shan's dates; she carries much the same ... It amazes me how well the Little Red Devils keep under these arctic conditions. Men are falling out of the line; we are using whips to keep the animals moving. Tojo appears to be tiring...

Towards the end of February came a great forward battle, war-lord troops having the temerity to engage us.

Hitherto it appeared that only the rearguard was seriously fighting. But now, our positions changing, the head of the column became the tail, and great batches of Central Column infantry under Chou En-lai moved past us up to the front.

"Now you'll see some soldiers," said Jo-kei.

"Real ones," shouted Tenga from the snowy mask of his face. "We reach the guts of Chiang wi' these," he cried, "an' I'm fightin' with them before he were born, eh, Jo-kei?" And he clapped Jo-kei on the back, sending him staggering.

All down the column the Fifth were coming out to see the Central Column pass: they were large, rangy men, their heads and shoulders encrusted with snow, their eyes unshifting in their big gaunt faces.

"*Hei, wei*, you bastards! – Suck a scabby tortoise – give 'em hell for Tenga, eh?" and he danced a jig in the snow. "Give 'em fuggin' hell for the muleteers, eh, my lovelies?"

The sun spread her last disclosing rays; beyond the distant battle line towered the slopes of the Loushan Pass, a pivot of the March: all about us was snowland, the tiny hovels of rotten thatch with their dwarf doors of corn-stalks and bamboo mantled white.

The cavalry came like horsemen straight from riding school, their short carbines at the ready. The artillery came, the one-mule eighteen-pounders wheeling in wide arcs to the flogging accompaniment of the whips. And even the snow turned scarlet to the flashing of the big two-point-fives a mile behind us. Men ran about us in the orange-crimson light; the bombardment of the war-lord troops barring our way merging into a single, stentorian roar split by the barks of the heavy machine-guns as the forward Assault Cadres sought to engage.

There came to me the usual sterile coldness in the numbing blare of the guns.

Before us, in the dying sunlight, smoke, earth and snow plummeted skyward as the shells found range. A growing fire, the creeping barrage, was wine-tinting the snow; star-shells exploded in showers of fire-work sparkle, lighting up the glowering peaks of iron Laoshan; the virgin fields of whiteness, girded by forests, were filled with running, shrieking men – the bayonet charges of the Twenty-First. I saw them in the outer portals of my mind, knowing no pity for the mercenaries being slaughtered. Tenga beside me swore obscenely, holding himself erect in an unknown cloak of pride, watching the snow-slopes of the Loushan Pass where the war-lord army of General Wang Chia-lieh, Chiang's opium-soaked puppet, was regimentally being mutilated.

This was the answer to the constant wandering around Kwei-chow. The dragon had turned at last. The tail, whipped clear, allowed the head to attack with ferocity: one moment we were a caravan of wandering nomads, next moment an attacker of terrifying fire-power. And above us, unable to identify friend from foe, the nationalist planes dropped their bombs hap-hazardly: below, caught in the pincers of Mao's strategy, three divisions of war-lord soldiers, Chiang's allies, were battered into defeat.

As if in assistance to the lords of evil, the gods themselves bombed us on the Taloushan plains. It was as if the artillery of the sky was turned upon us at the moment of victory. With a war-lord army of 15,000 being shot to pieces by our attack to blast a way to the Pass, there appeared at dusk a rent in the sky.

"Look!" cried Kwelin, and Pipa, forgetting animosity, clutched her.

We had removed the canvas awning over the wounded when this hole appeared in the clouds. Jo-kei roared, rushing up, "Get the canopy on the cart again, man – cover the wounded, Quick!"

For Jo-kei, as he explained later, had been to Taloushan before.

Fighting to get the cover back, I looked up. Thunder clouds red-shot in rolling blackness, were gathering to a single, focal point in the heavens, a phenomenon of the sky. And, in the middle of this fury, a single light, of extraordinary brightness, appeared, a golden gun-muzzle sending down a searchlight beam into the dark where the mercenaries were dying. Our field guns ceased their thunder; the snapping and barking of the small arms quietened. Friend and enemy stared at the sky. The hailstones shot down.

It was like the end of the world.

Leaping over the back-board I seized Tojo's bridle in the moment she panicked, pawing at the air. As the hail increased in size and volume, the carts diverted, the animals neighing and bucking, tearing free of the anchoring shafts. And the roar increased to a bombardment as the pelting hail grew in diameter, smashing down on to swarms of running men, stunning them, knocking them insensible. The roaring grew in ferocity, the lunar miracle of ancient Taloushan; hail the size of hand-stones poured in a deluge from the hole in the sky, drenching the vanguard with shock and pain. A stampede hit the Third, catching an advancing regiment of Chinese Mohammedans, the aristocracy descended from the sultanate of the family of Ma. These were the Islamic horseriders who stayed in the saddle when lesser horsemen fell. Now, galloping into battle abreast of the Sixth, they fell in tumbling heaps, their mounts practically shot from under them, and, on their knees, gripped their turbanned heads between their knees in wailing lamentation. Carts were overturning, gun-limbers racing in every direction, cutting lanes through the infantry; men and animals sprawled in the snow, backs turned to the tattoo of hail, and the night was filled with the shrieks. Tojo, throwing me off, galloped loose, spilling out wounded from the end of her cart. With Kwelin pressed into the snow beneath me, I watched the decimation of an army by Nature's artillery. Motionless, thrusting deep into the protecting snow, the Fifth lay passive under a flogging from the sky.

And then, through the thundering hail, the panic, the shrieks, I heard Tenga's voice yelling, "Get up, ye loony bastards – ye sons of sow-bellies – what you doing down there?"

Shielding my eyes from the hammering ice, I risked a look. Up and down the line men were sitting up, and Tenga, drunk again, went storming into those still prostrate, booting right and left and bawling, "Up off your jacks – what's got into ye? It's only *P'an Ku* – give 'im it back!" and he grabbed a rifle off the nearest muleteer and aimed it upwards, rapid-firing at the sky. The action caught the men, galvanising them into anger. Kneeling, standing now, every man in sight was suddenly yelling abuse, sending fusillades of rifle-fire into the heavens, making

166

beautiful patterns of tracer-bullets soaring into the clouds; and the broadsides of the Fifth grew apace, matching their anger.

Tenga bawled, amid the staccato crashes, "That's right – give 'im it back!" and he ran to a mound and cupped his hands to his mouth, roaring skywards, "*Hei wei*, you old bugger – it's us! Don't you know a Red from a Nationalist now?"

Instantly the hail stopped. All down the line men sank to the ground again, staring at the clouds, rocking with the pain of their cuts and bruises, for a golden light was suddenly emerging from the hole in the clouds. Holding Kwelin against me, I stared up at the phenomenon, and Tenga shouted skyward in the ensuing, awesome quiet:

"That's better, mate – you're miles off bloody target," and he pointed east.

As if in expiation, the moon came out in massive glory, decorating the clouds, distilling even the gun flashes of the far horizon.

Snow-clad, the crack Moslem regiment got to its knees; turning east, it flung up its arms and wailed its incantations to Mecca, imploring the mercy of its particular Allah.

Later, up on the Manchurian border, I saw these same Moslems; bearded, almond-eyed Chinese of the Caucasian faces, getting among the invading Japanese with great, sweeping strokes of their cavalry broadswords, yelling in their thick Ninghsia dialect:

"In the Fifteenth! After them the Fifteenth! *Ta Chung Kuo!* Moslems and Chinese are brothers!"

But now, rising from the snow with their turbans comically awry, all dignity gone, they were objects of derision by the watching muleteers. And, as they sheepishly turned, still kneeling, from Mecca to face the growing banter, they lowered their eyes: dignity, to a Moslem, being more important than life. And the muleteers, delighted, let them have it: ribald shouts and hooting grew to a crescendo.

"Stop!" yelled Tenga, and staggered out of the line; standing with bowed legs before the kneeling Moslems. With snow swirling about him, he yelled from his hairy face, "Aye, laugh, ye bastards! But there's not a mule-skinner here to shovel a bowl wi' them. An' not ten of ye with the guts o' one!" Raising his mule whip he cracked it over his head. "I piss the likes of you when there's a Moh in the line to back me!"

Plodding to the nearest Moslem officer, he hauled him to his feet. Straightening the man's turban, Tenga knelt, brushing him down.

It was a signal. Sheepishly (and I was one of them) the muleteers came over the snow in a body, caught the Moslems' vagrant horses, and commiserated with them on their cuts and bruises.

Later, we stood decently beside our carts while the Fifteenth Mohammedans, the pride of the Third, trotted past us up to the front. And Tenga stood at the salute, swaying dangerously, until Big One ran from the ranks to hold him up.

"*Ta Chung Kuo!*" bawled Tenga, and the officer he had helped drew his sword and lowered its point, then broke into a gallop. Never will I forget the sight of them, their great brown horses racing away in the moonlight.

Ta Chung Kuo! being translated, means "China!"

Later, men told me that Tenga had fought with them against the Japanese north of Chahar, but I never got the proof of it.

That evening an unusual Order of the Day came down the line, distributed by the Young Vanguards. It read:

> *Order of the Day No. 158*   General Headquarters
> *First Front Army*
>
> "Do not say the strong pass is guarded with iron.
> This very day with firm step we shall cross its summit.
> We shall cross its summit!
> Here the hills are blue like the sea,
> And the dying sun like blood . . ."
>
> *February 28th, 1935*   (Signed) Mao Tse-tung,
> (Loushan Pass)   *Political Commissar.*

"For my part," said Kwelin, screwing up Mao's Order and tossing it away, "I could have done without the poetry."

I agreed with her. Below the Loushan Pass thousands of enemy wounded were freezing to death while their High Command, led by their poppy war-lord, escaped over the Yangtse-kiang which we, in our turn, would have to cross.

Red Army casualties in the battle were negligible, as was Red Army concern for a dying enemy. Not once, at Loushan, did I use my instruments.

Certainly, I had only one casualty report in the Fifth Muleteers, that night, and this wasn't caused by war.

Shao Shan, as if celebrating the victory of Loushan Pass, decided to have her baby. None of us knew it would be many weeks old before we left the plain of Tal and turned our eyes south for Maotai, the town of wine.

We left behind us the wreckage of twenty enemy regiments.

Records were broken during the spring campaign in Kwei-chow: we circled and wheeled south of Tsunyi, as before: we marched north for sixty miles taking the Kuomintang with us, then drove south again, bringing them back. It was Mao at his best; for us it spelled exhaustion. We sent a feeler at Kweiyang, the capital of the province, and Chiang Kai-shek reacted with his usual panic, drawing Yunnanese troops over the mountains to protect it, so we left Kweiyang to him and struck him in force at Yunnan, now unprotected. Mao led Chiang, in the words of Jo-kei, such a bloody war-dance that he didn't know if he was in Tibet or China: Mao outwitted and out-generalled him. Out-numbered at fifty to one, he assaulted him, retreated before him in the Kweichow box (for Chiang had tanks) then wheeled and chopped his tail to pieces. His war-lord armies began to fail; we infiltrated their ranks, the communist Fifth Column rose against them; in areas of cover the partisans attacked. To retrieve the situation, Chiang flew with his wife to Yunnan and prepared to take his High Command over the border to Indo-China. Hearing of this, Lin Piao ran a battalion 120 miles in three days to attempt to capture him. Landing at Yunnan by 'plane, Chiang was told by terrified defenders, "The Red Army is coming", so he took off again. The Kuomintang and their puppet troops counter-attacked the new threat to the city; Lin Piao faded away and wheeled south-west, crossing the River of Golden Sand (the Yangtse-kiang) into the land of the tribal Yi.

Now he was actually behind the Kuomintang; they fled in panic.

Courage, audacity and Mao's elegant control of guerrilla tactics left his enemy standing.

It was Sun Tze's *Art of War*: Mao at his best, Chiang was outclassed.

There was now a deep change in the relationship between Pipa and I. Her growing dependence upon Yung, his fierce antagonnism to any sign of friendship I made towards her, had crystallised into the open hostility I had feared. And the presence of Kwelin, the growing bond between us, did nothing to salve the wound.

On a night in early April the column stopped outside Paisha. In twelve degrees of frost in the Kweichow box, blowing on frozen fingers, we formed camp in a blizzard, then found, near the lines, a tiny bombed cottage whose charred rafters framed the freezing moon. There, around a blazing fire in the middle of the kitchen we sat – Muchai, Jo-kei and the man from Kwangtung (who had lately adopted us). Bricko was there, his arm around Fool: Big One, gigantically hunched in a corner, watched with quiet eyes. Kwelin asked Fool:

"You will play a tune for us, little man?"

"He only plays for money, remember," said Bricko, fiercely.

"The money he gets will be according to his performance," said Jo-kei, and he wiped a fat finger around the rim of his rice-bowl and sucked it lugubriously. "Back in Honan I call a sing-song girl, and she dances taking her clothes off . . ." He puckered his face and snapped his fingers. "That's my kind of music."

Tenga entered, brushing snow from his fur cap; the mantle of flakes on his nose and eyebrows made him look ferocious.

"My granny's hole," grumbled Jo-kei, "not Mule at a time like this."

Instantly Kwelin rose and went to the cooking-pot. Pipa, from the other side of the fire, watched her with burning eyes as she filled Tenga's rice bowl.

Pipa looked pretty that night, as women generally do when carrying: her cheeks were bitten red with frost, her hair was black about her shoulders. And although, as she said, the Chans carry small, it was now clear by the swell of her that she was with child. Also, there was a sickness with her in the mornings when Yung attended her, hovering near in service. Once I heard him say, "See, my little friend sickens with child. Once she was my woman, now she is my wife." And he would put up a listening finger to Pipa's distant retching (for she always did this clear of the column) and say, "My wife, my friend – soon the son of my loins will kick within her belly. Who is the pansy now?"

It was the old Confucian language, a revolting exhibition of male insensibility in the face of Pipa's nausea, and I hated him for it.

Indeed, I do not know whether it was Yung's guileless stupi-

dity or his cock-sure sexual preening that I detested most. If he
didn't realise the deception being played upon him, he was a
fool; at twenty years old he was surely mature enough to understand the fertility cycle. Yet he used his time of late in boasting
of his prowess – the first time cock that rang the bell, and often I
saw Pipa watching his antics with ill-repressed disgust.

Also, his apparent success had undoubtedly made me small in
the eyes of the men. Pipa had exchanged me for the insipid
Yung. It didn't do a lot for a respected doctor: it made them reject Yung and pity me.

Now Tenga put his boot under Yung's bottom and slid him
aside as he sought a place near the fire.

"Shift over."

Sitting down, he began to eat in a sucking of chopsticks, dangling noodles and belches.

Said Jo-kei with equanimity, "And how are the hogs and swill,
my Yichi friend?"

"Leave him alone," whispered Kwelin.

Tenga lifted his heavy face; his dark eyes switched to Pipa,
and he said as Fool began to play his flute, "You still marching,
woman?"

"As good as you," said Pipa.

"O, aye?" his hands paused; the noodles dangled. "When you
done your time, then?"

"Four months."

"You got only two by the size o' that belly."

Jo-kei said, "Questions on midwifery will henceforth be referred to the sergeant." Tenga lifted his eyes at this, but went on
eating. Fool played on; there was no sound but Tenga eating,
the crackling of the fire, the flute of Fool. Suddenly, Kau Kau,
the mongrel, raising her head from her paws, crept out into the
circle, stood up on her hindlegs and began to dance.

Tenga wiped his mouth with the back of his hand, and muttered bassly, "I got a woman, remember, so I know. What you
say, Bone-man – she carrying one?"

"Let my wife be," whispered Yung, his eyes shining in the
firelight.

"More'n you done," said Tenga. "You put it up there smart,
and us on the bloody march." He reached heavily for his pipe.
"You got your brains on the end o' your belly."

"How dare you!" whispered Yung, getting up.

Unconcerned, Tenga filled his stub-pipe, an evil-smelling affair that he kept in his hat. Kau Kau danced with her mincing steps, teeth shining, jaws slavering to the smell of the food. Fool puffed on the flute like a snake-charmer: Kwelin had upon her face a most beautiful expression.

She glanced at Tenga. "Leave it, Sergeant."

"I ain't leavin' it, woman – I ain't even touchin' it." He levelled his smoking pipe up at Yung. "You done 'er, mate – so you bloody see to her."

"Tenga, *Tenga!*" protested Muchai, with tolerant charm.

Tenga took from his pocket a flask and drank deep; his glazed eyes swept the room; for the first time I was sure that he was drunk. He muttered, "Four months, eh?"

Jo-kei said, "Forget it, you bandy sow, it's woman's business."

"And she ain't goin' into the cart, neither." He tipped the flask high and I smelled his breath: rice-wine, the strongest in the business. "I'm having no sprog o' a womb riding wi' my wounded." He glared up at Yung still standing above him. "You hear me, poof?"

Jo-kei said, "Indecent, isn't it? And you talk about me!"

Yung shouted incoherently with anger; Pipa's face snapped up, but Muchai restrained all with a lift of his hand. "It would appear that you don't like women, Tenga?"

Kau Kau danced on; Fool played his music, a thin-reed, tuneless sound in the smoke-filled room: it seemed to change the subject: Kwelin actually sighed with relief. Unrolling my surgical instruments, I began to clean them with swabs and iodine. The night, I knew, was not yet finished.

The sergeant, jaw swaying, examined the faces about him with belligerent eyes. "You frit o' dying, old scholar?" he asked Muchai.

Muchai nodded, "Like the rest of us." He added, "And you?"

Tenga said, "Me? I'm browning my trews for turning me toes up in Lololand."

I wasn't surprised.

In saying this, Tenga was voicing the fears of the average peasant soldier – that of dying in a foreign place. We were now approaching the Yangtse-kiang, known in its lower reaches as the River of Golden Sand; north of it was an area inhabited by the Black Bone and White Bone Lolos, a fierce minority tribe.

"One place is as good as another to die in, Mule," said Jo-kei.

"It ain't," said Tenga, and drank again. "In Sansui, the priest tells fortunes . . ."

I interjected, "Tenga, it's all lies – you've been warned before about Kuomintang propaganda!"

Yung said, "Let him stew, the bloody savage."

Kwelin whispered. "Yung, leave him alone."

Pipa said, instantly, "He wasn't talking to you!"

I gave them a glance: Kwelin's expression was of unfeigned surprise; Pipa's face was dark with a hatred I hadn't seen before. Tenga said, draining the flask, "To the Jade Lady this one talked, and she don't give much for Tenga – says I'll end with an arrow up my jack."

"I sincerely hope so," said Yung, expressively.

Jo-kei scratched his nose. "Certainly, I could think of pleasanter ways of expiring." The music ceased. Kau Kau ran to the protection of Fool's arms.

"They're fairies, mind," said Tenga. "Every one of them Black and White Lolos is a fairy, they ain't nothing to do wi' me old *P'an Ku*."

He was a leader with a child's fears. The Jade Lady, his private god below *P'an Ku*, was the disreputable rag doll he hugged within himself: incarnate in earthly visions, she could not be ignored. Now he said into Muchai's face:

"An' me woman cryin' her eyes out, an' no bloody pension, is that right?" He perceptibly brightened, "Did I ever tell you about my woman, old scholar?"

"Not in here," cried Jo-kei. "We don't want talk of your woman in here."

"She were a good little crust," said Tenga, "eh, fat man?"

"I'm sure she was," said Muchai with docility.

"I got to tell ye, haven't I?" Tenga fell to mumbling, his face low. "I got to tell somebody about her . . ."

Jo-kei said, "There's ten listening, including a bloody dog – don't let yourself down, Mule."

There was no sound now but the simmering of the fire. Tenga said, "Perhaps those Lolo buggers'll get me, so I want all of you to know. Eh, dear me! You never seen a woman like I got, wi' a body on her like a sing-song girl, and filled to the throat wi' sons." He pointed a finger at Yung. "An' she's pretty in the legs for me – a man she gets, pansy, not a bloody Chekiang opera.

173

Beddin' first time, she turns me out a boy . . . !" He lifted his hairy face and his eyes suddenly danced. "I'm a father, ye know – did ye guess that, Bone-man?"

"Yes," I said, "you mentioned it before."

Tenga staggered to his feet, swaying above us. "Aye, Teng Ga-hu is his name, an' she makes him straight in her belly – she were a good little thing. I get her off a marriage broker on the Canton run – six dollars I pay 'im – not Han Chinese, 'o course – Tibetan, a little yellow chocolate . . . but she were sweet for me." He grinned at us with his big broken teeth: Fool, I noticed, was staring up at him, the spittle hanging in shining beads from his vacant mouth. "D'ye know somethin'," continued Tenga, "her name were Wun. And she were sittin' up in that broker's cart wi' a thing round her neck, sayin', 'Wun Peisha, virgin, age sixteen – six dollars.' An' she were – eh, old fat man? – she bloody were, didn't I tell ye last fall? 'Six dollar Mexican,' says this pimp, so I pays him four an' thumps him . . ." He stared around at the intent faces. "But she *were* a virgin, mates – a *real live virgin*!" Suddenly slapping his thigh he shouted bass laughter, kicking up his legs. "The stone lions in the fountain roared all down the street when I got 'er 'ome . . ."

"Right," said Jo-kei. "Enough – now leave it."

Unaccountably, tears were on Tenga's face. And Jo-kei, with an oath, broke from the circle, gripped him and knelt before him, his fist at his face. "Now, I tell you – no more! *Leave it!*"

Tenga rocked himself, grieving silently, and said, "They got to know, fat man, they got to know . . ."

"It belongs to *you* – they need not know!"

"But no bloody woman rides wi' my wounded . . . !" He pointed fiercely at Pipa.

"And don't blame every woman you see!" growled Jo-kei.

"They'm bad-joss, cheap women are!"

"Right then – that's the end of it."

Tenga flung away Jo-kei's restraining hands. "An' don't you touch me, neither, fat bastard – you take your bloody hands off the sergeant!"

"Don't you worry!" Jo-kei rose, hands on hips, staring down at him.

In the following silence, Fool began to play the flute again while Bricko clapped the time and Kau Kau danced. But the mood had been lost. Before Tenga followed Jo-kei out into the night, he paused at the door, saying, while I inwardly cursed him, "I don't like tarts on the loose, an' I don't like flash boys who sneak up an' do 'em." He pointed a shaking finger at Yung. "She were Chan Lin-wai's piece, an' you know it – she come first here wi' him, not you. But now you've gives her a puddin', so ye can see her off at Maotai, or she bloody walks."

Yung said, evenly, "I think you're disgusting!"

"Ay ay? You bloody think it, but she ain't riding it on my wounded, in or out o' baby."

After he had gone, Muchai said, "Do not worry yourselves, children." He took Pipa's hands. "You will ride, girl – Muchai will see to it."

"So will I," I added.

Fool and Bricko – even Kau Kau – stared up at us from the floor: there was no sound but our breathing. Pipa said, "You, Chan Lin-wai, will have nothing to do with it." She paused before Kwelin on her way to the door. "And neither will you." She glared into Kwelin's face.

We did not speak, Kwelin and I, as we walked slowly back to the wounded.

But at the cart, she said in a frosty breath, "Chan Lin-wai's piece . . . ?"

The man from Kwangtung on his way back to the Sixth, still silent, paused to smile at us, and we took the road to Maotai.

TWENTY

On to Maotai!

Rumours were now floating down the line – the Japanese armies were gathering in Manchuria for a march on Peking: that Chiang Kai-shek was preparing to make a concession treaty with them, leaving him free to obliterate the Red Army.

"My arse," said Tenga, "we'll take 'em both."

"That right you fought the Japs before, Sergeant?" cried Little Trip, falsetto.

"Matey ...!" and Tenga lifted him high and shook him to rattle. "This bloody ole Tenga, he was bayoneting Jehol Japs 'afore you was a twinkle in your papa's eye!" and he cracked his mule-whip down the column. And it was on, on, on to Maotai.

The seasons came late in 1935, the official *Beginning of Spring* starting nearer March, the *Feast of Excited Insects* began in late April. At the time of the Vernal equinox, great snows still covered the land; *Clear and Bright* (the old Chinese calendar) looked as if it would never get started. But, with *Grain Rain* the sleeping land awoke, and the sun raked us from the clutch of winter. The rich earth, thumped into white iron, began to melt. From the wounds in the mountain-sides sprang foaming water; the sky yawned blue in the face of summer.

Skeleton trees shook off their scarecrow hunger, the greening hedgerows became wind-alive, decorating the scars of war with spring flowers. Still the Kuomintang attacked us, of course; we still maintained the relentless retreat while the bombs rained down. But the Red Army, come that spring, was revitalised, new. Even Tenga temporarily stopped drinking and was actually heard singing. To crown this, he shaved, naked to the waist laughing at the sun.

Maotai, Maotai! The name was on everyone's lips.

The vicious hand-to-hand fighting was over; behind us the Kuomintang lay in heaps over the plains of north-central Kwei-chow. The bitter news of the retreat of Chang's Fourth Front

Army, once driving to join us, did not stem our joy at being alive in springtime: we merely labelled Chang Kuo-tao as a "flightist" and went on enjoying the sun. By March, still fighting in circles, we had crossed the Wu River again and struck south for Yunnan, capturing a car containing Chiang Kai-shek's plans of attack. Yet another report came from Kuomintang sources that Chu Teh, our commander-in-chief, had been killed, this time in the Battle of Pig Head Mountain, so he walked and rode up and down the marching columns to prove it false.

Unhappier news, and true, came that his second wife, Yu-chen, had been executed by the Kuomintang who had captured their home in Nanhsi. She had been beheaded (his first wife having met the same fate years earlier) her head being placed on a spike for exhibition.

But no news, good or bad, could dilute our enthusiasm for the march on Maotai by the Fifth Muleteers under their Sixth Regiment – the main bulk of the army having continued to drive to Yunnan.

"On detachment now, eh? We'll give it Maotai rice-wine," said Tenga.

Then came the Order of the Day by the Sixth Commander.

Comrades,
We have separated from the main army and have been given the task of capturing the town of Maotai intact. The footwater factory there is of vital importance.
Maotai ceased wine-making a year ago: it now produces a healing foot-water much needed by our comrades. The foot-water will be bottled as directed by company commanders. All bottles will be correctly labelled. The carts of the Fifth Mule-teers will transport them.
All ranks are hereby instructed that the water, while contain-ing healing properties, is extremely poisonous. On no account must the chemical be consumed.

Long Su-leh
(Adjutant, Sixth Regiment)

Jo-kei tore the Order into pieces, throwing them into the wind on the outskirts of Maotai.

"I'll believe it when I taste it," said he. "Wine and soldiers don't mix on the march, you can't blame Headquarters. My feet can have it after my stomach."

"You mean it could be wine, after all?" asked Yung.

"We'll soon find out," said Kwelin to the wounded.

At the door of the factory a tiny pickle of a man was standing guard, shivering on a forked crutch as if to lay his bones out, and he cried to Tenga from a wrinkled face, "Help me, help me for the love of Confucius. Twenty soldiers and a fat man have gone in by the back!" and he raised his skinny arms to the sky. From within came the sound of lusty shouting.

"That sounds like Jo-kei!" cried Yung, pressing in behind me with Pipa. The old man cried, begging before me:

"Listen to them splashing, young Doctor! Twelve hundred piculs of the best Maotai wine and they're bathing their bloody feet in it – the town will be burned, the women raped?" and he waved his stick at me, barring the way.

"Off with you, old prune," bellowed Tenga, and opened the door. We pressed behind him into the great fermenting hall.

Never will I forget the sight before us.

In a vast concrete area forty great vats were brimming with wine, and around every vat, sitting shoulder to shoulder, were the advance infantry of the Sixth, including Jo-kei: every man there had his putties round his neck, his trousers rolled up, and was splashing his feet in Maotai foot-water.

"By the balls of Buddha," whispered Muchai. "Jo-kei, surely, should know the difference!"

Soldiers were squabbling for seats at the vats now as more swarmed in, shouting with excitement. Sandals were flung off, putties wound down, the remnants of socks stripped away, and feet of all shapes and sizes went into the vats – wounded feet, blistered feet, feet that hadn't seen air for months went in with shouts of pleasure as the cooling wine flooded over them. Detailed squads kneeled at the vats now, filling bottles of the precious 'foot-water' and handing them up to Section Commanders for corking. The town was being ransacked for bottles and containers; muleteers were furiously loading their carts for its transport to Yunnan where the main Red Army was advancing.

Men stood waist deep in the vats, flinging the cooling wine over their aching bodies, washing their hair in it. An hour later the cry went up:

"Otto Braun! *Otto Braun!* The German is coming!"

"*Out!*" yelled Jo-kei, struggling out of a vat and pulling others after him.

178

"Captain Ho We-tei of the Sixth Detachment!" yelled a sentry at the door. "Coming with Otto Braun!"

Suddenly the men were stampeding, pulling on their socks and sandals, fighting their legs into their trousers, for the order had been to bottle the foot-water, not to bathe in it. And the very mention of the German's name brought a nameless terror to them – the Big Nose Ginger foreign devil that not even Mao Tse-tung could handle. In minutes the great wine vault was empty, with the last of the bathers racing for the back entrances with their trousers trailing.

"What brings Otto from General Headquarters?" I asked.

"Maotai wine," replied Muchai.

And as he said it Otto Braun entered the vault.

He was grossly fat; bulging in his plain, grey uniform: only his legs told his high rank; the fine Tartar riding-boots he wore reached to his knees. Over his shoulder, despite the warmer weather, was slung a fur-trimmed Mongolian cape; his bald head gleamed in the dim light of the vaults as he entered with Captain Ho behind him. He asked us, through his interpreter, "You are the Fifth Muleteers transporting this stuff?"

"Yes, sir!" cried Tenga, smartly to attention.

"And the Sixth have bottled the chemical as instructed, Ho We-tei?"

"Already on their way to Yunnan with the bottles," said Ho.

"Excellent. We can make good use of the produce of Maotai, eh, my Captain?"

We followed him deeper into the vault; to my astonishment he began to sing softly a German drinking song, and his voice, in that place of echoes, was deep and pure: feet astride, he stared round the vats, then stopped singing and knelt: cupping his hands into the wine he held it to his nostrils first, savouring the perfume of it, then buried his mouth in his hands and drank greedily, cupping up the wine again and again, turning his wet face upwards, gasping with pleasure.

"This, my Captain," he shouted to the door, "is the most excellent Maotai rice-wine. And if you ask my opinion, Ho, a very fine vintage." Beaming, he approached the door. "Come, everybody drink – you, soldier?" and he clapped Jo-kei on the shoulder.

Jo-kei sidled away with apologetic explanations.

179

"Then you, Old One?" and he gripped Muchai. "Surely you are not teetotal?"

"Not for all the tea in China," said Muchai.

Together we faded away to the door while the officers of the Sixth Regiment, galloping in, raced to the vats, to kneel there, drinking deep. Otto Braun, however, suddenly stood, a pained expression on his face as he probed his mouth with a finger.

"It appears to me," whispered Muchai, "that he might even have got a toe-nail."

"Come with me, my beauties," said Jo-kei. "Come, Bricko – bring Fool – where the devil is Tenga?" and he brought from under the foot-board of Tojo's cart a dozen bottles of clean Maotai wine, a truly excellent vintage.

Rejoining the main Red Army after a forced march of some fifty miles, we stopped the Fifth for morning sick parade.

There had been but one major casualty on the Maotai diversion – a young muleteer corporal, and he, I sent back on a litter to Sixth Casualty Clearing. Limb wounds, even amputations, I was beginning to undertake, but severe trunk wounds and major surgery of the skull, I usually shed upwards: this corporal was an example – a bullet near the heart.

It always astonished me that such casualties were accepted without demur because, officially, I didn't exist. Indeed, only battle necessity had brought me into being; Tenga himself had scrounged Tojo's long-cart, loaded in some fifteen wounded and told me to tend them. Kwelin, on her arrival from the Ninth Corps, had automatically been posted in as official Fifth Muleteer nurse by Dr. Nelson Fu, the Surgeon-General.

Now, to my astonishment, casualties from distant regiments were often sent up the line to me, their record sheets signed by a clerk in the Headquarters Military Commission, who elevated me in rank from Doctor-student to Surgeon of Muleteers. Even the feared Political Protection (who could, at times, be anything but protective) now designated my role as "Surgeon – Sixth Regiment" – and they were supposed to have their fingers on everybody. Kwelin said:

"If you carry on like this you'll finish up Master-Surgeon, Red Army, and get the pay of Dr. Nelson Fu who gets no pay at all."

The Army Paymaster seemed to be the only person in possession of the facts: my three-weekly pay of two dollars (which we sometimes didn't get) was, by some obscure calculation, a trifle less than Bricko's.

As Pipa mentioned (one of her rare responses to friendship) it doesn't say much for Shanghai University – you're getting less pay than the regimental eunuch.

But on that bright spring morning in early April, I most certainly existed, and not only on paper.

"There's quite a queue this morning," announced Kwelin.

A queue, I later recorded in my diary, of quite important people.

There was Yung, and he was among the first – for some time now I had been expecting him.

His constant vomiting I had put down to a psychological re-action; Pipa, also, was suffering even more from morning sickness; it was unusually virulent.

Yung, the hyper-sensitive, was never out of her sight, and her danger under the constant bombing was obviously affecting him; but I knew it went deeper than that. Traditionally, his family was tubercular; under these impossible field conditions he had the choice of medical discharge and an impossible journey back to Chekiang, or unspectacular burial during the retreat. Now he looked at me with his large, fevered eyes; the bones of his hand-some face were in high relief, the transparent skin stretched tightly. His pulse was rapid, his breathing hoarse, his tempera-ture compatible with swift caseation. Pipa, sitting in a chair behind me, waited under the hooped canopy with obvious con-cern. I said to Yung:

"You shouldn't be here, of course – that's the sum of it."

"I didn't come to hear that."

Kwelin, standing near, was holding Yung's shirt. Rising, Pipa deliberately snatched it out of her hand, giving it to him.

Yung turned away from the stethoscope, buttoning his tunic. From the start, I reflected, we had never really liked each other. Pipa said coldly, "If he won't tell you, I will – he's been spitting blood."

"Much?"

"A great deal." To Yung she said, "It's been going on too long. You've got to do something to help yourself, if only for my sake."

His disinterest in the affair betrayed him; obviously he had come solely to please her. Probably, living with the disease since childhood, he knew as much about consumption as I. The famous remark, "For tuberculosis is prescribed not medicine but a way of life," was never more applicable. I could do nothing for him here. Kwelin said, "May I suggest . . .?"

"You keep out of this!" Pipa turned to me with business-like authority.

The pair of them were still working with the wounded, Yung taking a great deal off my shoulders. Indeed, he could now be left to handle the simpler surgery – the daily routine of the marching army – without my supervision. Thus we were split into two separate teams: any hope of unity being utterly destroyed by Pipa's growing antagonism towards Kwelin, who, for her part, treated Pipa with unusual tolerance and gentleness.

"Well?" asked Pipa now.

I did not immediately reply.

She was another worry: she had been carrying too high for a week. In Kwelin's presence, I examined her every day now. Once over the border of Yunnan, the crossing of the Yangtse-kiang would soon face us; and the southern prong drive for Malung was on. Wuting was about 100 miles west. The nursing facilities at lesser places would be primitive, to rate it highly. It was frightening to anticipate childbirth complications on the march, despite Kwelin's knowledge of midwifery, ably demonstrated, I reflected now, during the birth of Shao Shan's baby.

I said, as lightly as possible, "You worry too much, Pipa – he's in better shape than you think . . ."

"But he can't be given the attention he needs," said Kwelin earnestly. From somewhere she had found a medical overall; in its snow-whiteness that put mine to shame, she portrayed authority. I asked:

"Look – if I recommended it – and I would – how about putting in at Malung, the next town west, Yung? You'd be with the partisans – they'd maybe get you into hospital."

"That's a hope."

"Pipa could even go with you," said Kwelin.

It stilled him; turning back at the door, he said bitterly, "And that's one way of getting rid of the pair of us, isn't it?"

"That's a disgusting thing to say," said Kwelin, her voice rising. "Anyway, what about your baby? Shouldn't you think of her?"

It was a passing kindness: Pipa wanted a son, Yung was nightly on his knees praying to Buddha for a girl. Now he said, coldly, "I came into the army for a purpose . . ." he gestured at me, "and he knows why. I've come this far and I'm not leaving it – my brothers can have it their way, but in this, I'm having mine." He looked at Pipa. "This is what we chose, you and me – the baby must take her chance."

From outside the tent came the mumble of grudging conversation; the rest of the sick were becoming impatient. Yung said, "You agree?"

Pipa stared momentarily at me, then closed her eyes. Her face, I remember, was ashen; the sickness rose in her throat, for I saw her swallow it down.

Hand-in-hand, Yung and Pipa left the canopy.

Sadly, I thought, I was unable to help her in this dilemma: Yung's love of her was insufficient for the sacrifice; his obstinacy embraced both her and the child. It was an unhappy reflection on the quality of what I once thought was absolute love, that at the time of Pipa's greatest need of me, I could not serve her. Indeed, it was an indictment of love that the sweetness of the Shengsu bed, where she had conceived, seemed now an improbable dream. My growing love of Kwelin, unexpressed, brought me fulfilment at a time when Pipa was but a frightening responsibility. And this baby, I *knew*, was mine.

Kwelin said, with her usual practical charm, "I fear that wasn't very conclusive." She then referred to her sick-list calling, "Soldier-Muleteer Pai Chun-ho."

The soldier entered with pale apprehension, standing stiffly to attention before me; he was a handsome lad for a muleteer and his appearance was clean. I judged his age at sixteen, though Kwelin, who had his records, said he was nearly twenty. As I approached him, he said with a stutter, "Will ye . . . are ye sending the woman away?"

"Of course not, she's the nurse."

He shivered as if with a sudden ague, and I guessed the reason. "*Please* . . . ?"

I glanced at Kwelin and she left us. I said, "All right soldier, let's have a look at it – down with your trousers."

It was, as I suspected, a mild case of gonorrhoea, one comparatively recently contracted for the swelling of the penis was

183

mild. But his fear was pathetic, and I knew the reason. The older soldiers made a hobby of terrorising venereal patients; the nightly insinuations, the lurid banter of the march instilled in the younger ones unnamed fears.

Actually, venereal cases on the march were few; there was never an official need for short-arm inspections. Later, in Yenan, I read a paper on it: Mao was probably right when he claimed that not a man was lost from the disease and few were incapacitated.

Apart from the odd case, such as this, it was mainly a virgin army: the average age of the Red Army soldier was under nineteen. True, older men – such as Jo-kei and Muchai – existed in large numbers, but these were balanced by the very young Vanguards like Shang Chi-pang and Little Ball . . .

"Has this thing anything to say for itself?" I asked the soldier, still to attention with his trousers down.

"N . . . no, Surgeon-General . . ." His cheeks were scarlet with shame.

The structure of the army was also of interest. Some forty per cent of the men were farm labourers or artisans, while over half were peasantry: about five per cent only were of the bourgeoisie – men like Yung and the man from Kwangtung.

"You've been putting this thing where I wouldn't put a walking-stick, Pai Chun-ho. Where would your father be if he'd gone around sticking it anywhere? Where would you be landed now?" I recalled, with some uneasiness, the town of Liping and the sweetness of Soong Lu . . .

"Will . . . will it have to come off . . .?" He gazed at me with anguished eyes.

"Do you smoke?" I asked Pai Chun-ho.

"Yes, Surgeon-General." His insistence on elevating me in rank did nothing to help his case.

"And drink?"

He answered with the alacrity of one old comrade to another, "Oh, yes, Surgeon-General, I like a quart or so." Plainly, he was recovering confidence.

I said, severely, "Now, listen to me. You're only twenty and you've got your life before you. From now on, you will neither drink, smoke, nor fornicate, you understand?" I held up the offending organ with a scalpel. "I might be able to save it this time, but if you're here again it'll certainly come off – you understand?"

He closed his eyes; sweat sprang to his face in a welter of relief. "Oh, yes, Surgeon-General!"

"Remember it. One day you'll meet a decent girl and that's the only one you've got."

Kwelin came in the moment he had pulled up his trousers.

"Methylene Blue?" she asked happily, giving him her brightest smile, and he again flushed to the roots of his hair.

Luckily for him, Lin Piao had captured a Kuomintang medical caravan on the road to Yunnan; Methylene Blue was aboard it: one grain, three times a day at least shortened the acute stage before damage was done to the urethral tissues. This was all I could do. Curative treatment would depend on the first available town, if he managed to survive that long under air bombardment. In the event, he didn't.

"Next," I shouted, sitting at my table, and General Chu Teh, the Commander-in-Chief of the Red Army, entered with a bow.

For one who always removed his cap when addressing his soldiers; for a man who completed the Long March on foot (save for marshalling) – often carrying one or more rifles – it was not surprising that he waited for medical treatment in my medical queue. This was no showpiece; it epitomised Chu Teh's natural humility. Of all the officers in the Red Army, this was the only man of high command who had actually laboured as a coolie – towing river barges like an animal with but a rag to cover him, so destitute was he through the curse of opium. Now, thirty years later, as Red Army commander, he had a price on his head of a quarter of a million dollars – not less than the amount Chiang Kai-shek was offering for Mao's.

Entering slowly, he stood before my table. His eyes, narrowed in his strong, brown face, moved round the tent and rested on Kwelin. She was entering his name in her precious sick register as if she was doing nothing out of the ordinary.

Originally of Kwangtung province, Chu was possessed of the Cantonese jaw, which, in itself, is an aspect of ferocity; he was a hard man, his eyes showed this, and as lean as a tiger. His ancestors had fled their farms during the Manchu persecutions after the White Lotus Rebellion at the end of the century, becoming theatrical wanderers beloved of the peasants: perhaps this had given Chu Teh his marvellous presence. Kwelin said, her voice official, "Chu Teh, Headquarter Regiment," and rose, approaching him. "Well, come on, what's wrong?"

Chu's eyes flickered over her with sly amusement; clearly now she had not recognised him. He said:

"A horse kick – bruising around the ribs. It needs re-strapping – shall I take my shirt off?"

"Of course, the doctor can't do much with it on." That morning she sounded unusually effective.

I said, "Kwelin . . . will you leave us, please?"

"Oh, no," said Chu, "she's charming – let her stay."

"By holy Buddha . . .!" breathed Kwelin, her hand to her mouth; turning, she backed away, colliding with the rest of the sick parade peering round the door.

Chu laughed softly. "That was unforgivable – you'll get it after I'm gone." Taking off his plain grey tunic (he had no badges of rank at all) he unbuttoned and stripped off his shirt. I began to unroll the bandage strapping around his waist.

This was the military tactician of the First Front Army who had linked his talents with Mao Tse-tung's political genius.

In middle age, and he was under fifty now (with the body of a man of thirty) he had so improved his lot that he had risen to graduation in the Yunnan Military Academy, been commissioned in the Modern Army and attained the rank of Brigadier-General. Resigning from the Chinese Army after playing a prominent role in the overthrow of the Manchu dynasty (which had persecuted his own people) he then sought political power, gained it, and indulged in the twin corruptions of public swindles and opium – the accepted roles of the successful public servant.

"This," I said, "is very badly bruised. Are you sure there's nothing broken?"

"I have to take the word of the Surgeon-General," he answered. "I was around this way – this is in the nature of a second opinion."

I pressed a rib and he groaned with pain.

"There's a break here, I can feel it."

His face creased up. "Dr. Nelson's going to be delighted."

His addiction to opium began soon after birth, I heard later – his mother indulged in the practice of most mothers in the opium-soaked Yunnan – she spread the drug on sugar-cane to stop him crying.

There was certainly no sign of it now; his body was muscled and tough under my hands. Talk had it that, to cure himself, he booked a six-week ticket on a steamer to Hankow, lay nearly unconscious for a fortnight in his cabin, survived the six weeks of agony and stepped ashore cured. Under this strain, most traditionally addicted men would die.

Now, while I strapped him again with fresh bandages, he looked around the room: the instruments on my table took his eye. "You indented for these, Chan?"

"Yes, Comrade-General."

"In the normal manner?"

"Through the regimental quartermaster to the Medical Commission."

He said, drolly, "For one who doesn't exist on paper, you're doing passably well – no point in interfering if something's going all right."

After his public swindles things certainly went all right for him.

With the profits of his plunder he built in Yunnan City a palatial mansion in which he installed many wives and concubines; at the age of thirty-five, he settled down to a life of dissipation – unbounded love, wealth, and the dreams of opium.

But, fortunately for communism, Chu Teh began to read.

In a city of 50,000 slave children, he also began to think. Pensioning off his harem, selling his assets, he gave the proceeds to the poor and travelled to widen his experience. In 1927, joining the National Revolutionary Army, he merged with Mao Tse-tung's forces through the influence of a comparatively unknown delegate, Mao Tse-ming, the brother of Mao Tse-tung. Thus began the famous relationship that was to write the history of twentieth-century China.

"Does that feel any better?" I asked, and Chu smiled and pulled on his tunic. "You always keep a good cook alive," said he, "but that's another story!"

A moment later the bombs fell on the Sixth.

To this day I claim they were after the Commander-in-Chief, for never had I experienced such accurate bombing. Running around Tojo's head, I leaped up to the foot-board and madly drove the uncovered wounded into a clump of trees. Over my shoulder I saw Chu Teh galloping furiously up the line to Headquarters.

They did not bomb us that bright April morning, they plastered us: the ground heaved to the concussive blasts, the air was filled with the shriek of metal. All down the line carts were making for cover, the mule-whips curling and cracking in a stampede of men and animals. With Kwelin helping me lift out the wounded, we settled them beneath the cart and watched the planned decimation of the entire Sixth Regiment. Right down the columns came the fighters, strafing the line, roaring up into the sun to flatten out a mile away and come again, machine-guns blasting. At a higher level the bombers swept over the sun. One moment peace, next bedlam: ground-fire added to the confusion as the Sixth fought back with small-arms fire. Craters appeared magically down the column, men fell flat, wounded animals cried; the new camels were loping away in shrieks, trampling the wounded. It was a fiendish corruption of our peaceful morning, and suddenly Jo-kei, leaping up from cover, dashed over open ground between us; breathless, he gasped, "Have you seen Tenga?"

Kwelin shouted against a sudden burst of fire, "He and Big One scattered with the Sixth – I saw them!"

White-faced, Pipa, great in the stomach, was lying in Yung's arms and he was propped against the wheel. I called above the din, "Is she all right?"

Yung nodded; hatred was in his face as he stared at the sky.

Muchai said, in a lull, "I saw Tenga run to the flank – Big One went after him." Leaping up, he gripped Tojo's bridle as she shied at a near miss.

"Tenga can take care of himself," said the man from Kwang-tung, and calmly lit a cigarette, smiling at the sky.

On his knees now, Jo-kei peered through the dust:

"They collected a stick of them right down those trees," he said.

"He'll be back," said Yung, bitterly. "Shaggy Yis like Tenga need bombs all to themselves."

It appeared, when we reached the line of trees, that Tenga had got one.

The attack over, Big One waved when he saw us coming, then knelt and beat his fists together; all the tuneless sounds of the mute he made. Tenga opened his eyes when I bent over him, saying, "Get me out of this fuggin' river, bone-man, I'm soakin' through."

"Lie still," I commanded, pushing Big One away, and knelt. Kwelin said, "He is lying in blood, Lin-wai. He can hear it trickling."

"Is it the old Wu again?" asked Tenga, struggling to rise.

I gently held him back, saying, "If it is then we're bloody crows, mate – the Wu's miles behind us. Where are you hit?" But I knew where he was hit.

"You should know – ain't you the doctor!"

Jo-kei was beside me. I said, "He weighs a ton, help me raise him." As Jo-kei did so I opened Tenga's shirt and my fingers were wet with his blood: baring my arm, I encirlced his waist, and felt the smashed vertebrae.

"What are you fuggin' doin'?" asked Tenga, pushing.

"Is it his spine?" asked Kwelin, and her eyes were shining.

"It is nearly shot through," I said in English.

Tenga's eyes switched away; he was listening to the running of his blood. "Are we close to the Gold Sand River, woman?"

"About a mile," Kwelin lied.

"I got me missus there," said he, and, hearing Big One's sobbing near by, he added, "What's wrong with him then?"

I said, "He is crying because you are going to die."

"Then why don't ye bloody say so?"

Muchai said, bitterly, "There's nothing like breaking it easy, Lin-wai."

"It's the way he'd want it," I said. "Go and fetch a litter."

"Ye're not fuggin' me about," said Tenga, "I'm dyin' here." He looked at Big One. "Hei, Jo-kei, fat sod – come here – tell him with the Hingsi language, you're better'n me at it; tell him I'm going back to the Yi? An' that he can 'ave this coat now – slit it up the back for him, eh?"

Jo-kei translated this, his fingers moving before the big man's face.

"I found him first, remember," said Tenga, and waved Jo-kei away. Pipa knelt, screwing her hands together, and said, "I wil cut it, Tenga – I will make your coat fit him."

"He's my friend, see," said Tenga. Jo-kei sighed impa muttering:

189

"Look, Mule, if you're going to kick it, can't you hurry up? The Fifth's waiting to move."

Tenga grinned wide; this was his language; he said, hoarsely, "Then you bugger off with 'em and leave Lin-wai wi' me."

All but Big One, who did not understand, rose and left us. In the distance I could hear the wheels of the Fifth crunching on the road and the bawls of the muleteers; the column was marching for Malung. Kwelin returned, waiting for me at a little distance. Tenga said, "They gone?"

I nodded.

His eyes closed. "That the Gold Sand River callin'?"

I said, "Kwelin lied to you, we are miles from the Yangtse, but the Fifth will be crossing it to the Yi tribe – your people."

"I'd 'ave been seeing that boy again, more'n likely?" he sighed.

Blood began to trickle into Tenga's beard. I did not give him a seed ... he was in no pain. He said, "When you gets to Sun village, ye dress up pretty an' go and see my boy, eh? Don't mind the woman – she's a good little piece, my Wun Pei-sha, but get the boy." He tried to raise himself, gasping, "*Shao-nin Hsien-fengtui* ...?"

"Yes," I said, "he will be a Young Vanguard, I'll see to it."

"*Hung chun* ..." he said. "Get Ga-hu, my son."

"I'll give him to Big One."

He nodded at this. Big One and I, kneeling together, watched him dying: near us the column of the Fifth was rumbling, but the muleteers were silent. One of the Fifteenth Mohammedans, wounded near by, was making an unusual lot of noise. I would rather it had been the virgin of the Golden Sand River, a dream-woman ... whispering to Tenga

Jo-kei returned and helped me get the coat; this, still blood-stained, we put over Big One's shoulder so Tenga would see him receive the gift.

"Go on, piss off," said Tenga. "The lads are away – what you all doin' hanging round 'ere?" And he died.

Big One wept and would not be comforted.

In my diary that night, I recorded:

7th April, 1935.

... has been a strange day. This morning, Chu Teh, the ... ander-in-Chief, called in at sick inspection; he has a cracked rib. I re-strapped him. While he was with us we were badly bombed: the Sixth and the Fifteenth Mohammedans had casualities. We had one, Tenga. The muleteers are quiet; it didn't seem possible that Tenga could die. When we reach Lololand I will go for his son. Big One weeps.

TWENTY-ONE

On the road to the Santai San range and Wuting, command of
the Fifth fell on to the shoulders of Jo-kei, who, though not a
muleteer, was respected by them for toughness and leadership –
the first qualification, in their eyes, being his years as a bandit.
Muleteer-Commander Ma Tai-chiu, destined to carve his name
on China's roll of glory, came down the line from our parent
Sixth to make the promotion.

Amazingly, on that day in April, two Gold Star heroes were in
the camp of the muleteers on the road to Wuting and Yuanmow, though none then knew it. Commander Ma, a wide-
shouldered man of Anhwei, darkly handsome, said in passing to
Bricko:

"Who is the man beside you?"

"He is Fool," replied Bricko, standing to attention.

"He looks it," said Ma. "Is he on the strength?" Gripping
Fool's chin he turned it gently to face him, saying, "Is he sane
or is he mocking me?"

Jo-kei, who had been sent for, then arrived, and said, "He is
neither sane nor on the strength, but he is staying."

"It is your command from now," said the commander, "but
can we afford such passengers? Is it even fair to the poor little
man?"

Apprehensively, Bricko turned Fool's face into his shoulder,
whispering, "Please stand decent for the commander, Fool?
Stand straight for me, eh, little chap?" But Fool chuntered and
dribbled, clutching Kau Kau and hiding his face.

"He marches like the others?" asked Ma, hands on hips.

"Every yard," said Jo-kei, and Commander Ma contemplated
this, then said to Bricko, "He is your friend, this little idiot?"

"His business, not yours," said Jo-kei instantly. "Tenga the
Yi allowed it, so shall I. Or take your chance with another commander."

But Ma, the soldier, did not appear to hear this. To Bricko, he
said:

"I have a sick father in Anhwei like this: it's excellent that such a man has a friend like you." It was then that the miracle happened.

As if understanding, Fool turned his face to Commander Ma and reached out his hand. Ma shook it, giving him a smile and a wink.

They actually met in our column, making history on that April morning.

Two Gold Star heroes, the highest award China can give.

Later, during a halt on the march, I wrote in my diary:

20th April, 1935.
The Red Army has split tactically into two columns, one racing north for Tehchang, while we of the southern prong attack towards Wuting through the Santai San range. We are in Yunnan province. Tenga's death is our only sadness. Truly it is springtime; the country smiles. We drive for the river of Golden Sand, the brimming Yangtse-kiang, the country of the Yi tribes. We have not been bombed for thirty-six hours (a *great* respite!) We travel more slowly. Even the rearguard, they say, is temporarily disengaged. Spirits are high. This morning the Fifteenth Mohammedans galloped past, a fine show of pace. The men sing, free of the long winter. The roads are rough, though, and the wounded are being badly shaken. I am worried about Pipa and Yung. The child she carries is much too high. Yung, obviously, is weakening with every day, coughing incessantly. If we get close enough, I will try to persuade them both to leave the march at Yuanmow. Kunming City would have been better for hospital facilities, but the Fifth struck too far north of it . . .

I repeated to Kwelin, "I am worried about Pipa."

"You're doing your best for her. Now Tenga's gone, she rides – often Yung rides with her. You can't do more."

Kwelin was marching at my side, our rifles slung: Tojo's head jogged between us. When Kwelin was about, Tojo was a reformed character: if Kwelin was away she played me up with tantrums. Kwelin's serenity, it appeared, had the same calming effect on mules.

I said, "Pipa's carrying very high."

She pursed her lips. "She's a little big for five months, and I admit it can be a dangerous time."

I jerked my thumb at the long-cart behind us. "She's being jerked to death in there."

It was the seventh month for Pipa, of course, and there were times when I was tempted to confide in Kwelin the truth of it – that it was seven months ago, not five when Pipa conceived; that it happened in a cottage in Shengsu not on this march: that the child was mine, not Yung's . . .

At times I actually took breath to tell her, but did not.

At other times, I wondered if she guessed what Pipa had been to me. Yung might be naïve; Kwelin was not.

That morning Shao Shan came past us on a mule with her newly-born baby in her arms. All smiles was Shao Shan, bowing and nodding right and left, accepting the soldiers' banter and congratulations as her right, and she brought to all there a new, sweet breath of home.

"One day your Pipa will trot past like that," said Kwelin, waving with the others, her face alight with pleasure.

"Not my Pipa – Yung's," I said. "He's her husband."

She sent me one of her secret smiles.

Leaving captured Wuting and Yuanmow behind us, we struck north for the crossing of the Golden Sand River and junction with our northerly prong at Tehchang. Pipa and Yung would not listen to my advice, they were determined to stay on the march.

Now, in open country, sweeping up to Chouping Fort near the little river town of Nisha, we adopted Mao's famous 'sinuous lines of motion', wheeling and circling in the night marches, to deceive enemy bombers, for now, with the Yangtse as our next obvious target, they were giving us little rest again.

But these days of warmth and sun were a glorious compensation for the constant air attacks. It was as if spring, in all her verdant clothes, was rushing up to meet us, decorating the hedgerows, tinting the grass, painting up the plum and cherry blossoms of the wayside farms.

The gentle winds instilled new life into the weary Third Corps. At every stop the men would be patching and darning their tattered uniforms, plaiting reed sandals, husking rice, even writing letters home with little hope of them ever arriving. And they had begun to sing again, bawling out their favourite *Eleven Bus* song, bringing waving villagers to the road.

Tranquil stood the cottages of the Shan people, tiny Yunnan aborigines akin to the Miao pygmies farther east. Originally racing away at the first sound of our coming, this minority tribe of Chinese blood had suffered the persecutions of the dynasties and had reason to fear us. Now, returning to their villages, they would listen with interest to the propaganda teams, bringing with them their produce and bartering this for weapons and silver (of which we now had an excess). And they would sit for hours in great circles, enjoying performances of Cantonese operas; makeshift affairs modernised to suit the times, every theme being the same – the persecution of peasants by landlords, the latter suffering the usual just and swift retribution. Hundreds of their young warriors enlisted with the Red Army and I often wondered what happened to their own landlords after our passing.

It was in Yunnan that we first noticed a change in the people's behaviour. Earlier believing the Kuomintang propaganda that the Red Army roasted children on bayonets for sport, the truth of us had now begun to spread by word of mouth: we had no advance propaganda working for us save rumours of our behaviour.

We took nothing by force, but left the equivalent in money or materials. Even to derelict cottages we returned doors we borrowed for sleeping. Bullion and money taken from banks – (and we ransacked everyone we came across) – we distributed to the people, retaining a percentage for bribery, should we prefer not to fight. Opium was harvested and hoarded for high-level barter – war-lords couldn't get enough of it, though in money they might be as rich as eastern princes.

We closed the Mist and Flower houses of the gentry, and the knocking-shops of the slums, leaving behind Political Protection civilians to enforce our laws: we redrafted provincial laws. Men, we said, no longer held traditional authority over women: with prostitution, for instance, the customer was punished, the whore educated.

Foot-binding, China's ancient curse on women, was outlawed; the Confucian claim that three-inch long feet were soft and elegant we ridiculed, distributing posters showing a foot-bound woman slipping on her backside beside a lithe Chinese girl running on natural feet: we condemned the lily-foot as a male lust-fetish. We hung examples of the Sung dynasty foot-bind shoe beside a normal shoe – putting carrots in one and flowers in the other. All over the provinces through which we passed, parents were unbandaging the crushed feet of daughters – incidentally, as agonising a process as the original binding, but feet were being saved in hundreds of thousands. In one Kweichos town where women were nothing but slaves, our Political Protection ordered the men to walk behind the women and carry the loads – reversing the traditional trend.

Contract marriage was condemned and 'free-partner' marriage encouraged; concubinage by the perfidious Custom Marriage (which allowed the practice of multiple wives) we immediately outlawed. (Decades later, this was still acceptable to the British in Hong Kong.)

The punishment for rape was death; a fair trial, instant execution. Even while fighting, Mao Tse-tung turned his thoughts to penal reform; we opened Primary and Middle Schools on the march.

And, with all these reforms, the peasants were armed and trained to defend these assignments against the pursuing Kuomintang; tough fighting men being promoted to cadres and left behind to lead them. In this way hundreds of pockets of resistance were created in the wake of the Red Army to harass the Kuomintang advance by peasants with something to fight for.

Never will I forget the day when the Education Commission came down the line to teach the muleteers to read and write.

The Young Vanguards came first, racing down the columns on their little Tibetan ponies: Little Ball was there, and Trip, also Shang Chi-pang – riding bare-back all three, and yelling hoarsely, "*Hao! Hao! Hao!*" and they leaped off the ponies and began to distribute pamphlets and thick, cardboard placards.

Next came the Education Commission with lessons on reading, and these were eagerly seized by the soldiers and read, mostly upside down, for if ten per cent of the Red Army had known a day of schooling, I would have been surprised.

Muchai, deputed as a teacher, fell out of the march; Jo-kei was there – also Bricko and Fool – until someone sent them back. Pipa, in the cart, took papers to teach the wounded; Kwelin took a horse up the line to the Assault Cadre and the Mohammedans (for they, too, spoke Chinese, if with their vicious dialects of Chinghai and Kansu).

196

The first lesson was in dates.

The Young Vanguards, most of whom couldn't brush a single character, hung a little placard around the neck of each man so that the man behind could see it. On each placard was written a numeric sign – one to ten; beside each numeric sign was written a date of a month.

Then a teacher would stand up in a pony-cart and trot up and down the line of marching men, shouting, One, two, three, four, five, etc., teaching the calendar. It was the simplest lesson devised, for all of them knew how to count, since they knew how to gamble; if not how to write.

Later, as a variation, the teachers would hold up a drawing of a dog. Beside it would be the character; holding this he would again charge up and down the line shouting the word, and the character would be there for examination around the neck of the man in front. Then brushes were issued and each marching man would try to copy the character of 'dog' – bellowing, while he did this, "*Kau, kau, kau!*" (Dog, dog, dog!) or "*Chu, chu, chu!*" (Pig, pig, pig!).

Muchai and Kwelin, Jo-kei and I – even Pipa in these early days, were going in and out of the ranks correcting the uneducated scrawling, shouting true pronunciations while teachers from the Education Commission went up and down the column holding up placards with drawings of dogs, cats, mice, horses, donkeys – every kind of household pet or appliance.

This activity went right back to General Headquarters where Mao himself, it was said, was helping to give lessons.

These were sunny days on the march north to Lololand, days of laughter. Although coming from every corner of China (less than a third were enrolled Party members) the men received this teaching with gusty humour: nothing seemed to divide them. The basic difficulty of varying dialects never developed into confrontations. I have seen Cantonese helping Moslems, tiny aboriginal Miao and Shan tribesmen mouthing the tongue-twisting syllables of Shansi, which the northerners handled with ease. The days echoed to patient explanations, happy ridicule, chorused repetitions.

And, on the third day of school, General Peng galloped down the column of the Fifth on a visit to his men of the Third.

He came as I had seen him before during the bedlam of the Battle of the Hsiang River – on the same big, brown stallion and going at the same speed. Seeing him, the men took up their usual cry of "Peng, Peng, *Opium Peng*!"

Lean, wiry, born to a saddle, he came with a cloud of dust behind him and his tunic flecked white from the bridle. Upraised he held a line drawing of a cat being chased by a dog, and he was shouting at the top of his lungs, unintelligibly to me, but the men heard it and took it up, a thunderous bawling, "The dog is chasing the cat! The dog is chasing the cat!" Shouted laughter now and banter as Peng sent the placard sailing away, and dismounted, going into the column.

Instantly, he was surrounded by the Young Vanguards who, for a better sight of him, climbed on the shoulders of the men.

This, I remembered, was the general to whom my letter of introduction was addressed – long, lost no doubt; this was the ex-bandit who had been sentenced to death at the age of nine for kicking over his grandmother's opium pot (hence his nickname 'Opium Peng') and escaped later to lead a peasant uprising against the polygamous war-lord, Ho Chien.

Appalled by a peasant massacre in Hunan seven years ago, Peng Teh-huai had directed the P'in-kiang Insurrection singlehanded, won, and established in the province the first Provincial Soviet Government long before many had hard of Mao Tse-tung

With an army of 8,000 peasants called the 'Iron Brotherhood', he had then attacked and captured the city of Changsa, destroying, while he was at it, the infamous interrogation headquarters in which, for a month, he had been tortured by the Kuomintang. Like Chu Teh, his comrade, Peng had marched ninety per cent of the way to date, often giving his horse to wounded men and carrying their rifles.

Now the men were shaking his hands, touching his clothes: it transgressed the social ethics of 'integrity of person'.

I doubted the wisdom of such familiarity: the peasants, withdrawn, reserved, rarely allowed such intimacy.

One thing was certain; Mao would never have chanced it, yet Mao Tse-tung was their god.

Stand-offish, men said; conceited, aloof . . .?

This, I suppose, was the business of being the Party Chairman.

"It is public error," said the man from Kwangtung finally, "to mistake friendship for weakness and aloofness for greatness.

198

History will judge Mao Tse-tung as lucky – he was merely in the right place at the right time."

Political Chang said, "That's an unfortunate remark – would you care to repeat it against your name?"

"He has no name," said Muchai with meek charm, "he is the man from Kwangtung. But I have a name and I will put it to this. When the blood-bath comes, history will judge Mao Tse-tung as a man China could have done without – not in this generation, perhaps, but by those unborn."

"You will hear more of this," said Political Chang, but we didn't.

Abroad in those days was an almost democratic brand of communism – unless, of course, one happened to be a landlord.

Nor did democracy apply to the People of the Yi, whose land, jealously guarded, was north of the Yangtse, which we were fast approaching. Our friendly overtures towards them (we released members of their tribe from Kuomintang prisons *en route*) didn't appear to have reached their forward patrols: these warriors, from Tehchang to Yuehsi, saw in our northern advance a threat to the independence of their fierce Lolo queen. Reluctantly I reminded myself that it was into this barbaric region that I would have to travel to fetch Tenga's son. The future, for me at least, looked a little insecure to say the most of it.

On the 25th of April, 1935, I wrote in my diary:

The halcyon days of travel are over. We now advance towards the Japanese (they say) at even greater speed. The slogan today is *'Pei-shang K'ang Jih'* (Go north to fight the Japanese). And, as if allies of Japan, the Kuomintang bomb us almost incessantly in the thick forests that guard the Yangtse-kiang. Tojo's long-cart is filled with wounded again; tree-splinter injuries are terrible – the splinters demand heavy probing, mutilations, pain. Today's Order says the Ninth and Fifth are again heavily engaged, our pursuers are punching high into our column flanks. Pipa is now in some pain. I am wondering if the child needs turning. This looks like being a difficult labour. Whether Yung likes it or not, I shall examine her tonight.

I said to Yung, "What the hell's wrong with you? Don't you want your wife to live through this?"

We were at halt by a stream some twelve miles south of the

Yangtse-kiang, having descended down the slopes of the Santai Shan and come to the edge of a tree-fringed range of hills; all about us the vast, tussocked land was excellent ambush country, and Jo-kei should have been aware of it.

Yung said sullenly, "You're not touching Pipa, you understand? I'm going back to the Sixth for a real doctor."

"Good – then go and find him."

"He'll have a job," said Kwelin, coming up with Jo-kei, who added: "News has just come from Commander Ma – we're isolated. We're to form camp here until the regiment arrives – they're eight miles behind. Bricko, get your Brown Contraption up."

"Thirty miles we've done today," piped Bricko from the ground, bathing Fool's feet. "What's the rush? There ain't no bloody sense in it."

"The Assault Cadres moved faster," said Muchai. "They're five miles up in front."

Jo-kei stared about him at the darkening hills. "One thing's sure," said he, "there's no Kuomintang up as far as this." He slapped my shoulder. "You take charge. I'm off to squeeze my head."

But he hadn't bargained for the Lolos.

In retrospect, I wondered what Tenga would have done in this situation; it proved a failure on Jo-kei's part not to put out guards.

Yung left us, going back down the line in search of the Sixth's surgeon. Pipa was groaning with pain: the wounded made tentative gestures in her direction.

"Yes, I know," I said, and stepped carefully down the avenue of legs to where Pipa lay: Kwelin came over the back-board, I recall. In the half-light we knelt above her.

For the first time I knew serious apprehension. If she failed to deliver the child naturally, I would be forced into a Caesarian, and I wasn't qualified for this. All around me were the white faces of the wounded; the glow of their bandages seemed to drift disembodied within the canopy, a phenomenon of floating limbs within my own weariness. I ached for rest Kwelin, exhausted by the day's march, swayed against me as Pipa opened her eyes.

"Where's Yung?" she asked instantly.

Kwelin answered firmly, "He's gone down the line for another doctor – is this what you want?"

"Yung's a fool," replied Pipa, turning away her face.

"As long as you realise it " said Kwelin. "You know what'll happen if he brings another doctor? You're not even supposed to be in here – you'll finish on the road."

I asked gently "Are you in much pain?"

"During the march but I'm better now."

"Then will you let Lin-wai examine you?" asked Kwelin.

Pipa answered "If Yung isn't here " and I realised then that she had sent him away.

The wounded did not look as Kwelin brought in water: I washed my hands.

It was as I had expected; the child's head was high. If things continued like this it was bound to be a breech-birth. It was a heavy sweating business for us both; Pipa made no sound during the examination; her eyes, filled with tears, were steady on my face.

I washed my hands, leaving the rest to Kwelin, and was at the foot-board when I heard Pipa say, "Oh, no, not you – you leave me alone!"

The wounded began a low, anxious murmuring; I heard Kwelin's gentle voice and Pipa's protests rise to a shriek. Pulling back the canvas, I saw her sitting up, struggling with Kwelin. Sweeping back her tangled hair, she shrieked, "Don't you touch me, you smug little bitch!"

And a moment later the Lolos attacked rolling boulders down the face of the bluff above us, stampeding the animals and sending every muleteer in Yunnan province rushing for weapons.

Later, Jo-kei said, "You've got to hand it to them, they were only a patrol, and they attacked a muleteer company."

Jo-kei, for his part, was not in a position to do much about it, for he was sitting with his trousers down on Bricko's Brown Contraption, and the first boulder down hit him clean off the thing, and I don't know who made more bloody noise, said Bricko, Jo-kei or the yelling Lolos.

They came in pairs from the darkness after the attack by boulders, swarming through the resting ranks of muleteers, slicing great wounds with their jungle knives, screaming their Lolo war-cries like women being mutilated. Two came for the medical cart, darting low over the ground in the moonlight, seeking entry, and I got the first one dead with my Luger and the second through the leg, and a shot fired by Kwelin from the long-cart finished him off. One moment peace, next it was bedlam, with mules rearing up to the growing gun-fire, Jo-kei cursing as he fought to get his trousers up, and muleteers bawling as the Lolos got among them.

Using their tiny height, they came in naked streaks, their oiled bodies glistening in the moonlight, their round, white eyes rolling in their tiny faces; getting into the carts, slashing at reins to steal the mules. Bright orange explosions lit the compound as the muleteers got their rifles going, but it was close-quarter fighting and soon we were down to knives and bayonets.

Jo-kei was yelling, "Come on the Fifth! Get into the little bastards!" and I saw him in the clearing, one fist sweeping a Lolo ceremonial sword and the other holding up his trousers. Bricko was behind him, locked in the arms of a tiny, naked Yi, and I saw Fool rise up and a knife come down; the man shrieked, falling. All about me were little squawking groups of fighters locked together in combat, and I ran among them, picking off spare targets in concussive jumps of the Luger as the pace of fighting rose. All about me, it seemed, were ochre-smeared, naked shapes and fearful yells: muleteers and tribesmen, fiercely entwined, rolled down the clearing slope into the stream, to rise, fighting viciously in a flashing of knives and water. One Lolo came for me unarmed, hands clutching for a hold, and I seized him, falling backwards into a heap of disordered fighters. In an indiscriminate confusion of attackers, the muleteers slowly extricated themselves and I discovered myself striking viciously with the pistol at a yelling face below me. In a troublous tumult of knives, the Lolos untangled themselves from the brawny defenders and ran pell-mell, shrieking into the night.

I stared at the dead man beneath me; rose unsteadily with blood on my hands and looked about me. People were making shape in the dim light. Jo-kei was near by, cursing profanely every Lolo down to the fifth generation. Muchai was crawling meekly out of his hiding place under a cart where six Lolos lay dead and another two dying.

I said to Kwelin, who jumped down from the medical cart with a rifle in her hands, "Are they all right in there?"

"Not a scratch." She bent to a twisting Lolo, pushing away Bricko who was preparing to despatch him.

"Pipa?" I asked.

A man shouted, his head poking out from under the canopy, "She were good, Doctor-student – she fight like a man – she were bloody good." Kwelin said, "Yes, Pipa's all right." She knelt beside the wounded Lolo. As if to herself she added, "Don't you worry, you won't kill Pipa."

Somebody came and dragged the wounded Lolo away; all about us men on the ground were softly moaning. I pulled Kwelin to her feet and turned her to face me. Her cheek, from eye to chin, was viciously scratched.

"How did that happen?" I asked.

Kwelin pushed me away; trembling with suppressed anger, she said, "If it comes to a choice between your pet sister and a Lolo – I'll take the savage." She pointed at me. "I tell you this, Lin-wai – she's as tough as a mule inside; outside she's a bitch. But I've got nails too – if she comes at me again – carrying or not – she'll get it."

I was not displeased: it was good to know that Kwelin was capable of a fight. She jerked her head. "Now get back in there, she's asking for you, as usual."

We did not speak again as we bandaged and stitched and the muleteers buried their dead.

We buried Lolos, too; they looked more ferocious in death than when alive. These were the savages I would have to face when I entered their country in search of Tenga's son.

Sitting under the canopy that night I cleaned and reloaded my Luger.

Kwelin watched me with very calm eyes.

TWENTY-TWO

At the approaches of the River of Golden Sand near the wayside hamlet of Lichi, Political Chang came to me on the march.

Yunnan was hot and sticky on that day in late April; many of the Fifth were marching stripped to the waist through the forest tracks of heavily timbered country. The hills swept up in baking, brown beauty either side of the column.

The air was perfumed with spring blossom, bees hummed, sun-shafts among the trees were filled with countless butterflies: it was Yunnan at its best, said Political Chang, matching my stride at Tojo's head.

"It's the best spring I have seen in many years," I replied, not entirely trusting him.

Political Chang's charming rotundity tended to lead one astray from the fact that he was there for a political purpose. He knew, of course, that I dispensed opium for pain – a technical disregard for medical regulations – but he had no absolute proof of it; now I wondered if this was the reason for his sudden friendliness.

He said, "You will please depute your nurse to lead the medical cart, Doctor-student. You and Sergeant Jo-kei are to report forward to the Assault Cadres."

"For what purpose?"

"It will be explained."

So the three of us left the column at Lichi, watched with unusual intent by a bantering Bricko and Fool, and I wondered what they were up to.

Pipa was standing against the wheel of the medical cart, white-faced with her usual pre-natal pains. Yung had never managed to fetch another doctor down the line – as I expected. Now I began to wonder what would happen if Kwelin, in my absence, had to play the midwife. Anticipating my fears, she said:

"Don't be long, Lin-wai, she ... she's not an easy patient." The sun was bright, pitilessly exposing the heavy scar on her lip and the red weals of Pipa's vicious scratches.

In the sticky heat, three miles south of Lichi, Jo-kei, Political Chang and I approached a landlord's mansion. From open windows came bass grumbles of men in discussion.

We entered the vast hall. Here was a dais and chairs like a children's classroom; at a desk, engrossed in papers, sat Chou En-lai; before him were combatant officers of the fanatical Red Cadre Regiment; young, lusty men with war on their faces.

With Jo-kei one side of me and Political Chang on the other, I sat. Chou En-lai rose to address us.

I scarcely heard his words.

It was his eyes.

Of magnetic intensity under their black brows, they burned in Chou's face.

This man, son of a great mandarin family, had always intrigued me. Once secretary of the Whampoa Academy (it was there that Muchai had been his teacher), he always was a champion of social change, and Chou had abandoned the Manchu philosophies of his family to follow a radical line; this led him into prison at Tientsin – following his part in the unsuccessful Student Rebellion of 1919. While there, he fell in love with Ying-chao, a young patriot also imprisoned, later his wife. Chou said now:

"Until today, your particular company has been called upon only to protect Party Headquarters, but now there's advance fighting in plenty to be had." He waved a sheet of paper. "This is a brief for a spearhead crossing of the Yangtse, and you are selected for the task." He stared slowly about him. "But you had casualties in Tsunyi and Tucheng – what strength are you?"

Their Commander replied, "A hundred and forty, vice-Chairman. Where do we attack?"

Chou said, casually, "Over the river under Chouping Fort."

"That could be risky, comrade."

"You are Red Cadres – that is why you are here."

The military briefing went on late into the afternoon. Neither Jo-kei nor myself were much concerned with the military planning: I was replacing a medico of the Cadres recently wounded; Jo-kei was there as a guide – he knew the land south of the river. But I was fascinated by the inner complexities of the man on the dais.

Originally in service to Chiang Kai-shek, Chou En-lai, as late as 1927, had engaged in a spectacular *coup d'état* on our enemy's behalf by leading a general strike in Shanghai of half a million workers: he seized all police stations, the arsenal, disarmed the city's garrison, and handed the Chinese City over to his superior. Chiang Kai-shek entered Shanghai in triumph, then immediately began his purge of radicals; Chou En-lai was first on his list as a possible revolutionary.

The briefing over, Chou En-lai left the dais without a backward look, mounted his fine black horse and galloped away into the sun.

Commander Hsiao of the Red Cadres rubbed his chin with veiled irony, and said, "History's changing fast. I never thought I'd take orders from a direct descendant of the Manchu murderers – how does one square one's conscience with the dead of the old Taiping Rebellion?"

Nobody answered this: I assumed they hadn't got the rank.

Fool won his Gold Star, China's highest award for bravery in the face of the enemy, at the crossing of the River of Golden Sand. He achieved it by accident; certainly he never realised his glory.

Indeed, had it not been for the perception of Commander Hsiao of the Red Cadre section, to whom Jo-kei and I were attached for this mission, Fool and Bricko would have been left behind with the Fifth.

The commander called, "Take a shot at the two men following us," and a sniper pulled out of the line, went flat and squinted along his rifle.

"Hold your fire, commanded Jo-kei, lowering his field glasses, "it's Bricko, Fool and the dog." The officer said:

"You know these men?"

"To my cost," said Jo-kei, sighing.

So the Red Cadre soldiers pulled into the side, waiting, their weapons cocked, for them to join us.

With six miles between us and the Fifth Muleteers (where Muchai had been left in temporary command) the sun was high, bathing the plains in gold. The Red Cadre, we found to our cost, marched with the precision of regimental guards; a contrast to the ambling muleteers.

Now the little column halted for Bricko and Fool.

"Are you both bloody insane?" asked Jo-kei, when they came

206

up, and he struck Bricko in the face. "You bring this tattered maniac with you at a time like this?"

Bricko said, his arm around his tiny friend, "Tenga is dead. You are Sergeant Jo-kei of the Fifth Mules; where you go, we follow," and he nudged Fool, still grinning, and the little man, now in a ragged army uniform sizes too big for him, hid his face in Bricko's shoulder and cackled from a toothless mouth. "Besides," added Bricko, "my little fool lives just beyond the Gold Sands river, near Chouping Fort, don't he?"

"What do you know of Chouping Fort?" asked Commander Hsiao, coming closer.

"We hear Doctor Lin and Jo-kei talking," replied Bricko, and Fool shook with silent laughter, dribbling from his chin. Hsiao said, turning:

"And how many other buggers heard you talking, Sergeant Jo-kei?"

I interjected, "We talked in the medical cart; these two sleep under it."

Hsiao nodded grimly. "Let's hope Chiang Kai-shek don't sleep there, too." He glared at them, hands on hips. "Are these two samples of Red Army muleteers?" He spat. "If they are, I'm changing bloody sides."

Jo-kei said, "All right, all right – they're here. What do we do with them?"

"Shoot them or bring them along – they're your responsibility."

"They come," I said. "We'll deal with them afterwards."

The officer returned my hostile stare. Of Tibetan blood, this one, and ruthless; his name for cruelty rang around the night-fires of the Sixth. Now his eyes narrowed in his yellow, high-boned face, and he said, "Have no doubt, mule-doctor, if security's been broken, I'll bloody deal with you."

On the march to the river (Bricko, Fool and Kau Kau walking in disgrace behind us) Jo-kei said:

"You notice, Lin-wai, that these Red Cadre bastards do not deign to speak to us? This is because we're muleteers and they are the army élite. Soon they'll be wearing sabre scars like the bloody Prussians." He glared at Commander Hsiao who was marching at their head.

"It doesn't particularly worry me."

207

"But it worries me," retorted Jo-kei. "I was soldiering for China before that ponce was a fart in his father; I was a bandit before he was born and a war-lord before he was weaned. In the days of Shanghai I talked with Chou En-lai of military strategy – that's why I'm here. But now I'm a muleteer, my so-called superiors don't speak with me." He turned. "When the New China is built, will there be such class distinction?"

"You can't expect equality in war."

"Nor sense when it comes to bloody intellectuals. I was wrong to discuss it with you."

I said, "The fighters are up front now. When peace comes, they will march behind us, and we'll have the time to root out arrogance and class. All genuine knowledge springs from direct experience, says Mao, and he's right. Hsiao lacks the intelligence to eradicate privilege; he is created for what he has to do."

Jo-kei said with a grunt, "You people are far too gentle – I'd mend him by kicking his arse. When peace breaks out and the guns start firing, the likes of Hsiao will give you dialectic bloody materialism in the shape of Red Guards."

We did not speak more of it for the track was steepening; the heavy medical pack became a burden and Jo-kei and Bricko took turns at giving me a spell with it. Fool, with Kau Kau trotting at his heels, lagged behind, his idiot face cackling at the moon.

It took that night and all next day to scale and descend Big Bun Mountain guarding the Gold Sand river, and at nightfall of the second day of marching Commander Hsiao stopped on high ground, pointing. Below us, between two great folds in the mountain range was the flash of moonlight on water – two little eyes, it seemed, watching us from the dark. Before dawn we were down on the beach of the wide river (called the Chinsa at this point), and to the right of us, stark and threatening against the pale stars, was the black silhouette of Chouping Fort, a towering giant above the huddled town of Nisha. Seeing this, Fool began to leap about, pointing, making incoherent sounds, until Bricko gripped him and clapped a hand across his mouth.

"What is wrong with him?" asked the officer, lowering his binoculars.

"It is his home, Cadre Commander," said Bricko, to attention. "Fool lives in Nisha town."

The commander licked his lips and stared at Fool, who was shaking with excitement, his eyes wild, pointing at Nisha on the other side of the river.

"Does he, indeed?" said Commander Hsiao.

Now, down at the edge of the river, Jo-kei and I waited while the Red Cadre men went into conference. It was still dark when Hsiao came and asked Jo-kei:

"Can the little fool man speak, Muleteer Sergeant?"

"O, aye, Commander," said Bricko, coming up. "But only me understands him."

"And he understands you?"

"He anna such a fool as he looks, mind," said Bricko, warmly, hugging Fool. Into his face he said, "You'm a right good talker to me, anna ye, chap?"

"But, in effect, he is dumb?"

"O, aye," answered Bricko.

"And his home is in Nisha, you say?"

Bricko nodded, wonderingly.

"Ask him, then, if he would like to go home."

Interjecting, Jo-kei said ominously, "What the hell do you want with him, Hsiao?"

"Ask him," said the officer. "Would he like to see his family?" This Bricko did, and the little man shivered with suppressed delight, chuckling idiotically.

We watched; we did not like it. I did not trust Commander Hsiao.

"Good," said he. "Now ask him if there is a ferry, please."

Bricko did this in a strange jumble of dialects, and Fool's eyes grew wide with understanding, and he stroked Bricko's face. Proudly, Bricko silenced him, saying to Hsiao, "Yes, there is a ferry, he says."

"Where?"

Fool, being asked this, mouthed hollow sounds. Bricko said:

"Beneath the Chouping Fort the ferry goes."

"And up-stream? – ask your fool what is there."

Bricko asked this; Fool wept in tuneless sounds and Bricko comforted him, eventually saying:

"Up there is another ferry. But do not go into Kuomintang fort, he says, or you will lose the tip of your tongue, like him, to change the Nisha dialect . . ."

We stared at each other. Bricko patted and whispered and dried Fool's tears with his hands.

"I am very interested in that fort," said Commander Hsiao. He studied his map. "And this confirms the map. There is truly another ferry, then – the main one – some three miles up the Chinsa."

"Out of fort-gun range," said Jo-kei.

"That is where the Red Army will cross?" said another.

"On the face of it," said Commander Hsiao, and, smiling, turned to Jo-kei, saying, "I contragulate you on this fool. It is fools like him that sometimes win a battle."

"These are our fools," retorted Jo-kei. "You'll meet some soldiers when I bring my sane ones."

Commander Hsiao chuckled, winking at Jo-kei. "Is there a sane one among you to take a false order to Chouping Fort?"

"You need a bloody idiot for that," replied Jo-kei, "you can get him from your Cadre."

Commander Hsiao did not smile at this.

The ferryman was no longer young. He chattered at the knife against his throat a moment after he grounded his sampan. "Right," said Commander Hsiao, and he took Fool's arm, "this little man has proved a blessing. He can have an hour to visit his home in Nisha." He picked up Kau Kau. "Here, little chap, you can even take your dog."

Bricko, measuring the leap into the sampan, pushed through the soldiers, saying, "I will come, too."

"You stay," said Hsiao, and called up his men. Eight went into the sampan with him, three rowing with the ferryman.

Bricko paced about on the beach, biting at his fingers as the ferry moved away; and Fool, on his way to visit his family in Nisha, danced on the sampan stern and waved at such important treatment.

I said to Bricko, "Don't worry – I'll see you're next across, stand in line with me." But Bricko was not listening; he stared fearfully at the receding sampan.

When the ferry-boat returned for the second crossing, we clambered in together with seven others, and Jo-kei heaved my pack aboard.

In dancing mist and spray we watched the enemy bank come nearer, the lights of Nisha growing big out of the dawn. From the fort on our right came the sound of music; the garrison awakening. Dim light filtered from its craggy turrets over the dancing face of the river.

Jo-kei whispered to me, "I don't like it – is he a madman? Eight men and an idiot to attack Chouping Fort?"

During that dark crossing of the river I looked at the men about me, the seasoned fighters of the Red Cadre.

Diligently cleaning their rifles and Mausers, these men made little talk save of war: of how a bayonet can more easily be pulled from a body by firing a bullet; that a man cannot shout a warning with a knife in his throat-box. They were scarcely human; never had I seen such men; the greatest hand-to-hand fighters of the East, at a time when the Western press claimed that Chinese soldiers went to war under festival umbrellas.

Up in Manchuria such as these fought the Japanese three years back in one of the greatest holocausts in history, when a million peasants were slaughtered and millions more ran before the flood of Japanese invaders, leaving such as these to stem the tide. Professional killers, they knew nothing of the bureaucratic corruptions, the political wires, the feuding lords, the raws on China's body; they did not even fight for China. They fought, with wolf-like ferocity, for one cause only – the right to own and till their land.

Sitting between Jo-kei and a frightened Bricko, I watched them; saw the flurry of their knives as the ferry ground the enemy beach; heard harsh cries as defenders were cut down. A booted door went back on the quay, and they were into the taxation office; moments later twenty policemen came out with their hands in the air. Commander Hsiao then ran up, giving swift, whispered commands. Seeing him, Bricko cried:

"Where is Fool? What have you done with my friend?"

"Your friend has gone to Nisha," said Hsiao. "His excellent service to his country deserves my generosity."

But the commander answered Jo-kei's question better. He merely raised his eyes to the Chouping Fort.

"You bastard," whispered Jo-kei.

Four days later, on May the 8th, I wrote in my diary:

The Red Army has begun to cross the river; the Fifth were the first mobile troops over; it was good to see Kwelin and Pipa safe. By seizing the ferry at Nisha and drawing away the fort's garrison to the Chiaoche Ferry many *li* distant, Commander Hsiao skilfully ensured that the crossing was unopposed. He actually forged a magistrate's seal, and with it obtained 100 boatmen and sampans; Chouping Fort fell without his firing a shot ... Meanwhile, the army made a feint at Yunnan City, drawing east Lung's war-lord armies. It is all astonishing military genius. I grieve for little Fool ...

Three hours after Fool had set off for his home the Red Cadre walked into an almost empty Chouping Fort. Jo-kei and I accompanied Commander Hsiao in search of Fool.

"You sent him to the fort alone?" Jo-kei asked, bitterly, and Commander Hsiao replied:

"I did no such thing. I gave him leave to visit his people in Nisha town, but first slipped into his pocket a false Order of the Day telling our intention to cross the river by the Chiaoche Ferry three miles upstream ..."

"Knowing that he would be captured in Nisha, when he got home?" interjected Jo-kei.

"And knowing he would be taken to the fort as a spy since he was wearing Red Army uniform?" I asked.

To both these questions Commander Hsiao nodded assent, adding, "That is why it had to be a fool. It is a tremendous pity, but the truth would have been forced out of a man who could talk."

"They must have thought him a particular hero," I said.

"And I think you're a particular bastard," said Jo-kei to Hsiao.

The officer spread his hands, unruffled:

"A thousand men are of no consequence, if it ensures the army's crossing of the Gold Sand River. To die in such a way is glorious," said he.

"Would you have done it?" asked Jo-kei.

"Willingly, for China." He added, "The outcome was success: the fort's garrison was sent on a fool's errand to the Chiaoche Ferry three miles up-stream. The rear party surrendered without firing a shot."

"Congratulations," I said, and spat at his feet.

We found Fool apart from some fifty other communist prisoners in the fort: none had been treated like he.

In a little cellar we found him, a place of torture. He was hanging by his toes and thumbs, which were swollen to the size of pears; his face had been pulled backwards by a strap so that it rested on the floor. The blow-lamp that had put out his eyes had been used to burn into his chest the words, 'Red Spy'. How long he had been in this position I did not know; he was still alive when we cut him down.

"Fool . . ." I said, kneeling beside him.

Kau Kau, unharmed, was licking his face.

A surgeon from the Sixth tried to chafe the circulation back into his limbs, but I pushed him away, saying:

"He is in my company, please leave him to me."

Even as they watched, I put two opium seeds into his gaping mouth; other doctors watched this breach of regulations, but none spoke of it. They just stood there, trembling.

"Goodbye, Fool," said Bricko, as he died. With Kau Kau in his arms, he did not weep. His face, stark-white, stared at his friend.

Leaving him with Jo-kei, I left the torture-chamber with others: an officer, a giant of red hair and a fierce face, cried bassly, "Why did you call him a fool? He who will win the Gold Star of China?"

"Please," I said, "it does not matter."

"But it does!" He gripped me. "How dare you, you bloody civilian!"

Coming up, Jo-kei pushed the officer aside: of high rank, the Mongolian glared down at us.

"He was ours!" said Jo-kei. "He was one of our muleteers – do you understand that, soldier? He was *ours!*" And he thrust them all aside.

Bitterly, I thought of the foolishness necessary to become so popular.

It was May the First. The Red Army began to cross the Yangtse almost unhindered, and the vanguard struck north into Szechuan Province of Tehchang and Sichang, which was the road to the Tatu Bridge.

TWENTY-THREE

Once over the River of Golden Sand, we marched into the region called Lololand, the country of the barbaric Black and White Lolos, one of the tribes of Yi; Tenga, a White Bone, was of their blood.

Kwelin said, on the march, "Will you go to Tenga's wife, Lin-wai?"

"If it is possible."

"Big One is asking to see Tenga's son – will you take him, too?"

"It is a great difficulty to take Big One anywhere – I do not know the finger language."

"Then shall I come?"

I replied, "No, you must stay and care for Pipa."

Kwelin made a very wry face.

This was a volcanic region; the baked earth flung up strange, scented smells, as if growing deep within the wide rock fissures were flower bouquets. And on the night halts the moon was the biggest I have seen, sailing above the land upheavals and sending slanting beams on to oceans of waving ferns: here the spit-gob spiders had woven webs of light, and in this silken sea the army moved like insect columns, its camp-fires flaring in the silver waste like struggling glow-worms.

Over such a camp-fire I watched Kwelin's sleeping face.

On that May night I became aware that I was falling in love with her. Naturally, I wondered if Kwelin could ever know love for me.

She was not beautiful, of course, as Pipa, but she was shapely, and I sensed that her womb was fashioned for sons. True, I expected resistance, but how can a man be fulfilled without sons? Into this woman, I contemplated, lying in the glow of the fire, I would put my seed.

I rubbed my chin. It would be necessary, of course, to put such a decision to Kwelin.

But what had I to offer in return, I wondered.

For a start, I thought reluctantly, I was quickly losing my hair for a man of twenty-two: taller than most, I resembled more a herring than a carp, the symbol of longevity: so, at this rate of wastage no woman was likely to have me around for long. Compared, say, with the man from Kwangtung, who sent the women shivering, I was scarcely a catch worth considering – a loping, moody student doctor looking twice his age; one always on the edge of aggression and temper.

It is excellent, my mother used to say, when a man can sit back and look at himself at the height of his maturity; for I was not a lad of twenty-two; with the assistance of this Long March, I was middle-aged.

Suddenly, to my amazement, I was aware that Kwelin's eyes were open, and that she was watching me.

Around us were the sleeping people: Pipa was sighing in the arms of Yung, men snoring bassly.

But Kwelin, as if my heart had called to her, had awakened. We talked, unspeaking, over the glow of the fire; a wordless communion. And Kwelin said, with her eyes:

"Chan Lin-wai, I'm in love with you. Why this is I do not know. After all, you aren't much to look at – no attractive Chinese gentleman should be over six feet tall. Also, you are moody and bad-tempered, and you drink: the test is this – could I put up with you in a kitchen? Would I abhor you in my bed when you sought sons in me?"

I answered her in my mind. "With you I'm at peace; I'd reform my arrogance; your child-birth would be easy, for I, who divided you, could also deliver you."

Kwelin virtuously lowered her eyes in the glow: the wind moved between us in a scent of burning pine; Bricko fitfully turned in sleep, and I dreamed that I heard Kwelin say, "You're a hard man, Chan Lin-wai; with each mile of this march you grow harder. You appropriate women, you do not woo them. At Liping City, Pipa told me, you sought the services of a whore. Sometimes love is in your face when you look at me? Why, then, oh *why* did you not seek me?"

"Because I respect you," I said, but none heard this.

Certainly Kwelin had not because she promptly went to sleep again.

I thought, one day, although you do not know it, I will rid

my heart of Yang Pipa, and take you home to Laoshan. But before this happens I will prove myself to you – the finest surgeon in the First Front Army, including Dr. Nelson Fu. In seven months of operating I have learned more on this March than in ten years at Shanghai University. What are good looks, anyway, compared to a man's ability? Ability and integrity, not morals, are the qualities a wife should seek: and can't a man take a drink at times? Come with me, Kwelin No-Other-Name, and it will be splendid.

Governed by a process greater than myself, I rose and tiptoed around the fire to where Kwelin was lying: she, like a tigress touched in sleep, instantly opened her eyes, but did not move.

"Kwelin . . ." I whispered.

It turned her; she had not rejected me: smiling, she knelt before me.

The glow of the fire cast her features in deep relief and long she stared at me, her hands clasped, then she said, touching my face:

"You know, Chan Lin-wai, you really do have the most beautiful eyes."

Naturally, this encouraged me, and I would have made a step or two in a very normal direction, but Muchai, looking over his shoulder from the ground, said:

"No, no, *no*! Now is neither the time nor place – in the name of Confucious, go to sleep."

Over the border of Szechuan, the land of earthquakes, we confronted new dangers. While this advance was another victory for Mao's guerrilla tactics – the Kuomintang, their air force grounded by low clouds, were floundering about looking for us 100 miles south-east in Yunnan – we were now facing the many Yi tribes who were hostile to anything Chinese. I had been constantly reminding myself that, once we entered Lololand, I would have to fulfil my promise to Tenga and fetch his son, enrolling him in the army as a Young Vanguard. This could prove difficult. Not only was this ostensibly enemy country, but the child might refuse to come with me. Tenga himself would be regarded as a traitor to his own tribe in fighting for Mao Tse-tung (an unhealthy situation for me). I was not looking forward to the business of entering Lololand, unless it was already occupied by forward elements of Red Army patrols. I was even less happy about the coming confrontation with the boy's mother.

Jo-kei said, eyeing, "Tell me the day you're off and I'll put in for a replacement of a dead muleteer doctor. I'm all for Tenga's dying wishes, but you'd do better to leave his offspring exactly where he is."

"But these Lolos are Chinese, also," said Yung, on the march.

"True," answered Muchai, "but they are non-Han Chinese, like the Miao and the Shans. They are to true Chinese what the Red Indians are to the American West. They hold no loyalty to China; they hold no brief for Mao." He added, "Their minority has been oppressed by China since the days of Kublai Khan."

"Whose passage to India through the Sikang Mountains we are now following," said Kwelin.

Jo-kei interjected, "Informative and very pleasant to contemplate, I'm sure! True, we are over the Yangtse, but Mao has landed us in a trap of three rivers: the Yangtse is behind us, the Yalung is to the west and the Tatu to the north. At the moment we are climbing the great Fire Mountain where the monkey burned his arse – will somebody tell me why?"

"It's a poor contribution – is that all you know of it?" asked Kwelin.

"For accurate legends, come to the scholars," cried Muchai. He was marching with his great, loping strides; near to seventy, he was now muscled, well-covered and hard, a contrast to the tottering ancient of Kuangchang.

Now, said he, "A classically educated monkey of the T'ang dynasty crossed Fire Mountain on his travels in search of Buddhist manuscripts: the hair on his behind was singed when he sat down to rest on the summit of Fire Mountain – that's why there's no hair on monkeys' bottoms today."

"We'll get more than singed bottoms if we fall foul of the Lolos," said the man from Kwangtung. "I've already had enough of them."

It was the day before I left the column and went in search of Tenga's son that we gained the trust of the Lolos, a race of natural thieves and filchers.

As we entered the drab streets of Yuehsi, the pygmies flooded out of their shanty mud cottages, greeting the Fifth like beloved relatives. This took the form of a running pillage: walking in

217

our ranks, they proceeded to confiscate everything in sight. Gun-limber flaps went up, ammunition was handed out; bed-blankets were unstrapped from marching soldiers and disappeared through doors: running among us with happy grins, their hands went into our pockets and our possessions were turned out for examination; they even lifted Bricko's belt, and his trousers slipped down. Muchai lost his cap and Jo-kei his money; they had the hold-all off Yung and his pamphlets off Political Chang; nothing was inviolate – they even started to unbandage the wounded in Tojo's medical cart until Pipa screamed and we hauled them out. And all was done with charming gestures of friendship.

From little cracked windows stared the pale faces of the White Bones, their slaves, and through every town we passed there was evidence of their ill-treatment.

But it was at Yuehsi, still occupied by an astonished Kuomin-tang garrison who fled at our approach, that we found evidence of brutality to Lolos, Black and White.

The Kuomintang prison, in the middle of the little town, was forced; a team of tough Assault Cadres men broke down the door with a battering-ram.

More than 100 men and boys lay in chains in a cellar reeking of excrement: naked, the living were chained to the dead, some of whom were in advanced stages of putrescence.

The Sixth went in and lifted them out; in such a manner were the prisoners chained that the first man (he was dead) could not be moved until the second was lifted.

We laid the tragic retinue outside in a circle and the armourers came to strike off their fetters. Of the men lying in the sun, sixty-one were dead.

One, an Elder, said faintly to me as I took his evidence:

"All of us here are of the tribes of Yuehsi or Ahou . . ."

Kwelin, I remember, wept as he continued:

"A few of us were brought from Kuochi by the Kuomintang. I myself have been here seven months – imprisoned on the 'shift' system, because my brother, who is clan head in Ahou, refused to supply more girls for the brothels . . ." He stared up weakly into my face amid the pounding of the armourers' hammers. "You understand, Red soldier, we had few enough women left for Lolo wives . . ."

The Assault Cadres found another cellar, then another; more

and more prisoners were brought out. The sun poured down on the bright, warm land. The old man said, "I have tried to stay alive because next on the 'shift' is my son, and when he dies, my grandson will be taken, and he is only twelve . . ."

Shao Shan arrived with a bowl of water and held it to his lips, whispering, "The army is going to see to this, not Mao Tse-tung."

She did not wait long.

Into the little square of the town galloped a company of the Fifteenth Mohammedans: behind every horse ran a string of roped Kuomintang soldiers, late to escape.

Before Political Protection could get down from Headquarters, the Mohammedans shot these one by one before the eyes of the Lolos.

For two days the army rested in Yuehsi, waiting for the General Headquarters, lumbering late as usual. Yung said, while I was preparing to go to Tenga's wife:

"I am worried about Pipa, Chan Lin-wai."

"I won't be long – Kwelin will be with her."

"Sometimes she cries with pain; yet the child is so high. Also, the sickness never leaves her."

"I know all this, and I'll be back by the morning – don't worry, I tell you – Kwelin is a trained midwife."

"She's not a surgeon."

"Neither am I – remember?" I glared at him.

Then Bricko mooched up like a murder looking for somewhere to happen, and muttered falsetto, "I'll kill him, Doctor Lin. He killed my Fool, so I'll bloody kill Commander Hsiao." His voice sang high in broken tears.

I gripped him, my hand over his mouth. "Bricko, you *fool*!"

But he tore my hand away. "Watch, then – I'll have him, the Red Cadre bastard!" and he left me, mouthing hatred.

Things were unsettled in the Fifth, to say the least of it.

"That you, Comrade Doctor?"

The opium-soldier came into the canopy-tent, pushed Kwelin aside and knelt, his arms out to me like withered vines, crying tearfully, "For pity's sake gi' me a seed, Doctor – only one?" he rocked himself. "The last one ... eh? I'm 'aving such a dreadful fuggin' war – nobody's 'aving a worser war than me."

Over my shoulder I said to Kwelin, "Get him out."

"Why, of course," said she. "Shoot him if you like – but he's still your responsibility."

I swung to her. "Well, it's such damnable hypocrisy! Mao barters tons of the stuff, and I can't prescribe a seed!"

"You shouldn't have done it in the first place!"

I stared at her. The opium-soldier was on all fours now, reaching for her hands; froth and spittle was on his mouth. "Eh, dear me, I'm 'aving it terrible, missy – the cramps, the cramps ..." He wept to her.

Kwelin walked past me to the medical pack, took an opium seed, knelt, pushed it into his mouth and steered him through the door, fighting off his attempts to embrace her. Returning, she said, "Yes, *out*! Whatever happens, you mustn't embarrass the respectable doctor."

"All right, he's had his opium – is all that necessary?"

It turned her, white-faced. "What with one thing and another, I'm sick of the situation here. I'm going back to the Ninth!"

"Because of one drug addict?" I put down the bottle I was filling, "or because of Pipa?"

She turned away, screwing at her fingers. "Right, then, if you want the truth – because of Pipa. I hear nothing these days but Pipa, Pipa, *Pipa*!"

My growing worry over Pipa had long been building a sickness in me; Kwelin's outburst was reasonable. Also, the lack of proper medical facilities – men were actually dying now for want of a bottle of iodine. (And in Yunnan there was a dearth of the herbs I wanted.) The constant marching, the eternal bombing, the mess of blood and suffering – most of which I could do nothing about – was beginning to affect my temper.

Kwelin, being handy, was getting the worst of it.

And Pipa, in her distress, was losing her control: even with Yung present and the wounded watching, she would try to rediscover in me some hint of love, rejecting with cat-like ferocity Yung's pathetic attempts to interfere. It was planting in Yung unknown suspicions, I could see it in his face: its effect on Kwelin, always present on these occasions (I saw to this) was a passive understanding of a very difficult patient: the likes of Pipa, she once mentioned, should never be tended by a blood relative. But I knew that, if Pipa insisted on raising my every appearance to an emotional confrontation, the truth of us would very soon be out. Yung, besotted in his love of her, was clearly hurt and confused: even the wounded with whom she shared the long-cart – usually behaving with splendid detachment when I visited her – were now showing unfeigned interest in our meetings. And Kwelin? She was too intelligent, I knew, to accept such a situation for long. And, if she guessed the truth of us, so might others: I could only wonder at the Party's reaction to an incestuous relationship. It could prove a public scandal I could not face – not only for myself, but for Pipa.

Now, Yung put his head around the door of the canopy, saying dispassionately, "Pipa is asking for you. Please come."

Kwelin groaned at the tent roof, her hands swifter on rolling bandages.

Desperately, I began to wonder if Pipa's unending vomiting, her intermittent pains, the position of the child, were proof of some serious internal malformation. One thing I knew – if she aborted on the march, she would likely die. As I prepared to leave camp, I speculated on the possibility of forcing a delivery before the crossing of the Tatu River, our next big obstacle that held the promise of another major battle.

The outrageous brutality of the Chinese to the Lolo prisoners – the slaughter without trial of their Kuomintang guards: the agony of the opium-soldier, for whom I was responsible; the death of Tenga, the torture of Fool – all built within me a numbing depression and a sudden, wild yearning to escape – from the Fifth, dirt, lice, war and women.

"I can't come now," I replied to Yung. "I tell you she'll be perfectly safe with Kwelin."

"Poor old Kwelin," said she, with mock irony. "Poor old bloody Kwelin."

I was a bit surprised. It was the first time I had heard her swear.

Strapping on my Luger, I went outside. Bricko had taken Tojo out of the shafts and saddled her. Pipa was lying in the sunset with the wounded, her face pale in its pitiless light. She called to me, but I did not answer.

"Take care," said Kwelin, touching my hand.

I heeled Tojo hard and we went at a gallop along the road to Yichi, to fetch Tenga's son.

Both Kwelin and Pipa waved goodbye to me, but I did not reply.

It was farther than it seemed on the map; indeed it was dusk when I reached the area of Yichi, recently, luckily for me, occupied by the Fourth Regiment. Here, in the main street, a beggar was sleeping, so I dismounted and shook him out of his rags saying:

"Old man," and I bowed to his age, "if this is Yichi, then where is Sun?"

He raised blind eyes to me, fumbling with fright, and croaked, "Dog's farts for awaking me to hunger! Now it will cost you money." He blinked red tears in his walnut of a face, scratching vigorously.

I said, dropping a coin, "I seek the cottage of Tenga the Yi."

The splintered moon kissed his shattered face in question. I added:

"The home of Tenga the Yi, who left for the war. His good wife lives by a stream in a red-roof cottage."

This rocked him with silent laughter. "*Good*? You speak educated yet visit a whore!"

"A whore? Tenga's wife?"

"Three cheeks on my bum," said the beggar, "do they come! Half the labourers of Yichi sew up Tenga's missus! – Good, you say? Good for a Mexican dollar – though some do tail her cheaper!"

I straightened from him ."You've got the wrong Tenga."

"And you the wrong woman," he replied, and pointed with his stick. "Down the village, turn right; take your place in the queue."

The stream of which Tenga had told was narrow; noisy in its brilliance under the rising moon. And by it stood Tenga's house, red-roofed, as he had said: yellow light from a window blazed over the fields. Tethering Tojo in shadows I moved silently, peering within.

About fifteen villagers were watching a cock-fight, the regional sport of the Yi: squatting in a circle under a lamp they were transfixed in a tumble of spurs and feathers; two cockerels,

222

locked in combat, leaped in squawks and blood; the air moved, bringing the heady swims of opium.

Tojo made a strangled sound; I hushed her.

At this, a skinny little boy as naked as birth, came from shadows, saying in Tenga's dialect:

"You want bed-woman, soldier?"

His large eyes rolled in a tiny face humped with bruises.

"You are Ten Ga-hu, lad?"

The men within roared; the cock-fight beat between us, and he suddenly frowned at the moon; instantly, I saw in that frown the face of Tenga.

"I am Hu. You want Mama?" he asked.

I nodded.

"Come?" he beckoned, leading me to a door at the back of the cottage; opening it, he said:

"Good jig-jig – one dollar," and held out his hand.

I remembered Tenga and closed my eyes.

"Go and fetch Mama," I said.

"No," said he. "One dollar first."

The spectacle of his ill-treatment held me with astonishing force.

I put the silver into his hand. Calling within, he opened the door wider.

"All right," said he.

The room was bare, a host to poverty. On a wooden table, rice-bowls and chopsticks were scattered, and the remains of a meal.

On the *k'ang* a naked man was lying. The half-dressed woman beneath him turned her head as we entered, indicating a chair: the man above her worked on industriously.

"Has he paid?" she asked the child.

We sat together, Ten Ga-hu and I, and watched.

Suddenly the man on the bed began to sing, a drunken bawdy of a song that battered off the walls of the little room: sitting up, he dangled his legs while Tenga's wife preened in a mirror; seeing us waiting, he began to curse in thick, Yunnanese dialect; clearly, in that dim light he had not recognised my uniform. I heard Tenga say:

"She were a good little crust . . . I got her off a marriage broker
– Wun Pei-sha was 'er name . . ."

"Who the fuggin' hell are you?" asked the man on the bed.

I looked at the hag that once was Tenga's wife; the powdered
face of the harlot, the smeared mascara, the scarlet mouth.

"Mind, she were not Han Chinese," said Tenga, as if in the
room. "She were Tibetan blood, a little yellow chocolate . . .
but she were sweet for me."

The man said, now standing naked before me, "Oho, eh? Two
yards of dirty grey cloth – look what we got, Pei-sha – a bloody
Yau Pat!"

He had mistaken me for the defeated Kuomintang. As I rose,
he shouted, "You'll be 'yellin' the road' next, woman. You so
hard up you drop to soldiers?" He turned to her.

Tenga said in my brain, "Aye, she were a good little piece, an'
there was honey in her loins for me, dirty ole' Tenga. An' she
made my Hu tall and straight in her belly . . ."

I tapped the shoulder of the man before me, and, as he swayed
to face me, I caught him with a hand to the neck; being big, it
didn't floor him, but drove him across the room until he barged
the wall. The woman shrieked as I brought his head down with a
smash to the stomach: as he staggered before me, I swung my
fist and hit him flat. He lay between the woman and I; his great,
flabby body heaving to the inrush of his breath: unconscious, he
snored bassly.

"That's for Tenga," I said.

We watched him; Tenga's wife, trembling beside me, her
hands pressed to her face, sighed like a woman in labour.

I said, pointing to Hu, "He came from your body, but he
doesn't belong to you. I am Tenga's friend; I am taking his
son."

Panic struck her. "Take him, and I scream for the men!"

I brought out the pistol.

"Scream and I'll kill you – him, too." I nodded at the man on
the floor. "I am taking the boy – this is what his father wanted."

We weighed each other. In the dancing light I saw her eyes,
large and slanted in her foreign face. Unmistakably Tibetan, she
was small and dainty beneath the dirt and tawdry clothes; her
breasts were that of a child, her arms round and smooth, her skin
the colour of rich, brown earth.

"Does Tenga live?" she asked softly.

"Tenga is dead," I said.

From the tavern room a cockerel crowed in victory.

"Dead, eh?" She moved away. "Then take him, and goodbye to the pair of them!" She stared at her face in the mirror.

The cock crowed again.

Hu twisted in my arms, calling to his mother.

At the door he cried, "Going to find Papa now, but I come back, Mama! *Ts'ing ts'ing!*"

She replied, "Go then, pimp! Go to a ghost!"

The cock crowed for the third time.

Outside the cottage door Jo-kei was waiting astride a fine Red Cadre stallion. He said, "I apologise for following you, but we were worried about Tojo. It is not every day of the week we get a mule of her quality."

"I see," I replied. "And now?"

"Now get the boy back to camp before I change my mind and shoot Tenga's whore." He leaned over as I lifted Hu on to Tojo's saddle, and added, "By the hair on my father's belly, he is the image of my dead friend – get going."

An unusual emotion assailed me on that ride back to camp.

With Hu's tiny body moving in my arms there arose within me a sense of possession that I had not experienced before: this was the son of my friend; in bringing him to the army I was fulfilling my promise to Tenga. But there was more to it than mere satisfaction of a duty done.

This child was not of my loins, but Tenga's, yet his presence, the touch of his thin limbs against me instilled in me a furious response of protection. Had I been opposed on that return to camp I would have acted like Tenga, tearing away any threat, giving my life that Hu should grow to manhood in his time ... as my own child of Pipa's body, might grow to his.

I saw, in the occasional trusting looks in this boy's face, the face of one unborn: it was a new and splendid emotion. A hedge loomed up in the moonlight and I gripped Hu against me with one hand, shouting at the sky with the boy's shriek of delight:

"*Hei, wei, up!*" and Tojo gathered herself for the spring.

"*Up, over* ..." Behind us we could hear the thundering hooves of Jo-kei's stallion.

Laughing together in this new-found friendship, I reined Tojo north. With Hu held hard against me and the midnight trees yawning about us, we galloped back to Yuehsi.

The muleteers were preparing to move when we reached camp: from their midst came Bricko with Kau Kau racing after him. Bricko asked, with a light in his face, "This is Tenga's boy?"

I nodded, and he lifted Hu down, saying, "You gives him to Bricko, Doctor Lin?"

I replied, "How can I?"

"Big One don't need 'im ..." He searched my eyes. "You beds me any stranger-woman an' I don't make sons ... but this one's already made."

"He is not mine to give," I answered, and took Hu from his arms. He said, his face low:

"Now I lost my little Fool, I only got Kau Kau."

Empty, I stood there; the sentries looked on. And then Big One came full pelt with his face turned up and his red beard waving, a galloping giant. Reaching us, he knelt before Hu, smiling into the child's face.

Jo-kei said, "I have told him that this is now his son; that it is what Tenga wanted." He made the Hingsi sign-language. Big One nodded, pushed Bricko away, and lifted Hu against him.

"And Tenga's woman – what of her?" asked Muchai.

I brushed him aside. "Don't talk to me about women," I said.

With Tenga's old Mongolian fur coat stretching at the seams about him, Big One carried his new son back to the Fifth.

Later, we followed.

With the Assault Cadres in the van, we took the road north to Luting and the Bridge of Chains, and, when the sun came up red and golden in the Sikang mountain peaks behind us, we found ourselves marching in a great valley within an ocean of camellias as far as the eye could see, and we sang:

There's a 'bus coming up, a Number Eleven,
And Mao Tse-tung says the seats are free.
So spin me along with a girl on my knee,
My pugs cocked up and me head in heaven.
Cool me shifters! Count me toes!
There's a 'bus round the corner, a Number Eleven.
Which nobody's seen and nobody knows.

I wrote in my diary:

I have been to Yichi and brought back Tenga's son, fulfilling my duty.
Now, over the Yangtse, we are through the Sikang range and on the road to the Tatu River and its Bridge of Iron Chains. Seventy years ago an earlier rebellion died there, the Manchus slaughtering the rebels to a man. The superstitious soldiers are getting very restless.
It is a glorious summer: we move – the entire army – in a sea of red, pink and white camellias . . .

21st May, 1935

Wong the corpulent, the only muleteer Tojo would allow to groom her, said to me:

"Comrade Doctor, I am afraid," and he stood before me in the medical tent on that first halt on the road to Anshunchang, shivering in his obesity, his white face puckered up. I asked, coldly:

"So afraid that it brings you to sick parade?"

He clutched his hands. "I speak for many, not for myself alone."

"Speak then." I added, "But no true soldier should be that afraid."

Said he, "But I'm not a true soldier, Comrade. I'm a student farmer of Fukien. Tell me, do the spirits of the slaughtered Taiping rebels haunt the Tatu River?"

"Of course they don't," I replied testily.

He said, "Of dead people I'm not afraid. When my parents were shot by the Kuomintang I set them side by side in a grave on the Hill of Han, near my village: seven years to the day I drew them from the tomb; not one Ching Ming festival did I miss, but always swept clean their grave. At the exhumation, all alone, I cleaned their bones and dipped them in oil and perfume; now they stand together in the jar with lucky red paper to keep away the flies, with wands of wattle and a flamingo feather to ban the evil spirits – it is a custom of Fukien."

I nodded. "Also of my province; you are lucky to know such simplicity of belief." I sat back, regarding him: in his regional superstitions he represented three-quarters of the army. Now he said, "I do not fear the dead, sir, but only the water-imps that swim in the River Tatu."

I spoke in the old language to put him at his ease. "What cares a man about devils in water, if he is dead already?"

Wong said, "Nor do I fear death by drowning – this is a farmers' army – few of us can swim. But there are many in the Fifth who tell that the souls of the dead Taipings have been born again as cockroaches, the oldest creature: these enter the stomach of a man through his anus; also by the ear, and crawl around the brain, looking at the world through his eyes."

Kwelin, briefly entering, heard the last of the sentence going out, and made a wry face: to Wong, however, this was most serious. I said, to cheer him, "Wong the Corpulent, you are more superstitious than a cross-eyed grocer. Does the Chairman tell you such things in his Order of the Day?"

It brought him instantly to attention. "Mao Tse-tung told us we would fly like birds over the Hsiang River, but we drowned in it like flies. Chu Teh has holes in his body that heal overnight, it is said, yet even here, in this tent, I saw you bandaging him."

"Well?"

He said, his face low, "Neither does Lin Piao catch bullets with his fingers – this is also a lie. Our leaders are but men like us. Now the soldiers are saying that history will be repeated: that Mao and Chu, and Lin Piao will die at the Tatu like Prince Shih and his Taiping rebels died: that many will be sent to Chengtu by Chiang Kai-shek for death by cutting."

This was the death Chiang had promised Mao.

Wong, I realised, knew more of history than was good for him. I said, "You read much, Wong?"

He straightened with pride. "To the men, every night, I read *The Romance of the Three Kingdoms*."

"And it is there that you read of the Taiping Rebellion?"

He nodded. I said, carefully, "Then you will remember that Prince Shih, the rebel leader, paused when he reached the Tatu, there to celebrate the birthday of his son, the imperial prince?"

"Three days he rested, Doctor-student!" He was delighted with my knowledge."

"But the child of Mao, who was born of Ho on this march, does not celebrate a birthday until December. We will reach the Tatu River within a week, and this is May."

It was wonderful to see his face; he brimmed with joy and relief. I added, "How, then, can history repeat itself? – unless Mao sits for seven months on the river bank waiting for his child's birthday? Prince Shih himself waited only three days – come, the idea's preposterous."

Wong said, excitedly, "How stupid I have been! Of course! I will tell them! Tonight, when I read again, I will tell them!"

"Excellent," I said, "and tell them this, too. Mao Tse-tung will fly them like birds over the River Tatu: that history will *not* repeat itself. Mao will be on his feet at Tatu; at the Hsiang crossing he was at the point of death with malaria – give the man a chance!"

It was a lie, of course, but anything would do.

Clear of the road that night I saw a little man kneeling in the camellias; he was a peasant from Hunan, he said, and lying before him among the flowers was a little iron crucifix. On the other side of the road, behind the drooping animals, knelt another; he was a factory fitter from Wuhan. Before him was a small red altar; in his cupped hands he held a faded Bell Flower, the Buddhist symbol of a dying soul.

To the first man I said, "To whom are you praying?" and he replied, "I pray to a crucified man, a god of the foreign missionaries – they of the large noses, the Big Red Gingers."

"Were you baptised?" asked Kwelin.

"In their faith," replied the soldier, "by Hose-pipe Fong, the Christian General, with 18,000 others. He bloody soaked us."

I asked, "And why do you pray?"

"That I might not drown among the water-devils of the River Tatu."

To the second man Kwelin said, "Why do you pray to Buddha, soldier?"

His face was hard and strong, and he was large; a man of the Assault Cadre.

"Because I fear the Tatu River," said he, and raised his eyes to us, "Before we reach Anshungchang, even, I will come to you like the others, for cotton wool. This I will push into the nine orifices of my body – before I swim."

Later, walking with Kwelin among the camellias, I said, "They are terrified of the Tatu; this is enemy propaganda."

"One thing's sure," said Kwelin, with unconscious humour, "Before we cross the Bridge of Chains you're going to need a cart of cotton wool."

It was on a tiny plank-bridge, a mile away from the resting army, that I said to Kwelin. "How are the lice?"

"They bite no worse than usual."

The late May moon was high above the Sikang range behind us; from the woods came the noises of summer, many nightbirds

230

sang. I said, "We could wash our clothes on this halt; it is a hot wind from Fire Mountain; they would dry within an hour."

She leaned on the bridge rail.

I can see her now as I write this.

She had grown her hair long, like Pipa, tying it with red ribbons: now she untied these and shook out her plaits so that the black strands fell over her stained tunic. Beneath us fish moved lazily in the shallows, flashing in trails of bindweed.

Her eyes were beautiful – better, even, than the eyes of Pipa; her face was tanned with sun and wind; the scar of her mouth was difficult to see in the reddening sunset.

"Would there be privacy, do you think?" she asked softly.

I looked around the glare of the camellias; I smelled on the wind the camp-fires of the army: the peaks of the Sikang speared at the big, May moon like hunters. "There is nobody within a mile, woman."

She laughed in nervous expectancy, and said, her face averted, "Then you go up-stream and I down-stream, and when we have made clean and washed our clothes, we will meet again on this bridge?"

"It is a marvellous idea," I said.

She knew, of course, that I would make love to her.

There were only the two of us in the world then.

"Kwelin," I said, and kissed her.

When I returned she was awaiting me on the bridge, as naked as I, and there was no shame in it. Hand in hand now, unspeaking, we went to a quiet place of flowers, and there lay down.

"You knew of my desire?" I asked.

She did not reply.

Her body was small and slim; as we lay in silence her hair wind-drifted over the white camellias, a lovely contrast of blackness. Her skin, I noticed, was not like Pipa's, which is of the Chans (dark-textured as the Hoklo sea-people who sail among the islands) but pale, as a girl of the north. Nor did she speak in the moment before love, as Pipa often spoke (a disconcerting business); nor call to another in tears as I divided her body, as had the woman of Liping, whose name I have forgotten.

But the instant of my touch brought her to a panic of fear, and she cried aloud, gripped by horror: her eyes opened wide and she stared into my face, then subsided into calmness, as if escaped from a cataclysm of her mind.

"Kwelin," I said, "Kwelin, it is I . . ." and the sound of me soothed her so that she turned away her face, becoming limp in my arms, at one with sacrifice. She did not reply; indeed, so quiet was she that, but for the swift inrush of her breathing, she could have been dead.

She awakened as I entered her body; this I did most carefully, lest it cause her pain.

And thus she lay as one removed in time: as once before she must have lain, limp in the face of savagery; a fraud of death.

"Kwelin," I said. "It is Lin-wai. Please . . ."

The kindness seemed to bring her from a sleep, and she smiled, reaching up her arms for me.

"Kwelin . . . Kwelin . . . ?" I said again, but she did not speak with me.

Mine was no desecration of her loins: within her body there was no possession, no conquest: it was giving, not taking, service, not spoils; a strange and mature gentleness. For it told within me, in stuttering breath, that this must not prove a corruption of her woman's dignity. Also, I felt pride – an emotion new to me – that she had permitted the gift – a perfect union, a rhythm instantly brought. It dispelled for her, Kwelin later told me, the bawdy obscenities of cock-fisted soldiers, waiting in line, aping her screams; the gobbling mouths and garlic breath: it silenced for her the shrieks of spreadeagled women, feet pinned by boys to the pitching lust of men: the rising dust; the opium-soaked faces, the market stinks. And the very act of love built in me a new and exultant hope that I might banish from her mind the raping Kuomintang. As if recognising this in the instant of her youth, she called my name loud and clear.

"*Lin-wai!*" The lightning flashed between us, forging us in heat and shape together.

I held her and would not let her go.

"Oh, Lin-wai," she said.

Her eyes were slanted and dark-humid when she opened them to my face. Kissing her lips after such tumult was like a budding of the earth amid a scent of flowers; the waving anemone, camellias pink, white and red.

"I love you, Lin-wai," she said.

Minutes passed, we did not move. Drugged by the moon we lay as one; like the lotus-eaters of Matapan who asked no more covering from cold than flowers, we grew alive in each other's arms.

Kwelin's hands moved: she smoothed back my hair and raised her lips to mine. In a moment, most strangely, her mouth was even more beautiful than Pipa's.

Later, when we returned to the bridge, Kwelin put her hands in her hair and laughed at the sky, saying against me, "Oh, Lin-wai, that was wonderful, wonderful! That was the first time for me."

"Kwelin," I said into her eyes, "that could have been the first time for me, too."

Hand-in-hand, smelling of damp clothes, we walked back to the sleeping Fifth.

But Muchai was not sleeping. He was standing a little distant from the medical cart, and as we passed him he bowed deep, whispered to me, "Now that, Chan Lin-wai, was quite delightful business . . ."

Clearly he had been at his morality spying again, but I could not accuse him because Kwelin was near. I envied his apparent ability to be in two places at once, and I said with unveiled sarcasm, "I am pleased that you approve, Muchai."

"Oh yes, indeed – most certainly – she will make a really charming wife." He smiled apologetically, "Besides, for one like me who is beyond the charms of women, I naturally find it more than a little entertaining . . ."

Neither was Yung sleeping. His eyes were black with shadow in the moonlight, his cheeks hollowed and flushed, his tunic tented pathetically over his wasted body. He said, bitterly:

"Where the hell have you been – Pipa's been asking for you – she's been in pain!"

"Naturally she'll have discomfort at times," answered Kwelin, calmly.

"Discomfort? She was biting her fingers."

Pipa was asleep when I reached her. One of the wounded had his arm protectively over her. Kwelin said, later, "She has had a show, Lin-wai, you realise this?"

I nodded. Kwelin said, "I cannot understand it – unless she is confused about the dates – is the child really Yung's?"

I did not reply to this. She continued, "I tell you again, it *must* be a seven-month child; Pipa did not meet Yung until early November."

I said, crisply, "We will not mark it off on a calendar; obviously it is a premature baby. If her troubles continue I shall take her to Dr. Nelson Fu."

Next morning Pipa was up and about again, helping Yung to organise the sick parade. Later, she walked over the fields with him, all quite naturally, gathering camellias.

The next day was known as the Day of the Camellias. The rocky peaks of the Sikang range glittered in the early sun: still the column rested while the vanguard, disengaged for once, closed up.

The brilliance of the morning brought people to see the ocean of red, pink and white camellias that lay around the Fifth and to the north as far as the eye could stretch.

First came the Assault Cadre, their outpost guard relieved, then the Headquarter clerks appeared; the Young Vanguards came in a body of scores, accompanied by the Communist League: from all directions, leaving the column, people came flocking to see the camellias.

The Central Committee came – even the austere Revolutionary Council; the grim, anti-Imperialist body arrived. On their stallions the Fifteenth Mohammedans galloped up with pennants flying, prelude to the arrival of General Peng of the Third and his staff: with him was Lin Piao and his aides of the First Corps. All stood in wonder, gazing at an ocean of camellias, opening to a sudden rush of the sun.

"My grandma's teeth," said Jo-kei, "it needs a bunch of flowers to make the Fifth important – look who's coming now."

We stood decently by the carts, holding the mules as Chu Teh walked up with his new wife, Kang – she who commanded a brigade of soldiers and fought like a man, an amazon among women. Ying-chao, the wife of Chou En-lai, followed with her friend, Tsai Chang – both transparently beautiful – in the middle stages of tuberculosis. Otto Braun arrived, on his legs for once, strutting with Prussian elegance, waving happily at our glowering muleteers.

"Mules are fine creatures for once, eh, my lucky?" cried

Shao Shan, waddling up with her baby, her husband, Man Kim following her. "Cheer up, lads, you look miserable to death," and she joined Ho, the wife of Mao Tse-tung, who was carrying her baby girl.

Many people I didn't know existed came to see the camellia fields on that summer morning, and a faint cheer gathered up and down the line as Mao Tse-tung appeared with his batman. Inscrutable, isolated amid the laughter and happiness, Mao was a man captured by thought, not the least interested in camellias.

Then, with Pipa and Kwelin leading them, the women began picking the blossoms at will, chattering to each other, holding up for inspection flowers of unbelievable hues. Within minutes every soldier of the Fifth was picking camellias.

I said to Kwelin, "If Chiang bombs us now there'll be a slaughter."

"If he can find us," said she.

For camellias were now a camouflage – stuck in the barrels of rifles, in sun umbrellas, tied in clusters to the ends of coolie-poles, bound to the ears of mules and donkeys, decorating ammunition carts: even the wounded lay with great bouquets of them, waving from the carts. The long-range artillery plaited them around the muzzles and tied them to the spokes of limber-wheels; Shao Shan even made her baby girl a cradle of them with spider grass. Ho, Mao's wife, was a walking pillar of flowers, holding up her child for all to see. In the end even Mao had a camellia stuck in the peak of his cap, grinning as he made his way back to Headquarters with Chou.

Later, when the bugles sounded the advance, the entire Red Army began to move like a decorated cobra through a land of flowers; the cart-wheels revolved in blurs of colours; and the energetic Political Scouts flashed the message by heliograph from the summit of Fire Mountain – the army, from that height, they said, was impossible to identify.

So we moved along the valley of the Sikang Range under a brilliant sun and an azure sky and the wind was perfumed; heading for the plains that led north to Anshungchang, and the Bridge of Chains.

For three days we marched unharassed by bombers. Pipa, during this time, was surprisingly well, with no signs of labour.

235

But I was becoming increasingly worried: if she intended to have a premature child I would rather she had it in the peace of the Sikang valley.

Now, clear of the mountains, our movements easily detected, bombing would again begin.

"Worse," muttered Jo-kei, "there could be a panic dash for the Tatu River."

Things were far too quiet, and I didn't like it: the pursuing Kuomintang who had hammered at us for over 5,000 miles were scarcely likely, in my opinion, to give up now.

The Magic of the Million Fish delayed us further.

There runs, on this Tibetan border area, a narrow river, a feeder to the flower riot of the Sikang valley. Here the column stopped again for the people to cleanse themselves of dirt and lice, and bathe their scabies. Therefore, an Order of the Day ordered the women to stay in isolation while the soldiers bathed and washed their clothes. The wounded – those who could be moved – were to be lifted out of the medical carts and washed on the river banks.

Kwelin said, "Well, I have seen one without his trousers – I take it they're all alike?"

I replied, "Obey official regulations – into the cart with Pipa, please."

She said, with an impish look, "The rules must have changed a bit since that walk among the camellias!"

"Do it for me," said Muchai, seeing her protests. "Consider my modesty and great age," and he laced up the canvas of Tojo's cart behind her.

Jo-kei joined us then, also Yung, Bricko and Kau Kau, and the man from Kwangtung: Little Ball and Trip were with us, I remember, also Shang Chi-pang, whom the boys called Prick: even Political Chang, at a distance and most shyly, removed his clothes as ordered: Muchai, his elongated body lean and well-muscled, was becoming pronouncedly plump, a contrast with Jo-kei's amazing loss of weight. Wong the Corpulent waddled along the river bank patting his stomach. All down the line naked men splashed into the cold, clear water of the Shi-ho River.

Bricko was the first to make acquaintance with the phenomenon; astonished, he stood waist deep holding up a fish: even

236

as I watched, he lifted out another – two silver crescents wriggling in his hands – a kilo each if they were an ounce.

Along the river fell silence.

Men were standing motionless, picking out fish; silver fish, golden fish – fish straight and long, chubby fish like those I used to catch as a boy in Laoshan.

Then Big One and Hu, Tenga's son wading in beside me, picked out more, staring at the light-spray from their hands. Something touched my body and I looked down into the crystal water. From my ankles to my thighs I was surrounded with fish, stubbing their noses against my skin, almost in a caress as if discovering the warmth of Man.

A buzz of disbelief spread down the river. This grew into awe; then realisation came to the soldiers – the fish were giving themselves up in friendship. Shouts grew into yells of excitement, for we had not tasted fish in months. Men were throwing the silver bodies out on to the river bank where they danced and leaped in the sun. Men were plunging their hands into the water and bringing out more and more. I was doing it myself – one had only to open a hand and a fish would jump into it.

Frightened by the shouts of men, the hooped canopy of Tojo's cart went back and the scared face of Pipa appeared: Shao Shan, ignoring regulations, came striding down the bank to investigate, picking up fish and examining them in disbelief. In the Fifth sector alone hundreds were caught, leaping out of the water as if to attract attention.

Years later, when the March was but a memory, Mao Tse-tung was asked for the most impressionable incident that happened between Juichin and Yenan.

"It's difficult to answer," he replied after thought, "but considering it all, I suppose it was the fish. It is hard to believe, but in one river – I forget where it was – they actually leaped into our hands."

We dried them in salt by the *picul*, loading them into the carts. It proved a very grave mistake.

TWENTY-FIVE

The call for speed came earlier than I expected; it was raced down the line by galloping couriers from General Headquarters while the animals were already under the whip. It read:

> Undetected enemy forces in large numbers have arrived east of Mapien and are moving north; already they have an advantage. The race is on for the Tatu Bridge. Failure to cross there will mean a long detour. Make all speed. Unfit animals will be slaughtered, their carcases poisoned. Leave nothing to the enemy: Ninth and Fifth Corps now also heavily engaged.
>
> Mao Tse-tung (Political Commissar, Headquarters)
>
> Distribution down to regiments; read and destroy.
> 24th May, 1935.

Had he told the truth the Political Commissar might have added that we had spent too long gathering camellias in the Sikang Mountains, and that failure to cross Liu's Bridge of Iron Chains into North China would mean the massacre of the entire Red Army – some 40,000 men.

Seventy years before more than twice this number of heroic Taiping rebels had been slaughtered at the very same place.

"A man can die but once," said Muchai. "In the same earth as one's ancestors is as good a place as any."

Now the summer sun burned down in regal splendour, flashing off the hides of the sweating animals, withering the remaining blossom of anemone and camellia. We did not trot, the usual pace of speed, but raced across the verdant country in the valley of the Anning Ho River sparkling along the foothills of Taliang Shan, the Guardian of Tibet. And, as the whips came lashing down, the wagons of the Fifth lurched and swung along the rutted roads to the commands of the Red Cadre troopers racing alongside, urging us on.

All that day we ran, stopping only when the mules, horses

and donkeys were exhausted; their breath back, they doused their heads into water, drank greedily and were dragged up again for the whip. Never had Tojo been so treated, and I hated myself for it. Rumour had it down the line that some drovers and carters were tipping the ends of their whips with wire and that others were prodding at created raws, which was against regulations – until it was officially ordered.

At dusk that day we were still at the gallop, spurred on by the Red Cadres who cracked their short mule-whips over any back handy: standing up in the saddle, cursing us, reviling us in the name of misbegotten mothers. At times we stopped the carts, being far ahead of the gasping infantry, men who could trot fifty miles with cat-naps before flinging themselves down to sleep where they stopped. These were the peasants of the curiously bouncing shoulder-poles; they covered ground at an astonishing speed.

In the first seventeen hours we covered eighty-eight miles: within the next twenty-four hours, by running and sleeping and eating on the march, we covered nearly ninety miles, and this through rocky terrain. This allowed the small enemy garrison in Anshunchang to be captured whilst playing *mahjongg* in their quarters. Miraculously, a ferry boat near the town was found moored on the south bank of the Tatu River; it was immediately seized by Red Cadre men, and a small force began to cross to the east bank. Thus, beyond Anshunchang, where the Tatu narrowed in her steep gorges, we were able to call to each other on the march. At night, now forfeiting all hope of surprise, we marched in parallel forces, our torches sending slanted red light on to the swirling river between us.

Jo-kei gasped, "It looks all right, but there's only a fraction of us on the south bank; we still need the Tatu Bridge if nine-tenths of us are to cross."

It was the last thing I heard before Pipa cried out in Tojo's lurching cart: her cry echoed over the river: men on the east bank actually stopped to listen to a woman's scream.

Kwelin said, in gasping haste, "I'm not surprised. I wonder she's stood it so long."

The column was still travelling at a fast walking pace, so we pulled Tojo's cart out of the line and lifted Pipa out. Things were so confused that I do not recall the exact chain of events:

to my knowledge she had been in labour for over twenty hours, and I had endured the groans coming from the back of the cart as it bucked and lurched at speed, and had known self-loathing.

Now, the moment after I swung Tojo out of the column there came a hoarse shout:

"What the hell are you doing? Get that cart back in line!"

A horse came galloping up from the distance. I ignored it as the rider wheeled around us.

Yung and I lifted Pipa over the back-board and laid her down on to the grass, and torches went up, flaring red about us. The horseman shouted down to us, "Get back into line! What the hell is happening?"

It was Commander Hsiao; he who had sent Fool into the Chouping Fort.

Yung said, "It is my wife; she is with child. She's not birthing in a ditch like an animal."

"That's right – fug off," said Bricko, and I saw the murder in his face as the torches sparkled. Jo-kei came, then, grim and purposeful, pushing Bricko aside, saying, "Is it the girl?"

Kwelin said, "She is near her time; she can't ride in that thing."

"Then get it back in the column," shouted Hsiao, furious.

Jo-kei said, "Nurse, get blankets out of the cart – all you need. We'll leave you the canopy – will a tent do, Lin-wai?"

I nodded, supporting Pipa's head. She was writhing in my arms. Bricko, kneeling, was saying, "Oh, you poor little woman ..." Jo-kei said, looking at the sky, "Right, the cart goes back into line, but the tent stays."

"There's wounded men in that cart," shouted Hsiao.

"Yes, and I'll transfer them." He grabbed the mare's bridle. "Now get out of it – these are my people – go and see to yours."

Magically, the hooped canopy was lifted over us; the night was obliterated as the gaps came down. In momentary darkness before Bricko carried in an oil-lamp, I heard Commander Hsiao shout above the rumbling carts. "Right – for now, Sergeant. But I'll see you at Tatu for disobeying orders." And I heard Bricko whisper at the door, "I'll bloody see you long 'afore that, mister," and he knelt again, taking Pipa's hand.

"Bricko, you go," I said.

"She was decent to Bricko ..."

"There is enough here – go."

I heard Kwelin say, "Lin, I think she's fainted."

Pipa's clothes, from waist to ankles, were heavy with blood she could not afford to lose. Yung stared at me, his eyes glittering with fever on the other side of the lamp. Kwelin said to him, "Yung, go with Jo-kei, it would be better . . ."

"I shall not leave her." The lamplight glowed in the caverns of his cheeks.

I said, "Best go, Yung."

He covered his face. Above Pipa's gasps I heard the obscene noises of the army, clattering hooves, whip-cracks; thundering wheels that shook the ground beneath her. Pale moonlight filtered through the open flap of the tent.

Kwelin said, "The neck of the uterus is scarcely opened, yet she's been in labour for more than twenty hours . . ."

"Nearer thirty," whispered Yung, still staring at me.

Kwelin brought red hands from under the blanket. "Look – see for yourself – it's no wider than three fingers."

I said to Yung, "Look, we can't work with you here, man – wait outside." He obeyed, first kissing Pipa's face; at the door he said "Save her for me . . . It doesn't matter about the baby."

"Go," I said.

Pipa was bleeding freely; Kwelin tried to staunch it with gauze her eyes calm in the wavering light. She whispered "She can't stand much of this, you know – you'll have to operate."

I was afraid, and Kwelin knew it. The intermittent nature of the pains, natural in the case of a first child, had misled me. Now I knew that their root cause was some obstruction; a deformity other than of the pelvis. One thing was certain, she would die if I let her continue like this. Kwelin said:

"She's conscious, Lin . . ."

"Give me two seeds," I said.

"Will her heart stand it?"

"We've got to take the chance. I don't want her conscious in the middle of this."

Kwelin opened Pipa's lips and pressed two opium seeds into her mouth. Grimly, I wondered what Political Chang would have made of it.

Together, we knelt there, staring at Pipa's white face; the home-made pill was rapid; the opium began to slow the twisting of her fingers.

Kwelin was baring the abdomen for the knife; it was all so

hopelessly inefficient – a far cry from the formal whiteness of the operating theatre and the precise, muffled voice of the surgeon. I tried desperately to recapture the rules of abdominal landmarks, the length of the incision, its precise location. Opium, I knew, was a poor substitute for anaesthetic by inhalation, but there was no alternative; to operate without deep sleep would inflict a dangerous shock. Vaguely, I remembered the voice of the instructing surgeon . . . "most difficulties are experienced in making the uterine incision too small . . . to pull the child by force can result in irregular laceration . . ." This, he added, is a fault general to the inexperienced; the perfect incision being about an inch and a half to the right of the navel and some six inches long . . . "I commend you to speed. Speed is the essence, the most important factor. . ."

Kwelin had swabbed the cutting area with disinfectant; she offered the scalpel, but I did not see her. She said softly, "Are you all right?"

I took the knife.

The danger would come, of course, immediately after the incision, especially if the placenta was situated immediately beneath; I had already decided to proceed with all speed and so reduce the complications. I heard myself say, "Gauze ready."

"Ready," said Kwelin.

Pipa began to snore defiantly, moving her sweating face from side to side. I said aloud, "The uterus is usually rotated to the right . . ."

"As quickly as you can," said Kwelin.

"Ready, then, and pack the gauze around the uterus . . ."

"You'll not bring it out?"

"No." I added, "Have you another seed in case it brings her round?"

"Two," said Kwelin.

I was sweating badly as I measured for the place of incision; lamp-heat in that confined place was sweeping over me in waves of increasing intensity. It seemed impossible that I should be kneeling here under a tent in the middle of nowhere operating on my half-sister, when, not nine months ago, we were lovemaking in Shengsu, 5,000 miles away: performing an operation I had never before seen beyond the confines of a lecture room in Shanghai University. Caesarean by the classical method, and not very classical, either, with few facilities, under impossible conditions. All about me was the numbing music of the marching army, the cracking of whips, the hoarse shouts of the drovers. It all seemed futile; the predicament I faced assaulted my senses so that I longed for escape. But Kwelin was there, unruffled; as if cutting out this child was the simplest act in the world. She distilled anger in me, yet confidence. Suddenly, she said:

"You haven't done this before, have you?"

I closed my eyes.

"You can do it, Lin," she said, "you'll be all right."

She was actually smiling.

I made the incision in the abdominal wall; and then deep through the thick muscle wall of the uterus; blood and water instantly gushed over my hands. Kwelin spread the gauze wide, packing it swiftly around the uterus; the bleeding lessened. Inserting fingers, I cut upwards, enlarging the incision; the membranes did not bulge through the incision because of the effluence of the water. The placenta was beneath my fingers. Pipa groaned and gasped.

"She's coming round," said Kwelin.

"Another seed, quick."

Blood was over the pair of us; never had I seen a woman bleed like this. Panic surged within me and I fought it down, slipping in my fingers below the placenta edge; if I ruptured this she would die of septicaemia.

So intent was I on swabbing with Kwelin that I was astonished to see a human foot appear, almost immediately to vanish; my fingers within again, I found the leg, seized it and drew out the baby. Kwelin made a little soprano sound, reached over me and grasped the uterus; then with her other hand reached into the uterus and pulled out the placenta and membranes. Swiftly washing her hands, she returned and closed the uterus and then I stitched the wound with horse-hair sutures, all we had. We did not speak. The umbilical cord Kwelin had already tied and severed; now she left me, working with silent speed.

The baby girl cried the instant Kwelin had cleaned her mouth.

Hearing this, Yung came rushing in.

"She's done you well," cried Kwelin, holding up the baby. "Here, Yung, take your baby daughter." She glanced at me.

Wonder was in his face; his arms were trembling as he took the child.

Kwelin said, businesslike, "And if you're very careful, you

can wash her while we see to Pipa – there's warm water in that bowl."

"And Pipa . . . ?"

I said, "You wash your baby, Pipa will be all right."

Momentarily, in the excitement, we were distracted from the tasks in hand. Yung carried the baby to the lamplight, peering into her face.

"Toiya . . ." he said softly, "that is what we will call her – *Toiya*."

Kwelin whispered to me, "Lin-wai . . . quick!"

Her face was stark white; a nerve in her temple beat violently. I found Pipa's pulse. Yung rose slowly to his feet.

"She lost too much," whispered Kwelin. "The shock was too great."

Pipa had died.

TWENTY-SIX

With Lin Piao's First Division advancing at speed along the River Tatu's opposite bank, the Third continued the race to the Bridge of Chains, the most vital obstacle of the March. But before Jo-kei returned for us with a cart, Yung, Kwelin and I buried Pipa clear of the column in a quiet bank of camellias.

Yung said, in the darkness, "Do not touch her again, Chan Lin-wai – I will carry my wife," and he took the baby Toiya from dead Pipa's arms and put her in the arms of Kwelin, asking, "You are a virgin, Nurse Kwelin?"

He stared into her face with blank enquiry: the army clanked past, the infantry cursing obscenely. Kwelin said:

"I am not a virgin."

"Yet you are unmarried?" He glared at me, then at Kwelin, adding, "Take care then, now I have washed her, that you do not touch my baby's face with your fingers."

In Yung's fevered eyes was a hint of madness. Kwelin bowed her head.

"In the name of perdition, man, get on with it!" I replied, and gripped Kwelin's shoulder.

It was the old hoodoos raising their ancient heads; old wives' tales of Chekiang, akin to Tenga's rag-doll god: even in my grief I reflected on the need to cleanse China of such lamentable beliefs.

Kneeling, Yung lifted Pipa against him; gasping, he held her, an amazing show of strength for a dying man, and said. "Now go for trenching shovels, and we will bury her. She has suffered so much; I am not having her pestered more, dead or alive, by this accursed march."

With trenching shovels, we followed Yung away from the marching army. He no longer carried Pipa in his arms, for this wearied him, but over his shoulder so that her arms hung down behind him, and her hair, once so lovely in the moonlight of the Shengsu cottage, trailed tangled and lifeless.

In this manner, with Yung still leading, we came to a quiet

place of bushes where bright camellias blossomed, and, as if considering us, the moon came out, painting the night silver.

We did not speak as we began to dig. Presently there came the sound of galloping, and Jo-kei and Muchai arrived with a cart and pony: Bricko also came, and the man from Kwangtung, and he went up to Kwelin, I recall, and took her shovel, first kissing her.

We did not speak as we dug Pipa's grave, but, in deference to Yung's wishes concerning the location and direction of the grave, fulfilled the demands of good *Feng Shui*, this being the Buddhist custom.

Therefore, we positioned Pipa in accordance with the Farmer's Calendar, which required that her head should point to the west and her feet to the east. Many unfortunate Divinities were resident at that time in the south and north.

Then Yung collected the little money we had (Jo-kei turning out his with ill-concealed regret) and tied the coins in a little red handkerchief, a most fortunate colour, red being lucky: kneeling, he crossed Pipa's arms on her breast and put the money in her hands: thus she would know some measure of independence, said he, on her journey to the Afterworld.

We had little else to give her, in our tribute to Yung's Buddhist beliefs.

Kwelin had a comb, and this she broke in half; one half she kept, the other half she put in Pipa's hair, symbolising the severance of all ties with a woman's mortal life. Bricko gave his drinking mug, placing it on Pipa's stomach since, in the Afterlife, women, as an expiation, have to drink all the water they have wasted in this one. Therefore, he first punctured the bottom of the cup, to mitigate this punishment. I, being Pipa's next of kin after Yung, found a white camellia, and this I put in her hair.

She looked beautiful, lying there in the grave, sprinkled with summer flowers we gathered by the light of the moon.

Yung knelt, kissing her lips.

"Goodbye, my precious," he said.

But, being my sister, it was not in accordance with respect for the dead that I should kiss her. Instead, I remembered the brightness of the moon over the cottage in Shengsu.

On this, the 28th of May, 1935, I recorded in my diary:

Pipa is dead. I can find no words to express my sadness, But my child, whom Yung christened Toiya, is alive: Yung appears turned to stone. Jo-kei and the others (who returned for us) buried her among the camellias of the Sikang plains. Yung will not allow the child out of his arms. I record here, lest none of us survive this march, that Toiya is mine; she is of Chan blood. I can write no more.

(The road to Anshunchang.)

Rejoining the Fifth in time for a brief halt, the torches on the west bank of the Tatu River were greater than 10,000, burning in the darkness like the incinerating souls of Taiping rebels of eighty years before. The camp-fire flickered into a glow beneath the rice-pot, red on Muchai's ancient face, and he lowered his bowl, belched and patted his chest.

"You still keep going, eh, old Bony?" cried Bricko, treble, "the old sod do eat for six, see?"

"It is essential that the stomach is well lined," said Muchai. "Lin-wai's medical attention and Bricko's rice will serve me until I get to Yenan, then I shall lay me down to die, being older than Confucius."

"I shall die on some high place, apparently, but not on the Bridge of Chains," said the man from Kwangtung.

We all looked up at this.

I thought I heard Pipa say, "You do not much flatter the woman who is your slave, Lin-wai . . ."

Hu, Tenga's son, was sitting in Big One's arms, eyes bright, ears shivering, being among men; and Big One held him like a mother bear at feed. Jo-kei said, "If the bullet stops you on the flat, Kwangtung, I shall wipe my bottom on your soul's premonitions."

"Last evening the Old Weaver of Sikang told me," replied the man from Kwangtung. "I am far too sensible to concern myself with mere folly."

"Come off it, man, you're worse than bloody Tenga."

"More than one the Weaver named. He was a mystic and his head was shaved, and I sat with him by the Shi-ho while the rest of you bathed."

"History is unimpressive without its dates," observed Muchai. "Didn't your Old Weaver give you these?"

"He gave me more," said the man from Kwangtung. " 'This peasant revolt of Mao Tse-tung' said he, 'has for its slogan *Share the Land*, and that was the slogan of the old Taipings.' "

I said, "It is not the only thing we have in common."

"Therefore, history will repeat itself at the Tatu River. 'Turn back,' he said. 'You will die in the Tatu by drowning.' "

Political Chang, sitting down in the circle, said, "Later, when we arrive at Yenan, I will come and collect this agent of the Kuomintang."

"No agent, Chang; the man was a mystic."

"I suppose," said Jo-kei drily, "that he gave you a list of names."

"He gave many – of those who are about to die."

"Me, for instance?" asked Jo-kei.

"You, for one."

Jo-kei looked disconcerted.

"Excellent," said Muchai, "now I shall see the back of him."

"You will not," came the reply. "Your name, old scholar, he gave second."

"How did your sister die?" Political Chang asked me later.

"He gave her opium!" said Yung, still weeping.

"Do you have proof of that?" asked Jo-kei.

Yung shrieked, his eyes wild, "Of course he gave her opium – he always gives them opium!"

"But were you *there*?" asked Jo-kei. "Did you actually see him give the opium?"

"But that is how she died!"

Jo-kei pushed Yung aside. "Off with ye man – only the surgeon can tell you how she died."

I heard Yung say, swaying above the grave. "Remember me, Chan Lin-wai! You killed the only decent thing I ever possessed."

It was Bricko, I believe, who broke the silence, and the man from Kwangtung said:

"Of all sitting here, three will live to see Yenan, and they will walk on flowers – this was the Weaver's message."

As the bugles rose up in scrambling haste, I said to him, "Now stop it – you are doing nobody a service."

"I have already recorded every word he said," added Political Chang.

The man from Kwangtung turned to me. "Of my friends who will live, you are one, Chan Lin-wai. Also, the Weaver saw in the glass a giant man and a child, a woman and a baby. How does that suit you?"

I left him; it was a poor time for magic; thumping Tojo out of her dream of sun and pastures, I pulled her into the line.

This was one good friend I would remember who would never walk on flowers.

Waiting in line for the bugled *Advance*, I reflected on what the Old Weaver had told. I made no sense of it. Of one thing only I was sure – much as I grieved for Pipa, much as I commiserated with Yung in his great sorrow, if the two of us reached Yenan alive, Toiya would be mine.

"You've still got your child, be thankful," said Political Chang. Jo-kei, I noticed, also glanced up at this; we were more than a little surprised at the absence of politics.

"O, *P'an ku*, pity me," said Yung, and went full length before them all, and wept.

But I could not weep.

In all my loss, I could not weep for Pipa.

Her grave, I recalled, we had filled with pink and white camellias; we did not speak while we dug that grave; there was no sound but the marching army, the treble sweeps of the trenching shovels, the bass thunder of the dropping earth; and Pipa said, "Could you not tell me that my lips are carmine, my skin like jade . . .?"

The army was beginning to stir from rest; Young Vanguards were racing past us with pamphlets; distantly, a bugle sounded. Soon it would sound the *Advance*.

The man from Kwangtung continued, "He told me, this old Weaver, of many rebellions – of the *Red Eyebrow* rebellion of 2,000 years ago at the time of the Emperor Wang, who put it down with slaughter. And, in the following twenty centuries, said he, there have been dozens of peasant rebellions all over China – the *Red Eyebrows*, the *Yellow Turbans* and the great

White Lotus rebellions, to name but three. Last of all was the *Great Peace* rebellion of the Old Taipings, whose footsteps we are tracing now."

"Just hark at that for bloody education!" cried Bricko, then wept.

But still I could not weep.

I heard Yung say, from a great distance, "You bastard, Linwai, you *bastard*, you killed her . . ."

"It would be better," said Kwelin later, touching my face, "if you could weep for this sister as Yung weeps for his wife."

I said, "I can only make tears for my mistakes. I am not a surgeon; I will never be a surgeon. Yung is right, for once; I killed her."

She turned me to face her. "You did not, neither by surgery nor opium. Pipa was dead from the moment she conceived – perhaps not even in a hospital would they have saved her, let alone on this filthy march." She peered at me in the light of a lamp. "But you loved her, Lin?"

"Once I loved her; now she is gone, I pity that love."

Kwelin said, with a smile, "It is enough, then, that you loved her once – think on that. Meanwhile my love for you should help you bear the loss, you think?"

The bugles sounded.

Now the goads were out, the raws created. It was a race for life to the Bridge of Chains. It was the Day of the Pointed Sticks.

With the First Corps ambushed and stopped on the Tatu's western bank, we lost sight of them under fire from the opposite side as we raced full pelt in thundering wheels and hooves. I refused the goad for Tojo, but I beat her as never before to keep her in the line. The speed was madness – we would never keep it up. In desperation, the Sixth infantry clung to the carts; to lighten load for them we stopped after an hour to off-load the wounded, with orderlies to defend them until we returned.

The order was now to secure the Luting bridge; nothing must supersede this order. Every Young Vanguard who galloped down the line was yelling, "Faster, faster, *faster!*" and the cracking of the whips rose above the wailing animals.

Men were falling with heart attacks; others, clear of the track, swayed off into a wilderness of mountains, their reason gone. When exhaustion halted the animals, more drovers came down the line with fresh relays of whips. Never have I seen animals suffer as these who carried us to the Bridge of Chains.

"Look!" shouted Kwelin. "Look!" and she pointed.

Gasping infantry were lying in the cart behind her. Holding Tojo straight with the reins, I followed the direction of her finger. On the other side of the river a mass of men and carts were galloping – part of the Kuomintang army that had stopped our First Corps. Occasional rifle-fire spurted red from their flank in their onward plunge, but few shots found us. The order came:

"Do not return enemy fire. Get on, get on!"

And, when dawn came up red over distant mountains, we were still at it, galloping, walking, trotting, galloping.

Mao Tse-tung was determined that the Red Army would not repeat the error of the Old Taipaings. In that dawn, astonishingly, a roving detachment of tribal Lolos ambushed the vanguard, but the Red Cadre fought them off. Again, in a narrow defile in twin hills, they bravely came again, this time with allies, the tribal Fan from the other side of the Great Snow Mountain, and we heard their terrifying war-horns calling them to battle, *WUNG-G-G-G-G-G! WUNG-G-G-G-G-G!* But we pushed on, sweeping them aside, with the Assault Cadres fanning out of the line at speed, their broadswords ringing out: the Fifteenth Mohammedans came next, the pride of Tenga, a magnificent tumult of turbanned horsemen lying flat on the saddles, their pennanted spears spiking out before their shrieking stallions. The Lolos fled.

Then came the bombers. They raked us all that day in the gallop to the bridge: we paid for our rest among the camellias; and cursed the Shi-ho River and its useless fishing. Down the line of galloping horses came the bombs, driving up great plummets of brown earth, blowing over carts, cutting red swathes out of the column, the machine-gunning drilling animals and men in a fighting mêlée among the spinning wheels. Detours were made as blocks were formed in the line, and again and again, until they ran out of fuel, the Nanking bombers plastered us at will: wounded were left to die with the dead: men falling from foot-boards were trampled by hooves: ammunition carts, the most heavily laden, were dragged to one side when their wheels collapsed in spiking struts. And the message came down:

Anshunchang is eighty *li* behind us. Keep going, *keep going*. It is but twenty more to the Bridge of Chains. *Faster*.

At dawn next day, the 25th of May, we reached it: the most hazardous obstacle since the battle of the Hsiang River where we lost 50,000: the bridge built by Liu over the savage Tatu River, the Bridge of Chains, the most famous bridge in China's history.

The planning was good.

As the animals collapsed and died in the shafts; as men fell asleep beside them, the toughest of all in the Red Army, the Assault Cadres who had been riding over the past twenty miles, came past the exhausted Fifth Muleteers and again took their places in the van.

We kept our heads down to the scattering fire of an enemy pill-box on the far anchorage of the bridge.

But of the Kuomintang who had raced us on the western bank, there was not a sign.

Kwelin lay beside me under sheltering rocks, and we looked down on the fierce Tatu boiling 300 feet below.

On this bridge was written:

Towering mountains flank the Luting Bridge
Their summits rise a thousand *li* to the clouds.

Given to extravagance of phrase (no mountain in the world is 300 miles high) Liu, its builder, nevertheless had caught the essence of the scene before us.

The bridge consisted of thirteen immense strands of chain, each link made of an iron bar as thick as a rice-bowl. And now, even as we watched, its 300 foot span swayed precariously in the wind, suspended between high cliffs on either bank: its foot-planks, I saw, had been removed by the enemy from the bridge middle to the Kuomintang machine-gun nest that guarded our western approach. And, even as we peered, this was spitting bullets: cracks and ricochets echoed and whined about us.

Muchai, crawling between us, stared out with fading eyes. "Are we going over together, Kwelin? Youth and age, child – hand-in-hand?"

"Rather you than me," said she.

This, the Tatu bridge, the escape road to the north: it held in its links the fate of communism.

For this we had marched 5,000 miles; with its help we would march another 2,000 to the caves of Paoan, from there to fight the Japanese.

We had crossed the Hsiang River for this, many mountain ranges – Tiger Mountain, Fire Mountain – these were the historic names. We had swept over the River of Golden Sand, come through the land of the Miao pygmies, the Shan people, the White and Black Lolo country, swept aside the opium-soaked war-lord troops. And, if we captured the Tatu bridge where the flower of China's rebel youth had died eighty years before, we could drive north to Shensi and safety, wiping from its history the shame of the great north-west famine.

Once there, we would have covered a distance equal to twice the width of the American continent. If we failed we would share defeat with the Old Taipings and lose our place in history.

"Are you going over now?" Kwelin asked Jo-kei.

"You can keep your national heroes," said he. "Jumping that bloody thing is a job for the young Red Cadres, not a fat old muleteer."

"It all sounded plush the way you put it," I said to Muchai.

Remembering the Old Weaver, we smiled at him.

"They're asking for volunteers, did you know that?" asked the man from Kwangtung.

"Tough men, dedicated soldiers?" asked Kwelin, "You seem about the size."

He looked good, his handsome face creased up against the sun; the dawn was blood-red, flowing over the hills on a chariot of fleece. I added, "Before you executed that communist general, he cried, *China! China!* – remember, Kwangtung? You are fighting for freedom, you say, not for Mao Tse-tung? That bridge over there is a marvellous opportunity to become a hero."

"Best a live hero," he replied, grinning.

I nudged him, grinning back. "Go on – take a chance. If you go, I will."

"Not you, my darling," whispered Kwelin, pressed against me.

"After all that fortune-telling? Not on your life," said the man from Kwangtung. "I'm to expire at a decent height."

Bricko said to me, "Doctor Lin, I'd go with my Fool . . ."

The volunteers to attack the bridge were coming down from

the Assault Cadres with a very different version of the Eleven Bus Song . . .

'. . . so spin me along with a girl on my knee,
Me pugs cocked up and me hand up her trousers . . .'
I said to myself, listen to them, the men who are about to die.

The morning dragged on. Jo-kei, seething, muttered, "What the hell did horses die for?"

It was near to mutiny down the line, men said: the same old story, the inefficiency of General Headquarters. Midday came; the sun dripped fire: we sweated and cursed – Mao Tse-tung, the bloody Central Committee, Otto Braun – anyone we could put our tongues to. Under cover we waited and the wind sang melodies in the Bridge of Chains. Somebody said, coldly, and I think it was Muchai:

"They're waiting for the Kuomintang to arrive, then they'll order the attack." Nobody replied; they lolled in attitudes of listless anger, cursing the bastards up at General H.Q. – we've seen it all before.

Bricko cried, shrill, "Hey, look at what they're eating – is that bloody fair?" He handed Kwelin and me rifles: Yung, sitting alone in a hollow, was diligently cleaning his.

Salt pork, a *catty* a man, said someone else, the greedy sods!

"And me a death volunteer?" cried a soldier from the Second Company, his legs cocked up. "Come off it, Eunuch, I gotta eat something to die on."

"Fug me," said Bricko.

They lounged about, ridiculing it all with planned arrogance.

I crawled from cover to the ruined wall, privileged to see them.

There were only twenty-two of them – big men, blood Chinese cast in the same womb-mould, quarried not born. They were square-faced fellows of narrowed eyes and shining teeth, their voices rough with banter – one victim after another of their group selected for the barbs of their obscene humour.

"Chi's got a girl up in Tientsin country, you heard?"

"It's a cold job, lad, jigging up there."

"Mind, he were better wi' the bawdy girls down in Singhi, though – fathered half the country, that right, Chi?"

"Now he's waiting for Chang Kuo-tao's 2,000 virgins."

"He'll do 'em as fast as they can pull 'em from under him, eh, cock?"

They bantered, cursed and swore profanely; they drew lots upon the future; two were writing home; one, a little way clear, was praying to a tiny red altar.

They were yellow-faced men of friendships, not the isolated, professional killers of the Red Cadre who took the Golden Sand, but standard Red Army soldiers, if the cream; they didn't molest women, they didn't kill prisoners; they spoke with regal understatement. Some were playing the finger-game like children, with big knives strapped to their putties and stick-grenades sticking out of their belts. Wandering among them was their platoon-commander, Commander Ma Ta-chiu, the finest soldier I have known.

This was he who had shaken the hand of Fool.

This was the soldier with the idiot father back in Fukien who had sired him well: the only idiot was China.

It began to rain.

The machine-gunners on the west bank were stepping up the fire; the Second Company crouched behind the wall, their faces taut, eager: behind them was their sister-company, the Third; these were fighting men also, but each man carried a plank to lay across the naked chains to repair the bridge flooring. Before them the iron links glistened above the roaring Tatu 300 feet below, that reached up white arms for the butchery of soldiers. Quills of tracer were streaking off the chains as the Kuomintang raked the bridge, splinters of wood flew up from the planks on the enemy left bank. Suddenly, there was a shout, and I eased back my rifle and raised my head above the wall. A suicide squad of Kuomintang infantry had run to the middle of the bridge, pouring kerosene on to the planks; they burned in quick, scarlet spurts, covering the bullet-spattered retreat of the men in smoke.

Young Vanguards were scuttling behind me, ducking to the whistling bullets; I counted a dozen of the boys, and each had a bugle to his lips as he lay behind the wall. And then, above the quickening small arms fire I heard the voice of Commander Ma Ta-chiu:

"We are going over . . . wait, men wait . . ."

A pause, then, "*Over!*" he yelled.

Twenty-two bodies hurtled over the wall. The Vanguards, lying on their backs, bugled a discordant blast. Vaulting boulders, the wreckage of bombed carts, leaping into a fusillade of enemy fire, the men of the Second charged down the slopes to the chain anchorages; some fell immediately, others leaped over them; I saw Ma Ta-chiu already on the lowest chain, miraculously swinging along it hand over hand, his fore-arms driving furiously through the links. Another followed, then another. A line of men were dangling over the river, and the air was suddenly charged with a chord of bullets and ricochets; the chains alive with blazes and sparks as the round struck. The Vanguards still blasted out a chorus: our staccato fire, small and accurate on the machine-gun nest, converged into a sustained, ear-splitting roar. The one-pounders barked behind us, shooting out their two-yard flames; a mile down the road the big two-point-fives pierced the thunder with deep-throated concussions: dirt, bricks, timber rose above the machine-gun nest on the north-east bank. The air choked with cordite; smoke rolled over the bridge; a blanket of fire as incendiary bombs struck the distant planks; the nationalist 'planes were bombing now, trying, belatedly, to destroy the bridge.

Then the Third followed in, crouched low, swerving with their replacement planks; mortars shredded the bridge approaches. I saw a man fall at the moment of mutilation, a plank and a head blowing sideways into the drop: men were shouting in shrill falsetto: Young Vanguards, disdainful of cover, leaped above the wall before anyone could stop them and rushed, flinging themselves down and rolling on their backs, short-blasting their bugles, the tempo of attack. Yung cried beside me:

"Ma's off! The commander's off!"

I actually saw him fall. And, as he fell I heard his voice, some unintelligible shout that belonged to China. The machine-gun nest, alive again, got the range; another man fell, another: in the space of seconds I counted five – into the rushing Tatu below, and still no man had gained the middle, where the planks were burning. More men fell shouting to their deaths, but others took their place, leaping into space, grabbing the snaking chains. The ground beneath me shuddered to distant booming of twelve-pounders: the enemy west bank was alive with sheets of flame – nothing could have lived in the inferno. Then, suddenly, at the very height of the enemy bombardment, the head and shoulders of a man appeared miraculously on the burning foot-boards of the Kuomintang side. He fell, then scrambled to his feet, plunging through the flames with his cap and hair on fire. Others followed this Commander Kiao of the Third. I saw them weaving in and out of the fires as they ran after him in quick swerves for the machine-gun post. Then all went flat as the west gate of the city, standing just beyond the distant bridge approach, suddenly detonated in a sheet of orange light: kerosene bins were ablaze, enveloping the end of the bridge. Men were falling off in squads now, toppling into the river as enemy small arms drilled them.

I glanced to my right: Kwelin was kneeling, squinting over the wall, loosing off rapid-fire with lightning knack-twists of her little breech-loader, an astonishing expertise. Yung, amazingly, was firing on my left, his frail shoulder leaping to the kicks of the butt. Beyond him was a jumble of Sixth infantry, shooting in broadsides at a command: near them, the big Shao Shan her baby elsewhere, loaded an ancient machine-gun with Man Kim, her tiny husband. Bricko and Muchai were there, as was Jo-kei, staring over the shattered wall, rubbing his beard in some distant contemplation, and I wondered what he was up to. Political Chang was with Wong the Corpulent, a replacement muleteer: beside him stood the man from Kwangtung: exposed to the waist, he was calmly sniping from the top of the wall, amid a song of ricochets. Beyond him, in a sudden fusillade, I saw Tojo's medical long-cart, its side-canvas rolled up and rifles projecting – even the wounded were firing from their litters.

As I knelt there in a hammering confusion, the swirling cordite, the personal explosions of my big, single-shot Ku-passa, I knew an inborn pride that banished the desperate weariness of the march; a growing exultation. I was one with these people in a community where loneliness ceased; something greater than the prosaic business of staying alive. The comradeship snatched me up and I suddenly shouted with joy while engaged as a healer in the crass art of killing.

And then I remembered another.

Remembering her drove me from my instant present, and I turned to the long-cart, shouting fearfully:

"Pipa!"

A hand came out and fastened on my arm. In the concussive blasts of the line-firing, I swung back to her in fear.

"Pipa is not here," said Kwelin. "Only I am here," and she went on firing.

The attack was faltering. The bravest gone, the reserves before me hesitated amid the Vanguards' frantic bugling; the Third were being picked off by enemy snipers as they tried to lash the planks.

It was the fire: justifiably, they were afraid of the fire.

And, in those moments when the reserves faltered, I heard the bombing thuds of the hand-grenades from the enemy bank. Men of the Second, their clothes alight, were attacking the enemy machine-gun post. It was impossible courage. I actually saw them lying in the fires of the decking, the over-arm swings, the fly of the bombs.

And then I saw Jo-kei.

Running from cover close by, he stood momentarily in a hail of bullets and shrapnel in front of the muzzles of our own high velocity guns, and he was shouting:

"Come on, the bloody Third! Come on!" and he ran. He held no weapon save his whip; this he cracked above his head as he ran to the chains, yelling, "Muleteers, muleteers, *muleteers*!"

Kwelin shouted, "Look – Jo-kei!"

And Muchai cried near by, "Wait for me, Jo – wait for me!"

Clambering over the wall, Muchai ran, tripped, scrambled up and staggered on, shouting, "Jo-kei, Jo-kei!"

I stood up, "Come back, you old fool, *Muchai*!"

I could not stay longer. Even from there I could hear the usual wailing of the wounded down on the approach; men were twisting, turning, their arms flailing about – shot down before they set foot on the bridge. The sight of Muchai had crystallised in me the need for action. I grasped my medical pack and climbed out of cover; momentarily, I saw Kwelin's frightened face.

"I'll be back," I said.

It was like running into a wind of cats; the howls and shrieks of injured metal enveloped me. The approach was a hall of carnage, and I went flat the moment I reached it: it appeared impossible to raise one's head and survive. Through the smoke and rolling dust I saw Jo-kei. He was standing between the chain anchorages, his back to the enemy, the mule-whip curling and cracking above his head like pistol-shots; in that baying redness the very image of Tenga. Then he stooped, picked up a dropped pistol and thrust it into his belt. I saw him next in the belly of the chains, followed by a procession of attackers, dangling over the drop. Others (later I learned they were men of the Third) were already on the charred planks, stamping out the fires and spraying the machine-gun slits with bullets while the grenade-men advanced. Even as I was tending a wounded man, I saw body after body drop into the foaming river far below: one, and I saw this clearly, was actually blown off by the wind, for I saw it tearing at his clothes in the moment before it ripped him away.

Now the enemy fire was subsiding. The Third, almost unhindered, were carrying over tree logs. Explosions were decimating the enemy gun-posts; I saw scuttling, grey figures racing back to their second line of defence.

Shang Chi-pang I found then, the little Vanguard of the head-boils.

He was lying in a fold of ground, waving faintly and crying: the bugle he had brought with him had fallen from his hand. In the lessening fire I crawled to him.

"Chi-pang!" I said, but he did not hear me.

Somebody was calling me amid the din, shrieking my name, and it sounded like Muchai, but he did not call again. I put my arm under the boy's head and turned him against me, running my hand under his tunic.

My fingers were webbed with blood.

"Doctor . . ." he said.

"I am here."

"I . . . I saw the muleteers go."

"You are with the muleteers," I said. "Do not speak, Chi-pang."

The dum-dum bullet had taken him in the shoulder as he crouched in the run; splintering, it had rammed down through his chest, taking with it bone, shreds of uniform, a dreadful wound. Rolling up my instruments I put them back into my shirt.

"Look," he said, and lifted the bugle; a round had shattered the reed. He wept.

I heard him amid the obscene muttering of the guns.

"Do not speak," I said, being careful not to call him Chi-pa. Presently, he died. But I held him. Even when the other wounded, seeing me through the thinning smoke called to me, I held him; I could not let him go, and could not see him for tears.

The bridge fixed by Liu, ancient in China's warring, was taken.

It cost me Jo-kei; it cost me Muchai. Only the Tatu River cascading from the Great Snow Mountain to the Plains of Chengtu knows where they lie: in the arms of her sister Min, perhaps, under the stars of West Szechuan?

A long cry from the sedate rooms of the Whampoa Academy and the bandit lairs of Honan, where Jo-kei, fat man, held court among his concubines.

Others lost more than I: China lost her best.

Commander Ma Ta-chiu, Hero Gold Star, perished with his men: the blood deluge that won the Bridge of Chains (which could have been destroyed by the Kuomintang by a single stick of dynamite) paid for the lives of thousands more. Had this bridge not been won, the Red Army would have been forced back through Lololand and Yunnan, in order to continue north: it could have spelt the end of the Long March which paved the way to communism. The Kuomintang air force continued unsuccessfully to bomb it, even while the Red Army crossed.

It cost Chu Teh, men said, an hour of his existence: it also nearly cost him China. During the attack he did not speak; a man turned to stone.

A captured enemy Order of the Day stated:

Now is the time to eradicate the Red bandits. We will trap them like oysters in the sands of the Tatu River. Kill them to a man, but spare the leaders. These, like Prince Shih of the old Taiping rebels, we will take in carts to Chengtu, for death by cutting.

May 30th, 1935

General Liu Wen-hui,
4th Division,
Kuomintang.

TWENTY-SEVEN

We barracked but a few days in Luting City: sufficient time only to bury the dead of the Tatu fighting and help the First Division under Lin Piao drive out the enemy forces of the Kuomintang General Liu – he who had foretold our defeat. The city had been thoroughly looted by the nationalists; all food had gone; nothing had been left in the tailors' shops to buy; we would have to climb the Great Snow Mountain to reach Moukung with the tattered clothes we stood in.

And immediately the fighting vanguard began to arrive, it became heavily engaged, with a hammering Kuomintang army behind it. Furious at not having destroyed us at the Bridge of Chains, Chiang Kai-shek threw everything he possessed against us. Had we stayed to fight in Luting to the end, the civil population would have died with it. Even so, the bombing was around the clock, as great as at the Juichin Encirclement; the water supply was cut: raw sewage flowed down the streets from burst reservoirs; slowly, methodically, the city was flattened: long-range shelling added to the chaos. Chiang's armies, now out-numbering us at twelve to one, seemed more confident than ever before.

So we fought our way out of Luting, leaving behind us a shambles of a city and the hatred of its people. The man from Kwangtung said, in a lull in the bombing, "Muchai was right, Lin-wai. I often wonder if the freedom we bring to the people is bought at too high a price. They greet us with flowers and we leave them loathing us."

"They will remember us, though, at the final victory," replied Kwelin. "Peasants have been killed, but not one by our direct action, except criminals: we have not looted, we've taken nothing without permission; not a woman has been violated. We have bartered with money squeezed from landlords; burned deeds of title, re-distributed land, closed brothels, outlawed foot-binding."

I said, "Now there's a speech from a Buddhist Red!"

Kwelin replied, her eyes glowing. "The people suffer now, but they will remember us when we get to Paoan and Yenan."

"*If* we get to Yenan," said the man from Kwangtung.

For my part, as we dragged ourselves out of Luting City on that first day of June, my mood was not political; nor was I fervent in allegiance to the Party. After thousands of miles of ignominious retreat, we had escaped the fate of the Taiping rebels only to be confronted with a killing, artificial winter in the middle of summer'

Barring our retreat to the north (and our longed-for union with Chang's Fourth Army – which was executing its own Long March) was the Great Snow Mountain of over 16,000 feet.

It could be the end of many of us, certainly poor old Tojo, whom I had grown to love. Still quarrelsome and defiant, the mule now plodded with her head low, her balding hide tenting her bones.

Soon, I knew, would come the order to shoot the animals: for them a welcome death after the floggings, raws and sharpened sticks of the road from Juichin.

On the night of the 3rd of June, on the road to Yaan, I wrote in my diary:

Jo-kei and Muchai are dead: Chi-pang, too; also Tenga. Everything I possess, save Kwelin and Toiya, seems to have gone. Now we are to climb the Great Snow Mountain. It is 16,000 feet high. Mao must be mad to bring us to this. We are in rags and covered with lice; Kwelin has the most painful scabies between her legs, yet she insists on marching, and does not complain. The latest official recommendation is that we boil chillies to keep ourselves warm when we get among the glaciers! Surely Toiya will die. What baby can survive such arctic heights?

The man from Kwangtung said, "Be reasonable, we've come this far, we might as well finish it. I can't see the Kuomintang doing much pursuing up the side of the Great Snow Mountain. The move is wise."

I said, "But I can see us doing an awful lot of dying."

But the pursuit eased after we abandoned Luting to its fate – Lin Piao's First Corps had inflicted a decisive defeat on the oncoming Kuomintang; our retreating vanguard was given relief. It must have been a change for them. The average life of a communist soldier in General Lo's now famous Ninth Corps was said to be less than sixteen hours: only by the shrinkage of other corps was it kept intact. Yet the big General Headquarters still lumbered on, demanding a full army corps to protect its flanks.

"One thing's sure," said Kwelin, "it'll have to dump some of its typewriters when it comes to the Great Snow Mountain."

We feared this climb into the clouds; it was on every tongue, in every mind.

These days we had a stranger in Tojo's cart. Political Chang, having faced the enemy for the first time on the march, had managed to collect a bullet in the backside. Many were openly delighted. However, it was a bad wound; the bullet had shot away part of the hip joint, severing the sciatic nerve; I knew the agony. Apart from Yung, Chang was my only patient; all my wounded had been left behind in Luting to fight to the death – it was a singularly efficient prescription – two of them had broken backs.

Now, five days out of Luting, with the gradient increasing, the tattered vanguard stumbled towards Dream Pen Mountain, the gaunt Paotung Kang and the Chung Lai Range – all fearful obstacles: and, behind these, their glacier peaks spearing through the surly clouds, the bastions of Great Snow and Big Drum mountains challenged ascent. The June morning was bright with warm sunlight, the heat of it slanting on our backs: yet the air was cold and filled with tiny particles of ice that beat on our half-naked bodies like rain, drenching us, an amazing phenomenon.

Kwelin marched on my right, Bricko on my left at Tojo's head; behind us in the cart Political Chang was groaning, an accompaniment to Yung's continuous coughing: it was a mobile sanatorium, said Kwelin.

It was more like a mobile bomb, for we were temporarily carrying forward ammunition.

Yung was a perpetual worry to me. He was entering the final stages of his disease; blood-flecks were on the inside of the canopy, yet he insisted on nursing Toiya day and night, spending

263

his waking moment in paternal admiration, coughing into her face. I began to wonder if she would survive the coming ordeal by cold only to die of Yung's consumption. Kwelin said now, ever logical:

"Yes, but you can do nothing about it, Lin – the child is his." Sighing, she added, "Had you reported his condition in Luting, they'd have kept him behind with the wounded."

"And Toiya with him?"

"Why not?" She spread her hands at me. "The decision would have been his – he's her father." She was watching me.

I closed my eyes, trudging on, and we turned our faces to the mountains.

My baby was pretty; her name Toiya suited her: for she was tiny when I took her from Pipa's womb – scarcely five pounds, said Kwelin, balancing her on one hand.

Toiya's eyes, like Pipa's, were deep brown; her hair – and of this she had much – had the black shine that was her mother's. And Pipa had fashioned her beautifully, paying careful attention to her feet and hands, which were delicately shaped. At times, when Yung was absent and Chang groaning in sleep, I would go into the cart canopy on some pretext; there, watching for Yung's return, I would hold her in my arms, smelling her all over for the baby-smell, like the brown-faced peasant women of Laoshan do – another way of kissing. When Yung returned I would be back at Tojo's head with Kwelin, mentioning that I was even more worried about Political Chang.

Apart from Yung's coughing, it was an ideal life for a baby, being nursed all day and rocked on the march, so she rarely cried. Even the feed times were well organised; three times a day to the minute, Yung would put his head through the tent flap.

"Toiya is asking, Kwelin," he would call (he rarely spoke to me) "listen to her whimpering."

The business of calling our mobile milking mother was impressive.

Kwelin would blow on Shang Chi-pang's bugle, which Bricko had repaired, and a great, wobbling Shao Shan would trot up the line on her mule. On arrival, her tiny husband would assist her in climbing from the mule to the foot-board of our cart: there, gravely, she would sit in the driver's seat with Man Kim on one side of her and Yung on the other and proceed to unbutton her tunic; shirt and vest were then parted (all especially cut to assist milking mothers) and she would expose her mountainous breasts – each, according to Kwelin, a good half-gallon. On one of these Kim would place their baby girl, now four months old, and Yung would put Toiya on the other.

There, with the sun on her face and a baby cradled in each arm, Shao Shan, Commander of the Women's Detachment, would smile at the world, taking as her due the court men paid her, though they only came, said Kwelin, to see the biggest pair in China. And she was, after all, explained her tiny husband, the only mother on the Long March now with true, communist milk.

And Yung, everything forgotten in his joy of parenthood, would lean forward, pressing first one breast, then the other, until one day Man Kim, Shao's husband, very reasonably, said, leaning over to him. "Young man, kindly leave my wife's tits alone – I will tell you when Toiya is on an empty one." After this poor Yung would sit quietly, his eyes fixed to the baby's face, oblivious of everything.

I often wondered if I was the only one in the world grieving for Yang Pipa.

On the seventh day out of Luting the June days faded for us; we stumbled upward, like men hell-bent on winter.

Eastward lay below us the verdant basin of the Chengtu rivers: westward, as we trudged on the roof of the world, lay the vast lunar panorama of ice that guarded Tibet; a turbulent ocean of crystal peaks of unimaginable, cold beauty. And on to this unbounded moon country, like the ceiling of the Universe, the sun, naked in a sky of gold, fired down slanting rays: mist rose, and into this was born a pattern of rainbows, blue, pink, scarlet.

"This," said Kwelin, "is where the world was born."

There was growing deep in me a bond with this woman; her inborn poetry, her sensitivity called to me. If anything beautiful happened on this filthy march, Kwelin was there, the first to see it, bring it to life: it seemed she sought out every small brightness of a day, as if to alleviate suffering; every triviality she would beautify.

At the time of the camellias, I had made love to her: she was not the first woman to grant me physical relief; nor, perhaps, would she be the last. At no time had I told her I loved her, but I believe, in that climb into the Tibetan moon-country, that the respect in which I held her was fast changing to love. Her serenity of face, her gentleness, brought calmness to our days: her courage seemed boundless. There were other women on this march, many of importance, the wives of leaders, but none were treated in the manner men treated Kwelin. Reaching out, I took her hand, and she said:

"This is the world of my Kuan Yin, who lives with rainbows!"

I said to her, "I am beginning to love you," but she did not hear this; instead, she whispered, her hand to her mouth:

"Oh, listen, Lin . . . listen!" She lowered her face. "Oh, how terrible!"

I did not reply because down in the valley great fires were burning. Below a horizon of incandescent flashes, the fighting rear-guard were beating out of Luting, and in the canyons and gorges about us dull gun-thunder boomed; and, horribly, by some strange phenomenon, the glacier ice played the sounding board, bearing in its canyoned throat the echoes of internecine war, the shrieking of ricochets, the screams of wounded brothers.

In this enveloping whiteness, with these cries, it seemed to contain us in a crystal coffin, a burial alive.

We marched in silence, listening: Kwelin, I saw, was weeping.

And on the mountain road below us there bloomed scarlet new explosions and a great thunder; the Red Army, preparing to assault the Great Snow Mountain, was at last destroying its surplus equipment.

It was a road that wound serpent-like across the minor peaks, crazily upward, covering fifteen miles in a madness of curves and bends in order to travel five. Standing here, we of the middle vanguard could see six-tenths of the Red Army crawling in a termite exodus against the snow: a writhing dragon that spat fire from its flanks at a dozen minor ambushes, its tail lashing its way out of Luting, where battle fires lit the clouds. Looking up at the eternal whiteness, I could see, but two miles away, the other two-fifths of the columned army. And leading it, distended at the mouth, the Assault Cadre, the Red Cadre and the gallant pole-charge engineers bombed and blasted a path through the roadblocks, the major Kuomintang resistance. Then great shafts of flame leaped from the muzzles of the mule-drawn two-point-fives: this was the tongue of the dragon.

"Look!" and Kwelin pointed.

"They are blowing up that bloody General Headquarters at last," said the man from Kwangtung.

"That's the last we'll see o' that old bugger," cried Bricko.

The dragon, distended at the waist where the rat had been swallowed, was purging out the needless weights: the propaganda presses, the portable mint that had never been used, the chairs, tables, typewriters, tailor's dummies, useless ordnance that had run out of ammunition; the pails and latrines of the anti-Capitalist league, sewing machines without needles, water carts carried empty from Juichin – sieved with bullets, beyond hope of repair; the personal furniture of the High Command that only marched when it had to, but not the litter of Otto Braun, who continued to be carried.

Now the carts were being abandoned, with kerosene to hasten their burning. They were sliding them in hundreds down the snowy slope into the valley. Discarded ammunition, too heavy to be carried, exploded in deep-throated booms up and down the line. The Red Army was becoming a free-foot army, for the ascent of the Tibetan mountains. And, at the height of the destruction, Little Ball came up on his little Tibetan pony.

"All carts over the top, Doctor-student; ammunition to be piled."

I asked, "What about the wounded?"

"We've got no wounded." The snow was on his heavy lashes, painting up his face; the puppy fat of his body was disappearing, he was growing into a man.

"I have," I said. "I've got Political Chang."

"Got to leave him, Doctor, lest he can walk." He put his hands upon his hips in challenge.

Yung said, later, "Political Chang is calling for you, Chan Lin-wai." Toiya, still in his arms, was muffled against the wind.

"I've done all I can for him."

"Can't you relieve him a little?"

"What do you advise?"

Kwelin said, "He could have an opium seed, but he wouldn't approve of that."

To this Yung made no reply, but closed the flap of the cart. I said, "What a situation! Soon he will beg for opiates, and he has already reported me for using it on others."

"Are you sure about that?"

I nodded. "He has done more – a page of my diary is missing."

Kwelin stared at me. "An important page?"

"Too important – it was critical of Mao Tse-tung. I was a fool to have left it around. No doubt Political Protection have it by now."

She asked, "But how could he have taken it? Chang can't walk."

I smiled at her as we trudged on. "You are feckless, Kwe – this is part of your charm."

"Yung...?"

"Who else?"

Little Ball suddenly wheeled his pony trotting back to me calling, "Ah, yes, Doctor Chan – report to Central Headquarters next time we halt – Political Commissar."

"Well, I'm damned," said Kwelin.

But, that afternoon, before we stopped, Yung called again, and I climbed into the cart. Political Chang was in the last stage of pain before the scream. He had bitten his lips; blood was on his throat. His ashen face rocked and trembled to the ice-rutted road. He said, "Doctor Lin-wai, if you have any pity...?"

"The poppy will pity you," I said.

"It will kill him," muttered Yung, clutching the baby.

"Please...?" whispered Chang. "I beg you!"

I took four seeds from my medical box and put them between his swollen lips. Holding his hand, I watched. Political Chang sighed and entered the bright pastures of his opiate dream: immersed in red, cooling waters, his feet swung over the galaxies of the opium stars, bringing him sleep.

Yung said, his eyes wild with his inner fever, "That is how you killed my wife."

"He will die, anyway," I replied. "Like my Pipa he will die in peace."

Yung put his head on one side and peered at me.

That night (we did not officially halt until the following dawn) Kwelin and I lifted Political Chang out of the cart; while he was still in his brightly coloured dreams, we put him gently down on the side of the road. A mile farther on we unharnessed Tojo from the medical cart and waited for the engineers. These piled the ammunition – it was needed by the rearguard – and ran the

268

cart over the berm: we stood, Kwelin and I, watching it career-
ing to destruction into the valley 2,000 feet below.

"Give me Toiya, Yung," said Kwelin. "I will carry her first."

He shivered in his rags. In his approaching madness he had
taken off his underclothes and wrapped them round the baby.
Half naked now, he backed away from her, "You will kill her – I
know you two, you will kill her!"

"Let me take her," said Shao Shan, coming up with her plodding mule. "See," said she, "I have made a pretty cradle on
either side of the saddle – one for your baby, one for mine."

We stood hesitantly; the column, still advancing, was bunching about us on the frozen road. The icy wind from the mountain
sang about us in flurries of snow. Man Kim, Shao's husband,
took Toiya from Yung's arms, and put her in the cradle. Yung
stood staring at Toiya, his arms still cradling, a baby no longer
there.

"There, now," said Shao Shan, "you have two babies, one
each side of this old mule – would you like to lead it?"

It was the evening that the Tibetans came galloping down a
crevice: on fine white stallions they came from the secret trails of
Tibet, saw the advance of the Fifth and ten muleteers coming
around a bend, and believed them to be wandering bandits invading their territory. They came in scores first, then hundreds,
a full regiment of Tibetan braves: broad, squat men of flattened
features; mercenaries sent to reinforce the Szechuan war-lords
blocking our advance to the north. With them came their baby-
faced concubines, beautiful young women plump from good
eating and love; the men wore fur-lined uniforms and carried
driving muffs on their fleet Tibetan ponies: the women were
swathed in fine, white furs, wore jade beads and bracelets: the
captain carried on his saddle gold and silver bullion of pillaged
Luting.

They had unwittingly walked into the mouth of the Red
dragon. It swallowed them whole.

It was sad to do it, but we badly needed winter clothes. The
Fifth, without firing a shot, pulled over their shivering bodies
fine, Tibetan fur. The gold and silver was sent back to General
Headquarters, the Tibetans and their concubines went back to
Luting in our lice-ridden rags. For the lice still flourished; they
die only on the corpse of the host. And Shao Shan, mountainous

in fur, waddled up and down the muleteers, in a clanking of gold earrings, jade beads and bracelets.

I managed to get a coat for Yung; he actually allowed Kwelin to put it round his shoulders. Later he took it off and cut it down the middle, wrapping up each baby as they rocked in sleep each side of Shao Shan's mule.

"At this rate he shouldn't last much longer," said Kwelin.

Kwelin, of course, had watched what had happened but taken nothing for herself. Standing on the edge of the frozen track, she was shivering in her torn jacket and trousers, the standard summer issue. With a little white fur coat in my hands, I approached her.

"Oh, no," said she, backing away. "There are others."

"Perhaps, but this time it is you."

I put the coat around her and it was wonderful to see her face.

"My, there's a beauty!" cried Shao Shan, stomping up. "*Hei wei*, men, look at the little nurse, ain't she lovely?"

They came to her, thronging about her with gestures of admiration: womanlike, she smoothed the fur with her hands, delight in her face.

Later, I held her against me, and she said, "Oh, Lin, it's wonderful to be warm again . . ."

I held her for a long time, and would not let her go.

It was the morning that I went back, as commanded, to General Headquarters.

TWENTY-EIGHT

Political protection in the Red Army – of which Political Chang was a minor unit representative and Mao Tse-tung the Commissar – operated individually and was autonomous. In the last analysis of any debatable situation, it was the final authority. Mao Tse-tung was not the Commander-in-Chief of the Red Army – Chu Teh performed this function – but Mao, as its Political Commissar, possessed absolute control. The spy condemned by a unit and hanged by that unit did not die by order of the army but by its political arm. Likewise, the investigation of disruptive elements was instituted by the Political Commissar, not by the General Officer Commanding.

Therefore, Political Chang, when he reported me for breech of regulations by dispensing opium, did so to Peng Teh-huai, the general commanding the Third Corps: but when he reported my apparent political defection – the denigration of an individual Party member – he did so to the offended person via Political Protection.

Unfortunately for me, this happened to be Mao Tse-tung.

This was the theme of the March; everybody was of equal rights, if not of equal importance.

Ever since missing that vital page of my diary I had expected a call to General Headquarters. It came, however, sooner than I expected:

To Doctor-student Chan   Headquarters, Political
Lin-wai, Fifth Muleteers,   Protection Department.
  Sixth Regiment, Third Corps
  (Advanced units)
  Present yourself at the Department to explain written attack upon the undermentioned person.
  Attend at 1200 hrs, 15th Inst.
  13th June, 1935   Mao Tse-tung
                      Political Commissar.

For a man with hundreds of thousands of dollars on his head, the Political Commissar was not well guarded when I came down the column to General Headquarters – now a slimmer version of the elephant we had dragged by the tail for thousands of miles. Indeed, only a languid sentry and Mao's faithful batman, Chen, received me. Mao himself was standing within at a desk, poring over maps; he glanced up briefly as I approached and stood before him. As a man bored, he sighed.

"Ah, yes – Doctor-student Chan." Sitting down, he regarded me with heavily shadowed eyes.

Malaria had taken toll of him. He was wasted and huge-eyed. His thin body, upon which his plain, black tunic sagged in folds, seemed to increase his height, and he moved with the lethargy of a man approaching death, his large-maned head thrust forward. Only his eyes were alive – fevered and bright, like Yung's; they switched over me in assessment.

"Be seated, please," he said, and picked up a paper I instantly recognised – a page of my diary. He read:

"'It appears to me impossible that the Tsunyi Resolutions should have included Sun Tze's theory of "sinuous lines of motion". We plod on and on, admiring the tactical genius of Chu Teh working within the political insanity of a constant drive north-west. We are like sacrificial actors delivering ourselves into the hands of waiting executioners. If this is the *Art of War* as practised by Sun Tze, I suggest Mao confines himself to his role as Political Commissar and leaves the business of retreat policy to his field commanders who better understand it.'"

Scanning the page, Mao added, "That was written on June the 8th – but a few days ago. Presumably you still hold these views?"

"I heard myself say, "I do, Commissar."

Yung, I reflected, had certainly picked the entry which would have the most effect. To my astonishment, Mao said, "Naturally I disagree with your views, but I don't take issue with them. The northerly march has become a necessity through no fault of mine – both the Kuomintang and Chang's flightist Fourth Army continue to limit us." He got up, sighing, "Had it been possible I wouldn't have marched at all."

I did not reply: on the face of it he was substantiating his tactics; later, I knew that he was really speaking to himself, a habit that gave the impression of arrogance; as his apparent isolation contributed to allegations of his rudeness and conceit.

A silence entered the room; he appeared unaware of me. Sitting down again he unbuttoned the top of his flies, turned out the waistband of his trousers and began to examine the seams for guests. Once, in the presence of Chu Teh and others, he had removed his trousers and conducted the interview in his underpants, for coolness. His present bug-hunt was as normal an action: Mao Tse-tung was a peasant. It considerably put me at my ease, and I vaguely wondered if it was planned. Suddenly he said, not looking up, "You keep a detailed diary, Doctor?"

I straightened on the chair. "Daily entries, if possible."

We fell to quiet again. With a grunt of triumph he picked out a flea, crushed it between his fingernails and went in search of others. "You are aware that Meng-chiu is a casualty?"

I said, "Hsu Meng-chiu, the official historian?"

Mao nodded. "Frostbite. By the time we reach low country he'll be lucky if he still has legs." Finding another flea, he despatched it with finality, buttoned his trousers and added, unexpectedly, "This retreat will count as a military defeat, and the country, like you, will blame me for it. But, since we are at it we might as well record it."

I watched him; he had again lapsed into singular, personal isolation; it was disconcerting. I didn't know what to say. Clearly he was now unaware of me.

This, I reflected, was the man who had not replied when they informed him of the butchery of his sister soon after Chiang's White Terror. Now, out of context he said, "Until we get protracted proletarian support – and we haven't got it yet – we will have to continue to adopt flexible lines despite the haggling of the uninformed – bloody people like you. The Army wasn't ready for positional war – we've always been at our best on the move. Are you interested?"

"Not in detailed military tactics Commissar."

He was instantly impatient. "No – in assisting with the historical records?"

"Certainly, comrade." I rose.

He picked his teeth reflectively. "Meng's a good historian, you know."

"So I've heard."

"He'd appreciate it." He added, "And keep the entries simple. Some of you historians are fussier than a hen's arse."

I nodded, waiting. Giving no indication that the interview was at an end he leaned forward at the desk, beginning to read: I must have stood in silence for over five minutes before he said:

"Passivity is the real enemy, of course. The failures at Juichin cost Kiangsi a million dead." He stared at me. "Terror, violence and death aren't always the midwives of freedom – Juichin Soviet, as I predicted, turned out to be a graveyard. Did you see the size of that headquarters we pulled out? The Russians wouldn't listen – Otto Braun wouldn't listen, but it's always the political leadership that takes the blame – from people like you up." He cursed silently. "When our masters fart I'm supposed to say it's perfumed, but I wouldn't agree again."

I asked timidly, "On the size of the headquarters, Commissar?"

He straightened. "Good. I'll arrange for you to join Headquarter staff. Meng'll want a daily record, of course – most of his stuff has already gone, apparently – you'll like Meng – he's collating all that's left."

He was rolling a cigarette with one hand, staring past me at the wall of the tent; a man isolated.

Somebody was holding aside the tent flap. Mao returned to his desk, shuffling papers. A voice said, "You can go now." It was Mao's batman.

As I wandered away from the tent the batman followed, calling me.

"You'd better have this, hadn't you?" and he gave me the page of my diary.

It was a somewhat unusual interview.

Now the artificial winter of the ice-bound peaks was into us; dolefully the mules and horses plodded, most of the little donkeys had long since expired. And we climbed upward, ever upward into the freezing mist where hung clouds in gorgeous haloes, painted by the sun. And this rained golden on the glittering, white wastes about us, reflecting into our eyes a vicious sunglare that sent men blind. On the morning of June the 23rd I recorded in the diary:

The toughest among us are faltering. News comes that Lin Piao, left with a weakened heart after the long-distance run on the Yangtse River assault, has had to rest; men say he is constantly fainting. Mao has malaria again – I'm not surprised. Kwelin's legs are raw and painful; I try to get her on to Tojo but she insists that Yung belongs there. She also has a bad ice cut on the side of her heel and is limping badly. Soldiers are dying on their feet, mainly from heart attacks – the eternal climbing through sleet and blinding blizzards. Yung, I believe, is going snow-mad . . .

Big One, as compensation, was a walking barrel of strength. Labouring on without complaint, he was always ready with a smile; a most genial giant now we had given him Hu. Hu, dressed in his white fur coat (stripped from the smallest and prettiest concubine I had ever seen) laboured up the icy tracks hand in hand with his adopted father, shouting shrilly as he made the Hingsi sign-language into Big One's face: their laughter, piping treble and booming bass, echoed down the chasms. And in the delighted laughter Yung, rags fluttering about his frozen body, would shout in mad chorus. His hair was matted and reached almost to his shoulders. Any covering we fashioned for him, he immediately flung off: it seemed impossible that he would survive each bitter, howling night, yet he was always first out of sleep in the mornings, shovelling up the rice Kwelin cooked in gasps and grunts, bawling unanswered greetings to imaginary people up and down the tracks. As if the appalling cold made no impression on his wasted body (you could now track Yung in the snow by the patterned blood-flecks of his coughing) he demonstrated astonishing reserves of strength. His brothers, dying, as he, on the verandah of their Chekiang mansion, would have knighted him with pride.

Bricko made show of neither pain nor courage, but plugged on in his concubine furs, up to his elbows in his pockets, his face-wounds livid and scarlet, his eyes simmering on Hu and Big One. Behind him, Kwangtung, the man with no name, trudged in the same fluttering rags as Yung.

Shao Shan, leading her mule, came next of the Fifth; on this were ingeniously slung the tiny weave cradles, Toiya snug and secure on one side of the saddle, Shao's baby on the other: to her own child, for easy identification, she had tied a chicken's claw, this being necessary at feed times (both being unidentifiable bundles of fur with slobbering mouths); also, it served the main purpose that if this child should die, it would be able to scratch a living of sorts in the Afterlife. Behind the mule plodded Man Kim, Shao's husband, one arm outstretched, fist on its flank. In the stumbling progression he occasionally thumped and cursed.

Kwelin, now limping badly, walked with me. I had my arm

about her, partly to help take her weight, but mostly to try to keep her warm. The fur coat I had given her was gone; within a day she had laid it over a Sixth infantryman dying on the roadside. Now she leaned into the icy wind coming down from the mountains with nothing but her summer tunic to protect her. Earlier, Bricko had run down the line and returned with an armful of straw: this I had pushed between the tunic and her ragged vest; her body was so chilled that she did not feel the coldness of my hands.

"Kwelin, you're an idiot," I whispered, kissing her secretly.

"We are all idiots," said she, "or we wouldn't be here."

"And I love you."

She was buttoning up her tunic; her fingers ceased instantly, and she raised her face: there was in her eyes a look of sudden, inexpressible happiness: the wind howled between us, the column shoved past; but we did not move. Snow-flakes, swirling about us, had decorated her hair, riming her lashes so that, with a swift movement she dashed them away. I will never forget the widening happiness of her eyes. Reaching out, she gently touched me. "You ... you love *me, Kwelin* ...?"

I saw behind her a plateau of lunar ice and the ice-capped peaks of the ferocious Bayan Kara: all about us were the curses of slipping, sliding men, the whip-cracks, the obscene chatter of the march.

I smoothed the snow from her cheeks, uncaring, save for her.

Suddenly she pulled me against her, burying her face in my coat.

June 25th, 1935

We are at 14,000 feet now, crossing the Ta Hsueh Shan. These mountains, this cold will be the end of us. Hundreds are dying daily. The snow-slopes are littered with the dead and dying, the summer-uniformed southern region men simply can't stand it; their blood is thin and disordered by malnutrition. After every stop men fail to rise. Some go to human sculptures of ice: often I rub snow from frozen faces and shout "Are you alive, man? Are you alive in there, P'eng yu?" And then comes the business of chipping away the iced clothing and blowing warm breath into the red ice-holes that betray the mouth. Kwelin is wonderful. The insides of her legs are worse with raw and ice-burns, and some have cracked, causing her agony. Every night, huddled in the little snow-caves, I treat them with ointment and bandage them while Big One and Hu stand guard. Yet still she tries to mother poor Yung. Only yesterday we found him flopping about in the snow like a man drunk; he has the most terrible frostbite, too. Soon after this I found Kwelin kneeling with him by an ice face; she was warming his blue hands in the divide of her breast.

The man from Kwangtung said to me, "Are you hungry, Chan Lin-wai?"

"Sometimes I think I will never eat again."

"Are you cold, Lin-wai?"

"Ice is lying between my skull and my brain."

We lay together, shivering on an ice-crest, listening to our breath crackling in the frost of twenty degrees below, and there rose from the resting column a gentle mist that veiled the lantern stars above Great Snow Mountain. All about us men were crying with the cold: Kwelin, hugged against me, whimpered in her frozen sleep.

The man from Kwangtung said, "But I am not cold, my friend. I am lying in the arms of my little plump Kiangsi wife, and she is soft and warm. It is all a matter of the subconscious, you know. Only an hour ago she cooked for me a fat Peking duck, like I used to eat as a student in Camozan: she served the skin with it, you know – not separately, which is barbarous cuisine. Afterwards she chopped the breast and put it in little brown, savoury pancakes."

"I enjoyed that very much," said Kwelin, though I thought her sleeping.

Hu, from beneath Big One's furry arm, piped up, "Live boiled crabs and bamboo shoots, my papa cooked me when I was four, and roast pork in fingers, an' me teeth cracked and crunched on the crackling, wi' the fat drippin' off me chin, eh, damn!"

Shao Shan, with the babies on her belly, sighed like the well of life going dry, and Man Kim said, "I'm giving hell to a big red cock when I return to Shao Farm, Kingsi: I'll stuff him with garlic and sage and walnuts and slice him sizzling on the stove with shredded celery. Maotai wine will wash him down, and not a mouthful will I give to fat Shao Shan."

"Then I shall eat you, little husband," she said, dreaming, and Bricko cried, his shrill voice echoing down the pack-track:

"When I get clear of this bloody army I'm buying me a ton o' Foochow crystal prawns served up with a cart full o' chow mein. An' I'm ploughin' up one side o' that and sliding on me backside down the other in soy sauce an' a sea o' sharks fin oil."

"That," said the man from Kwangtung, "would be a reasonable finish to a decent meal." Sitting up, he bowed to Kwelin as he took from her one of the little dried fishes she was handing round. Munching it, his breath rose in little spurts from between his frosted fingers; his eyes were dancing as he looked around the peaks of Great Snow Mountain, and he said, "We've all eaten well: we're warm and we're together – you're not having us, you big white bastard."

A man on the track, above a great couloir, stopped the Fifth column, and shouted above the wind:

"Are you the commander of the Fifth Muleteers, soldier?" He was wearing the shoulder flashes of Political Protection. I shouted back, "We lost our commander at the Tatu – nobody is appointed yet. I am the unit doctor."

He put his arm around me, steadying us against the blustering shoves of the wind. "Have you ever had a Commander Hsiao of the Red Cadre down this part of the line?"

"Whom?" I yelled.

"A Commander Hsiao – he was with an advance unit that crossed the Gold Sand River."

"What of him?"

"He is dead, comrade."

"He's in bloody good company," I said.

"Shot at close range, though."

I remembered Bricko, and replied, "Why ask here?"

The man bawled in the teeth of the wind, "It was said he was owed a grudge by the muleteers – it is either murder or suicide. Do you know of anyone here . . ."

I hauled him into the shelter of a crag, and yelled into his snow-flecked face, "He was Red Cadre – the muleteers loved and respected him. Don't you come down here looking for murderers – you look among your Cadre. Commander Hsiao was a fine man, one of China's heroes."

"He was a load of shit," said Bricko. "I killed him for Fool."

278

I said the day after this, to Yung, "Yung, my friend, I need Tojo for Kwelin, you will have to walk."

The wind had dropped: even my low voice echoed and clattered over the tilting slopes and bottomless depressions: powdered snow lifted from the pack-ice, billowing in slow, drifting clouds up and down the plodding columns: in quick blazes of a sun dripping molten fire, we sweated and stank in the momentary heat. And Yung, as I held Tojo's head, glared down at me from the mule with maddened eyes. He said, his voice amazingly modulated, "I will certainly come down: Kwelin can ride behind my Pipa. They are not large women, the mule can easily carry two."

"Excellent," I said, helping him out of the saddle. "Kwelin's legs are very bad."

He said, "She is very kind to me, is Kwe; she warms my hands against her breasts. Her breasts, you know, are much like Pipa's, eh, my darling?" He stroked Kwelin's face.

"Then you will not mind her having a ride?" I asked.

"Of course not," said Yung, and laughed happily, dismounting and leading Kwelin to the mule. Patting the mule's saddle, he cried, "Do you mind Kwelin riding behind you, my love?" He trudged over to Shao Shan who was leading her baby-mule; taking its bridle, he said to her, "You have a rest, woman, I will lead that. Just look at those two in front, Shao Shan – aren't they the two most beautiful girls in Szechuan Province?"

Even in his madness he was beautifully articulate.

"It is all right, woman, it is all right," whispered Man Kim, patting a weeping Shao Shan.

We were nearly at the summit-track of Big Snow Mountain when it happened.

Yung was still leading Shao Shan's mule; she and her husband (now in pain with his legs) were plodding behind it. We were negotiating a blade-like edge and the animals were slipping and sliding: earlier, Man Kim had tried to take the rein from Yung, but he had shrieked and kicked, and it had needed Kwelin to get off Tojo to quieten him.

All about us, I remember, the crazy, criss-cross slopes and hollows glinted the dull blueness of the pack ice: the powder layer smoked and whisped above the snow-filled crevasses; some, men said, filled with a hundred feet of snow, a very deep burial for a single mistake, said one; a warm sleep in the arms of eternity, said another.

Yung slipped first, hanging on to Shao Shan's mule; this pulled down the animal's head, and its hind legs began flailing on the edge: over-balancing it collapsed on to its belly and wallowed momentarily, floundering on the ice-pack like a dying walrus. And the moment after I left Tojo's head and began the run to help I saw one of the babies fall out of its cradle, unwrapping its fur covering as it rolled down the couloir, raising a line of snow-dust in its wake: to the very edge of the slope it rolled, coming to rest on the brink of the precipice.

It was at least a 1,000 feet drop through the clouds to the snow-filled canyon below.

After the commotion, the warning shrieks, came silence.

The column stopped, frozen by the event.

Then Shao Shan screamed, and the scream echoed and re-echoed shrilly around the crystal peaks. Then, suddenly, we heard the baby whimpering: still rolled in its blanket, it was fisting the air, kicking on the edge, and its faint cries came to us above. Shao Shan's frantic sobbing. Yung shouted, happily:

"All right, Toiya, all right, I'm coming," and he slid over the blade of the couloir on his belly and the gradient took him, piling up the snow against his chest.

He came to rest two yards from the child.

There was an emptiness in us.

The column was motionless, watching.

Slowly, inch by inch, Yung paddled forward to the baby; reached out once to grip the edge of its shawl; an inch short, he moved forward again to the brink of the drop. He called, and we heard him clearly in constant echoes, "All right, Toiya, all right . . ."

Kwelin, I remember, had her hands over her face: Shao Shan was on her knees, staring wide-eyed. Yung's finger touched the shawl. A man beside me gasped.

The baby was rocking on the edge of the drop. Yung's out-stretched fingers were gathering in the shawl. Gently, he pulled. The baby unrolled in its shawl. He pulled again, infinitely slowly; the baby turned on the brink, its tiny, red fists waving in space.

Yung was cool and sane; none could have bettered it – he lunged – all that was left to him. And, in the moment before his hands touched her, the child slowly rolled out of sight: Yung's descending hands clapped down on snow.

And, in the suspended second before Shao Shan screamed again, Yung turned to face the column high above him: gathering his legs beneath him, he looked momentarily at the bronzed sky, calling:

"Pi'pa!" the correct pronunciation of her name.

There was on his face an expression of infinite peace.

"*Pi'pi . . .!*" with his arms outflung.

The mountain snatched his cry upwards, echoing it shrilly around the peaks.

Then Yung waved briefly and fell backwards over the drop.

Later, Kwelin came to me, saying, "Shao Shan is down with the Sixth. She is holding a baby and will not release it. The child she nurses has no chicken claw around its wrist – it is Toiya."

I stared into her white face. "Let me see!"

She cried, "Yung was mad. He did not know his own child. Shao's baby is dead – Toiya is alive."

"It can't be! I saw Toiya fall – she was on the left of the mule, woman!"

Kwelin brushed snow from her face. "Then somebody changed them – was it Yung, at the last feed?"

I whispered, "But Shao Shan herself would have told us – if not Shao Shan, then Man Kim!"

It was the last halt of the day. Thunder clouds were gathering, booming and hissing among the ice-bulges: we shivered in the deadly cold, clinging to each other. Below our feet the ice-pack moved in bucking protest to the mountain's shoves. Ice tinkled from the crags above us; the air was thin, we breathed in gasps. The sun had set in a glory-blaze, a vast, reddening tribute to Yung and a baby dying in snow. Ice, splintered by the heat, fell into the valleys like crystals of shrapnel.

We found Shao Shan half a mile down the line with the Sixth infantry: they were crouched together clear of the track – she and Man Kim, her husband: seeing us, he came belligerently, his fists tight and he said:

"Get back, get back! Leave her, the Fifth is bad luck for us."

Kwelin called to Shao Shan, who was feeding Toiya, "But she is not your child. Keep her, if you like, but do not call her yours, woman."

"Come, Shao Shan, face it," I said.

Shao did not move when Kwelin took Toiya from her arms.

We stood together, watching as Kwelin put her back again and she suckled to Shao Shan, did Toiya, knowing the mother-smell. Many people had gathered, as people do at an altercation. Man Kim said to me, "Let her have Toiya, Doctor Lin. It will kill her now if you take Yung's baby away."

"She is the only one with milk," said Kwelin, as we went back up the line. On the way Kwelin stopped me. "Think, Lin," said she. "You are my husband now you have loved me. Just think how wonderful it would be if I could one day feed your baby?"

I kissed her: the innocence was in her face. How could she possibly suspect that Toiya was mine?

"One day," I said. "When this dirty march is over. One day."

Hand in hand we went back to the Fifth.

TWENTY-NINE

With dogged courage, following us up the snow-packed mountain trails of the Seven Ranges, the Kuomintang were after us.

Chiang Kai-shek, flying in fresh troops from Kweichow, landed these not forty miles from our rearguard, linked with the war lord troops of four mercenary armies, and attacked us in west Szechuan in the south and on the flanks. Well-clothed, they were led by hardy, mountain fighters of Tibet with nationalist officers fat from the big eating of Luting. And we, caught in the snow-glass bottle between the Great Snow Mountain and the Paotung Range, were herded like sheep through the narrow, treacherous passes in air almost too thin to breathe: the Nanking bombers plastered us in every hour of daylight, skidding their eggs down the deep-walled passes into the massed columns of struggling men and animals.

Communism will die, said Chiang Kai-shek, between Mowkung and the blood-spattered road that leads north to Yaan: the final slaughter-ground will be east of the Tibetan border, and here I am building a Kuomintang abattoir.

For once we got an Order of the Day signed by Chu Teh, the Commander-in-Chief, and to this day, with the printing presses abandoned, nobody knows how it was reproduced: it was printed, mainly, on Red Lucky Paper left over from New Year celebrations: it told, in Chu's eloquent prose, the history of the Chinese-Tibetan minorities dwelling in these arctic-like regions, and said:

This march is nearing its end; the victorious Red Army will never be defeated. We have conquered Great Snow Mountain, we will leap over the Paotung Range and Big Drum: we will set the Red Flag flying above the ice-summit of great Dream Pen. The Kuomintang pursue us with fresh troops – but what are knicker-soldiers against we hardened veterans of the Red Army? They have bribed the tribes of the Fan People to ambush us ahead, but we will brush them aside on our drive to

Mowkung and lovely Maoerhkai. We will unit with the Fourth
Army under our fellow-General Chang and sweep Chiang
Kai-shek and his corrupt war-lords off the face of China.
Have courage, comrades! Long live communism, long live the
triumphant Red Army!

"Bollocks!" said Bricko, when this was read aloud by the man
from Kwangtung.

"Listen to this, Doctor Lin!" cried Hu, and he broke away
from the Big One's hand and held a text before him. I was astonished; his worthless mother had, at least, taught him to read.

"Tenga would have been proud," said Kwelin, softly.

Hesitantly, Hu began, so I took the paper from his hand, and
read:

Mountains, O mountains,
I urge my swift horse, unmoving as it gallops,
Lift my head, surprised that Heaven
Is three-foot-three above me . . .

"Everybody's composing bloody poems," said the man from
Kwangtung, shivering. "What I want is a good square meal of
millet and corn, with a good slice of red meat off the rear of a
Hunan pork-seller cooked brown and sizzling by my little
Kiangsi wife."

Bricko, his face-scars livid in the embers of the fire, said,
"Three-foot-three, says he—? under the sky?"

Kwelin said, "That is Dream Pen Mountain. The old people
tell that the gods cut a hole in Heaven and poured down icebergs,
then stitched up the sky with white and blue thread."

"Well, I never!" said Bricko, amazed.

"That'll mean taking the saddles off the mules and horses,
when we go over its top?" asked Hu, his eyes round with wonder.

"Undoubtedly," I said.

Little Ball, slipping and sliding down the road with more pamphlets from Political Protection, cried, handing them out, "Just
heard Mao say that the snow has confiscated his feet," and Kwelin replied, reading one:

"He's lucky finding such pretty words to express it – mine are
bloody frozen."

I glanced at her in the blue light of the moon.

There was growing in Kwelin's eyes the same, strange light that I had seen in the eyes of Yung.

Kwelin said huskily, at another freezing halt, "Yesterday, when I went to bring back Shao Shan and Man Kim, I met a woman of the old partisans, the only one alive of six. Can you hear me, Lin?"

I heard her above the shrieking of the bitter wind of Paotung and held her closer in the snow. Kwelin said:

"She had a brother in the forward propaganda teams, her twin brother, said she – aged twenty on the day he died. Last week, he and five others went in front of the Cadre, up a slope of Paotung, to drive in flag-poles and lay down ropes to guide the way. Can you hear me, Lin-wai?"

I was not really listening; the cold was in my bowels, my belly; icy hands were beneath my arms, which were soaked through and freezing, making it difficult to raise my hands. And this, occasionally, with a new fever of my body, would melt, so that it was like standing in a world of bitter coldness while a torturer poured icy water down my held-up sleeves. Sometimes, although Kwelin's face was before me, I saw it only in a mist of pain: the cracked skin of her cheeks I saw, the riven lips, the thin red trickles that ran from these wounds over the iced glaze of her chin. Yet snow-flakes had painted her up most prettily, lying heaped above her eyes, and her hair was the hair of a snow-maiden, tufted and peaked and preened with icicles: starched and frozen was that face: it amazed me that it actually spoke. She said:

"And when they reached the summit of Paotung they had no strength to plant the flags they carried. So they slid down the mountain on the rope, one by one, at intervals of a mile, each one resting on his flag-pole, with one arm outstretched until the frost took it, pointing the way, the dead ice-men of Paotung. Are you listening, Lin-wai?"

I will die with you, Kwelin, *Kwelin*, I said to myself; we will lie together in a glaze of ice: seeing my lips move, she added, "She herself – this woman, you understand – I think she was of Pak Sha Wan where the little fishes go – this woman, with Chu Teh beside her, pinned the Medal of Courage upon her brother's breast. Did you not see them last night, as we climbed to Paotung?"

I shook my head: now, because of the snow, I could scarcely see her face.

"The ice-statues of Paotung! Will they point the way for ever, do you think?" She stared up at me, and I knew again that I loved her. I wept.

I put my arms about her, rubbing her frozen face, breathing on the snow to melt it, kissing away the reddened ice, trying to heal the wounds of her mouth.

We took the Paotung Range in our shivering, shuffling plod of weariness, the remnants of a broken army. But we were the middle echelon: up in front were the indomitable Red Assault troops still of enormous fire-power, blasting at everything that moved. In the rearguard the fighting redoubled in ferocity as fresh Kuomintang troops were flung in, disregarding losses.

In the middle of the Paotung group came icy swamps with flatboards of ice an inch thick, and into this morass tumbled men and animals, hooves and hands flailing about until the swamp sucked them down. These pie-crust bogs appeared intermittently, and all had to be temporarily bridged with timber cut from nearby forests. From these forests many soldiers failed to return: a rescue squad sent for them came under the arrows and blow-pipes of the ferocious Fan tribe, whose country we were now approaching. But the flank assaults persisted, and scores of men died mysteriously, until reports came back from the Surgeon-General that they had succumbed to poisons. For this we repaid in full. The Red Cadres came in a body down the flanks and blasted every yard of wood and forest with short-range high explosives.

This Fan tribe, apparently, was brother to the one that had attacked us before the crossing of the Tatu, and the *W-u-u-u-ng*, *W-U-U-U-U-NG*! of their battle horns pestered our waking moments: at every gorge sliced through the icy banks these dark-skinned warriors would appear on the crests, showering us with arrows, killing off the heroes of the propaganda teams who preceded our advance. Then would come the boulders, rolling down on to the columns to crush us; or, worse, blocking the mountain passes so that engineers had to be brought up to remove them under fire. In the narrow defiles they had positioned hollowed tree-trunk guns filled with stones and metal; charged with gunpowder, these were fired by tribesmen volunteers: these home-made guns, carefully concealed, could strip a platoon of advancing infantry down to their skeletons.

Sometimes, when crossing Dream Pen, the road itself was engulfed with great hollows and piled drifts, and we gripped the guide rope the teams had laid, our hands lifeless with cold; icily hauling one another up in blizzards that forbade sight, so that all floundered around like drunken men in their own darkness. Some of the slopes, where the road had been dug up by the Fan tribesmen, had to be negotiated by the hand-holds cut earlier by the propaganda boys, who, with fearless courage, stood on high ground, waving flags to encourage us. Exhausted men, sickened of it all, crawled away from the columns to die in peace; the deep, ice-hole breathing that brought a numbing death: others went blind, and were led by comrades – long trails of them following one with sight: others went mad, as Yung, rolling around the tiny red encampments in the last stages of life, bawling and singing until the crack of the inevitable bullet.

On Dream Pen we crossed the chasms of dizzy height with knocked-up bridge ladders, and the muleteers of the Fifth, encouraged by the worn Red Cadres, inched their bodies over yawning crevasses, whimpering with fear. Hu, I recall, went over one of these on Big One's back; Kwelin followed, with me behind her, whispering pleas that she should not look down. Man Kim traversed one lashed to a board, with Shao Shan pushing it before her, the slim bridge bending ominously above the drop, groaning to her weight.

Man Kim, Shao Shan had been saying lately, was having trouble with his legs . . .

In this manner the Red Army crossed the Great Snow Mountain and the Chung Lai Range, the Paotung Range and Ta Shan; Dream Pen Mountain, where the stars were so big they fell out of the sky, and Big Drum, which we hated: also Chiachinshan, the tallest peak, which was 16,000 feet.

At the time I recorded in my diary:

Medical Record, from 28th May to 11th June, 1935, Fifth Muleteers, Sixth Regiment, Third Corps.
RATIONS: 1 lb rice daily; a little dried meat, dried fish; water from melting ice. Boiled water and chillies; orange squash. Much diarrhoea and vomiting. Snow blindness, tem-

porary and permanent. Men constantly urinating, bladder disorders. Malnutrition the curse; men are losing teeth and hair. Scabies rife – lice prolific – they thrive in thin air, it seems. *Frostbite amputations*: daily average three fingers; a hand or two every week, with my own fingers blue with cold. Sixteen amputations below the knee – seven above, a few to hip-joint; as stretcher cases, few of these will survive – body action is the only way to get through this. And this is only one regiment in the First Front Army of five army corps and a central column. They are saying that the Kuomintang are collecting specimens from Great Snow Mountain (Chiachinshan) to Big Drum – mounting fingers on string in alcohol!

Man Kim got it as bad as anybody. Outside a deserted Fan village on the road to Mowkung, I amputated both of his legs. He was astonishingly cheerful about it. He is a tiny man – one big opium seed put him subconscious. Shao Shan sat outside the old, ragged mule-tent while we did it, Kwelin and I. It was scarcely classical surgery; I had been turned into a butcher. We had done so much of this wayside cutting that, if we were warm enough, we actually laughed and talked of other things in the middle of it.

Kwelin, at the request of Man Kim, when he came round, wired together his amputated legs and laid them in the snows of Big Drum for collecting at a later date, said he, for use in the Heaven of Perpetuity, when, with luck, he could walk in golden places on the arm of Shao Shan.

He walked in her arms all right.

Later, at Paoan, Lo's rearguard reported that they were after the money, for the label Kwelin wrote announced:

These are the legs (up to hip-joints) of Man, a soldier of the Third. Finder rewarded – apply Shao Farm, Kansi Village, Kiangs – after the revolution.

Are they still there, I wonder, mirrored in the ice along the track that leads to Dream Pen Mountain, under the stars?

Man Kim was in excellent company.

About the time I was removing his legs, Meng, the official Party historian, whom Mao Tse-tung had mentioned to me, was losing his as well.

Hearing this, I reflected that it was only a matter of time before, as Mao Tse-tung had promised, I would have a call ordering me to join General Headquarters.

Now, with the trials of the Great Snow Mountain and the Chung Lai Range behind us, we descended through the foothills of Big Drum, leaving thousands of dead in the snows behind us.

Under a faint sun, with spirits reviving, we again marched northwards to the fertile lands of Mowkung and Maoerhkai.

Here the ordeal by ice was forgotten amid the growing warmth of a lowland July: southerly winds caressed our bodies: we cleansed ourselves of vermin in the flowing, white-crested streams, marching with new strength and vigour among the endless wheatfields and paddies. The rice-fields and young bamboo, decorated with poppies, moved like a tempestuous ocean in a thousand patterns of sunlight with each fresh rush of the perfumed wind.

Within this watering-place lay Fupien, where General Chang Kuo-tao was marching to meet us from the east. Farther north, they said, the land awaiting us was hostile and impoverished, its people numbed by privation: for this was the gateway to the Grasslands, which we would have to cross to reach the resting-place of Paoan and Yenan.

But here it was a land of honey and kindness, with the well-fed peasants running shrieking from their villages to greet us as we passed – and a more doleful lot of tattered savages were never to be found, said Kwelin. Covered with sores after the ravages of hunger, the itching madness of prickly heat and scabies, we marched bare-footed; the dejected survivors of a once great cause. No wonder the people's greeting changed to awesome stares as we passed. The peasants of these northern villages had been told of an invigorated revolutionary army marching north to Yenan to form a Government of the People. Our advance propaganda teams, skilled in the art of political persuasion, had led all to believe that we would arrive with banners waving; turn out the landlords and burn the title deeds: that we would perform, for their pleasure, the beloved Cantonese operas with artists of dance and song.

Instead, these villagers saw stumbling past them soldiers making a pitiful attempt at close-order marching. We carried no banners save the tossing wounded, red-patched, on the backs of drooping mules. We did not 'yell the road' as other armies;

we did not sing: indeed we did not have the enthusiasm to return their waves.

Once, 6,000 miles away and nine months earlier, we had broken out of Huichin Soviet 100,000 strong and more; losing at the Hsiang River nearly half these forces. Local recruitment had swelled our ranks but battle casualties, hunger and exhaustion had daily thinned them. Now the Seven Ranges had decorated its snows with the iced statues of our dead – target practice, men said, for the oncoming Kuomintang.

Past these silent, flat-faced villagers lining the road to Mowkung with their red flags limp in their hands, shuffled 33,000 living skeletons, the remnants of a once great Red army of communists who, but three years earlier, before entering the Juichin box, was nearly 300,000 strong.

But there were advantages. The forces of the Kuomintang, also decimated, were far behind us, fighting their own battle against frost and ice: the gallant Ninth Corps, for once, was disengaged, and also clear of the mountains. Communism, the pamphlets said, was still intact. Before us lay only the ferocious Fans, and these we would easily brush aside.

By day and night we marched to Fupien, passing on our way the temples of the Lamaistic Buddhas: outside the dark, insanitary cottages of the border, Tibetan-sculptured figures sat in stony contemplation: in a place near Lifan, I remember, there was a fine, stone-built missionary church whose priests, possessing the biggest noses I have seen on human beings, presented us with boxes of tinned fruit from California.

At a stop outside Fupien we rested in the sheeting rain. In the shelter of a deserted, half-burned barn, Kwelin came to me and we sat together while I entered in my diary:

2nd July, 1935.   Village of Erhokou
                                                  near Mowkung

Tomorrow, according to a Routine Order, we will meet the Fourth army under its commander General Chang. They, suffering a major defeat at the hands of the Kuomintang, ran fast from the Soviet Base on the Chialing River, so there is already talk that Mao has labelled him a 'flightist'. If this is so, why are we uniting with such an army under such a commander? We can serve as gun-fodder for the Kuomintang very well on our own . . .

Kwelin, reading what I had written over my shoulder, said, "If you're aspiring to be the new Party historian, that's scarcely the way to begin."

"I'm aspiring to nothing," I replied, closing the diary. "Mao says he wants me as the March diarist, so presumably he'll send for me – at the moment I'm content to stay a muleteer and enter unofficial opinions."

She said, "I shall miss you if you go to General Headquarters."

Her face, I remember, was smudged with mud, her cheeks riven with rain: her hair, usually so tidy, had lost its string and lay in matted strands about her tattered tunic. I found a piece of bread in my pocket, and this I gave to her (having been saving it for a time of greater need). Although she was starving, she ate it delicately, poising it between finger and thumb.

I remembered the *cheongsam* women of Hong Kong: the vivacious chatter of their painted mouths and their slim, silk-stockinged legs clip-clopping on the pavements; their fingers dipped in blood before their toothpaste smiles. I remembered the lanquid elegance of Pipa and I wondered, sitting there with tattered, skinny Kwelin, how I had ever loved Pipa. I did not know. Once I had thought of Kwelin only as a comrade: if I had treated her as a man since that love-making at Sikang, this was because she deserved the tributes one accorded men; but now I was in love with her. And it was a testimony to the power of that love that I could lie thus with her unpestered by desire. Suddenly, inevitably, she had become mine: in this new happiness I could wait for her. Although she had modestly tied together her broken tunic with string, I saw her breast, and it was no longer beautiful; it was the breast of someone old. Yet it held me with rooted force. Lying there in the silence of the barn, contained, as one, by the rhythmic beating of the rain, I knew no wish to relieve my manhood; my longing was not of this. But there was a thriving will in me to lose myself in her; to make her singularly mine in marriage amid all the dirt, blood and squalor of this endless marching.

Had I been given the choice between this woman and a mist and flower girl of perfect symmetry and grace, I would have chosen Kwelin. Indeed, given the exciting Pipa, who made demands on love, I still would have chosen this smudged and tattered Kwelin. The night was suddenly cold and she shivered momentarily.

"Come, sleep," I said, and put my arm about her.

She slept, but I did not sleep, at least, not until close to the dawn.

Such was the joy of having her near me.

She awoke in the night and looked into my face. All around us, discovering late this haven from the rain, soldiers had crawled in and were lying in the straw about us: Bricko was there; Big One and Hu were side by side, the giant's snores spouting up from his belted belly, a thunderous noise. On my other side Shao Shan slept beside Man Kim, Toiya between them: earlier, the man from Kwangtung (who was awake, watching the door), had helped Shao lift Kim down from Tojo, where he travelled strapped on his back. Corpulent Wong, dressed in his female blouse and skirt, was asleep at the feet of the drooping mule.

In that barn straw on the road to Fupien I knew a warm companionship about me: by some trick of fantasy I seemed to hear the bass voice of Jo-kei, the eloquent, modulated words of Yung. Obscene with his oaths, Tenga was there, squat and shapeless in the moonlight; also Chi-pang, the child I loved in memory. Pipa's face I saw in that dreamy consciousness before the fall into sleep, and heard Muchai's scholarly articulation; even Politcal Chang was there, watching from a corner.

Toiya made a whimpering cry and I opened my eyes as Shao's hand went out to her.

These men and women, I thought: all my comrades.

And the best of these was Kwelin.

I did not know, as I lay there wondering about the future, that before us were the most dangerous of hazards: the most exacting trials we were to suffer lay in the last 1,000 miles between here and Yenan.

The figure of Little Ball was beckoning at the door.

"Doctor-student Chan Lin-wai . . . !"

I sat up, bringing Kwelin with me. We heard the Young Vanguard say, "Tomorrow, first light – report to General Headquarters."

And so, before dawn, we woke them – Shao, Kim, Toiya, Wong the Corpulent, Big One, Hu and Bricko.

With Man Kim strapped on Tojo's back and Shao Shan leading her, we went back down the line.

For the first time in a year I felt complete; Kwelin was beside me, Toiya was in my arms.

In the absence of the historian Meng, now crippled and to be left behind in Fupien, I was granted the unpretentious title of:

Diarist Chan Lin-wai, Fifth Muleteers, Sixth Regiment, Third Corps; assistant to Hsu Meng-chiu (Official March Historian) for March reports after Fupien.

A little reduced in terms of ego I gathered my small entourage and we retraced our steps back to the Fifth Muleteers where the man from Kwangtung, with a bow and no questions, received us.

It was a slight, if significant, punishment for stepping out of the political line, but one thing was sure – Political Chang would have approved.

"Never mind," said Kwelin, "if most of the early records have been lost, yours will be the only ones that stand – who knows, one day you might even write a book about it."

THIRTY

On the 6th July, I made my first official entry in the diary:

> Today, in a brief meeting with one of the aides of the Political
> Commissar, I was confirmed in the post of Assistant March
> Historian, and have taken over what current papers Hsu
> Meng-chiu possessed. His accounts are excellent, but I am a
> little surprised at the few facts I have got. In Meng's absence
> (he is recovering from his amputations in Field Casualty) the
> aide told me that valuable papers, the most important records
> have already been lost on the march – in swamps, river cros-
> sings, in battle. It is a terrible loss, and I wonder if Mao Tse-
> tung knows of it. Luckily, I have recourse to my own diary
> records, but in these there are few statistics or high level deci-
> sions. (Nothing, for instance of the vital Liping and Tsunyi
> Conferences) – mine is but a soldier's diary of events, nothing
> more . . .

Outside Fupien village at five o'clock the next afternoon (the
Fifth Muleteers being well forward), we found ourselves infiltrated by General Headquarters and waiting in the rain for the
meeting with Chang Kuo-tao's Fourth Army. Mao Tse-tung
and Chu Teh were huddled in their ragged, soaked clothes (Mao
had only recently recovered from another bout of malaria) under
a tarpaulin; paper-silk umbrellas were in evidence, and the road
was crammed with the famous people.

Chou En-lai was there, as imperturbable as ever, and suitably
smart. The hero of the fighting rearguard, General Lo, had come
to greet the Fourth, though privately it was said that he despised
the Fourth Army commander as a 'front runner'. Kwelin, beside me, whispered, "Look, Lin-wai." She nudged me. "Who is
that with our General Peng?"

I said, "It is General Yeh. His friend, Teng Ping, was killed at
Tsunyi." Young and handsome looked Peng of the Third; Kwelin, it appeared, was still sufficiently alive to notice handsome
men.

Lin Piao, the tactical genius of the First Corps was there, ashen-faced with his constant fainting spells: beside him was the fanatical Chen Kung of the Red Cadres, also Tung of the Fifth Corps: and clustered about these leaders of the First Front Army were the heads of Political Protection, Personnel Works (whose coolie-battalions had died on Great Snow Mountain during road-making). All the chiefs and heads of every department one could put a tongue to were there that morning, to unite the First Front Army with its comrades of the Fourth. The man from Kwang-tung whispered into my ear:

"By Confucius, if the Devil were to cast a net now he'd pin some lively souls," but to this I did not reply.

I did not reply to this because I saw, in the far distance, a great army approaching. Its size and magnificence took my breath.

We of the First Front were represented by hundreds, from general officers to humble coolie-carriers, but across the fields were coming thousands in the pouring rain.

"By my grandma's tits!" exclaimed Skinny Wong, in his bright red blouse. Corpulent Wong, now skinny, his nickname had changed.

"Just look what's comin', Doctor Lin!" piped Bricko.

"It would delight the soul of Jo-kei," said the man from Kwangtung, "to see as many females as that on one street."

And females they were – a fraction of the Fourth Army's Women's Detachment of 2,000 – the fighting amazons of Sze-chuan – they marched in the foreground, a galaxy of colour, carrying banners that stretched above the oncoming army; on these, in blood-red characters, was inscribed:

WELCOME TO OUR COMRADES OF THE FIRST FRONT ARMY!

and

TOGETHER WE WILL BUILD A NEW PEOPLE'S SOVIET IN NORTH-WESTERN SZECHUAN

and

UNDER THE LEADERSHIP OF THIS FOURTH ARMY OUR GENERAL CHANG WILL BUILD A NEW CHINA

"Will he, indeed," said Kwelin, softly. "Hasn't he heard of Mao Tse-tung?"

"There is going to be trouble," said Man Kim, whispering down from Tojo.

"If there is I'm going to be in it," said Shao Shan, shifting Toiya on to the other breast.

The Fourth Army slowly approached, its banners and pennants flying in the rain and blustering wind.

For me, it vied, in size and splendour, with the tented armies of Kublai Khan. Mounted on fine horses the front rank came, and in the middle of this was General Chang, his sword held perpendicular in rigid salute beside Hsu, his lieutenant. And, some twenty paces away from Mao Tse-tung, he raised his sword high. The Fourth clattered to a stop behind him.

Chang Kuo-tao of the Fourth Front Red Army was waiting for Mao to receive him; Mao Tse-tung of the First Front Red Army was waiting for him.

Deadlock.

The rain teemed down upon us, steaming down my neck and over my body. I sensed the strain of this importance. Communism of two breeds had met at a wayside village: the communism of one would prevail. Confrontation, internecine war could ensue if jealousies, personal dislikes, vendettas were not abandoned.

Both armies were of roughly equal strength – some 30,000 to 40,000 men apiece. But Chang's army looked like men who had never seen a battle; it was an army that had bolted before the war-lords on the march to this very meeting point, and Mao had already labelled it as 'flightist'. Once the rulers of northern Szechuan, they had now marched from Honan for this historic meeting.

We of the First Front Army looked no longer soldiers, but destitute beggars. In place of smart uniforms we were drooping in rags: our bodies were emaciated, thousands of us were barefooted, many of us had even lost our weapons on the Seven Ranges. Mao himself was in tatters, with long hair straggling over his shoulders and the sallow countenance of a man half dead.

With a fine bodyguard of some forty cavalry, Chang started forward, clanked a few paces then stopped, waiting for the tribute Mao Tse-tung would accord him.

Mao accorded it.

Lowering their tarpaulin, he and Chu Teh walked slowly out

into the rain. Gathering their rags about them they stood, fists on hips, glaring over the space between them until Chang Kuo-tao dismounted, slowly approaching them on foot.

As he did so I looked this army over.

They were square-shouldered men, plump with good feeding; sitting on their great black stallions they seemed born to rule; the true representatives of communism. Kwelin spoke then, and her voice rang out with astonishing clarity in the silence.

"What lovely horses, Lin-wai," she said.

Instantly, Mao turned, sweeping aside his hair. "Don't envy the horses . . . not on this march."

He glared at Chang Kuo-tao again. A little sheepishly, Chang saluted, then offered his hand.

The spell was broken.

Men about us broke ranks and ran over to Chang's army, embracing the women standard-bearers, back-slapping the men: these were large, brave fellows, local conscripts whom Chang had saved from slavery under mandarin landowners: they would have died for him had he lifted a finger. Kwangtung put it into its right perspective when he quietly said, "That was a close thing."

He was right. Had Chang, in that split second of indecision, decided on war, the two armies would have been at each other's throats and only Chiang Kai-shek would have benefited.

Kwelin said later, "I knew it; I sensed it. Chang Kuo-tao had come prepared for a battle against Mao. Perhaps Mao expected it, I do not know."

History was made in the village of Fupien that day. What could have been a fight to the death, was turned into a union of brothers. Mao Tse-tung became the accepted leader of these brothers, and the figurehead of Chinese communism.

THIRTY-ONE

The talk was all of Yenan now. But for nearly three weeks we
rested in the area between Maoerhkai and Mowkung while the
Party officials conferred: day after day the meetings went on
while the eager Kuomintang, delivering themselves of the ice-
mountains, built up an iron pincer about us. And the longer we
stayed in these fertile regions, the nearer they came. But more
and more food was brought in, the result of forays by small units;
abandoning Mao's general rule that nothing must be taken from
the peasants, these raided the barns of local landlords.

Kwelin said, "Now he must be making up for his honesty in
the past."

Later, Mao told me, tongue-in-cheek, that this was the only
occasion he gave men licence to loot. Said he, "We will return all
we have taken," but I don't think he ever did.

Shao Shan said, feeding Toiya, "I've never eaten so well in
my life. Did you see that convoy of ducks and chickens yesterday? There can't be a quack-quack in the whole of west Szechuan."

Skinny Wong (who had lost considerable weight) brushing
down Tojo, said, "Night 'afore last I see another load come
through – reckon it carried nigh 50,000 *catties* o' wheat, an' 200
head o' lamb. We seeing any, Doctor-student?"

"He's better than the Old Weaver of Tatu for predictions,"
said Kwelin, "look what's arriving!"

It was the daily distribution of rice. The ration cart stopped
outside the ruined shack we had commandeered and a pig leaped
out in squeals and went hell for hooves with its nose-cord flying,
and Hu went after it down the village street: next came ducks
and chickens in clouds of feathers, with the ration-gorgers tossing them out and the recipients after them: Big One was
wrestling with an enormous porker, Kwelin despatching a
chicken, Shao Shan was into the ducks, and I hadn't heard such
a commotion since the Battle of the Tatu River. Sacks of pearl
rice were off-loaded outside that shack, tied rolls of bamboo
shoots, more dried fish and it stank in the midday heat; 100

catties of salt, most precious of all, was distributed among the personnel within the confines of the main street.

Man Kim said, from his palliasse on the floor, "Well, old Mao don't reckon to loot, lads, but when he does he do it proper!" His face was bright with anticipation – legless he might be, but he was making a fine recovery. Indeed, he was becoming a pest with Chi-pang's bugle.

Vaguely, I wondered if the same food distribution was going on all down the line – if, for instance, the fighting rearguard would receive so ample a share . . .

I also began to speculate if this fine fare was looted especially for the feeding of the many foreign guests visiting General Headquarters.

To date, I had seen but one radio in service with the Red Army; a primitive affair captured early. Presumably, this had been used as a receiver-transmitter, for now the most unexpected visitors were coming in: Party officials with arm-bands of varying colours – a deputation from Ho Lung's great Second Army (the third part of the Red Army with which we expected to unite farther north) – apparently it was undertaking its own Long March, and enduring fearful privations.

Standing with me at the shack door, Kwelin said as another group passed, "That lot, I heard, are from Chang's revolutionary military council." They looked it; small, secretive men of stern faces, marching in step with militaristic bearing towards the landlord's mansion, the seat of conference. Another group of six walked past, jabbering in whispers.

"And those?" asked Shao Shan, giving Toiya to Kwelin.

"Those are Russians," said the man from Kwangtung, "flown in from Moscow this morning."

"Are you sure?" I asked.

"Look at their uniforms – I heard it last night; it's not another rumour."

"Talk, talk and more bloody talk," grumbled Bricko. "You hear those soddin' guns?"

He was right. Day after day now the booming of the enemy advance shelling was creeping nearer and nearer.

Somebody said, "The Commissar's got malaria again, you heard?"

"That's why we're piddlin' here."

"Aw, balls – it's the conference, ain't it?"

"They gab and we fight."

"Pay 'em credit – Mao walks, too."

"Well, bollocks to 'em all – I want to go home."

"*Aiya*, man, do I itch!"

They waited, bored: they gambled, grumbled, they fought among themselves.

"I wish I were back in Kiangsi."

"That fuggin' place?"

"Good women there, mind."

"Balls, soldier – the best screws come from Shensi."

"That where we're going, ain't it?"

"Who says?"

"Political Protection."

"They don't know the time o' bloody day."

"Mao knows."

"He don't – he's got malaria."

"Another sod to carry."

"Aw, come on, Sarge – when're we off?"

They speculated in Fupien; they drew maps of the next advance: one even said we would retreat back to the Tatu. Some wrote home: others sat with the blank faces of a couldn't-care soldierly acceptance.

"Back over those mountains?"

"Shoot me toe off first!"

"You 'eard that. Goin' to shoot his toe."

"Well, I anna goin' back over that bloody Snow Mountain."

"Nobody'll ask you to – stop talking rubbish," said the man from Kwangtung.

Some died in Fupien: these were mainly the wounded we had carried after the battle of the Tatu; many, too, were frostbite cases brought down from the Seven Ranges. But scores – even in Fupien – died from septicaemia – the result of numerous open chilblains and wounds that had frozen. A few of these, some I was still attending, were being moved out of the village to die together for lack of village space. These we laid in a sepulchre near a great Lamaistic monastery, and Kwe and I visited them: entering the great cold tomb to pay them last goodbyes. Later (and they had to be disposed of early since it was now high summer), great bonfires lit up the streets in the mass cremations

– the refuse of the Great Snow Mountain. The night air was sickly with the smell of the pyres.

The dying, I discovered, did not protest as much as the living, but perhaps, said Kwelin, everybody in Fupien is also dead or about to be: it is simply that we do not know it.

Bricko said, unaccountably, for earlier he had been feigning isolation:

"If I catches it proper some time, Doctor Lin – will you give it to Bricko for keeps?"

It quietened me. I answered, "Let me understand this – you wish me to take your life with opium if you are too badly wounded to live?"

"Opium or bullet, I don't care neither." He scratched his cheek, fighting for the sense of it. "See you don't leave me alone to die, eh? I be much too lonely to die wi'out Fool . . ."

"Are you leaving me in Fupien, Doctor Lin, when the troops move out?" This the legless Man Kim asked of me when Shao Shan was temporarily away.

Kwelin said to me, "I keep telling him no, but he doesn't believe me."

I knelt by Kim's palliasse of straw. "When Mao moves out of here you come too."

"Half a man?"

Kwelin pondered this. "It has advantages you know – only half to feed."

"It's my woman, see," said Man Kim.

"Shao? What of her?"

"Got a pain in her belly."

I smiled at him. The bedlam of the road beat about us; the clash of iron-wheeled carts, the obscene banter of marching soldiers. "Most of us have, Man – it's the rich food."

"Womb pain – I know – she 'ad it before; six children come out of Shao, remember – she can carry her babies, but she can't carry me."

"What are you talking about?" said Kwelin testily, "you'll be on Tojo!"

"Not in the Grasslands, I won't." He licked his cracked lips. I asked, "Are you in pain, Kim?"

I examined him again; the stumps of his legs were healing but, with the chafing of Tojo's saddle, they were raw and badly inflamed, and the anchoring straps must have been an agony to him. He said now:

"I got no pain, mister, just my woman . . . see?"

Kwelin squared up in a fighting stance and put her fist against his chin. "You see to yourself, Three Foot, I'll see to Shao Shan."

Otto Braun, peak-capped and leather-booted, strode past the shack door; in his arms was a Fupien urchin child and he was pushing back her ribboned hair and kissing her face, bellowing at her in German, and the child was shrieking laughter, her eyes clenched against the sun. He saw Kwelin, and bowed low, clicking his heels, then bawled:

"*Mama hsiao hai tzu, Papa hsiao hai tzu, eh?*" Clearly, he was trying to learn Chinese.

Kwelin bowed back, shaking hands with herself. She said, "I think he's going to adopt her. For my money," she added, "he's a good human being. Can one believe everything one hears on this accursed march?"

Hu came in from the street then, carrying a pannier of water. Kneeling beside Man Kim, he raised his head to drink.

"That's right, Uncle Kim, that's right . . ." he said.

I remembered Yung who tended me at the Hsiang River.

Strangely, at that moment it was Yung I remembered.

I also remembered the comradeship of Jo-kei, the friendship of Tenga. I thought of the men I had never touched, yet loved to the full.

It was a good business, this love of fellow men, I decided: unlike the love of women, it needed only death's requitement to make it everlasting, and no fair words to bolster its sincerity: it existed unspoken, unattached to romantic situations. To most of the world it was beyond comprehension.

I closed my eyes. *Muchai* . . .

Also I remembered Pipa, lying in the Sikang Mountains among the camellias . . .

"What are you thinking of?" asked Kwelin, peering into my face.

I answered, "I was wondering, if Tojo goes down, how we can possibly carry Man Kim?"

"It was something more important than Man Kim. Will I ever know your thoughts, Lin-wai?"

She looked pretty then, with the youth returning to her face after the heaven-sent rest in bountiful Maoerhkai.

I replied, "You'd be a little surprised if you knew them now."

With her hands clasped under her chin she walked around the barn, looking at me prettily over her shoulder: Bricko, near by, groaned in sleep. Big One snorted deep, and turned over.

"One day we will be alone in here, woman," I said, "then it will be a very different story."

That night, while the others were sleeping, I wrote in my diary:

It is the 25th of July, 1935. Tomorrow (the Order has just arrived) we move out of Fupien: the eternal conferences seem to be over. Apparently, the two armies are to divide: the Fourth, under Chang Kuo-tao, is to act as rearguard for the enemy is nearly upon us again: we of the First Army will be in the van: two distinct armies marching northwards, but Chang Kuo-tao leaves later. For some time, however, he will base at Fupien . . . Chu Teh, commanding some 15,000 of our men, is to stay behind with him! This is astonishing news. Clearly, something is seriously wrong. Awaiting us on the other side of the Grasslands is a Kuomintang double army. With only some 20,000 soldiers left to Mao Tse-tung, has he any hope of cutting through these and striking north-east to Paoan and Yenan? Has Chu Teh even defected? . . .

Reading this entry next morning, Kwelin said, "Well, you've entered some pretty things at times, but this is the first time you've recorded something that is bound to get you shot."

"There is more freedom than you think."

"Let's hope so. Diaries can be dangerous. I'll pray they continue to restrict themselves to landlords."

Young Vanguards were racing down the village street blowing bugles for the advance and distributing hand-bills.

So much for the appointment of March Historian, I reflected: for the last fortnight or so I hadn't even set eyes on Mao.

There was a time, indeed, when Kwelin and I were nearly alone in the barn. Earlier, I had been operating; the wounded were men from Chang's Fourth Army, also a woman, one from his famous Two Thousand Regiment of female volunteers. She was quite beautiful and well formed for a peasant bond-maid; these usually being ungainly creatures, broken by droughts, famines and constant labour.

The girl had taken a bullet through her right breast; blood poisoning had set in from the nickel deposit.

Heaped with bruising and contusions, it seemed impossible to save.

The peasant girl said in her high-pitched, sing-song Anwhei speech.

"Please do not cut it off, Doctor."

We were alone in the barn: Kwelin, I, the peasant.

"But you will still have one," I said, with male detachment. "Will you risk your life for the sake of good looks?"

Kwelin said instantly, "Would you do the same to me?"

She glared at me, she and the woman of Anwhei. No men were near, and I was in a minority. The girl wiped sweat from her face, and said:

"If you take a breast from me, you steal one son. How can I suckle before my mother if I am deformed? If I could reach it with my mouth, I would suck away the poison."

"Don't worry," Kwelin said, "I'll do that for you now. Cut if you like, Lin-wai – but cut lightly. It is important to us – two good breasts – you don't understand this, being a man."

I cut enough to release the poison, and Kwelin sucked: for two hours, lying beside the woman of Anwhei, she sucked and spat, and I left them: when I returned to the barn they were still lying together, and the peasant girl was clean. I stitched her with the greatest care, using the finest sutures. "There now," said Kwelin, and stroked her face. "It's as good as new. He will be delighted."

The man from Kwangtung said to me, "It is possible, Chan Lin-wai, that you are a man of means."

I answered, "Actually, I'm a financial vacuum. Perhaps there was a time, when my father meant me well, that I would be reasonably well off upon my return to Laoshan. Now I'm a communist I doubt if he'll leave me a bean."

"Wealth is comparative, of course," replied he. "One man

304

might consider riches as nothing less than 10,000 *yuan*; to another, this sum would mean less than a student's grant."

"Assume me to be in the former category."

He was persistent. "You have no investments in America, for instance? – This, you know, is the latest thing."

"If I have, I am unaware of it," said I.

It appeared to intrigue him. He wandered away, looking at the stars.

The column was filling the street; mules and horses were being whipped in line. Skinny Wong brought Tojo to the door of the shack, followed by Kau Kau, Bricko's dog. Big One and Hu were there, standing ready for the march; Kwangtung, alone as always, was staring towards the north. Kwelin had Toiya slung on her back; Bricko and I knelt beside Man Kim, and Shao Shan whispered to me, "You are really taking him, Doctor-student?"

"He be too much bloody trouble if we leave him behind," said Bricko, and we lifted him without a grunt; Man Kim was as light as a feather when we replaced him horizontally on Tojo's back and strapped him in that position.

"You can't take him!" cried a staff officer, passing. "All wounded must be left, man – this isn't a picnic, you know – we're going through the Grasslands!"

I replied, "Special dispensation, Captain." I showed him my headquarter pass. "Official historian – this man is a material witness."

"That's right – you fug off," said Bricko.

THIRTY-TWO

North of Maoerhkai, bounded on the east by the Place of Many Rivers and on the west by the snow-glaciers of Tibet, the dream-lovely country of flowers borders the Grasslands that guard the road to Sungpan.

Here bloom the endless fields of poppy, the fragile flowers of red, white and purple, the juice of whose pod men call the Tears of China. Here the water-lily floats majestically, larger than the *Victoria regia* of the Amazon, capable of withstanding the weight of a man, and the sacred lotus flares white at the sun. All is beauty here, a million *mou* of coloured flowers waving above the tangled bindweed spiked with rushes and cypress. The labourers' tracks through this paradise are firm, beaten along the narrow dyke-passes to the consistency of concrete. And here live the tiny tribes of Tibetan and Chinese blood. It is the home of the primitive Fan, who, like the Shans and Lolos, hate nationalists and communists alike.

Beyond the Country of Flowers lay the Grasslands, and death.

To escape from the Kuomintang (now clear of the Seven Ranges), who were mounting furious assaults to the east of us, west of us and behind us, we entered the Land of Flowers in late July: it was the final lap of the Long March. Mao Tse-tung's Order of the Day to the remnants of his First Front Army (we were now less than 20,000) was to cross the Flower Lands, then the Grasslands, in order to attack the Nationalist divisions lying in wait north of us.

"It is madness," said the man from Kwangtung, "not one will be left alive."

"It is magnificent," said Kwelin, "but I wish it wasn't us."

It was Yenan, Yenan, *Yenan*.

General Chang, our commander of the Fourth Army, who soon turned back in the face of floods, remarked, "It is to be condemned; the stupidity of a snake wriggling out of its skin, sacrificing its tail to save its head."

But we of the First and Third Army corps under Mao could

have done without such grudging admiration: Mao's intended sacrifice fell on stony ground, for the main body of the combined First and Fourth armies under Chang Kuo-tao, with our Chu Teh virtually his prisoner, retreated back to the Sikang Mountains to spend a year among the camellias.

Did they tread over the grave of Yang Pipa, I wondered?

Doubtless they did, said Kwelin, for they were there long, enough.

Later, when our General Ho Lung led his Second Army into the camp at Sikang and joined with Chang's Fourth Army, there totalled in that camp some 50,000, yet it took them a whole year before they joined Mao in Yenan. History will one day relate it, said Skinny Wong.

I relate it now. The only man who rejected all temptation to retrace his steps was Mao Tse-tung. It was he, with his comrade, Chou En-lai, who maintained the spirit of crusade, the cause of *The Long March*. Beyond the Grasslands was a greater enemy – the Japanese, with whom Chiang Kai-shek with a million men had bargained territory while he conquered us. This was Mao's target; this was why he marched: to get to Yenan.

And, after Yenan, the Japanese.

Mao Tse-tung said to me, "Why am I marching, you ask?"

"For war against the Japanese?"

"Of course," said he.

We were approaching the true Grasslands. Miles behind us lay the Land of Flowers and the ground was already squelching under our feet. Considering the difficult conditions, I was astonished that he agreed to talk with me. We walked together. All about us was the light equipment of a bare-foot army: long since the giant caravanserai of the General Headquarters had been abandoned. Few animals, even, remained; most mules and horses had been eaten on the march.

Chou En-lai was leading his horse and Ho Tze-nien, Mao's wife, was in its saddle: half Mao's age, she looked young and beautiful that day in July, and she carried her baby girl (now six months old) with a marvellous dignity, her hair tossing in the wind about her torn, mud-spattered tunic. She was the third of Mao's four wives; in their nine years of marriage she bore him five children.

We trudged on; mist rose over the grasses. Occasionally I

could see Tojo's head bobbing up amid the marching army; once I saw Man Kim, strapped there, waving, as if at the sun.

I did not pursue the subject of Yang, his second wife: she had been executed three years ago by the Kuomintang, in Changsa. I recalled his poem:

My proud poplar is lost to me . . .
. . . The lonely goddess who dwells in the moon
Spreads her white sleeves to dance . . .
In the boundless sky . . .
They break into tears that fall as torrential rain.

We marched on, and I chanced occasional glances at him. Despite his recent attack of malaria his step was strong. But the march had taken toll of him. His gaunt body upon which the rags loosely hung, his cavernous face with its high, pinched cheeks and dark hollows of eyes betrayed the burdens of his decisions. We spoke in starts as we marched, and I took brief notes: as before, there was little cohesion in the conversation: he switched subjects with mercurial ability.

I asked, "Would you call this March a success?"

"History will record it as an error."

"Yet you undertook it readily?"

He sighed, "There are pressures, domestic, political. A million dead in a year of siege is enough wastage for any ideology: our loss of nine-tenths of the counties we held was another." He made a wry face at the sun. "Blockade of the sea routes was final – we are also fighting the Fascism of Hitler, remember: no man can stay alive without salt."

"And the rewards of this retreat?"

He had gone again: a man remote, he was lost in an isolation he had built for himself. I had noticed this earlier. In any group he was always the one devoid of gesture. I recorded somewhere later that Mao Tse-tung was a 'shut' man: one who talked to the world at the entrance of a brass tower.

I repeated, "Will there be political rewards in Yenan?"

He appeared surprised, "Certainly. The March is in itself a manifesto of courage – it is already three times longer than that of Xenophon's Greeks; *Ch'ang Cheng* – and this will be its name, will take its place in Chinese mythology. Generations will boast of it."

This I was noting in my diary; he added, "It has announced

to 200,000,000 Chinese in twelve provinces that the Reds are fighting for their liberation: it has sown the seeds that will yield the harvest."

"And after Yenan?"

We plodded on; there was no sound but drovers urging the horses, the shout of an occasional passing Young Vanguard, and the faint crying of a child.

Mao began to roll one of his eternal cigarettes; this he did skilfully, one-handed, after knocking out some foul, home-dried weed, a tobacco substitute, into the palm of his hand. Cupping his fingers against the wind (they were deeply stained by nicotine), he lit the wonky cigarette, inhaled deeply, and said:

"In the summer of 1929, I visited the famine areas of Suiyan – on the border of Mongolia. The Western press, with its usual inaccuracy, estimated the deaths by starvation at something over 1,000,000: it was probably four to six times as much." He spread his hands. "It was a horror the mind could not comprehend. Men, women, children, were dying at my feet, and I could do nothing, do you understand?" He slowed his steps. peering at me from under his cap, instantly hostile, "But how can you understand; you who were raised in a family of rich élite."

"I understand better than you think."

Mao said, "I saw women lying in filthy corners with babies dragging at paps; yet women are a saleable commodity in Old China. Long before they end like that they can usually get a year or so in the Kuomintang brothels. The children were skeletons, their bellies filled with tree-roots tenting out like growths. Somebody had to do *something* – these were Chinese, my own people . . ."

There was a silence, and I swiftly said, "But what made you think the average peasant would fight?"

He replied, "I didn't consider it – I knew it. You threaten the land of the average farmer and he becomes insane with anger. But he needs organisation; he needs arms and hope. Famine is popular with the gentry: it allows them to buy up their estates – and with the money of extortion, remember – the peasants actually buy it for them: up in Shensi taxes are paid thirty years in advance and represent seventy per cent of income. It will stop."

"How?"

"By removing landlords. There is scum on every brew; the way to cure China is to cream ours off."

He became silent.

I briefly reflected that the cause of communism could not only be laid at the feet of the landlords. There were 1,000 guilty war-lords and concession-hunters of the west. In a Shanghai park there was once a notice put up by foreigners, "No dogs or Chinese allowed."

"You go," said Chen the batman.

Compared with what I later experienced, it was quite a moderate dismissal.

Now the Country of Flowers began to sink into the mountains behind us and an acrid, yellow mist began to fill our world of the March. The bog-earth below us began to squelch with every step – *pu-chi, pu-chi*; an unsynchronised chord of obscene music. This sound, even as I write this, sings in my ears ... *pu-chi, pu-chi, pu-chi, pu-chi* ... It was the noise of muddy sandals and hooves sucking at the excrescence beneath us: with each step foul odours whisped up, polluting the wind. The runners of the rifle-sledges, upon which our arms were stacked, left knifing cuts across the bogs, wounds which brimmed with a stink like static urine.

Within endless sight was flat, desolate marsh; not a single habitation was to be seen, not a human being. And, within but a few miles of entering this filthy sea of mud and slime, the surplus rations we had garnered in Maoerhkai had to be abandoned on platforms in the stalk-patches for others coming on behind us. Thus, for the first three days in the Grasslands, we all ate our fill, chewing *chingko*, dried fish and buckwheat until our stomachs were distended. Knowing that later we would need this, we treated ourselves like human camels.

Starvation faced us within the first six miles of plodding travel. Each man clung to his little ox-hide bag of rice, his life-line. Over that soggy, putrid earth, Kwelin clung to me.

Looking back on the scene, we must have appeared a tatter-demalion company. A change of clothing in Fupien might have momentarily tricked the lice, but we now looked the least like soldiers. Gone were the cooking utensils, wash-buckets – all had to be abandoned after entry into the Grasslands. The only pot we had now in our Headquarter Section was a cracked, fire-blackened basin and a spoon to stir the rice, and from this we ate communally. It was a transition from comparative riches to a beggarly poverty, now we were losing the pack-animals. Also our appearance had changed considerably. I was wearing a landlord's overcoat of Shantung silk: Kwelin had stolen a bright orange gentry gown that reached to her ankles; Bricko was clad in a flowing black cape and Skinny Wong had on red pantaloons – filched from a Mohammedan, with a girl's summer blouse most beautifully flowered in orange and gold: this readily earned him the nickname of 'Sister'. Once used for performances of Cantonese opera in the villages through which we had passed, the fabulous operatic costumes of mandarin red, the scarlet gowns and Court tunics of kaleidoscopic colours now adorned anybody who could get hold of them. Some – people like Shao Shan, quick to see the humour of it – wore tall, ornate head-dresses; she, with her tiny husband propped up before her on Tojo, swayed in majesty, her gorgeous paraphernalia of bells and trinkets tinkling in the wind, aping the old, vitriolic Dowager Empress.

Thus, in pairs, gripping hands in case of a fall, what was left of the Red Army began the trek to its final battle before we opposed the Japanese in the north.

Said Kwelin, "We are dressed for the part. Actually, you know, it isn't really happening. We are mad people led by a madman into the final act of a play. Soon a bell will ring and we will awake and that will be the final act."

Later, the man from Kwangtung said to me, "Record, in your diary, that we entered this bloody place on an empty stomach: that 15,000 of us began this trek, and that only the blessed will ever fight for Yenan."

We had no food.

The Grasslands terrified Kwelin; the unending mud with its pestilence of flies induced in her a horror, and she would not let me out of her sight. During the day I went with my arm about her; at night I held her against me while she shivered with cold and her terror of the bog beneath us. Sometimes she actually wept with fear, and I would stifle her sobs lest the men heard.

"We got food all right," said Skinny Wong, "we got old Bricko's Kau Kau, a joint on four legs."

"You leave my little wonk be," said Bricko.

"He's good insurance, though," said Wong. "In my county we fancy a couple o' joints o' dog, eh?"

"You keep your hands off Kau Kau, 'cause he's Fool's wonk," said Bricko. "One bit out o' my little Kau Kau and I'll bloody eat you, eh, little son?" and he picked up the mongrel and buried his face in its fur.

We plodded onwards across the wilderness of nothing, leaping from tuft to tuft on to the strange coarse hair of the bogs. The bogland bubbled and sucked; the outraged earth farted up its filthy smells; it was airless by day and by night the mists rolled endlessly over us.

Kwelin, leaning against me, prayed, "Oh, Kuan Yin, *Kuan Yin* . . ."

The man from Kwangtung said, "Once there was food here in this wilderness – see, I have found wild celery and scallion," and he opened his hands.

"If there's that much there should be more," cried Shao Shan from the mule.

"There was more once," I replied, "but the vanguard have swept it up. Now we're discovering the disadvantages of arriving late."

"Otto Braun seems to be eating," said somebody.

They recriminated, they insulted this leader and that: soon, I knew, they would fight over the food.

We plunged onward in a filthy, slimy column, mile after mile: the Kuomintang bombs blew out great ulcers in the earth, showering us with the muck of rotting vegetation.

There was a place of swamp where a man's arm stuck out and his open hand gave us greeting; and dawn gob-spiders had weaved an intricate snare of webs spittled with dew: within the span of each long skeleton finger sat a spider, preening itself in the sun. It was rather as if the hand was held up to us as we passed it on the track, boasting of the phenomenon.

And it was near this place (men used the arm as a signpost) that I set up a small medical centre. In terms of efficiency, this was a pathetic echo of what I had been able to do for them in the past. But, to date, I had managed to keep my surgical instruments clean, with the canvas roll within my ragged shirt and tied around my body: also, the medical pack was intact, Bricko, Big One and Hu taking turns in its carrying.

In that squalid place of mud Kwelin and I awaited the men;

they came to us in single file, squatting on their haunches, hugging themselves against the bitter night wind.

"Hei up, missus, I ain't been for six days."

"That isn't important, you've not much going in," said Kwelin, who was at her best on such occasions. He was of Honan; stringy and misshapen.

"You givin' me nothin', then? I'm as tight as a bloody owl, woman."

"Did you eat mandrake potato?" she asked. "O, aye," said he.

"This time tomorrow you'll be running for it," said she. "Get your trousers loose – next, please."

"Got toothache, lady." This one was boy-man, not a Young Vanguard but scarcely a soldier. "Sit here," said Kwelin, "and open your mouth," and she called over her shoulder, "Trip! Little Ball!" The latter came pelting over the tufts. Bricko slyly handed Kwelin the forceps.

"Which tooth, little chap?" asked she. "Come on, open up."

With Bricko on the victim's head and Little Ball on the bugle, Kwelin, at her best, could achieve a really painless extraction.

At all times I respected her, like the rest of us; at times like this, I loved her best. She was like a bright light among us in this mood; among her soldiers, entering their banter (they rarely used obscenities with Kwelin near) she was more the man than many. "Next please!"

A few had bullet wounds from encounters with the Mantzu, and we did what we could for them; usually, however, within a day a wound was septic in this putrid place.

That night, the eleventh day in the marshes, it rained, but it did not rain. It bucketed, it tub-washed from a sky of lead: it pelted us with such ferocity that we had to shield our mouths and nostrils to snatch our breath. It dropped in sheeted water that instantly flooded the soggy earth, creating great ponds of still-water about our little camps. Drenched, we wandered in a foul wilderness, crouching under the lightning forking out of the heavens with our hats thrust out. And, when it had finished and we stood uncertainly, we discovered that we had not trapped a single drop of drinking water in the fight to stay upright.

Man Kim, from the enveloping embrace of Shao Shan, said,

"I'm shiverin' to have me bones out, Doctor Lin. Can't you order up a drop of sun?"

His courage was like a flame among us: in agony, he joked and shouted encouragement from his straps, and Tojo, as if to save him pain, planted each hoof as delicately as a Jenny donkey.

He called for sun once, but he did not call for it again.

The leaden skies cleared on the thirteenth day in the Grasslands and the sky became blue by dawn: marching still, our clothes steamed in its life-giving rays. We were revived, refreshed: with courage returning, we shouted our love at the sun; made camp in the warmth of a hungering day. Little Ball cooked our last hot meal of wheat and *chingko*, using the last of the firewood, and we sat around on the stinking earth, laughing with a new gaiety and hope, again gregariously Chinese – handing round the spoon one to the other, dipping into the blackened pot on its tripod.

And, at midday, it was as if a sun-spot flared a sword of fire. Within minutes the temperature raised ten points: in that damp place the heat grew painful and we lay outstretched, shielding our faces. I heard men crying aloud in panic to this sudden, onslaught of wet heat. Hotter still by early afternoon, it became an inferno before the cool promise of sunset: the sun was white-hot in a sky of incandescent rays, dropping on to the heated swamps a liquid fire that scorched our half-naked bodies. The sweat ran out of us with the profusion of humans being boiled. Shao Shan, crouching protectively over her husband, wailed at the sun, saying:

"Soon it will be better, little man. Soon the cold will come, with evening."

I lay above Kwelin, trying to keep her cool while the sun blazed down upon me: then she would insist on turning, to protect me: clutched together, we slowly dehydrated, the sweat of us mingling in streams. For as far as one could see there wasn't a single leaf of cover.

On the march (it was the sixteenth day of swamp, this I entered in my diary) Kwelin shrieked and fell full length: turning on an elbow, she snatched up her stained orange gown, her eyes filled with horror.

On the inside of her thigh, locked fast into her skin with claws, was a brightly coloured spider the size of a baby's hand.

"Wait, do not touch it," said the Man from Kwangtung.

314

Kwelin began to sob, her face turned away.

"Keep still," said he, and knelt beside her, one hand uplifted in silent warning.

Men gathered about us. With her naked leg outstretched, Kwelin lay shuddering in the circle of our feet, one hand quietly tearing at tump-grass, the hair of the bogs. And the spider lifted his hairy jointed legs in strange, dancing gyrations upon her thigh, his many tiny eyes switching about him in the sunlight, as if intrigued by this sudden attention from humans.

"It is a male," said the man from Kwangtung, and picked it off.

Lifting Kwelin to her feet, he momentarily held her. "Come, little girl," he said, "it was only a very small spider."

With the evening came coldness; an hour after sunset it was mid-winter. We were on the march again now, a bitter wind blustering into our faces, its ice-needles stinging our sun-blistered skin. And, as midnight approached, the temperature dropped so that we marched on a frozen ice-layer over the swamps, skidding and falling. Snow fell – great wavering flakes as big as orchid petals that clothed our chests and faces, as once, in my childhood, they fell on Laoshan. In mantled whiteness, with our bare feet rhythmically thumping on ice, we marched shivering and chattering into a frozen dawn.

And, when the sun rose again, the night frosts vanished: the bogs steamed, the cycle of heat and burning was renewed.

Soon the soldiers began to die.

Mainly, they died of dysentery.

We were now, we said, a 'Brown-Patch Army' – the sons of diarrhoea; men with bright brown patches on the seat of their trousers. We joked about this, there was nothing else to do – certainly, there was nobody around to complain to.

The cause was largely an enormous sweet potato which we discovered just below the soil, a thriving mandrake: one, we found, would feed six men for a day. But we had no kindling wood to make a fire, so there was no alternative but to eat them raw. They produced immediate ulcers on the lips and in the mouths and I was suspicious of them from the start.

What modesty we still possessed vanished with the arrival of this inedible food. Our route through the bog was now lined by squatting men relieving themselves in the last stages of dysentery: gaunt, yellow-faced soldiers with their trousers down and their shin-bone limbs stuck out defiantly, yet covering their faces like children at the sight of Kwelin and Shao Shan. Sometimes Kwelin would flounder across the mud towards one, kneeling beside him with words of comfort and a scrap of rhubarb or Ginseng root which I had managed to hang on to in the medical box.

"I'm coming, soldier. It's all right . . ."

"Sorry, missus!"

"It's all right, I say, hold on to me, man."

"*Hei wei*, soldier – turn off that woman!"

I heard Kwelin say, "Don't strain, man, please do not strain . . ."

"Women up, men – watch the women!"

"Eh up girl, 'ave you got a tail like mine? *Aiya!*"

The inbred shyness of the peasant forbade exposure, until Shao Shan and Kwelin got dysentery, too.

"You know," said Bricko, as Kwelin stumbled away to the side of the track, "there's no need to cry, woman. Who cares, anyway?"

"All bottoms look the same out here, Shao," said the man from Kwangtung. "Laugh and call it a full moon, girl. Get your trousers down like me."

"You'm a good old woman," said Man Kim, reaching down to pat her. "Don't you worry about the men."

It was the sweetness of people in comradeship. We actually supported each other towards the end of it: I held Kwelin steady; she held me.

"This," said she, her eyes serene, "is the business of falling in love."

We lost hundreds of men to bullets in the Grasslands, which was thought a record since we saw no enemy guns. The tribesmen were marksmen.

For this was Mantzu land, the fierce clans of the Tibetan border, and these warriors withdrew before us over the bogs, knowing the hidden tracks like the veins in their arms. Indeed, soon after we had entered the Grasslands the Mantzu Queen issued an order to her subjects to kill any Han Chinese, White or Red, who entered her domain: failure in this, she added, would be punished by boiling alive: this, presumably, is what happened to many of our soldiers who were captured. It became a rule to 'keep one bullet up the spout . . ."

There was no opportunity to explain communist policy to these barbaric people: such had been the cruel repression of the nationalists and the force of their propaganda preceding us, that there was no hope whatever of trade or barter with them; so, we had to take.

We stole, for the first time – raiding parties, penetrating deep into the forests that skirted the marshes, often returned with a few sacks of *chanpa* (griddle cakes made of flour-barley and butter) but it soon became evident that we were paying dearly for this: a sheep became worth the life of a man.

Bricko came back from such a raid; he was a walking mud-man, his rifle just a muddy stick, and he said, gasping, "We comes across a little *yurt* hut, me and the commander, an' sittin' at a table were fourteen of our men – Sixth infantry they were an' the commander goes up and gives one a shake. 'What the 'ell are ye doin' sittin' here?' says the commander, an' the fella he pushes just keels over dead."

"Dead?" I echoed.

"He were dead as a bloody mutton that fella – an' all the thirteen others dead 'an all, the commander says. Just sittin' there around a dead fire – freezed bloody solid."

He omitted to say that all had bullets in their backs: not frozen any of them, when the report came through – *rigor mortis*, and I mentioned this.

"Call it what you like, mister – those fellas was dead," said Bricko.

"Help me, help me!" cried Kwelin from darkness.

I heard her stumble in the darkness of the obliterating mist, heard the tell-tale sucking as she sank waist deep. In a swirl of night-mist I saw her not ten feet away, steadily sinking into the oozing mud with Toiya held above her head. In a moonflash I saw her mud-stained face, the terror of her eyes.

Bricko, being closest, got her first; using his rifle as a lever, he went flat and slowly crawled towards her.

"Kwelin's down, Kwelin's down!"

I gasped and rolled on to a thick patch of vetch-grass, the needle hair of the bogs. Bricko got Toiya's foot and pulled her backwards in a deep slush of the suffocating mud: I straddled my body across another grassy tuft; lying on an elbow, slowly sinking down, I felt the cold wetness sucking up my forearm; and in the moment before it reached my head I heard the subterranean calling of the bog. There then occurred, in the bridge between terror and cry, the phenomena of the Grasslands: many lights suddenly appeared, illuminating the mist with a roseate glow. And in an ensuing, muffled explosion a candle of a flame made shape to the right of Kwelin's floundering body. The heat of it was warm to our faces, the candle-power of its tremendous light banishing the mist so that all appeared in black silhouette – Bricko's muddy arm as he pulled Toiya to safety; Kwelin's horrified eyes as the bog sucked her down. I myself was shoulder-deep at the moment I grasped her forearms, but my grip slipped on mud to her wrists. I hauled, driving myself deeper; the mud slowly filled my mouth and I gasped for air, seeing, before the corpse-candle drifted away, a hemp rope slicing through mist. Grabbing it, I twirled it around my hand; Tojo's hooves scrabbled, flinging up mud as Big One backed her away.

They pulled us out like mating fish, and we lay together, Kwelin and I, gasping like fish from a pond.

I stared at her in the misted moonlight: she was no longer human but a shaking figure of mud, tiny below the crouching men: one most beautifully shaped in symmetry. Only her eyes, red-rimmed and starting from her mud-cheeks, told her terror.

"Rather you than me," said Shao Shan, trying to wash the baby's clothes. "It would have needed the Fifteenth Mohammedans to fetch me out."

"That light was a sign from the Old Weaver of Tatu," said the man from Kwangtung. That night Kwelin said to me, "Leave me, Lin – I will not walk in the morning."

"Oh, yes you will," I said, and kissed her. She clutched at me, sobbing quietly. I held her breasts; we knew a brief and earthy sweetness.

Day after day we floundered on, and I did not see Mao Tsetung. I did not see any high official, nor did I see Otto Braun being carried on his litter: it was rumoured so, but it was a lie. The Grasslands sometimes allowed a man to support his own weight; he now could never have supported another's.

More and more horses and mules were lost in the bogs: more and more soldiers slipped silently into water and were sucked under before they were able to take a breath for the cry. Nearing Panyu, on the Kansu border (where, it was rumoured, reactionary Moslem cavalry was waiting to receive us) a mud-stained Order of the Day arrived, yelled at the top of his lungs by Trip, who miraculously appeared when I had given him up for dead.

"Shoot all animals," he cried. "All animals to be shot. Horses first, then mules!"

Skinny Wong came to me, his manner outraged. "If Mao wants that mule shot he will have to do it himself!"

"Ignore it," I said, "at least for a while."

At night the cries of frogs, bull-throated, was a deafening chorus. With the soggy ground beneath us, we slept on our feet like horses, in twos, threes or fours, back to back. It is an interesting experience to sleep upright in the bedlam of another man's chokes and snores, with the horn-beetles using legs for ladders to swarm over your face, and you dare not brush one off for fear of waking the others. In this strange, vertical bed the gecko lizards with their adhesive toes and a marvellous sense of humour, walked up your trouser leg in search of your privates: Shao Shan was particularly annoyed with one, I recall, who managed to reach the most intimate of places.

When I awoke one morning Kwelin was sitting on my feet, rocking Toiya against her and crooning in a strange, discordant voice: it was eerie. And as she peered up at me I saw in her eyes an unusual, vacant light.

A madman two miles south of Kansu said to me, "You got a live mule, commander?" and he prodded Tojo in the ribs. "I'm going to eat that fuggin' mule, mister Commander, an' nobody's stopping me."

"Put a hand on that mule and I'll bloody kill you," said Bricko, coming up.

He was a shadow of the arrogant Bricko of Juichin, the man who wept for Fool: but his spirit was alive with an undiminished flame. The man said, "Listen to me, comrades, an' you'll never believe it . . ."

We were at camp, I remember, lying back on a ragged palliasse of vetch-grass, gasping with fatigue, unrecognisable as humans, having the bulged outlines of female gorillas. After a seven-hour slog through the bogs, when we had nearly lost Tojo, we were unspeaking, save to curse. "I don't believe it," mumbled Bricko, "you'm a liar – you lied once before, 'cause I heard ye – you got that monkey story, eh? You'm a useless, lying twat!"

"On the contrary," said the man from Kwangtung, "they are extremely useful."

"I was scavenging around for a mouth of somethin'," said the madman, "and I comes across the skeleton of a donkey sticking out of the swamp. Most o' the lads had been at it, of course, an' it fair reeked putrid . . ." He warmed to his tale, his hands cupped before him, shuffling about on his knees in the mud. "But I reckons that old donk owes me a bit, so I scraped off a cupful from between his shank an' his hooves. One cup I got, remember, by the light of the moon. An' I was just stealin' away with it for a feed and up comes a bloody monkey and snatches it from me hand." He glared at us with his baleful, reddened eyes, the face of hunger.

"Monkey, my arse," said the man from Kwangtung.

"I tell you, mister – it were – I bloody see'd it sure!"

"It were a fuggin' communist, that's what," said Bricko.

"Mind you," said Shao Shan, nursing Toiya, "I've seen a few up that Headquarter alley that look like monkeys, eh, Mister Man?" and she prodded her little husband lying beside her.

"I tell ye, it were a real, live monkey – I heard him hollerin'."

"Then you go catch him and we'll eat the sod," said Bricko.

We slept a little, dreaming of Yenan.

I had found a stub of rock; behind this I put Kwelin, pushing myself against her to keep away the cold. In the night I awoke to find her kissing me; her lips were warm on my face.

Shao Shan said, pressing her breast, "It is finished."

"Oh, no," whispered Kwelin, terrified, and she snatched the baby from Shao's arms and staggered up, stumbling about. Reaching me, she stooped, peering into my face in horror. "What shall we do, Lin . . . no milk?"

"Look at the old things," said Shao Shan, shaking them. "Not even a lick on the tits."

It was near dawn, I recall. Near Shao sat Skinny Wong, once corpulent: beside him sat Big One, his head in his hands, mud-caked from head to foot; Hu was asleep against him.

There was no sound but the bitter wind sighing over the marshes: all down the column people were waking from fitful sleep:

the sky was flaring red, and bronze to the north where lay the haven of Pahsi. Man Kim spoke:

"We lose that baby and we lose everything, Doctor Lin."

I took Toiya from Kwelin and cradled her in my arms.

Man Kim said, "My woman's got to eat, see? Don't matter who it is – there ain't a woman in the world can make milk without eating."

Kwelin said with great sincerity to Shao Shan, "You've got to eat, girl." She took Toiya from my arms.

"Nobody likes that idea more'n me," said Shao.

"Take your pick," said the man from Kwangtung, though he appeared not to have been listening. "It's either a dead mule or a dead Toiya – I know what Yung would have done."

We stared at each other in the brightening day. Kau Kau, as if hearing this, whined against Bricko's leg, pitifully shivering. Big One, I noticed, licked his thick lips.

Shao Shan said, "Knock off that mule and you'll have to leave my man behind, an' that ain't happenin', Doctor Lin – not for you, your sister, Yung, or his baby. I'm taking my man to Yenan, 'cause he ain't never left me."

Kwelin said, in whispers, something quite out of context, "Poor little soul . . ." she hugged Toiya against her. "Her poor little bottom's red raw, too – in a dreadful state." This served us: we all gathered around, looking at Toiya's bottom, making parental sounds.

"She's asleep?" I said.

"Poor little darling, she ought to be dead. Perhaps she is dead, Lin-wai?" She smiled sadly into my face and I saw again the hint of disorder in her eyes. "Are we all really dead, you think . . . ?"

I said, "Nobody here will die, I won't let you die . . ."

The sun was reflecting vicious red rays over the sombre outline of a distant forest: it was as if the trees were afire, like the ending of the world. From somewhere in the darkness a man was sobbing.

The man from Kwangtung said:

"Shall I tell you something? The Red Army will capture Yenan if this baby lives: she is a symbol of life. If she dies in the Grasslands, so will this army." He rose. "There's no hoodoo in it, it has nothing to do with the old Weaver of Tatu: if Toiya dies, we will, too."

Bricko lifted the mongrel and held it against him.

All stared at Kau Kau who was whimpering in his hands.

I said to Kwelin, "Nurse Toiya until she cries for food. We will make our decision then."

Bricko retreated with the bitch staring fearfully over his shoulder.

Hu was making frantic finger-signs before Big One's face: the giant man watched with a stained, bearded smile. Smiling wider, he rose, went to Shao Shan and pushed her aside: kneeling, he picked up Man Kim in his arms.

"It is easy," said Hu. "Big One will carry him."

Calling Bricko back, I gave him my pistol, and he went and shot Tojo. An hour later Tojo, save for her bones, had vanished. We began again the onward slog: before us, behind us, were the jogging shoulders of sweating, cursing men; the bogs steamed.

There was a bull of a soldier of the Sixth and his name was Tung Yuen: a bullet had shattered his forearm as he was trying to steal a sheep from a Mantzu encampment.

Neither did he bring the sheep, losing it on the way.

"This arm will have to come off," I said, and he replied, fiercely:

"But I am Tangar – from Yentai. I will lose my junk if I lose my arm!"

"You'll lose your life if I leave it on," I said, and he pondered this.

"See sense, man," said Kwelin, coming up.

"It bloody stays on," said he.

Toiya began to cry in Shao Shan's arms then, and the man from Yentai said, "That could be my own baby son back on the junk. My wife, you know, is a Hoklo – they are really only sea-vermin – but from her belly has come three fine boys, also a daughter for the deck-scrubbing."

Kwelin said, with cool practicality, "Then you must return to your little sea-cow, and, with your fine seed, she will fetch out more." She was baring his arm for the knife, and she added, "Come, what is an arm when it comes to a family? What is pain when it comes to a sea-cow of such quality? Four bouncers, man – think of the pain of that – and in your belly, remember – forget your arm!"

He stared at her. She said, "You are skin-afraid – prove it different – you big cockerels are all the same. *Kneel!*" and he knelt.

"Now lie," said she, "and I will lie beside you – on your side, so the sun will not blind you," and she turned him so that he could not see the knife. Bricko came; swiftly, I rolled out my instruments.

I heard Kwelin whisper into the wounded man's face, "Now think that I am your wife: put your right arm around here and dream you are making a son in me."

She never ceased to astonish me. I took off his left arm at the elbow and he didn't make a sound. Afterwards, I said to Kwelin, "It appears to me that you've done that before – I heard every word you said."

"Why not?" asked she in pale surprise. "It works with arms, anyway – it always did in the Ninth. With the surgeon on one arm and me on the other, they don't get a lot, you know."

They came down from the Sixth infantry; big, ragged men and starving, and they bantered with us, calling the tune, a hideous, forced humour, and when they left, Kau Kau, Bricko's mongrel, had gone.

Bricko and I, Shao Shan and Big One went after them, catching them as they were pegging the dog for the club.

Bricko went in first; swaying across the vetch-grass, he felled one with his fist and dragged another down.

"Oh no, you bloody don't, you bastards!"

There was six of them, and Big One took three, and the hullabaloo of the fighting brought their comrades around: in a dazed circle men watched us while we fought, and Kau Kau, an inch off the beating to make her tender, yelped and leaped, tethered in the bog. One came at me; he was a big man and tough, and we wrestled fitfully together without strength until we fell, me uppermost: it was only a glancing blow I caught him but he sagged into unconsciousness. Men were screaming, others doubled in choking coughs; we were mud-men, kneeling in it, covered in it, with the slime flying off our tremendous aimless swings. Somebody was beating Bricko with the club and between the sickening thuds he was crying, "He's Fool's dog, he's Fool's dog, don't you see?"

An officer came, a pistol levelled: his command cut through the weak gasps and sobbing.

"On your feet – you ought to be bloody ashamed, the lot of you."

We staggered up, bent and swaying, exhausted by the fight.

"What's it all about?" demanded the officer: he was pale, thin and trembling with hunger. I said, wiping away the mud, "They . . . they were going to eat our dog . . ."

Instantly, he swung the pistol at Kau Kau, and a voice said:

"Shoot it, and I'll blow your stomach into the man behind you." The officer put away his gun. The man from Kwangtung knelt and cut the cord that tethered Kau Kau.

"Any dog-eating," said he, "will be done by us."

We followed him back to the Fifth Muleteers with the walking joint. When we returned I found Kwelin standing alone: the sun was stoking up coals in the sky, and Kwelin smiled at me, not even mentioning the appalling state I was in. She said, "It looks like being a beautiful day . . ."

I wiped the mud from my eyes and stared at her.

Drought.

On the twentieth day in the Grasslands we were still making north, the plunging feet of the soldiers leaving black wounds in the thin crust that covered the decaying vegetation. Many of the following Sixth infantry were crying for water.

For six days now it had not rained.

It rained once, I recall, and Bricko shrieked, "Look, it is raining!"

But it wasn't raining on us; it was raining on the scattered remnants of the Sixth fifty yards behind us. We ran. The man from Kwangtung was leading. And, as he chased the rain, begging for it to stop, it receded before him. Little Ball was there, leaping from tuft to tuft over the bogs, shouting with his bowl thrust out to catch the sparkling water. But the rain eluded him, sweeping with increasing speed over the shouting column, to vanish over the horizon. The sun burned down. We fell on our faces, sucking at the putrid mud. Men of the Sixth raced up – some Red Cadre people were there, too, and they hauled us up, pushing us away, yelling:

"It's our rain, it's our rain – piss off, go on, piss off!"

Bricko was first out of the mud, flinging himself at a commander, but others tore him away. The commander grabbed a rifle and crouched, levelling it at the eunuch.

"Go and find your own rain," he said.

Somehow I had managed to contain a handful of clean water: this I took to Kwelin, treading carefully. We knelt. "You first," said she.

The rain was evaporating in my cupped hand. I made Kwelin drink first; when it was my turn my hand was dry. At this she wept, holding me.

The sun flared in its molten sky. It dehydrated our bodies, it pumped up enormous blisters on our naked skin; spied through the rents in our rags and brought up scalds. Earlier, we had cut great hunks of flesh from the shanks of the mule and hung them to dry from our belts. We moved now attended by individual swarms of flies that stung and bit us. We went automatically, blindly swaying after the man in front, our sun-hats tilted to flash away the violet burn of the sun. Below our bare feet (not a man was now wearing sandals) the matted bog was of the consistency of concrete; to change instantly to liquid mud at the first shower of rain, bubbling in its depths, belching up foul odours. But the rain did not come, and we stumbled forward, seeking always the mirage of Panyu which the propaganda teams called an oasis: here, they said, wallowing about us in the mud, was a paradise of pearl rice, chunked beef, ice-cold, sparkling water. They were magnificent, appalling liars. Somebody – I think it was the man from Kwangtung – said he saw Mao fall in the swamp: Chen, the batman, ever watchful, was first in after him. Others said Mao was being carried, but this was a lie. One report had it that both he and Chou En-lai had been captured by Mantzu tribesmen and been boiled alive.

"He ain't got nothin' on us," mumbled Bricko.

We staggered on, staring ahead for the paradise of Panyu. For days now we had held no sick parade; we held one once, but nobody came. The men didn't care about dysentery now, or broken limbs or wounds. All they wanted now was water and food, and in that order.

Shao Shan said, "Last night I went back for a bit more of Tojo – the whole of General Headquarters must have been at her – she was picked as clean and white as that prehistoric monster up in Shanghai museum."

"Mao's all right," said Skinny Wong. "He just fell in the bog. And the moment he was out he was pulling bits off a donkey."

"But all the animals have been eaten now," said the man from Kwangtung.

"It's disgusting," whispered Kwelin, staring at nothing. "It's disgusting." She turned to me. "May I have some water, Chan Lin-wai?" She stared up at me, her eyes filling with tears. "Please . . . some water . . .?" She was a piteous sight now, formless, dehydrated.

"*Come*," I said.

There was no water; either that day, the next day, or the day after that. The column was on the move again. Kwelin's strength was failing. I half-carried her now: Big One wanted to help, but I pushed him away, I wouldn't let anybody touch her. Come night I was almost dragging her, gripping her around the waist with her arm hooked round my neck. "Let me go," she said once, "Lin, let me die." I shook my head. "I will not let you die."

The mosquitoes buzzed their sing-song war-cries in the night fastness: it was a world of blood-hunt, of the leech, man-killing hornets and mantis-prayers: the days were sun-scalds, the nights arctic; the dew was the formic-acid sprays of tribes of great-ants; at dusk the purple fur scuttling of moon-rats became our staple food. It was a bright green flowering, and loathsome paradise, and I shall never forget it: a bog-burial ground of thousands of our best: skinny ignominious corpses were these, shroudless, a multitude of starved soldiers in tatters, their choking faces suspended grotesquely above the Grassland mud.

Now men in the column were dying of thirst. The main cause of this was the dried fish we had salted and brought from the miracle of the Shi-ho river: now our last resort against hunger, it laid crystal salt upon our lips; it cracked our throats, inducing a premature and agonising thirst.

Our skin tented over our bones.

The sun blazed down.

On the fifth day of the drought we drank our own urine.

The face of my lovely Kwelin was now the face of a venereal beggar; her drum-stick arms projected indecently from the rents of her Cantonese gown: she walked in gasps, leaning against me. With one arm I supported her, in the other I carried Toiya, who, protected, fed by Shao Shan again, was better off than any of us.

My baby had become, in this nightmare of the Grasslands, a symbol of life: her faint, croaking cries of hunger were a clarion call to any man within ear-shot. Soldiers as far forward as the fanatical propaganda teams and down the line to the dying in-

326

fantry would send by the indefatigable Young Vanguards morsels of food for the Muleteer Girl. Shao Shan also received many scraps, being a mother in milk.

But the one thing nobody had was water.

Often, I wondered how Mao Tse-tung's baby was getting on . . .

"What are you talkin' about, ye fools," mumbled Bricko. "I got water . . ."

He took the bowl from Little Ball by force, I remember.

It was midday. The sun was incandescent, a thermal ball of cremating light. Men were dying in hundreds of a raging thirst; their sprawled bodies lying where they had fallen out of the column. With protruding purple tongues sticking out of their blackened face, they were a new carnage: many of the dead were actually sitting up on the stones as if enjoying the comedy of watching the Red Army march, their opaque, blistered eye balls transfixed; their mouths wide open for the last, dreamed gasp of cooling water.

"Ay ay," said Bricko, "I got water. Ay ay!"

And he pushed Little Ball full length in the mud, wheeled about him as a scarecrow in the hot wind, and picked up the rice-bowl.

We watched. Holding Kwelin against me, shielding her face in Toiya's clothes, I watched: Kwelin made a small, complaining sound.

We watched, all but Kwelin and Shao Shan, who also turned away her face.

Big One, on his knees with Man Kim strapped to his back, watched as did Hu. Skinny Wong watched, also the man from Kwangtung.

Bricko was on his knees, opening his flies.

The swaying column of mud-scarecrows was bunching behind us, now spilling past us in haggard disregard. I saw their faces, the tear-stained rivulets decorating their gaunt, mud-stained cheeks. Seeing Bricko with the bowl, they stopped; drooping about me, they stared at him with incredulity.

"Why, you filthy bastard!"

"Oh no, oh no! Just look what he's doing!"

They pestered, disbelieving, pushing faintly at their neighbours.

"It needed a fuggin' muleteer!"
"I anna doin' that, soldier."
"Bloody die first . . ."

They moaned together, appalled yet fascinated: the tongues of many had swollen from their mouths in violet plums: these stood stupidly speechless. Some just pointed at Bricko in mute complaint as he knelt there filling the bowl. And Little Ball said apprehensively, "We gotta use that pot for rice, ye know, soldier."

Somebody said, "Water . . . water . . ." Kwelin heard this and stiffened in my arms, trying to look. "Water . . . ?"

"I got water," said Bricko, and drank.

Later, in darkness, I called to Shao Shan, and she turned her face to mine, shivering. There was great activity down the line: men were calling faintly to one another; it was like the murmuring of some distant, fancied ocean. I whispered:

"Shao . . . help me, eh?" I gave her the bowl and she stared at it with haggard eyes. "Come on, now . . . ?"

"What you damn want?"

I said, affronted, "How is Kim?"

"He is dying."

The bog sucked and belched about us.

I gasped into her face. "You fool! He need not die!"

Shao Shan put Toiya on the earth and took the bowl, staring up at me with peasant obedience.

"Help him," I said. "It must be his own."

Shao Shan said, face low. "By the blood of my mother's womb . . ."

"When you have finished with it, bring the bowl to me."

I saw her face as a pale mask in that moonlight.

"You had any, doctor?"

I said. "And then you must help me with Kwelin . . ." I shook her for sense. "Understand? She is dying. You must help me. With Kwelin. I can't lift her . . . I can't do it alone."

Toiya had ceased to cry. I wondered if she was dead.

Later, all down the line men were using their rice-pots; I

could hear them clanging about, an indecent lust for water. With Kwelin in my arms I soaked a rag of my uniform in the pot and moistened her cracked lips. The urine stung her into consciousness: I held the bowl to her mouth. Gasping, spluttering, retching, she drank.

Shuddering, moaning, she drank.

And, as she did so, weeping, it rained.

"Seui a! Seui a!"

This they shrieked about me in a growing chorus. "Water! Water!"

Men screamed delight, a frog chorus; the frogs stopped to listen to the guttural croak of thirst.

"Tai, lohk yuh la, lohk yuh la!"

Those standing flung out their arms to the pelting moon, danced in delight to the thunder of the sky; others whirled in mad circles, hopelessly gyrating, spending their last strength in a dervish tribute to rain. Others, the more than half-dead, stirred face down in the fissured bogs as the water-holes filled about them, and prepared to drown. All down the column men were shouting, mouths wide to receive the deluging rain. Lightning lanced the glowering clouds; the moon lifted her black skirts and shone her great, silver backside over the dull, parched country, lighting it with instantaneous searchlight beams.

The Red Army sprang to life; naked men splashed up and down the watery tracks, shouting their gratitude to the heavens: others sat in the lethargy of approaching death, too far gone to know the life-giving water: some I saw flopping over in waving arms, languidly flailing in the marsh that soon would suck them down.

I sat with Kwelin in my arms and watched Shao Shan gather Toiya to her breast: Kim, her husband, was blowing on Chipang's bugle and waving his arms; Bricko called in delight to him, a shrill treble. Big One was holding Hu high in his arms, shaking him as if in sacrifice to distant gods.

Kwelin said. "Lin, it is raining . . ."

I held her. Rocking her in my arms, I held her in the rain.

Shuddering anew, she screwed up her fists and held them against her mouth.

THIRTY-THREE

PAOAN! *Yenan!*

Now, with the rearguard emerging from the Grasslands, the anus of China, the tattered skeletons of the once great First Front Army stumbled along the flinted roads to the north. And before us, shimmering like a mirage across the lunar Kansu plains, the oasis town of Panyu, the Place of Water, glittered golden in the sun-raging day.

A few hours after leaving Panyu, with our thirst quenched and a little food in our stomachs, we again saw Mao at his best, the brilliant student of Sun Tzu's classic *Art of War*. It was a bitter, ironic experience.

Once clear of the Grasslands, renewed attacks by Chiang Kai-shek's Kuomintang awaited us: this phase of the March, when at our weakest, the enemy would use as a killing-ground – this Mao anticipated.

So now, with a mixture of anger and pride, we lay exhausted north of the Panyu oasis and watched long columns of the famous Red Cadre infantry march past us to engage General Hu Tsung-nan's Nineteenth Division, the waiting butchers astride the road near Pahsi.

Only once before had I seen such men as these, the pride of the Red Army, and that was under Commander Hsiao, when I was ferried with them over the Gold Sand River for their attack on Chouping Fort. True, they were mud-covered soldiers – as all who entered the Grasslands; but no walking skeletons were these; they were muscular from good feeding, and none, I suspected, had gone short of water: the rest of the army had been sacrificed to keep them strong. And now they marched past us with their usual lust for battle, rank on rank, with weary Sixth Infantry dragging their marsh-sledges: on these were stacked the rifles and automatics, the canisters of water, the food boxes of a provisioned army: to provide these, we of the muleteers and a dozen other units, had died in hundreds. And, as if aware of their role of superiority, accepting the sacrifices as their due, they marched with almost regimental pride, looking neither right nor left at the riff-raff of the old Sixth and the remnants of the Fifth Muleteers lying along the road. Bricko reacted first as we watched them pass: raising himself to his knees he pointed a mud-encrusted arm at them and croaked.

"You bastards! You bloody bastards!"

Kwelin, lying beside me, weakly restrained him. The Red Cadre ignored the growing chorus of indignant bawling. I stood up, waving my arms, and in our area the shouting stopped. Men began to remember, perhaps, that these fresh soldiers had been held in reserve to die.

Not three hours later they were into the Kuomintang Nineteenth, cutting red swathes through the enemy defences, spreading their usual ferocity in the vicious hand-to-hand in which they specialised. And so, while the main army rested on the road to Pahsi, Chiang Kai-shek's ambush was pinned on the bayonets of Mao Tse-tung's tactical brilliance. Later still, these same Red Cadre, weary and blood-stained, returned to us with captured food.

Food!

They brought it in mule-carts captured from the enemy: salted pig in wooden casks, barrels and barrels of the finest pearl rice, and these they rolled down the road towards us with cries of victory. There was *chingko* by the *picul*, buckwheat and the wild celery the Kuomintang loved. There was a strange chopped beef in tins, which the enemy called "bully" – and these we prised open with our bayonets: one cart, with a dead Kuomintang still trapped in the driver's seat, was filled with cans of delicious orange squash called "California", and this we guzzled in the cold, grey dawn, weakly cheering the Red Cadre victors. Clear of the rest, while the muleteers and Sixth advance infantry fed until they bulged, I cradled Toiya in one arm and gripped Kwelin with the other, taking them to a little arbour of trees: soon, I knew, the sun would come up, turning the dawn into scalds of light. The provisioning Red Cadre, realising this, were beating their captured food column back down the line to the last tattered survivors just emerging from the Grasslands. Away to the north the ambush battle still raged, in a thunderous painting of the night sky, but scattered engagements east and west of the road told of the gradual defeat of the Kuomintang Nineteenth. From somewhere Bricko had actually got a tin of condensed milk: this, diluted with water, we fed to Toiya while

Kwelin, revived by the food, began weakly to tend the Red Cadre wounded.

"You rest, woman," said Shao Shan, coming up.

"Leave her," I commanded. "She is a nurse – this is her job – here, you take care of Toiya."

Amazingly, this worked. With Hu and Bricko's help I formed a small casualty station. I heard a soldier say:

"Leave it, girl – you're a bloody sight worse off than me."

Kwelin was kneeling above him with his first-aid packet in her hands. I went to them. It was a bayonet wound: the stab had taken the man over the bicep; blood was rushing, unstemmed, from the veins under the elbow.

His eyes were fierce upon me, the usual Cadre arrogance. "You a doctor?"

"Which is more than you are," said the man from Kwangtung.

"This woman's half dead."

"Shut your mouth," I answered quietly, "the woman's a nurse."

It settled him. With a tremendous effort, Kwelin stemmed the bleeding; I heard the soldier call out to me while I was probing a bullet out of another. With one arm bandaged he was yet supporting Kwelin. The patients were reversed.

"All right, Doctor, I'll see to her," cried Bricko.

"You got some woman there," said the Red Cadre soldier. "What's her name?"

"You were lucky to get her," I said, holding a mug to Kwelin's lips.

"She starved for you, mate," said Bricko. "For you she's got no name – now take your arm and piss off."

"Here, Kwelin, come with me," said the man from Kwangtung.

I had to let her go; there was so much to do. The effect of her weakness was intermittent fainting, but there was more to it than that: Kwelin's face was slowly adopting a dark, unhealthy pallor and she was shivering.

I wanted to be with her, to wash her clean, to cherish her, but the Red Cadre wounded were still calling to me from the litters as the dawn broke in flashing light and heat. The sun bulged molten in a sky of fire; Kwelin, conscious again, was working on the wounded as fast as I operated: it was an unwholesome business of sprawling limbs and screams, for I had no anaesthetics save five precious opium seeds, and these I could not spare. The warning shouts of nearby men told me of Kwelin's constant fainting, but the moment Shao Shan revived her with a mugful of water in the face she was back on her knees over the wounded: her presence, her indomitable courage, calmed them: it enforced their own, personal stoicism. I was doing dreadful things to them with the knife but now they bit on their rags and stared at Kwelin, in wonder.

On that bloody morning outside Panyu she was like a beacon of fire among us.

With dusk the sounds of heavy fighting ceased; the Red Cadre wounded lessened to a trickle: more, two surgeons of the Sixth came down to help in the afternoon.

With the coming of dusk and coldness I held Kwelin in a quiet place away from men: Shao Shan, squatting near by with Man Kim beside her, nursed Toiya. Here, infinitely slowly, for I, too, was exhausted now, I washed Kwelin clean, and passing soldiers looked away.

Once she awoke and touched my face: Bricko – I think it was he – came and covered us with Kuomintang blankets. In my arms Kwelin slept; in the bitter cold of the Kansu night, under a sky shattered with stars, I held her, and the faint shivering of her thin body, I knew, was not caused by the cold.

But, when we awoke with the dawn she appeared momentarily refreshed, and the shivering had stopped. The star-shells of the forward battle had long faded into the new dawn; the thundering of the Kuomintang artillery had ceased.

All about me men were stirring on the ground; the few wounded still left with us were groaning from sleep, facing the first searing pull of the stitches. A man was standing above me; there was about him a quiet authority. He said:

"Surgeon Chan Lin-wai, of the Third?"

I sat up, nodding. "I serve the Fifth Muleteers."

"Compliments of Third Casualty Station – you did well." He bowed.

I did not reply to him, for Kwelin had opened her eyes to me.

"Come," I said, and put my arm about her.

The officer persisted, "The Surgeon-General himself would like to compliment you and the nurse."

I raised Kwelin to her feet and put my face against hers.

"Shall ... shall I call back?" asked the officer. And Bricko shouted:

"Tell him it's too late – they ain't gettin' our doctor and nurse."

"Tell him to go to hell," said the man from Kwangtung.

The officer rubbed his chin, grinning. "I'm sure he'll understand," said he.

Pahsi followed, but we dared not rest. It was on, on, on – a race for the Liupan mountains. Day after day the remnants of the decimated Nineteenth Kuomintang harried and ambushed us, and their bombers plastered us along the road to Paotso. The reformed Red Cadre fought like animals in the van, and we of the Fifth and Sixth supported them; we lost no prisoners, we took none; scruples vanished on that march to Paoan where the Twenty-Fifth Army was awaiting us – they who had earlier endured their own Long March – as a score of units from army corps to mere regiments were still suffering theirs: but all arrowing to a single target – Yenan in the province of Shensi; there to build a new base for war against the Japanese. The column plodded onward; autumn winds blew into our faces.

"War against nobody," said the man from Kwangtung. "When I get to the loess land I'm putting my feet up."

"*If* you get to Yenan," said Skinny Wong, limping along.

Hu, his thin face bright in the sun, cried to me, "Mister Linwai, when I gets to Shensi Province, me and Big One's starting for farmers."

Kwelin gave him one of her slow, sad smiles; I was still worried about Kwelin on the march to Paotso, though some of her strength had returned.

"Aye, *aiya*!" cried Hu, all four feet of him and as bony as a starved monkey, "when we gets there we're knocking off a landlord and dig the farms, eh, big fella?" and he walked backwards in the column, his little hands fiercely sign-telling before Big One's face. The giant man stumbled on, incoherently chuckling from his matted beard.

"You're comin' for a farmer, Hu lad?" cried Man Kim from the back of his donkey: this we had filched on the road to Panku, and this is one little bastard we're not taking in barter, said Bricko. Shao Shan, with Toiya slung on her back, led the little moke; Kim, strapped horizontally on what was left of

Tojo's saddle (we had boiled the rest for chilli soup outside Pahsi) had a Hakka sun-hat shredding over his face to protect him from the glare. The clip-clop of little hooves beat on the rutted road.

"Ay ay, Uncle Kim – me and the big fella," cried Hu. "And up in Wuchichen wi' the Commissar, we'll mate up goats for udder milk to feed to Baby Toiya, for we're always wanted for farmers, 'anna we, man?"

Big One grinned amiably, patting Hu's head.

Bricko shrieked, "Sounds good, young 'un, but what you doin' for a woman, eh? You start the hoein' and sowin' and ye bound to need a good woman for the heavy labour, an' hens." His shapeless, naked feet spurted dust. All down the column great billows of dust were rising to the steaming, onward march.

"Clearly you're a dedicated Marxist," said the man from Kwangtung, standing alone. "Equality? fraternity? love?"

"Ay ay!" shouted Hu, delighted, and he patted Man Kim's stomach up on the donkey. "I thought o' that, so I'm fetchin' my mama. You lend me that moke to go an' fetch my mama from Yichi, Uncle Kim?"

"You can have Mao Tse-tung's bloody dun horse when we get to Yenan," replied Kim. And he waved his thin arms and shouted at the sun.

I looked behind me, momentarily steadying Kwelin. The column of men was swaying along the dusty road: behind us lay the bath-steaming Grasslands: the mountains seemed to follow us, their peaks granite-red and burnished by the sun. All about us were the flat fields of loess land interspersed with humps and hillocks, good ambush country. Every day now the Moslem cavalry took us – the reactionary brothers of the old Fifteenth Mohammedans, once the pride of the Sixth. Now, horseless, with beards to their chests, their turbans hanging limply, the refuse of the arrogant, once great sons of Kansu were entering their homeland to do battle with knives, son against son, father against father.

But they fought with the same fury, their broadswords swinging under the bellies of the great, brown chargers, slashing at the levelled spear-pennants, chopping down dismounted riders: they always fought in the van, for in ambush the van is often the flank: standing stock-still, swords held high, yelling their war-cries as the double line of Kansu Moslems bore down upon us, and their unison shouts I will always remember:

"*Shang ma!*" ("*Mount Horse!*" – *though they had no horses*). Down would come the crude sabres as they leaned against the shock.

"*Ma-ti Ma Hung-kuei! Ma-ti Ma Hung-kuei!*" And as they cut and lunged in a mêlée of flying hooves and shrieking horses, they defiled the name of the old Moslem war-lord, whom once they had served: he who had stolen their lands, taxed their families out of existence and stolen every son but one in a family, a puppet of the Kuomintang. Now, on the north road that led to Yenan, our Moslems kept their pride – the first to engage the cavalry because, though fighting on foot, they lived in dreams of cavalry.

Usually, we left them to it: nobody could help much among those flailing sabres: nor would we transgress their Moslem-Turkish creed – the man who rides in cavalry dies under cavalry.

On we went, tramp, tramp, tramp; with Kwelin leaning heavily against me, we swayed down the road to Latsu.

Shao Shan, one great breast bared, was feeding Toiya, the only being in the First Front Army instantly recognisable as human: how many soldiers, I have wondered since, died on the Long March to keep her alive? Shao said into Kwelin's gaunt face:

"Soon, love, soon ... Not long now, little nurse – soon we will get to Yenan." We staggered on through another molten day.

It was Yenan, always Yenan, and the caves in the loess hills of Shensi province. But Yenan was still 500 miles away, and before us stood a final barrier, the narrow Latsu Pass lying between the headwaters of the rivers Pailung and Min.

This narrow defile was two miles long; the whole length of this defile was defended by a Kuomintang division entrenched in depth.

We met some Han Chinese peasants – a true Chinese minority living in the middle of the fierce Mantzu clans. We broke ranks and ran to them; we embraced them (breaking the rule, 'respect for person'). We even kissed in this tremendous joy at finding brothers and sisters in that barren place: we knelt in their fortified houses: forgetting communism, we kissed their red altars to hoodoo gods; we buried our mouths in their soil. They said they thought we were mad crow-starvers come from another world: dancing, we cried and laughed.

But Kwelin had not joined in these celebrations. Leaving the laughing, excited people, I came to her with Toiya in my arms.

"They are Hans – they are true Chinese, don't you understand?" I asked, but she did not reply: indeed, she just stared past me.

"Kwelin ... ?" I put Toiya against her, but she did not take her.

"Kwe ... !"

Her complexion was changing; her face was further darkening, as if she had mixed her blood with Hakka, the Guest People from Anwhei. People were rushing past us, shouting in delight. I said into Kwelin's eyes:

"O, *P'an ku*, your god pity me."

Like people escaping, I hurried her to a remote place and there sat her down. Automatically, she took Toiya into her arms, but her eyes, great orbs in her high-boned, dusky face, did not move to Toiya's uneasy cries. Kneeling before them I stroked Kwelin's hair, saying, "Oh, Kwe, do not leave me now – not after all this – don't leave me." Putting my arms around her, I began to rock her to and fro.

Soon we marched again, and Bricko took turns with me in carrying her.

Night fell and the column camped. Many came to me, offering help, but I sent them away. I could not bear them to share her. With the food run out again, all I had left was some old *chingko*, and this I chopped into little pieces for her, feeding it to her with my fingers, saying stupidly, "You will be all right, my darling. You see, when we get to Paoan we will feed you up. Do you know there is Maotai wine in Paoan?"

Toiya was screaming for Shao Shan's milk, but I scarcely heard her: I was saying ridiculous things to Kwelin, such as, "But you were all right outside Panyu, weren't you? You were all right then – you even helped me to operate on the Red Cadre, remember how the officer came down from the Surgeon-General? *Kwelin ... !*"

The moon was rising and I shuddered with the cold, holding her closer. Kwelin raised her face once and smiled at the moon. I said, in growing panic:

"And remember the man of Yentai, whose arm we took off?"

I laughed, shaking her by the shoulders. "You were certainly on form with him!"

I sensed, rather than saw the presence of Shao Shan. Toiya had cried herself to sleep. Kneeling, the woman picked Toiya up and slowly came to me, her bulk obliterating the moon. Kwelin, in my arms, lay across my lap, yet her eyes, wide open, were fixed upon my face; she was breathing deeply, awake, but asleep; a frightening phenomena.

Nothing in my medical studies had taught me how to handle this. My inadequacy brought me close to terror. I began to wonder if she might die; so many had died, but it had not crossed my mind until now, that Kwelin could die. I thought, if Kwelin dies I will kill myself.

I called upon her Goddess of Mercy, to whom I had found her praying on that summer day in Tsunyi.

"Kuan Yin . . . *Kuan Yin*, heal her . . .?"

Shao Shan, still cradling Toiya, leaned over me, whispering, "Let her go, man, let her go, you are squeezing her to death."

"Is it malaria?" This I actually asked of a peasant, and one of low intelligence at that. "She is sweating – look how she is sweating! Shao, help me!" I grabbed at her leg, pulling her nearer.

"She is not sweating," said Shao Shan.

I held Kwelin aside; my legs were soaked, even the grass was wet.

"But look, look – she is soaking me!"

"It is a new sickness," said Shao Shan.

Kwelin was not sweating; she was incontinent.

That midnight we marched again; Bricko and I carried Kwelin on a litter; it was a rough litter, but it served us, and men of the Sixth, who loved her, came up the line to the muleteers to take a turn with her weight. They found little gifts of food for her; they helped me wash her in wayside streams, and when the Nineteenth Kuomintang attacks came, they surrounded the litter, using their bodies as stop-butts lest a bullet should come her way.

Earlier Mao had been overheard talking to another – I believe it was Chou En-lai, but I may be wrong. "The women on this march," said he, "have proved more courageous than the men. People like Kang, the wife of Chu Teh, are not women, but super-men. When the column is resting, the women do not rest, but set about the cooking. When the column is sleeping the women do not appear to sleep, but are out, armed, looking for food. We even have a lily-footed woman (bound-foot) and she has walked many hundreds of miles. Look to that for courage – look to Kang, the amazon woman – look at my own wife, Ho; look at the women who have carried the wounded on their backs..."

"Look at Kwelin," I said.

"Aye," said Bricko, "it don't matter about them other buggers."

Gaunt, skinny, hollow-eyed: this was Kwelin before the Battle of Latsu Pass. Now she lay on her litter by the roadside on the way to Latsukou and stared at the shuffling men with the eyes of a woman lost. The last four miles of the Grasslands had raked her; in those miles, in the drinking of the urine, Kwelin seemed to die.

"Your hair is still beautiful though, my precious," said Shao Shan now. "When we get you to the Twenty-Fifth, I will plait it and tie it with pretty ribbon. You see – you'll be beautiful again, when we get you to Paoan."

Later, Shao Shan said to me, "I have seen her on this march doing disgusting jobs on howling men – sucking out poison from their sores, cleaning filthy wounds – wiping their backsides – there was nothing she would not do for them. On Snow Mountain she was thawing frozen fingers on her breasts. Now she is ill. Can we do nothing?"

I emptied my hands at her, and she shrieked into my face, "Is that all? You're a damn doctor, aren't you? *Do something*!"

Vaguely, I was wondering if they sold black ribbons in Yenan, Kwelin's hair now being white ...

We were running out of food again; there was little to be gathered in this barren country: any we found went to feed the Red Cadres again.

On the road to Latsu we went like automatons; indeed, there is much of that journey that I cannot remember. Usually, in the lurching columns, there was some attempt at a marching order; some semblance of discipline. But now the men were nothing but ghosts with the mirage of Paoan floating before their staring eyes; stumbling on under the shoulder-poles, falling to their knees to lie there gasping, some actually weeping in the

forward plunge. Once, back at the Gold Sand River, such as
these had run eighty miles in twenty hours: once, indeed, Lin
Piao (who was still busy fainting, the word came up) had, with a
regiment, marched faster. With the wagons under the lash, at
the race to the Tatu Bridge of Chains, more than fifty-two miles
had been covered in a non-stop twelve-hour rush. Now, swaying
on blood-stained feet for the Battle of Latsu, I doubted if we
were covering fifteen miles a day.

Men were committing suicide; rumour had it from Headquarters that the wastage was becoming important – certainly,
most nights, Kwelin and I, huddled together, heard unexplained
solitary shots. Young Vanguards coming up from the rearguard
told of lessening engagement: some said the glorious Ninth
Corps was free of the pursuing Kuomintang, who, though flogged
on by their mounted commanders, could not match our pace.
And now, at every halt, men would come to me and say, "Is it
Paoan? Surely it is Paoan!"

"Don't be mad – we are bloody miles from Paoan!"

"But you said, Doctor, you said – you told him, remember?"

"Get off!" I roared once, and Kwelin shuddered against me.
"I told him nothing. Get away, you bloody ponce! Soldiers?
Soldiers, you call yourselves?"

I could have wept for their courage.

The cadres were reforming for the attack on the Latsu Pass,
one of the few obstacles left that barred the way to the solace of
Yenan; one of Chiang Kai-shek's last hopes to destroy us, men
said. This was a narrow defile on the Min Mountains at the
headwaters of the Min and Pailung Rivers; in the defile was a
narrow bridge between high, vertical cliffs: below the bridge
ran the swiftest river in the province; the sounds of its waves
echoed thunder. To look down at the raging water could bring
dizziness, the Daily Order said, and death.

Later that day I recorded:

20th September, 1935.   Latsu Pass.
The men are in a terrible state. Truly they are no longer
soldiers, but tattered, lantern-jawed skeletons. Many have lost
their hair. The Grasslands have given them huge, gnawing
ulcers on their legs; the flesh left to them is mounded with red
swellings, bites from the insects of the bogs. We all have acute

dysentery; we commonly pass motions even while marching. No longer do we sing; indeed, we rarely talk. Thousands lie dead and dying in the marshes behind us – how many we shall never know. We of the Third (what is left of us) walked on the corpses of those who had died farther up the line, using them as stepping-stones. A woman of Headquarters told me "I put my foot into the mud and something squeaked. Kneeling, I pushed aside the grass. My foot was on the face of a dead man. His tongue was stuck out, as if he was putting it out at me. Now I dream of it."

Kwelin was dreaming of it. Staggering on my supporting arm she went automatically, staring before her, her long white hair blowing out behind her. Her mind seemed to have left her. Often I spoke to her endearingly, but she did not reply. I knew I could hope for no improvement until we reached the peace of Paoan.

On the road, within sight of Minshien, a Young Vanguard came to me; in his hand was a gift. "Look, Doctor," he cried. "I have found a snipe's egg for the little white nurse."

The soldiers called her this after Minshien.

At a halt on the road to the Battle of Latsu, there was a little polluted spring which men, by weak gestures of friendship, left to the women for their toilet.

To this place I carried Kwelin.

I had in my pocket a few grains of buckwheat, a little *chingko* and some pine cones and fungus I had found: this I pounded on a stone with the butt of my Luger, making a mash with water from the stream, and fed it to her with my fingers.

Kwelin chewed, staring beyond me.

"Kwe," I said, patting her face. "It is I – Lin. It is Lin ...!" but she did not reply. After a minute of this mechanical eating, she began to vomit, and I realised that we were sitting beside a dark pool of marsh drainage that looked like horses' urine; the foul smell of this I had grown used to, but Kwelin had not, so I took her farther down the bank of the stream, coming up to a sagging *yurt* hut of departed Mantzu tribesmen: here was shade, for the sun was coming up; in this hut I laid her down.

"Kwelin ..." I called, patting her cheeks, but she did not reply.

341

The vomit was staining her ragged gown, and I knew that this would distress her when she returned to consciousness, so I found fresh grass by the stream and wiped it away, cleaning her mouth: inside her mouth, on her lips, were large white ulcers from mandrake eating; these I rubbed with salt.

Her eyes open now, Kwelin did not protest while I did this, nor make sound of pain.

It was her legs that worried me: even if she were deranged, she might recover if I could get her to Paoan, but something would have to be done about her legs; no one had the strength to carry her far.

Outside the *yurt* hut I made a fire with sun-glass, in the communal bowl, I boiled water. While it was bubbling, I went back into the hut and bared Kwelin's legs.

It was then that I noticed her face.

In the short time since I had been away, the colour of her skin had changed to an unusual dusky hue; and, even as I knelt there, to my astonishment, it slowly turned as black as a Negress. In a moment, though of classical Han features, Kwelin was no longer Chinese: the nose was flatter, the brow overhung, the cheeks swollen and broad; her lips thickened, enhancing the hare-scar which gleamed sinewy white in the sun-glare knifing through the roof. Appalled, I stood up, staring down at her, then again knelt, feeling her heart: this thudded on with ruthless intent, as if defying the phenomena. Kwelin opened her eyes then; they were incredibly white in the changed pigment of her skin.

"Papa," she said. "Papa, you make me cool . . .?"

Never before had she spoken of her father.

I bowed my head.

Kwelin began to shake: it began with a trembling, a betrayal of weakness that grew slowly from her hands to her arms, and then to her whole body. It was a shaking akin to physical hysteria, and I took off my coat and covered her with it; then, in desperation, I dragged her out into the sun. Sweat began to pour from her: in a moment she was a shining bath of water that ran in rivulets, soaking the ground beneath her, yet she was ice-cold to my hands. In my weakness and desperation, I lost all faculty for medicine: as a child who no longer knows what to do, I snatched her into my arms, rocking her to and fro against me while the sweat of her ran into my legs. While doing this,

I heard sudden footsteps and Bricko appeared, bare-footed and ragged against the dark rushing of the stream.

"Come quick, Doctor Lin!"

He stared at the boiling water, and then at Kwelin.

I said, vaguely, "What has happened now?"

"The fellas are goin' down, that's what! – they got faces the colour o' her." He pointed at Kwelin's face. "What's wrong wi' 'em?"

"Go back to them," I said. "Tell them I will come ..."

"But ... they got faces ...!"

"Yes, I know; they've got the black malaria."

His hand went slowly to his mouth: Bricko backed away, then ran, with Kau Kau at his heels.

Hearing his passing, Kwelin said, her voice clear and firm, "I am dying, Papa?"

Turning her to face me I put an opium seed into her mouth: after a minute she sighed like a woman in death, and slipped easily into a gorgeous dream of life.

I had to do something about her legs.

Without clean legs she would never get to Paoan.

First I dipped a rag from my shirt into the boiling water, sterilising it, then I pulled up Kwelin's dress to her loins.

The sores from which she had suffered earlier had infected downwards from the inside of her thighs to her knees; below her knees, spreading outwards, the skin was humped and red with swellings from insect bites; fertile ground for serious ulceration: the old ice-cut on her heel was heaped blue with poison.

Each individual sore I treated with boiling water, taking care not to injure the skin beyond the confines of the infection: Kwelin slept on in her scarlet dream; indeed, at each application of the scald she even smiled, seemingly grateful for the balm of cooling water.

How much I owed to opium on that March!

After the infections were treated, I dragged her nearer to the stream, and, bandaging her legs with the rest of my shirt, washed her body to cool her: even her hair I washed: supporting her shoulders, I untied its string and let it fall in the stream, watching it sway in the brackish water: her hair was probably dirtier still, but the water refreshed her.

343

Very strange she looked with her black face and snow-white hair.

When all this was done, I dried her as best I could, then lay beside her with my arms about her, saying, "Oh, my little love, my little love," but after a bit of this I thought it bloody stupid to be saying that when there might be something else to do to help her.

Also, I could hear the sounds of firing far down the line – probably another spasmodic attack from Mantzu tribesmen. I stared about me at that desolate place: it could even be dangerous there.

Finding a piece of branch to bite on, I treated my own leg-sores with the boiling water, an effective, if agonising cauterising.

A very frightened Bricko – he was actually shaking with uncontrolled fear – put his coat over Kwelin as I returned to the column and laid her down on the grass.

I looked at the sky once, I remember. The heat of the sun was building up for another attack. It was an astonishing autumn for pain.

I was glad that Pipa was dead.

Soon, I supposed, all of us would die.

With nothing to aid them, I went down the lines of the Fifth to visit the soldiers with the black malaria.

Later, the man from Kwangtung said to me while I was carrying Kwelin on the road to Waxy Mouth Pass (which was another name for the Latsu).

"Do you remember, Chan Lin-wai, the tales of the Old Weaver we met south of the Old Tatu?"

I chanced a look at him. He was marching with a spring in his step, a man of gigantic courage. Much earlier – at the time of the camellias, I think it was, I had seen the women of Headquarters watching him with the same unfeigned admiration.

I said, "Legends and prophecies confuse me at a time like this. Frankly, I'm doing my best to stay alive."

The sun shone brilliantly, but on the road to battle the air was cool with new hints of autumn. All down the line men carried comrades with the black malaria. But this didn't prevent the fierce Red Cadres from making pathetic regimental formations, calling for volunteers to scale the cliffs behind the Latsu Pass to outflank the dug-in Kuomintang division.

And there came down the column that day a fine soldier: his shining appearance made me wonder if he had flown above the Grasslands on Perseus' sandals and a Greek legend: this was Colonel Yang of the famous Fourth Regiment (later, after the liberation, he became Acting Commander-in-Chief of the Red Army). Now he was personally selecting men who were not afraid of heights. The pace of the marching slowed as he moved among us.

The man from Kwangtung replied, "The Old Weaver made a prophecy, do you recall? Did he not foretell the deaths of Jo-kei and Muchai, also Tenga? Did he not also say that but three of us, of all friends here, would one day walk on flowers?"

I marched on with Kwelin lolling on my back, my eyes narrowed against the fierce sun. The flies were worring Man Kim; Hu had a long vetch-grass stick, a fan to keep them away as Kim lay strapped on Moke Donkey. Bricko and Big One were either side of me, waiting to take their turn to carry Kwelin. In this carrying Kwelin, with her hair flowing out behind her, went pick-a-back, her wrists tied and hooked under my chin: with my hands linked behind her, she went drunkenly in my staggering gait, her bandaged legs stuck out grotesquely from beneath my arms, preceding me. Little Hu had decorated her toes with wayside posies. The sun reflected brilliantly on the flowers.

Shao Shan, leading Moke Donkey, limped badly.

I prayed for the miracle of Yenan, but to whom I prayed I do not remember. All down the column men were weakly crying for food. The man from Kwangtung said, though I scarcely heard him:

"Every man some time must reach his destiny. Waxy Mouth Pass is mine. Do you know that I have an excellent head for heights?"

"Don't be a fool," I answered. "Leave the climbing to the bloody heroes – there's a few in the Red Cadre just dying to die."

He said, "Should you survive this march, Chan Lin-wai, here is my authority that you shall own what I possess," and he gave me an envelope.

This, in itself, was not unusual: he was the fourth man to have willed me his possessions.

"Shall I open it now?" I asked.

"Not now, read it when I am free." He frowned into the sun. "It is little enough, in the mess of it all, but it is my wish. I have

345

cared for my wife already; my house is in order. You will understand that I do not wish this to become an emotional issue?"

"Of course." We marched on. His shoulder touched mine; instantly, he drew away.

"Dispense what little I have to the poor of China – to Taoist and Buddhist, communist, nationalist, Red Army soldier and Kuomintang renegade – I have no religion, I know nothing of politics. Have the grace to visit my little wife at the address I give, if you please?"

I bowed to him. The men lurched by as I stood before him.

"Remember me," said the man from Kwangtung.

I watched him go down the road to the Tenth Assault Cadre and their Colonel Yang.

I saw him once again.

Where is he now, I wonder? He who valued only freedom, seeing little difference between Chiang Kai-shek and Mao Tsetung in terms of patriotism and tyranny – he who executed the communist hero Fang Chih-min, yet fought the Japanese for China, up in Jehol.

"Where is he going?" asked Shao Shan, turning to watch.

"Where's that bugger off to?" cried Bricko, hands on hips; staring, he stooped, presenting his back to me, to carry Kwelin.

I did not reply.

Outside the village of Lanti, before the battle for the Pass, we laid Kwelin down and Shao Shan and I swilled her body with cool water to reduce her temperature, which was raging. At every stop we did this, and sometimes at unofficial stops – racing with her clear of the column while Bricko rushed after us with water; this we poured into her hair, and Shao washed it over her with her hands, swiftly drying her before the end of the sun and the onset of night-cold: a medical orderly of the Fifth Battalion versed, like Muchai, in the gathering of herbs, gave me the powderings of a wayside plant; excellent, he assured me, for reducing temperature.

At night Bricko and I would lie with our arms around her, giving her our warmth, to wake at dawn stiff and cold, with her thin body like a fire between us.

Gradually her temperature subsided.

On the road to battle, while on Big One's back, Kwelin suddenly straightened against his shoulders and gathered up her hair.

"Aunt Kwe's looking!" shouted Hu, shrilly. "Aunt Kwe's alive!" His cries brought the drooping men back to life; they gathered around Big One delightedly, laughing and chattering, while he, with a human returned from the dead upon his back, grinned down at the road with the passivity of a donkey.

An hour before this battle the opium-soldier came to me. (At this time I thought him lost.) "You there, Doctor-student?" and he peered at me through the dark.

"Oh, no," groaned Bricko. "By my aunt's fan – just look what we got 'ere!"

"Oh, please, Doctor-student," begged the opium-soldier, his eyes red-rimmed; his face, in that shimmering lamp-light, was that of a haunted ghost. "Just one little seed, matey, I'm 'aving such a terrible bloody war!"

"You're having no worser war than me – so bloody hop it," Bricko cried.

"Is it you, Doctor-student?" the man pulled at my sleeve.

"I am not here," I said. "I am dead. You are looking at my soul."

"Oh ...!" and he pestered me until I could have screamed. Kwelin, nearly fainting with weakness, was in my arms. "Oh ... I nearly kicked it in the Grasslands, mister. I was down in the mud and they walks on me – you know that?" He leaped about, stamping deliriously. "They just bloody walks on me! Horses' arses, I was near clapped an' they put their bloody feet on me. Nobody's 'aving a more 'orrible war than me."

He was clinging to Kwelin now, she who had succoured him before, until Bricko furiously hauled him away.

I said to Shao Shan, "Listen, woman – now *listen* – Kwe will have to ride on Moke."

"O, aye?" whispered Shao, eyeing me, and she spread her legs and bunched her fists like a man. "How can she ride wi' my fella up there?"

"It's time your fella come down," said Bricko, and men peered at us from the darkness as the Cadre went by for the climb to Waxy Mouth.

"Then you try takin' him down," said Shao Shan. "That's my man up there on my Moke, and up there he stays."

Bricko said, "He's half dead, anyway, poor old bastard." He

peered up at Man Kim who was smiling meekly at the stars. "Hey, me old fella – will you jump off an' give our little Kwe a ride?"

Reaching out, Man Kim touched Kwelin's hair. "For you, little woman, I would walk on my hands."

"Oh, no you bloody don't – you stays, husband," said Shao, and she put Toiya under one arm, a big fist threatening. Man Kim said:

"For once you will do as you're told, woman. Help me down."

Hu cried, "You can ride on Big One's back again, remember, Uncle Kim!"

"Leave him!" roared Shao Shan, as Bricko came nearer, and she struck him in the face, sending him sprawling in the road.

Man Kim said, "How dare you, you have struck my friend. How dare you!"

Bricko rose, his hand to his face. Trembling, Shao Shan stared about her, Man Kim added: "You'll do as you're bloody told – you hear, Shao? For the first time in your life you will do as you're told."

And Shao Shan replied, saying, "I shall not. You will stay where you are. I'm getting you to Yenan, husband, and you can't do nothin' about it."

There was no sound but the wind and Kwelin crying with the pain of her burns.

I whispered, "It is all right, love, it is all right."

"Oh, yes I can, woman," said Man Kim, "I can die. You hear me? If you don't take me down, I shall die – up here, tonight."

They glared at each other.

We watched, silent save for Kwelin's sobbing.

"Get him down, Bricko," said Shao Shan. "The old sod means it."

That night, while we camped at the foot of the cliffs, the Red Cadre climbed up to the cliff to the enemy defences. The man from Kwangtung climbed first, for men told me this: they tied together their putties and flung grappling irons in a hail of fire: there, on the top, they hauled up a gun and shelled the little bridge. And, as the Kuomintang wheeled to them in the dark, the Sixth infantry went in on a frontal assault. The battle was short and brutal; 200 Kuomintang dead clogged the river.

Our own dead we dared not count.

I said my own private farewell to the man from Kwangtung, whose body I found in the thickest of the waste, beside the broken gun.

There, kneeling beside him, I opened the envelope he had given me and read it by the light of the moon.

It was a legal and authentic will, with my name entered apparently at the last minute as his sole executor to the poor of China: the value of stock invested in a Manhattan bank was not inconsiderable – subject to confirmation it was a little over $4,000,000.

The ornate and flourishing signature, so readily accepted by his bankers years later, was quite indecipherable.

That night we crossed the bridge he had died to secure: he who was poor in his mansion back in Canton, but rich beyond dreams on the road to Latsukou.

THIRTY-FOUR

Through the rock country of Chingming, clear of the marshes, we turned our faces to the distant Liupan Mountains, the last natural barrier between us and Paoan. Into the lands that harnessed the Golden Rivers, we marched with a new spirit.

For this, compared with the Grasslands, was bountiful country; a grazing land of countless sheep which we bought from local farmers and slaughtered on the spot: wild scallion and celery grew here in abundance, young cabbage and parsnips, tangle-root and beet, and we ate our fill beside the roadside bivouacs; washed ourselves free of vermin, tended the wounds of the marshes. We even roasted an ox in the Fifth, eating until we bulged in a gigantic, moonlight feast. That smell of roasting ox, said Bricko, must have nipped on the wind right back to Headquarters, tickling the end of Otto Braund's nose.

In this land of Golden Rivers, Kwelin, unknown to her, held court.

Because of the pushing of the excited muleteers and the heat of the roasting-fire, I had taken Kwelin to a little hollow in a rock face, and there sat her down with Shao Shan beside her. Then I went back to the fire and cut from the carcass sweet pieces of meat with which to tempt her: these I chopped finely with a scalpel and brought them to her on a banyan leaf.

She ate slowly, smiling sadly, swallowing the food as if swallowing chaff, but I was delighted: Shao Shan beamed and fussed; Bricko came and squatted at her feet. More people came; soon we were encircled by a great swathe of men. All sat silently while Kwelin ate; I thought she looked beautiful in that moonlight with her white hair lying on her shoulders and Toiya in her arms.

Even more men came. The feasting at the ox was forgotten.

Silently, they came in tribute.

They came from the ragged Sixth Infantry, they who had fought with Mao at Chingkangshan, and they brought with them their comrade bandits. Men came pushing through the woods about us, those from the Fifth, the walking wounded Kwelin had served. Men of the rearguard came – officers visiting General Headquarters, the scarred warriors of the famous Ninth, hearing of her work with the assault troops who beat the Nineteenth, they honoured with their presence the rough muleteers. Many came of whose regiments I had never heard, on that halt before Liupan: three women arrived – one of these was the peasant fighter of Chang's Fourth Army – whose breast had been saved.

They came on the wind of rumour – not by order – to pay tribute to a muleteer nurse: one was the man of Yentai, the bull-Tangar of the junks, with whom she had lain while I stole his arm. They made no sound, these people, save to cough, for many were tubercular: they arranged themselves on the earth before Kwelin and Shao Shan, and watched while Kwelin was fed.

Little Ball came, also Trip – indeed, many Young Vanguards – perhaps too, the soul of Chi-pang, who died at Tatu.

Then, at the back of the squatting soldiers, came another, and he had come on orders.

Slowly, the people got to their feet, staring.

He was a man of immense strength and size; not even Big One matched this man for height and shoulders; I had met him once before – at Chouping Fort. Slowly, he entered the clearing. Looking neither right nor left, he said bassly:

"I am Red Cadre."

I didn't like it, and I sensed the men's hostility; they had starved while the cadres fed – to the crack troops was given official recognition; many common soldiers had died to cut the way. And, while the grumble from the muleteers and infantry grew to a crescendo, I rose and called to this man:

"What do you want with us?"

"I seek the white nurse," said he.

There was no sound but the wind and the crackling of the fire.

We watched.

The giant man came slowly forward. Reaching Kwelin, he went on one knee: she, holding Toiya against her, smiled into his face. Taking from his pocket a cloth badge he offered it to Kwelin; when she did not take it he reached forward, and placed it in Toiya's eager fingers.

It was the Red Star: within it was stitched the head of the wild bull, the symbol of the Cadre.

"From my comrades," said he.

None moved. He returned the way he came.

With strength and hope returning some of the vanguard, triumphant after their victory at Latsu Pass, began to sing, for the next day was glorious. A new hope, a new enthusiasm for victory began to spread down the line.

In the ranks before me men had kept a space; this was for the soul of the man from Kwangtung, though none mentioned this.

Even the Young Vanguards, their sores and ulcers healing, began again to run down the line, distributing pamphlets, happily calling. One such pamphlet I recorded; it was a poem by Mao Tse-Tung. Because it was about peace, men treasured this poem about the Great Snow Mountain. I read it in a drone of heavy bombers against a mackerel sky:

Towering aloft above the earth, Great Kunlun,
You have witnessed all that was fairest
In the human world.
As they fly across the sky, three million dragons
Of white jade freeze you with piercing cold.

In the days of summer your melting torrents
Fill streams and rivers till they overflow,
Changing men into fish and turtles.
What man can pass judgment on all the good and evil
You have done these thousand autumns?

But today I say to you, Kunlun,
You do not need your great height,
You do not need all that snow!
If I could lean on the sky, I would draw my sword
And cut you into three pieces.
One I would send to Europe, one to America,
And one I would keep in China.
Thus would a great peace reign through the world,
For all the world would share your warmth and cold.

352

And on that day, with a faint song beginning in the ranks of the tattered men ... the *Eleven Bus Song* which once they sang in Kiangsi ... I entered in my diary:

1st October, 1935

All that lies now, before Paoan and Yenan, is the barrier of Mount Liupan. We are bombed at least twice a day now, but it no longer matters. The men are singing again: sometimes, on high ground, we can see the purple outline of the Great Heap before us. Beyond this mountain lies the Great Wall of China. Our spirits are higher. Even Kwelin seems to be returning to life. Today Mao Tse-tung sent us an unusual Order of the Day in poetry – it was a message of peace, for us, for the rest of the world.

Later, as we neared the Liupan Range we were repeatedly attacked by nationalist bombers, ambushed and flanked by warlord mercenaries and the Mantzu tribes, but nothing could destroy our new spirit. Life was flooding into us with every step: we cleaned and polished our weapons again, tied up the worst tatters of our clothes, plaited litters from the hedgerows to carry our sick and wounded. On every mouth were the names, Paoan and Yenan, *Yenan and Paoan*.

Get on. Get on!

On the third day of October, organising the wounded, treating the sick with fresh herbs gathered on the roadsides, I found Kwelin sitting on a bank.

Earlier, Shao Shan had borrowed from me my little sun-glass for making fires; this, with wheel-grease and dust to back it, she had propped against a stone so that Kwelin, if she wished it, might see herself in a mirror. Very pretty she looked sitting there, with Shao Shan combing out her white hair with her fingers, plaiting it and tying the ends with string.

"There's no doubt about it," I said, coming up, "the woman's very attractive."

Kwelin smiled wanly, but did not reply. Shao Shan said, "Make the most of it, Doctor Lin. By the time she gets to Paoan she'll be chattering like a hundred cats, eh?"

"How are the feet?" I asked.

"They're worse'n my old man's," said Shao. "D'you know the old sod ain't walked a single mile in the last nine hundred?"

353

I looked at Kwelin. Aimlessly, she sat, but her fingers were on her Red Cadre badge, and the sight of this heartened me.

Shao Shan, with motherly intent, was putting wild flowers in her hair.

This woman astonished me. In a march of 7,000 miles to date I doubt if she lost a stone of weight. In the privations, her ordeal of child-birth, the taxing night marches, the sun's dehydrations and the constant hunger, she was now little less than the wobbling immensity she had hauled out of Juichin. I had seen muscular men of powerful physique go to a shadow and premature death under less, but Shao Shan, mother of six, just kept on marching – the Kiangsi camel with humps forward, as the man from Kwangtung once so aptly called her.

Shao lived for one goal – singularly, and with resolution – to get her husband to Yenan; had he expired on the way she would have carried him mortifying, with the latent ferocity of a meat-fed tiger.

Now she was bestowing her motherhood on Kwelin, crooning to her in a voice one uses for a child.

"Kwe . . ." I said, and lifted her face to mine.

Kwelin's features were Chinese again; her flawless skin was no longer dark-hued, but golden: her expression was in repose, as if her inner being, battered into submission by the fists of the March, was now requited by an endless peace.

I said to Shao, "Has she spoken to you at all?"

A perfumed wind moved between us.

"She will speak when she's good an' ready, mister – she'll come to it, don't pester!"

Bricko arrived and knelt at Kwelin's feet, crying, "*Hei wei*, little missus, how ye comin'?"

He took her hand and held it. Kau Kau was trying to get on to her lap, and Shao pushed the dog away.

Big One stood in gigantic apathy, his face low, screwing at his hands. Hu regarded her with tear-filled eyes – flowers in his hands. Skinny Wong hovered near.

And Shao Shan said, helping Kwelin to her feet. "What are ye all staring at? Away wi' ye – go on . . . !" and she swept us up with her arms. "*Away!*"

"Go easy, woman," said Man Kim, watching her. "Go easy . . ."

354

I raised my head; there was a dryness in me, yet water was in my throat.

"Do not go, Shao," I said, "I want to do her legs."

"They'm nearly healed, Doctor Lin – look," and she lifted Kwelin's skirt, swiftly unwrapping the bandages, "... it's all good skin!"

"Then take them off, let the air get to it."

This she did, tossing the bandages away.

"Now leave us, please."

I sat on the bank with Kwelin and there was about us the activity of a rushing army. Bugles faintly sounded: sledges, on which our rifles had been carried over the bogs, were being unloaded for the broader fights ahead. Up and down the column of revived muleteers, breeches were being eased: sheep-fat was warming in the thunderous rat-a-tat of the bolts; the sun flashed on dust-rubbed bayonets.

"Kwelin," I said, deliberately kissing her lips.

Amazingly, she smiled, and I saw in her face, the face of a starved ghost, an unusual light, though it might have been a trick of the sun. And then, as if seeing through the mirror of my features all the scenes of the day, Kwelin rose and wandered away.

I pressed my fist against my mouth to stifle the indignity.

THIRTY-FIVE

Now, as we began the slog of twenty miles up the gradient foothills of the Liupan mountains, the flame of revolution spread like a prairie fire over expectant China.

For the first time in history, the seed-beds of discontent arrowed north. In every county, copying our example, men were on the march. From Shanghai in the east they came: west to the Tibetan border and south to Canton the people were on the move. Slowly the middle provinces began to ferment.

The people came individually, the lonely farmer with his possessions bouncing on his shoulder-pole; they came in families, in groups, they came in small armies. For the first time since the fall of the Manchus the non-Han Chinese looked north for succour against oppression. The ancient minorities like the tribes of Yo, the Fans, the Miao pygmies – the fierce Black and White Bone Lolos, who worshipped their gods on the trails of Kublai Khan – all came to the protection of the Red Army.

The Long March, for these, ceased to be a fighting retreat: the name of Mao Tse-tung became a password of victory, one to compare with China's ancient glories: the peasant soldier of the March was no longer two yards of uniform-grey but a crusading saint; the Kuomingtang became a brutal enemy.

Minor rebellions began to spark against the authority of the Nationalists: principally Chaing Kai-shek's failure to oppose Japan was criticised. More, the Long March, catching the imagination of the oppressed, became the symbol of China's will to cleanse herself of the Chaing Kai-shek corruptions.

9th October, 1935.
This must be recorded, lest I have no chance to do so when we reach the Twenty-Fifth Army Corps at Wuchichen, the outpost of Paoan.
The Chairman claims this March as a victory, here I state the truth – that even if we succeed in building a new fortified

soviet in Paoan, the whole Red Army is now but a tenth of its 300,000 strength of a year ago; that membership of the Chinese Communist Party, at less than 50,000, is at its lowest ebb. This is *not* victory, it is defeat. All we have gained is the transfer of revolution's seat from the south to the north, and the laying of the bones of our bravest and best along the road from Juichin.

Yet, I concede that the people are *aware* of us – they trust our *intent*. Could it be, as Mao claims, that this March will prove the seeding-ground of all China for new and vital successes to come? I do not know. All I know is that I am desperately tired, and that my loved ones seem to be dying about me: that in my opinion, the Red Army is finished.
(Hapatu Village)

But the people were on the march, building communism into something larger than life.

Yenan, and its caves in the loess hills (though still occupied by the Kuomintang) became the ultimate land of promise – its dream and magic name sounded a clarion call to a country longing for change. And the new Shensi-Kansu soviet base at Wuchichen, already in being and defended by 10,000 communists of the Twenty-Fifth Army Corps, was commanded by a romantic figure, one Colonel Liu. Reinforcing his Party members with secret societies, bandits, troops defecting from local war-lords, he had formed the nucleus of a garrison of sufficient size to sustain resistance for a year from Kuomintang air and ground attacks.

It was to this tiny soviet base of Wuchichen that we now marched.

And we were but one of many such columns, each completing its own Long March by arrival in Shensi. Earlier, the famous Twenty-Fifth Army had come from the old soviet base of Oyuwan, also the straggling remnants of the Twenty-Sixth and Twenty-Seventh. General Ho Lung, commanding the Second Army, was now striking westward to join the Fourth Army under Chang Kuo-tao in Sikang; subsequently, these combined forces reached the tiny garrison, which we were now approaching.

But first, still a few hundred miles from safety, we had to fight our final battles against the Kuomintang in the Liupan

Mountains. Beyond lay the bastion of all hopes – the loess lands of Yenan and the Great Wall of China.

Our spent and depleted column contracted like a concertina for safety on the ascent of the Liupan Mountains, but we returned every sniper's bullet with a side-blast of concentrated fire, dropping them out of trees, spinning them over the crags to the plains beneath. And, on the top of the range, I paused to look back.

"Look!" I called.

Big One, lumbering along with Man Kim strapped behind him, turned too; also Skinny Wong, who was carrying Toiya; Hu turned, tugging at Shao Shan. Bricko put it in a nutshell, saying:

"It ain't the same Red Army that pulled out of Juichin!"

Below us on the plains, the Red Army followed us up the long ascent. Gone was the elephant of the baggage train, the thick swathes of disciplined Assault Cadres, the jogging field-grey cavalry led by the Fifteenth Mohammedan. It was, on this last, desperate lap, a straggling, peasant band that wound not fifty miles over the horizon (the spitting dragon I had seen ascending Great Snow Mountain) – it was doubtful if it stretched for two. And in the weary, staggering columns of armed men great gaps of open road punched by weariness appeared; it was an army in the final stages of exhaustion.

In the other direction – northward towards Central Asia – lay the purple haze of the mountains guarding the Gobi Desert, straddled by the Great Wall.

"Look," said Shao Shan, and pointed forward.

Beyond the Six Twists of Luipan the sun flashed fiercely over the patchwork plains in sudden light-blaze – always proof of cavalry. The Mohammedans saw this, too, and bunched about us, fingering the edges of their crude sabres. The Red Cadre saw it, and came up, staring through field binoculars.

A small army of Moslem troops, the horsemen of the puppet Ma Hung-kuei, awaited us north of the moutain: it was fine, flat country for cavalry charges.

Ignoring the sniping and spasmodic bombing, the soldiers crowded about us, looking down at the plains. Mao Tse-tung came to our position of vantage: Chou En-lai joined him.

All stared, unmoving.

"It's a chance to get some bloody good horses," said Mao.

From river to river the sun gleamed and flashed on lance, spur and stirrup. The yellow loess lands of the Yellow River Basin stretched away to the horizon. I heard distant hooves as the enemy horsemen wheeled about, seeking positions of advantage for the attack.

With but a few hundred miles to go, we were standing on the lower Ridge of Dividing Waters, a most propitious name.

I heard Chou En-lai say, "The cavalry of General Ma, eh? Let's get down and into them – we'll eat them in the foot-hills, it's a bloody bean-curd army."

It was a masterly understatement.

These, and he knew it, were the best and fiercest soldiers in the whole of the Kuomintang.

Suddenly it snowed: the clouds obliterated the mountains; an unexpected and advantageous pall covered our movements. The rest of the Red Army, now climbing in the face of a blizzard, fought its way for twenty miles up the gradients of Liupan.

"Are you there, Shao?" I called.

Like the rest, I was nearly on all fours on the slopes; all about me men were sliding on the icy rocks, somersaulting, floundering downwards in shouted warnings, colliding with comrades on the way up and pulling swathes of men out of the advance. Moke Donkey II – a thin beast presented to Kwelin by an anonymous soldier before we began the climb – slid about, her tiny hooves scrabbling, and Kwelin was lurching precariously in the saddle. Shao Shan stopped, gasping against the donkey's head.

"You about, Doctor Lin?" cried Bricko.

"Yes, here – come, give a hand."

He came on hands and knees, a snow-flecked ghost arriving timorously out of the mountain mist, and on the end of the rope he pulled came Big One, a lumbering bear with its mate on its back, and this was a snow-man, Man Kim. We rested on our knees, beating our rags for warmth, while Hu and Skinny Wong shuffled up, hoarsely breathing, men with heads on fire. I wiped snow from my face and looked at Kwelin, seeing her against a sudden glow of the sky: she sat erect on Moke Donkey, her face low against the baby, and I pulled aside the ragged cloth:

359

Toiya, her eyes wide in her tiny, cold-pinched face, saw me and struck the wind with little red fists, crowing with delight.

Kwelin watched Toiya with expressionless eyes.

"Hold her tightly, Kwelin – tight, remember?"

"It got to be tighter 'an that," said Shao Shan. "Any time now that moke's goin' over."

"Last time we lost a baby it were on a mule," said Bricko, hauling up Kau Kau by her scruff.

I will always remember Bricko as I saw him then: gone was the boy they had emasculated on the road to Yutu; this one was a man.

Broader, iron-hard with the drudgery of the march, there was about Bricko now the peasant confidence of one who had found himself. Nobody shouted falsetto after him these days; no man was quicker into the thick of it and slower in retreat. Sometimes, in repose (and he was invariably alone) he would play Fool's flute tunelessly, and Kau Kau, head on paws and trembling, would watch him, awaiting the vital melody he could never find. But a quality wonk like Kau Kau, Bricko often said, "would only dance for Gold Star Heroes, mind, and this ol' eunuch fellah's just plain rubbish."

Sometimes, in his absolute disdain for death, I wondered if Bricko sought it since the martyrdom of Fool; the idiot beggar of Nisha, whom he loved.

Now Hu cried treble, attracting the attention of men lumbering past us, "Give me Toiya, Uncle Lin. Let Shao take the moke – I will carry baby!"

"Later," I said, and took Toiya into my arms.

In this fashion, with Big One carrying Man Kim; Hu and Scraggy Wong helping Kwelin, and Bricko coming behind to catch any rollers, I followed Shao and the donkey up to the peak of Liupan.

I felt unusually close to Pipa as the sun came out.

Yung I remembered, too, also Jo-kei and Muchai: Political Chang I saw in the eye of my mind up there on the crest of Liupan, also little Chi-pang; the slobbering face of Fool, I saw; the dark eyes of the man from Kwangtung: all my friends returned to me in that rock-strewn place in the bright October sun.

How many more would I lose, I wondered, along the road to Wuchichen and Paoan?

360

"Close ranks, close ranks! Make formation! Prepare for attack!"

With Shao Shan on the moke with Toiya, just for the nearness of her (lest it proved the last time) I actually carried Kwelin in my arms.

The commands rang out; the bugles of the Young Vanguards were singing among the peaks as we descended into the valley.

Now, with the nationalist air force swooping among the peaks, we jog-trotted down to battle with the Assault Cadres leading us: throwing ourselves down under cover, we awaited the sledge-guns and the bog-rafts towed by slogging men; these carried the machine-guns and cased ammunition. As the distant Ma cavalry recoiled like a spring for the first charge, we of the Fifth, preceded by the Sixth fanned out in semi-circular wedges across the spattered loess country, taking up position. Strapping Man Kim more securely on to Moke's back, we tethered her behind a boulder; settling Kwelin with Toiya, we moved in a group among the infantry.

"*Take position! Cavalry out!*" (and we had no cavalry).

The Fifteenth Mohammedans (men we rarely saw) came out of the van and shouldered past us; big men, and broad. In their bearded faces was the hatred of the reactionary General Ma Hung-kuei and his warriors on their fleet Ninghsia ponies: this was the enemy general who boasted that when the Reds entered Kansu, he would cut them to pieces.

Our Moslems, unlike those who faced us, were unhorsed: but, also, like the enemy cavalrymen, they were untrained in the art of the phalanx charges: their role, on the horse, was to dismount and fire. Now, scowling from their fierce faces, they took up the role as shock infantry, kneeling to form the advance line with their great blunt sabres held like impaling spears before them.

"We chop 'em bloody mince-meat," said Bricko, furiously, and he unsheathed his bayonet and ran down the lines to join them.

"Come back!" I shouted, but he did not.

Hu ran after him, but I caught him by the collar and handed him over to Big One, grabbing the giant and pointing to Kwelin and Toiya.

"You stay here – Hu – tell him! Both of you stay and take care of Kwelin and Toiya!"

"Aw, Uncle Lin . . .!"

I remember him now, with the sun on his face, protesting.

"Tell him!" I commanded.

Hu waved his hands magically before Big One's face. The man grunted, gathering Kwelin and Hu with a huge enveloping arm; Man Kim shouted from Moke's saddle.

"And me, young doctor? You let me go?"

"You stay, ye hear me?" yelled Shao Shan, and she tried to grab the reins.

I did not wait longer. With Wong beside me, I checked the Luger loading and entered the gathering crush of Sixth infantry and muleteers in the jog-trot down to the plains.

The bombs began to fall in roaring clusters as we gradually filled the open ground: we lay under this air bombardment waiting for the Moslem cavalry.

It was a golden day. Beside me was the blunt profile of Wong, the humped cheekbones of his cavernous face. He looked ridiculous, awaiting this fight to the death, dressed in his girl's blouse and skirt. Before me were the packed ranks of the Sixth, lying, kneeling, casually easing their rifle-bolts. And, half a mile beyond him, ranged rank on rank, in jigging, jogging cavalry, the Moslems of Ma awaited the signal to attack.

I pressed my face into the earth; hearing, magically, the faint commands, the stamping hooves of the uncertain line: squinting up, I saw a sword flash down: the front line of prancing horses drew up to the rein, their forelegs dancing in light. Ear to the ground again, I heard them coming in a faint thunder. Now faster, gathering momentum, the drumming roar increasing. And I saw a bright array of charging horsemen; heard their soprano shouts mingling into a sustained roar of hooves; horses shrieked; the ancient strangled war-cries of cavalry.

"Hold your fire! Hold it! Hold it!"

It was one of the Red Cadre officers. Before our crouching Moslems he stood in his tattered uniform, one arm upraised.

The Mohammedans came on at breakneck speed, abandoning their usual fall and fire tactics, in a bid to break our line. I heard the officer call:

"Wait men, *wait!*"

Still they came on, in packed ranks, saddle to saddle, their spear-pennants lowering, sunlight flashing on reins and spurs.

And, as the gap between us closed, a turbanned officer ran forward, turned and faced our Fifteenth Mohammedans, crying:

"*Shang Ma! Shang Ma!*" and he screamed, his sabre waving "*Ma-ti Ma Hung-kuei!*"

Again the war-cry defiling the war-lord General. It buffeted the plains; the old war shout I had heard before.

"*Ma-ti Ma Hung-kuei!*"

A Sixth infantrymen yelled, "Into the traitors, into them! Moslems and Chinese are brothers!"

The turbanned officer turned and faced the oncoming cavalry: he was in rags save for his fine, plumed turban; a giant of purpose, his naked arm upraised, whirling the sabre; then he raced to meet the charging horses; instantly spitted by a flung lance, he staggered on, slashing and lunging until trampled beneath the hooves. And even then I heard his voice:

"*Ma-ti Ma Hung-kuei! Ma-ti Ma Hung-kuei!*"

Behind him the short volley-guns of the Fifteenth blasted into the mad ranks of men and animals; these instantly overturning on impact with the Sixth who were standing now, blazing rapid-fire fusillades into the wall of attackers whose impetus took them onward over the dead and dying, spilling into the ranks of the Fifth Muleteers.

The battle was filled with thundering hooves, the cries of wounded, the frantic neighing of horses. Felled by the initial charge, the Sixth rose as on a command, clawing at the horsemen, plunging among them, striking down those who sought to rise; it was an insane gyrating, chopping-block of yelling figures and waving pennants, the ringing of sabres, darting of swords: a fight initially of squat, bearded fanatics that slowly spilled over into our muleteer ranks, beating down our line like an oncoming avalanche. It was a mêlée devoid of planning; a fight to the death in a symmetry of blood. Over and over rolled the clawing contestants; we forbidding an advance, the Kansu-Moslems determined to get through us. Daggers and bayonets were out now, a vicious hand-to-hand; the gilt and grey tunics of the enemy Turkish-Moslems clashed with the tattered, mud-caked skeletons of the Sixth. Too tough to die, these clawed at the beautiful Mongolian ponies, the all-black and all-white remnants of the Nanking First Cavalry.

Now these horsemen were systematically pulled down to the blood-stained earth the infantry knew, into a mud-hacking, vulgar fight. Spreadeagled, they were clubbed into submission. Removed from the dignity of the saddle in which they were trained, they rose desperately reaching for reins, only to be dragged down again into a tumult of fists, knives and close-quarter bullets that never breathed air. The Red Cadre were in the fore, silent, gliding through the battle-smoke that funnelled through the packed ranks of squawking soldiers, shot-fire spitting methodically from their long Mausers. And the Sixth, like hunting wolf-packs decimated their prey in individual squabbles, the bayonets rising and arcing down to Moslem shrieks. But still they fought on, legs braced on the bodies of their writhing horses, their sabres sything down. Those who escaped reformed.

Remounting, with their paste-jewelled turbans flashing in the sun, they charged again.

This time they got through the Sixth.

They were through the Sixth and into the muleteers, and we knew it.

It was then that I saw Shao Shan.

She was standing on an outcrop, her legs splayed like a man's on the shining rock: arms bare to the shoulders, her scarlet opera gown stained and in tatters, she was flourishing a Ninghsia sabre, and her shrill voice cut through the bass shouting:

"Come on the Fifth! Where are the Fifth? Get into it, you bloody Cantonese!"

She was at once, gloriously, the image of Tenga.

Moke Donkey, free of her hands, ran amok among the scattered Kansu ponies, and Man Kim, strapped on his back, was blowing Chi-pang's bugle in quick, violent blasts, calling the bayonet charge. Bricko I saw then, pulling men to follow him, and they mounded about a shrieking Shao Shan in a flash of steel as the bayonets came out. And as Shao leaped down they followed her in the charge, right into the heart of the Moslem fighting.

I gripped Skinny Wong beside me.

"Come on!" I yelled, and we shoved into the ranks of the advancing muleteers.

It was a craggy fight, and brief.

Hopelessly locked, friend and enemy were gyrating in weakening strength: the dying stabbed up vainly from the ground, the living fought for air in a chorus of lunatic cries: unaccountably, fires were burning; the tinder-growth of the plains flared horizontally underfoot, scorching the packed ranks: in crackbrained confusion men on fire shrieked to be free. One, his blood-stained rags alight, leaped at Wong, bearing him down, and I lifted my Luger and shot him in the head. Dragging Wong up beside me we forced a path through to the isolated Mohammedans, following Shao Shan. Wong his girl's blouse and skirt nearly torn off him, was almost naked; we hacked and mauled our way forward, directed by the unmistakable voice of a woman. But now, men of the Sixth had dragged her back and she was penned by muleteers, struggling to be free: Shao's hair was down, and she was bleeding from a body wound, but still waving her captured sabre. Automatically, I was firing my pistol at retreating Moslems. In a moment, forced on from behind, I was now in the van in this climactic battle with cavalry: and the muleteers, seeing a new leader, followed me into the enemy's thinning ranks. We were climbing over the mounded dead and dying, animals and men: all about me were bawling, blackened faces, the inhuman foliage of men at war. Suddenly, Bricko was running beside me with Kau Kau at his heels: loading and firing a rifle from his hip as space cleared, he was shouting, "That's for Fool! That's for Fool!"

The fight was over: the cavalry was dispersed: scrambling on to their remaining horses, the Mohammedans of Kansu were in flight. Over our heads the sledge-guns pursued them with whistling iron, until there was nothing but their galloping dust to tell their passing.

That day, on the road to Wuchichen, I helped to shoot the impossibly wounded: it was the first time we had done this in the whole of the campaign: there were no medicines, no opium left, no way to succour them: we could not even carry them, for we could find no branches for litters.

And, even while we were collecting the dead for burial (and these were hundreds) the nationalists renewed their old, spasmodic bombing; their squat bi-planes weaving at low level among us like searching fingers.

Blood was upon my hands after the battle of the Liupan plains: my tunic, knotted together so carefully by Shao Shan in the mountains, was nearly torn off me, yet amazingly, I was unhurt.

Blood was everywhere; on rock ledges removed from the fight, on the blackened scarecrows of the burned undergrowth, on the brown earth which thirsted in wide patches, the littered killing-ground. Turbanned brothers, Kansu and communist, lay locked together in scattered swathes, some faintly moving; ashen-faced in a final love-play of mating death. Wounded infantrymen of the Sixth, their campaign rags torn away, lay in isolated groups; a trampling by horses.

Three hundred and twenty dead, eight hundred wounded.

All over the battle-field pistol shots were sounding: horses and men ... men and horses.

The enemy wounded we did not shoot; to die of thirst and wounds, if the Kansu willed it, was their destiny.

While the bombing went on by a single plane, dropping its bombs with desultory ineffectiveness, we buried the dead: also, we collected the stray Ninghsia ponies in scores, and bolted their wooden saddles to the siege-guns – for them a tremendous indignity. On these, in a red-patched moaning caravanserai, we hauled the lightly wounded.

We did not speak much. Shao Shan had collected a sabre graze in the thick fat of her waist, and I did what I could for her: Kwelin I found unhurt, still faithfully guarded by Big One and Hu; she sat apathetically, unmoved by the shock and noise of it, giving me no greeting as I came to her.

Man Kim, his hand gripping Shao's while I bandaged her with the hem of her mandarin gown, was weeping soundlessly. Hu held Kau Kau against his face; Little Ball, dying with a wound in the stomach, made no sound when I tended him. Others wept I remember.

Kwelin did not weep.

I could not have wept, even had I tried.

Bricko.

Earlier, I had gone in search of him with Big One.

We found Bricko lying alone. The Kansu sabre cut had taken him low; rarely have I seen such a wound from a knife. Kau Kau lay beside him, one paw on his throat: she bared her teeth and snarled as I approached.

Near him, among many, lay Skinny Wong, who had gone to

succour him, and in doing so, died. He had gone easily, the round had taken him clean.

Bricko smiled as if expecting me: it could have been a meeting of two men in a field, one resting in the sun. He said, and his voice was clear and strong:

"You remember what you promised, Doctor-student?"

"Do not talk," I said, and knelt.

There seemed only two of us in the world.

I said, examining the wound, "It's a fuss about nothing, man. This time next week, I'll have you on your feet in Paoan."

"When that time come, mister, I be playin' the flute wi' Fool," said Bricko.

I pushed Big One away, saying, "He is going to find a litter. Is the sun in your eyes?" I put my cap over Bricko's face.

"Aye," said he. "It's a bit – you got a drop o' water for me, Doctor Lin?"

"Coming up," I said, and brought around my water-bottle: with the other hand I slid back the automatic cock of the Luger, but Bricko heard the click.

"Make it good, Doctor Lin," said he. "Make it bloody good."

The solitary explosion momentarily silenced the day.

THIRTY-SIX

We halted six miles from the gates of the new Shensi-Kansu soviet, and the road over the gentle, snow-covered hills wound in slow curves to the north. It was a pathetic attempt to "clean up" before the official reception from the garrison of the new seat of communist government.

On that brief stop I wrote in my dairy:

20th October, 1935.
What is left of us has halted. I am a little hazy as to why. Somebody has said we are to clean ourselves up before we enter the new soviet outpost at Wuchichen. All around me, men are washing in a wayside stream: Mao, indeed, has come quite close to us, and is blowing and gasping in a little canvas bucket. Near him, on a stretcher, lies his faithful batman, Chen, too weak to walk – malaria. Chou En-lai is wearily arguing some point of organisation with a junior. The Young Vanguards (not Little Ball or Trip, both of whom were killed in the Moslem charges) are carrying bags of millet down the line – a last feed to bolster us, I suppose, so that we march with some precision. But nobody seems to know how to cook golden millet – it passes right through a man. Indeed, said some-body, with care you can collect it and cook it again ... little Man Kim has truly awful dysentery. But Kwelin seems better ... and Shao Shan gets tougher and more formidable every day, despite her wound.

"What are you writing this time, Uncle Lin?" asked Hu.
Earlier, unbidden, Kwelin came and sat beside me, but did not speak.
Her hair, as white as the snow beneath us, looked beautiful – from somewhere, just like a woman, she had managed to get some wide, black ribbon and Shao Shan had plaited it on her shoulders. She looked Scandinavian: a woman, not a girl of twenty-three – Kwelin, on this march, had lost her youth. It was as if the blood had left her face.

Now she held out the plaits for me to see, letting the strands fall through her fingers, smiling at them like a child.

"They are very pretty," I said. "Shao has done you well – you must admit it. Surely, that is the most beautiful hair in the whole of Shensi."

Kwelin did not reply, but took my hand and lifted it against her face. I said, "Woman of light, I love you . . ."

I thought she was about to speak; long had I awaited this, but she did not. In pale, almost transparent beauty, she looked past me.

She just sat there with my hand to her face, looking down the road to Liupan. I kissed her lips. "I love you, I love you," I said.

Leaving her, I went to tend the wounded.

Later Shao Shan came to me, saying, "Me and my chap will ride into the bloody old soviet done up fancy – Hu has just collected a fine Ninghsia cavalry mare and he has called her Tojo: I shall go in like a queen, with my man sitting in front of me. People will know that we're grand in the south."

"But Toiya?" asked Hu, all eyes.

Let my son be as Teng Ga-hu if a woman serves me well, I thought: a man-child, tall and straight; a son of which a man can boast, as Tenga did.

Meanwhile, of my daughter I spoke:

"Toiya rides with Kwelin," I said.

And so it was that, when the column took the road again in the falling snow, we of the Chan contingent gradually worked our way up the line to the van: many of the Fifth Muleteers, realising the ruse, followed us, shouting rude banter at Shao Shan, who sat her mare like an Amazon queen with Man Kim in her arms like a mothered child. Proudly went Shao down the white road to Wuchichen, unaware of the laughter. Her faded and torn mandarin gown was still a scarlet splash of colour: the Cantonese headdress she wore, a foot tall, flashed its paste diamonds in the weak sunlight. Magnificent in dignity and purpose Shao Shan looked that day; taking over Wuchichen like the Dowager Empress; people took note of it, whispering and pointing, or standing hushed as she went by.

After Shao came Kwelin on Moke Donkey II, a sleeping

Toiya in her arms. Hu, his face alight with excitement, marched between Big One and I.

Kwelin looked serene and beautiful in her rags, with her long white hair blowing out behind her.

In this manner we entered the new Shensi-Kansu soviet.

We looked neither right nor left, entering the outpost where the Twenty-Fifth fighters, men and women, lined the road in silence, staring. We came, not as a weary, bandaged rabble, but as a disciplined army, for all the dirt and rags and wounds.

Later, the people began to clap, but we did not acknowledge this. Many of us, like the welcoming people, would have wept for the joy of it, but we did not; nobody in the world was having us as easily as that. When we approached the middle of the outpost village we saw great banners of red with white characters announcing:

WELCOME TO CHAIRMAN MAO

and

THE CHINESE COMMUNIST PARTY LIVES
FOR EVER!

and

WELCOME TO THE GREAT CENTRAL
RED ARMY!

and

EXPAND THE SHENSI-KANSU AREA OVER
ALL CHINA!

I saw it all, remembering my friends I had lost: others must have been thinking the same, for I saw many move over in the ranks, making empty spaces for their comrades' ghosts. Walking at the head of Moke Donkey, with Kwelin in the saddle behind me, I remembered Pipa first.

And I thought I saw marching in the ranks the wraith of Bricko.

Was the calm, scholarly Muchai marching too, I wondered? Did Jo-kei, bandit, war-lord, hero, march with us, unseen? Where was the man from Kwangtung? Was he here with us this day, or amid the earthly riches he had sacrificed for what he called freedom?

And where was Fool? Did he, too, walk, seeking the friendship of Bricko? Or did his Gold Star Hero spirit still hang under torture in Chouping Fort?

I saw so little on that march; unshed tears blind the most.

Did Fate conspire that Skinny Wong, once corpulent, should die in the place of the opium-soldier, who, even now was pestering at my elbow?

"Oh, mister . . . Doctor-student! Just one? I'm 'aving a bloody terrible war."

Where was Little Ball, aged eleven, and Tip, aged nine? – dead for China before they had learned to live; and Shang Chi-pang, whose bugle Man Kim was blowing now . . . ?

And what of Commander Ma of gentry China? He who had leaped at the Bridge of Iron Chains and swung hand over hand over the haunted Tatu? Is he gone on the rush of his father's tears, the Idiot of Kiangsi?

Does Tenga live again in the brightness of his son? Or does his soul still yearn for his little virgin Tibetan, the Prostitute of Yichi?

Where is Yung? Does he sleep in the great white couloir of Snow Mountain, within touch of Shao's baby? Or does his spirit wander endlessly among the glaciers of Dream Pen Mountain, in search of Pipa, who sleeps in camellias?

Now the people thronged about us: our very silence had swept them into life. And they began to run through our ranks flinging over us the petals of winter flowers: the children had great baskets loaded with pink and white blossoms. Excitement grew: women lining the way began to sing, and I heard Hu's voice shrill above the growing tumult. Turning, I saw Kwelin, and she was laughing. Young girls, fighting to see the baby, had pushed great bunches of flowers into her hands, showering petals over her and Shao Shan. And now she was crying something unintelligible to me and I went to her.

"Lin, Lin – I want to walk!" She stared about her. "Where am I? Where is this?"

Shouting with the joy of it, I lifted her down, and the girls pestered about her, trying to get a look at Toiya.

Kwelin cried, "Oh, the flowers, the flowers!"

Her face, in that moment, came alive.

Bending, she settled Toiya down so that she touched the road with her feet, and Toiya shrieked and gurgled with delight, kicking at the petals, a carpet beneath us.

I remembered the prophecy of the Old Weaver of Tatu; I remembered again the man from Kwangtung.

Kwelin, Toiya, and me – we were the three who walked on flowers.

Now there grew about us a great concourse of men, and this was the garrison of the Twenty-Fifth Army home soviet: these came among us to help with our wounded. Seeing Shao Shan, they followed her in a body, bawling up to her.

But Shao Shan gathered Man Kim in her arms and did not spare them a glance. Little Hu, astride Moke Donkey, was covered in flowers: Big One's eyes were shut, I saw; his face was low, his bearded mouth in the boy's hair. Was he grieving for Tenga? I wondered. Or did he dream of Jo-kei the man he served?

On, on. The snow was falling in great, wavering flakes, as big as the snowflakes of Laoshan. The shouting grew louder. A band was playing martial music. The village square was packed with thousands.

I remembered Pipa, and heard her say:

". . . you do not much flatter the woman who is your slave. Could you not tell me that my lips are carmine, my skin like jade . . ."

I heard her voice above the tramping army. Clearly, I heard her, and smelled again, amid the snow, the scent of camellias. And I saw, with Kwelin's hand in mine, a sea of white and red and pink blossoms stretching to the boundaries of the universe.

I spoke her name, but none heard me.

The column was stopping. By good fortune the crowd pressed us back, still together, but within a few yards of the Central Committee. Mao, indeed, was so close to Kwelin that she could have touched him. And, as the soldiers made an entry into the crowd, I saw a small deputation approaching. Chou En-lai was there, I noticed.

The crowd was stilled: there was no sound but the coughing of the tubercular refuse we had brought from Juichin.

The officials approached Mao Tse-tung. One, leading the rest, extended his hand.

"Welcome to the Shensi-Kanus soviet," said the Twenty-Fifth commander.

"Is this Comrade Liu?" asked Mao, shaking his hand. He smiled. "It was good of you to come so far to greet us."

The Long March was finished.

In a year and four days since leaving Juichin, we had marched nearly 7,500 miles. Over 100,000 men and thirty-six women had begun it; of these, only 9,000 lived to enter the Shensi soviet.

According to my diary, there was a fight of sorts with the enemy almost every day: sixteen whole days were confined to major battles.

We had marched 252 days in daylight and twenty-one in darkness and averaged twenty-six miles a day.

We had crossed twenty-four rivers, passed through twelve different provinces; made contact, politically, with 200,000,000 people and entered six different aboriginal districts; we had gone where no Han Chinese army had penetrated since the days of Kublai Khan.

We had climbed eighteen mountain ranges, five perennially snow-capped, and occupied sixty-one cities; fought the armies of eleven different war-lords, and defeated in pitched battles, a million Kuomintang.

The crowds were dispersing.

Alone with Kwelin, who still carried Toiya, I found a little ruined hut away from the main army. Night was falling.

It was warm within the hut, Toiya made a sweet, complaining sound, calling for Shao Shan, then pressed her face against Kwelin, nuzzling her for milk.

I put my arms around them saying, "Soon, when the fighting is finished, I will take you home."

Distantly, we heard the chanting of the armies, "Peking, Peking, Peking . . . !"

Kwelin said, "Here, Lin-wai, take your baby."

The window glowed red. Her face was shadowed in the light of the torches.

I took Toiya. "You knew, of course . . . ?"

"I knew," said Kwelin.

We stood uncertainly, listening to the sounds of men. I said: "Will you come home with me, Kwe?"

Kwelin answered, "One day, when you are really sure of your love for me. One day, when Pipa is dead, I will come with you to Laoshan." Then she whispered to Toiya. "What a pity Aunt Kwe has no milk for you. Yes, I know, my love." She turned to me, smiling brilliantly. "Look, wait here for me. I will try to find Shao Shan."

I would have waited there forever.

The stars of Shensi were as big as little lanterns in the window of the hut; the moon round and full after a heavy meal of summer: shining, perhaps, over the Sikang mountains where Pipa lay? Did a perfume scent the air, I wondered, where the land was bright under this Shensi moon? Did this fragrant concubine walk the lanes of Shengsu where we made love near Caladal, and the little streams of home?

I can see from here the black outline of the Shengsu forests. I can hear the singing of the Hakka Guests from the paddy fields of old Kanti. Are the love-pavilions of Laoshan standing like wraiths among the trees? Is the wheat still flying from the barns of Chenyuan? Does the Bridge of Chains still cry in the wind above the Old Tatu where our Gold Star heroes died?

Bricko and Jo-kei; Muchai and Tenga; Yung, Little Ball and Trip; Wong, Chi-pang and the man from Kwangtung . . . all my friends.

Where are they now?

And Kwelin?

Shao Shan entered silently. She said nothing, but took Toiya out of my arms, sat down in a corner and unbuttoned her tunic. I said to her:

"Where is Kwelin . . . ?"

She looked up, saying, "Wake up, man. It's a bloody big place, you got to look sharp."

I snatched open the door and ran into the darkness. The opium-soldier, catching sight of me, yelled, "*Hei wei*, Doctor *Doctor* . . . ! but I easily outpaced him.

I saw her white hair through the massed shapes of men: they greeted one another in the moonlight with the fierce banter of troops at war: they had made little fires in the dark, sitting around them with their bowls of tea, shovelling up the noodles in chopsticks and gasps, swilling down rice-wine, telling their endless, boasting stories. The Fifteenth Mohammadans were there, the heroes of Liupan, their white teeth gleaming in their bearded faces; the Red Assault Cadres sat apart, glowering in their usual isolation. Men I knew gripped me, shouting into my face, pulling at me as I went in search of Kwelin.

"Kwelin ... *Kwelin!*" Soldiers, bantering, took up the cry.

I found her walking down an empty road.
"*Kwelin!*"
It stopped her, but she did not turn to me.
Face lowered, she waited, twisting her fingers.
"Oh *no*!" I said, and turned her into my arms.

THIRTY-SEVEN

Now I sit here in Laoshan, in the room where my mother taught me of the poets. I have but this chapter of the Long March to record, and then it is finished.

I should, of course, have started this earlier; my service with the Eighth Route Red Army, with which I served until the capture of Peking in 1949, precluded me doing anything with my house, and there has been much repair needed since Kwelin came here with Shao Shan and the children: in fairness, this has kept me occupied to the exclusion of everything else.

A little whole ago, before I began this final chapter, I saw Big One lumbering past my mother's grave with a sack of coal for the kitchen: Shao Shan, who rules there, is upbraiding him for bringing in the snow: like the rest of us, I suppose, she is getting old and touchy. I keep insisting to her that he really doesn't understand, but she takes no heed.

Earlier he brought me a telegram – the thing had been in his pocket for the best part of a week.

To:
Surgeon-General Chan Lin-Wai   Staff Headquarters
Estate Office, Laoshan,   People's Liberation
Kwangtung.   Army, Peking.

   Hasten completion Long March (Fupien-Paoan in detail) for incorporation into official Party records long overdue. Transmit direct.

                                                   Hsu Meng-chiu,
   11th December, 1966.   Official Historian C.C.P.

Life is simple for us here in Laoshan. The cicadas' song, the rain on banyan leaves is louder in this peace, than all the guns of our youth. And a doctor's life in a village, even under the stringent regulations of the Peking government (which demands such constant revision of study and Barefoot Organisation) is of necessity pretty quiet.

Kwelin is reading poetry in her chair by the window – earlier – as if I hadn't enough interruptions – she quoted me passages from the Wang River collection: *Willow Waves* and *Huatzu Hill* being sufficiently arresting to completely divorce me from the work in hand. The winter dusk is upon her face; her lip for me, shows no scar, though Toiya's little ones insist on fingering it and asking questions, as children do.

Maturity has brought to Kwelin a marvellous serenity. Her eyes are calm; she has plaited her white hair in a bun at the nape of her neck, held by a fan-comb of ivory. She too, is prematurely aged, but nothing can steal her from that queenly dignity.

Nor, it appears, is she as tired as I.

On reflection, it was a good decision to send her back to Laoshan with the children after the March, while I fought on with the Eighth. If Toiya and Hu are straight and tall today it is because of the protection of my father's house: also Kwelin found her mind again amid such harmony.

Now there is a great commotion going on. Every time Toiya's family comes, it is the same.

How can one work in such a barn-yard?

Kwelin said, "Yes, yes, I know – but they are only children once – come, you are being perverse. Surely you can put it aside while Toiya's here?"

"And where the devil are my spectacles?"

"Up on your head. Oh, Lin – don't be cranky. After all, the family don't often come."

It's apparently useless to tell her that I must get this finished.

"I will go to meet them," said Kwelin, rising.

Dimly, in the dusk, I can see Big One waving. Toiya and Hu are coming across the garden: how tiny looks Toiya beside her tall, broad husband! Tenga would have been grateful, I reflected; the Tibetan of Yichi made his son well; as Pipa made Toiya beautiful on the road to Tatu . . .

Any attempt at writing is now impossible. They are all at the kitchen door in shrieked greetings, with Kwelin hustling them in: Shao Shan is scolding the children for something or other – she is becoming particularly crusty in advancing age, yet she has the audacity to complain that I'm getting crotchety. I never would have believed it – the things one puts up with from servants these days. Man Kim is making a confounded noise on Shang Chi-pang's bugle: it's impossible to create anything amid such a bedlam.

377

Before me is Mao Tse-tung's last Order.

Order of the Day No. 369   General Headquarters,
             Political Protection.
             Shensi-Kansu Soviet.

Comrades,

The Long March is finished. After rest and recruitment we march on Peking; the fight is only just beginning

I command you on reaching Paoan, but there are bigger struggles to come.

This March, remember, was only the prologue of the Chinese dream. It is in Peking, not in Shensi, where we will forge our destiny.

        Mao Tse-tung
        Chairman, Central Committee
20th October, 1935   Chinese Communist Party.

The dream, I reflected, the destiny ...

Did men die too willingly, I wonder, for the birth of such ideals ... ?

But Mao was right, as he was invariably right.

Yet it was fifteen years before I stopped fighting, and some of my contemporaries are fighting to this day.

The house is still.

A little while ago, after tea, Toiya and Hu took the children home: in truth, their twin six-year-olds are delightful: I really should try to be more amiable with them. The boy, named after Hu, is his image, the girl, Pei-sha, tells me of Pipa; the same flashing eyes and mercurial defiance, the same sweetness ...

Earlier Toiya came to me. Thinking me asleep, she put a rug around my legs. This house is a draughty old place – she is perfectly right – I must give thought to better heating. Kwelin seems perpetually cold ... she who survived the Great Snow Mountain.

Now she has gone to sleep over her sewing. Our world is silent, as if it never lived. Shao Shan has taken Man Kim in his wheel-chair over to see their relatives: the fire burns low, the little flames are shining on Kwelin's fingers – I smell pine-needles ... the logs came from Shengsu, where Pipa lived.

It is infuriating to be so tired when there is so much to do.

The wounds of the old Eighth Route seem to have drained me of vitality. But the Central Committee don't ask for something unless they really want it: Meng is such a reasonable man. It is necessary that I make some effort.

They haven't come to pull the curtains yet . . .

The moon is shining in the window above the woods of Shengsu. Once the moon sailed like this above a lane of waving poplars . . .

Above the hiss of the logs I can hear the wild geese calling from the village . . .

Kwelin has just awakened. She is all my dreams. What would I do without Kwelin?

She spoke, I think. I don't know what she said, but she kissed me.

It is quite wrong that I should sit here dreaming, when there is such important stuff to get down on to paper.

Unaccountably, in the eye of my mind, in brilliant colours of white and pink and red, I can see an ocean of camellias. They stretch as far as I can see in this dying light across the peaks of Sikang and the little streams of Caledal . . .

"Kwelin . . . are you still here?"

"I am here, Lin-wai. I am here."

I am cold.

"Kwelin . . . Kwelin . . ."

The brush is heavy in my fingers.

ALEXANDER CORDELL

THE BRIGHT CANTONESE

Half-Chinese, half-English, with hair the colour of gold, they called her the Bright Cantonese: Mei Keyling, member of the new Red Guard, agent for Central Intelligence. Dedicated to the glory of China with a courage that was to be tested to the full in a vital mission, a mission that was to include an epic journey as leader of a band of stricken refugees fleeing from the devastation of an atomic bomb, the betrayal of a lover, dangerous intrigues – and, finally, a terrifying confrontation with the sadist Hamer.

CORONET BOOKS

ALEXANDER CORDELL

RAPE OF THE FAIR COUNTRY

Set in the grim valleys of the Welsh iron country, this turbulent, unforgettable novel begins the saga of the Mortymer family. A family of hard men and beautiful women, all forced into a bitter struggle with their harsh environment, as they slave and starve for the cruel English ironmasters.

But adversity could never still the free spirit of Wales, or quiet its soaring voice, and the Mortymers fight and sing and make love even as the iron foundries ravish their homeland and cripple their people.

"Ribald, bawdy, exciting, tragically violent"
New York Times

"A tremendously lusty story...a splendid novel.'
Sunday Express

Alexander Cordell's masterful trilogy is continued with
HOSTS OF REBECCA
SONG OF THE EARTH

CORONET BOOKS

ALEXANDER CORDELL

THE FIRE PEOPLE

THE FIRE PEOPLE was inspired by, and climaxes in, the inglorious Merthyr Tydfil riots of 1831 and the hanging of Dic Penderyn, the first Welsh martyr of the working class.

It is a book of great power and vividness, peopled by a host of fascinating characters – Irish immigrants, European refugees, Welsh foundryworkers, whores, soldiers, miners, preachers, policemen – all lending to a backcloth that is alarming and appealing at one and the same time.

But most important is the story of Dic Penderyn – his warmth, his understanding, his dignity, his love for his wife, his loyalty to his friends, his courage in the face of helpless adversity.

CORONET BOOKS

ALEXANDER CORDELL

RACE OF THE TIGER

He left the grinding poverty of the Old World for the jungle-law life of the New.

Born to the riveting penury of Nineteenth Century Ireland, Jess O'Hara and his high-spirited sister, Karen, flee their wretched homeland for a new life in America.

Exhausted after a nine-week crossing in an over-crowded, disease-ridden "coffin ship", they arrive in Pittsburgh – the thrusting, turbulent steel capital of the United States. Surrounded by smoke and fire-belching chimneys, deafened by the beat of giant hammers, they struggle to adapt to this alien world.

At first resisting the tug of easy wealth, Jess forsakes his fellow immigrants and bulldozes his way to fame and fortune, exploiting the love of two women to become a financial tiger in a city where mere jungle-law prevails.

"The most compelling book I have read for a long time ... dramatic on a breathtaking scale"
Manchester Evening News

"Vastly entertaining, fast-moving, full of splendidly full-blooded characters"
Books and Bookmen

CORONET BOOKS

ALSO AVAILABLE IN CORONET BOOKS

ALEXANDER CORDELL

☐	15383 0	Race of the Tiger	45p
☐	20515 6	Rape of the Fair Country	85p ⎞
☐	20509 1	Hosts of Rebecca	85p ⎬ trilogy
☐	20516 4	Song of the Earth	85p ⎠
☐	20803 1	The Bright Cantonese	70p
☐	15476 4	The Sinews of Love	80p
☐	17403 X	The Fire People	£1.00

R. F. DELDERFIELD

To Serve Them All My Days

☐	17599 0	Book 1 – Late Spring	40p
☐	16709 2	Book 2 – The Headmaster	40p

ELLIS DILLON

☐	18802 2	Across the Bitter Sea	£1.25

MALCOLM MACDONALD

☐	20010 3	World From Rough Stones	£1.00

All these books are available at your local bookshop or newsagent, or can be ordered direct from the publisher. Just tick the titles you want and fill in the form below.
Prices and availability subject to change without notice.

~~~~~~

CORONET BOOKS, P.O. Box 11, Falmouth, Cornwall.
Please send cheque or postal order, and allow the following for postage and packing:
U.K. – One book 19p plus 9p per copy for each additional book ordered, up to a maximum of 73p.
B.F.P.O. and EIRE – 19p for the first book plus 9p per copy for the next 6 books, thereafter 3p per book.
OTHER OVERSEAS CUSTOMERS – 20p for the first book and 10p per copy for each additional book.

Name ....

Address ....

....